BETRAYAL

JOHN LESCROART

A NOVEL

BETRAYAL

DUTTON

DUTTON
Published by Penguin Group (USA) Inc.
375 Hudson Street, New York, New York 10014, U.S.A.
Penguin Group (Canada), 90 Eglinton Avenue East, Suite 700, Toronto, Ontario M4P 2Y3, Canada (a division of
Pearson Penguin Canada Inc.); Penguin Books Ltd, 80 Strand, London WC2R 0RL, England; Penguin Ireland,
25 St Stephen's Green, Dublin 2, Ireland (a division of Penguin Books Ltd); Penguin Group (Australia), 250
Camberwell Road, Camberwell, Victoria 3124, Australia (a division of Pearson Australia Group Pty Ltd);
Penguin Books India Pvt Ltd, 11 Community Centre, Panchsheel Park, New Delhi – 110 017, India; Penguin
Group (NZ), 67 Apollo Drive, Rosedale, North Shore 0632, New Zealand (a division of Pearson New Zealand
Ltd); Penguin Books (South Africa) (Pty) Ltd, 24 Sturdee Avenue, Rosebank, Johannesburg 2196, South Africa

Penguin Books Ltd, Registered Offices: 80 Strand, London WC2R 0RL, England

Published by Dutton, a member of Penguin Group (USA) Inc.

 REGISTERED TRADEMARK—MARCA REGISTRADA

ISBN 978-0-525-95039-4

Printed in the United States of America
Set in Adobe Garamond
Designed by Leonard Telesca

PUBLISHER'S NOTE

To Lisa M. Sawyer,
Who shares my life and owns my heart

"A man's death is his own business."

Aaron Moore, First Sergeant, U.S. Marine Corps

"Injustice is relatively easy to bear; it is justice that hurts."

Henry Louis Mencken

PROLOGUE
[2006]

On a Wednesday evening in early December, Dismas Hardy, standing at the thin line of dark cherry in the light hardwood floor of his office, threw a dart. It was the last in a round of three, and as soon as he let the missile go, he knew it would land where he'd aimed it, in the "20" wedge, as had the previous two. Hardy was a better-than-average player— if you were in a tournament, you'd want him on your team—so getting three twenties in a row didn't make his day. Although missing one or even, God forbid, two shots in any given round would marginally lower the level of the reservoir of his contentment, which was dangerously low as it was.

So Hardy was playing a no-win game. If he hit his mark, it didn't make him happy; but if he missed, it really ticked him off.

After he threw, he didn't move forward to go pull his darts from the board as he had the last thirty rounds. Instead, he let out a breath, felt his shoulders settle, unconsciously gnawed at the inside of his cheek.

On the other side of his closed door, in the reception area, the night telephone commenced to chirrup. It was long past business hours. Phyllis, his ageless ogre of a receptionist/secretary, had looked in on him and said good night nearly three hours ago. There might still be associates or paralegals cranking away on their briefs or research in some of the other rooms and offices—after all, this was a law firm where the billable hour was the inescapable unit of currency—but for the most part, the workday was over.

And yet, with no pressing work, Hardy remained.

Over the last twenty years, Wednesday evenings in his home had acquired a near-sacred status as Date Night. Hardy and his wife, Frannie, would leave their two children, Rebecca and Vincent—first with baby-sitters, then alone—and would go out somewhere to dine and talk. Often they'd meet first at the Little Shamrock, about halfway between home on Thirty-fourth Avenue and his downtown office. Hardy was a part owner of the bar, with Frannie's brother, Moses McGuire, and they'd have a civilized drink and then repair to some venue of greater or lesser sophistication—San Francisco had them all—and reconnect. Or at least try.

Tonight's original plan was to meet at Jardinière, Traci Des Jardins's top-notch restaurant, which they'd belatedly discovered only in the past year when Jacob, the second son of Hardy's friend Abe Glitsky, returned from Italy to appear in several performances at the opera house across the street. But Frannie had called him and canceled at four-thirty, leaving a message with Phyllis that she had an emergency with one of her client families.

Hardy had been on the phone when Frannie's call had come in, but he'd been known to put people on hold to talk to his wife. She knew this. Clearly she hadn't wanted to discuss the cancellation with him. It was a done deal.

After another minute of immobility, Hardy rolled his shoulders and went around behind his desk. Picking up the telephone, he punched a few numbers, heard the ring, waited.

"Yellow."

"Is the color of my true love's hair," he said. "Except that Frannie's hair is red. What kind of greeting is 'yellow'?"

"It's hello with a little sparkle up front. Y-y-yellow. See?"

"I liked it better when you just said 'Glitsky.' "

"Of course you did. But you're a well-known troglodyte. Treya pointed out to me, and she was right as she is about everything, that growling out my name when I answer the phone at home was somewhat off-putting, not to say unfriendly."

As a lifelong policeman, Glitsky had cultivated a persona that was, if nothing else, self-protectively harsh. Large, broad-shouldered, black on his mother's side—his father, Nat, was Jewish—Glitsky's favored expression combined an unnerving intensity with a disinterested neutrality that, in conjunction with anomalous ice-blue eyes and the scar that ran through both of his lips, conveyed an impression of intimidating, barely suppressed rage. Supposedly he had wrung confessions out of suspects by doing nothing more than sitting at an interrogation table, arms crossed, and staring. Even if the rumor wasn't strictly true, Glitsky had done nothing to dispel it. It felt true. It sounded true. So it was true enough for a cop's purposes.

"You've never wanted to appear friendly before in your entire life," Hardy said.

"False. At home, I don't want to scare the kids."

"Actually, you do. That's the trick. It worked great with the first batch."

"The first batch, I like that. But times change. Nowadays you want the unfriendly Glitsky, you've got to call me at work."

"I'm not sure I can stand it."

"You'll get over it. So what can I do for you?"

The connection thrummed with empty air for a second. Then Hardy said, "I was wondering if you felt like going out for a drink."

Glitsky didn't drink and few knew it better than Hardy. So the innocuous-sounding question was laden with portent. "Sure," Glitsky said after a beat. "Where and when?"

"I'm still at work," Hardy said. "Give me ten. I'll pick you up."

PERVERSELY, TELLING HIMSELF it was because it was the first place he could think of that didn't have a television, Hardy drove them both to Jardinière, where he valeted his car and they got a table around the lee of the circular bar. It was an opera night and *The Barber of Seville* was probably still in its first act, so they had the place nearly all to themselves. On the drive down they'd more or less naturally fallen into a familiar topic—conditions within, and the apparently imminent rearrangement of, the police department. The discussion had carried them all the way here and wasn't over yet. Glitsky, who was the deputy chief of inspectors, had some pretty good issues of his own, mostly the fact that he neither wanted to retire nor continue in his current exalted position.

"Which leaves what?" Hardy pulled at his beer. "No, let me guess. Back to payroll."

Glitsky had been shot a few years before when he'd been head of homicide, and after nearly two years of medical leave from various complications related to his recovery, he got assigned to payroll, a sergeant's position, though he was a civil service lieutenant. If his mentor, Frank Batiste, hadn't been named chief of police, Glitsky would have probably still been there today. Or, more likely, he'd be out to pasture, living on his pension augmented by piecemeal security work. But Batiste had promoted him to deputy chief over several other highly ranked candidates.

In all, Glitsky pretended that this was a good thing. He had a large and impressive office, his own car and a driver, a raise in pay, an elevated profile in the city, access to the mayor and the chief. But the rather significant, in his opinion, downside to all of this was that the job was basically political, while Glitsky was not. The often inane meetings, press conferences, public pronouncements, spin control, and interactions with community groups and their leaders that comprised the bulk of Glitsky's hours made him crazy. It wasn't his idea of police work; it wasn't what he felt he was born to do.

Glitsky tipped up his club soda, sucked in a small ice cube, chomped it, looked across at Hardy. "Lanier"—the current head of homicide—"is retiring, you know."

"Nobody's that dumb," Hardy said.

"What's dumb? I'd retire myself if I could afford it."

But Hardy was shaking his head. "I'm not talking about Lanier," he said. "I'm talking about you."

"I'm not retiring."

"No, I know. What you're doing is thinking about asking Batiste to put you back in homicide. Isn't that right?"

"And here I thought I was being subtle."

"You and a train wreck." Hardy sipped some beer. "You talk to Treya about this?"

"Of course."

"What's she say?"

"You'll just do that eye-rolling thing you do, but she says whatever makes me happy makes her happy." At Hardy's reaction, he pointed. "There you go, see?"

"I can't help it," Hardy said. "It's eye-rolling material. Have you talked to Batiste?"

"Not yet. He did me a favor making me deputy chief. I don't want to seem ungrateful."

"Except that you are."

"Well, I've already put in three years there and it's not getting any better."

"And homicide would be?"

Glitsky moved his glass in a little circle of condensation. "It's who I am more. That's all. It's why I'm a cop."

FINALLY GETTING TO the reason they'd come out in the first place.

"It's just so different," Hardy said. "I mean, two years ago, I've got two kids and a wife waiting for me when I come home. We're playing Scrabble around the kitchen table, for Christ's sake. Watching videos together."

"If memory serves, you couldn't wait for that to end. It was so boring."

"Not that boring. And even last year, the Beck's off at BU but at least Vince was still around at home and we'd give a nod to a family dinner a few times a week. Now he's in San Diego and Frannie's a working fool and . . . it's just so different."

"Empty nest," Glitsky said.

"I thought I was going to love it."

"Well, there you go. Wrong again." He shrugged. "You'll get used to it."

"I don't want to get used to it. I want to love it the way it should be."

"How's that? Should?"

"You know, like go out on dates with my wife, and do fun nonkid things on weekends, stay over places, go back to being my carefree old self."

"Who? I don't believe I ever met him."

"You know what I mean. It just doesn't seem right."

"What? That Frannie's working?"

"No. No, she's wanted to go back to work forever after the kids moved out. I've been totally behind her. Going back to school and everything. I mean, we've been planning on it."

"But you just didn't think it would take so much time away from you?"

Hardy sipped beer, swallowed, blew out heavily. "She's a good woman," he said. "I'm not saying she's not."

"Few better. If you do something stupid with her around this, I'll hunt you down and kill you."

"I'm not going to do anything. I'm just trying to get my head around where we are now. It's like her job is her life all the sudden."

"You ever hang out with yourself during a murder trial? Miss a few dinners, did you?"

"That's not the—" Hardy's tone hardened. "I was bringing in all the money, Abe. I was supporting everybody. That's not the situation now."

"Oh, okay. You're absolutely right. It was different when you did it."

Hardy twirled his glass on the table and stared out across the dimly lit bar. Even going out with his best friend to talk about himself wasn't turning out to be such a party. Things were going to have to change, and as Glitsky said, he was going to have to get used to it. Hell, things had already changed under his nose and he'd barely seen those changes coming. "It's never easy, is it?" he said.

Glitsky chewed some more ice. "What was your first clue?"

AFTER YEARS OF AGGRAVATION and frustration, Hardy had finally broken down and rented some enclosed parking space in his neighborhood. The full double garage was still a long block and a half from his home and it cost him nearly four thousand dollars a year, but its door opened when you pushed a button on your car's visor, it was closer than most of the parking spots he would wind up finding on the streets anyway, it did double duty as a storage unit, and, perhaps best of all, it removed both the family cars from the immediate threat of theft or vandalism, both of which his family had been the victim of three times in the eighteen months before Hardy had plunked down his first rent check.

The walk home tonight wasn't bad, though. He'd stopped after the two beers with Glitsky; his caseload was light at the moment and so he was unencumbered by his usual forty-pound litigator's briefcase; the night was brisk and clear. His two-story "railroad" Victorian on Thirty-fourth Avenue up by Clement was the only stand-alone house on a blockful of apartment buildings. It sported a white picket fence and a neatly maintained, albeit tiny, lawn. A flower-bordered brick walkway hugged one side of the lawn; four steps led up to the small porch, a light on by the door. More flowers grew in window boxes.

Hardy let himself in and flipped on the hall light. The house was called a railroad Victorian because the ground floor was laid out like a railroad car. All of the rooms—living, sitting, dining—opened off the long hallway on Hardy's right as he walked through the house to the back rooms.

Turning on more lights in the kitchen and family room behind it—the house was dead still—he automatically checked in on his tropical fish, sprinkled some food on the water's surface, and stood in much the same attitude of passive repose he'd adopted after his last round of darts earlier that night. After a minute of that, he took a few more steps and found himself in the corner that held the doors to both Rebecca's and Vincent's rooms.

He opened the Beck's first. She'd slept in this room only a couple of weeks before when she'd been home for Thanksgiving, but there was, of course, no sign of her now. The bed was neatly made, the bookshelves organized. Vin had been home, too, and his room was pretty much the same as his sister's, although somehow louder in his absence—it was more a boy's room, with sports and music posters and lots more junk everywhere. Mostly, now, both of the rooms just seemed empty.

Checking the phone for messages (none), then his watch, Hardy called Frannie's cell and got her voice mail. She turned her phone off when she was with clients. He said, "Yo. It's quarter to nine and I'm just starting to cook something that I'm sure is going to be fantastic. If you get this and you're on your way home, let me know and I'll hold dinner. If not, you snooze, you lose. Love you."

Hardy's black cast-iron frying pan hung on a marlin fishhook over the stove, and he took down the ten-pound monster and placed it over one of the stove's burners, turned the gas on, grabbed a pinch of sea salt they kept on the counter next to the stove, and flung it across the bottom of the pan. Whatever he was going to make, salt wouldn't hurt it.

Opening the refrigerator, he rummaged and found mushrooms, an onion, a red pepper, some leftover fettucine with a white sauce he remembered as having been pretty good. He threw away one heavily mil-dewed tomato, but that still left two that were probably salvageable if he cut them carefully. Unawares, by now he was humming the tune to "Baby, It's Cold Outside"—driving home, he'd been listening to Steve Tyrell's standards on his CD player. The freezer held a four-pack of chicken-and-basil sausages that he loved.

In five minutes, he'd chopped all the ingredients, put them in the pan, added some random herbs and spices and several shakes of Tabasco sauce and a half a cup or so of the Zinfandel he'd opened. He'd just turned the heat down and covered it when the phone rang. Certain that it was Fran-nie, he picked up on the second ring. "Bob's Beanery."

A male voice replied. "I must have the wrong number."

"No, wait! I'm sorry. I thought it was my wife."

"Mr. Hardy?"

"Speaking."

"Mr. Hardy, this is Oscar Thomasino."

"Your Honor, how are you?"

"Fine, thanks. Am I bothering you at an inopportune time?"

"No, but whatever, it's no bother. What can I do for you?"

"Well, admittedly this is a little unusual, but you and I have known each other for a long time, and I wondered if I could presume slightly upon our professional relationship."

This was unusual, if not to say unprecedented, but Hardy nevertheless kept his tone neutral. "Certainly, Your Honor. Anything I can do, if it's within my power." A superior court judge asking an attorney for a favor was a rare enough opportunity, and Hardy wasn't going to let it pass him by.

"Well, I'm sure it is," Thomasino said. "Did you know Charles Bowen? Charlie."

"I don't think so."

"You'd remember him. Flashy dresser, bright red hair, big beard."

"Doesn't ring a bell. He a lawyer?"

"Yes, he was, anyway. He disappeared six months ago."

"Where'd he go?"

"If I knew that, he wouldn't be disappeared, would he? He'd be someplace."

"Everybody's someplace, Your Honor. It's one of the two main rules. Everybody loves somebody sometime, and you've got to be someplace."

During the short pause that ensued, Hardy came to realize that he'd overstepped. His tendency to crack wise was going to be the end of him yet. But Thomasino eventually recovered to some extent, even reverting to his own stab at not-quite-cozy informality. "Thanks, Diz," he said. "I'll try to keep those in mind. Meanwhile, Charlie Bowen."

"Okay."

"Yes, well . . . the point is that he was a sole practitioner. No firm, no partners, but a reasonably robust caseload."

"Good for him."

"True, but his disappearance hasn't been good for the court. Or for his wife and daughter, either, to tell you the truth. His wife's hired her own lawyer to file a presumption-of-death claim, which, between you and me, has very little chance of getting recognized, in spite of the fact that it would be convenient for the court."

"Why's that?"

"Because when sole practitioners die and go to heaven, the bar inherits the caseload and has to dispose of it."

"What if they don't go to heaven?"

"Most lawyers argue themselves in, don't you think? I know you would."

"Thanks, I think. Your Honor."

"Anyway, I know it's just housecleaning, but Bowen had a ton of work outstanding, and that work needs to get done. And while we're not going to issue any presumption of death until he's been gone a lot longer, last month Marian Braun"—another of the city's superior court judges—"ruled that his disappearance rendered him legally incompetent, and just yesterday the state bar suspended his ticket at the court's request."

"So now they've got to farm out his cases. If he hadn't returned my calls for six months and I was his client, I would have fired him by now."

"I'm sure some of his clients may have done just that, but not all by a long shot." Thomasino sighed. "Charlie was a friend of mine. His wife's going to need whatever he still has coming from his cases. I'd like to be sure that the bar puts those cases in the hands of somebody who I know will do the right thing by her. Anyway, bottom line is that I ran into Wes

Farrell today at lunch." This was one of Hardy's partners. "He said things at your place were a little slow. The good news is that you can probably count on some percentage of Mr. Bowen's clients hooking up with your firm. Not that any of 'em will make you rich."

Reading between the lines, Hardy knew what the judge was saying— that this was grunt administrative work. The court probably had appointed the majority of Charlie's clients, indigents up for petty crimes and misdemeanors. Nevertheless, the court would pay for every hour Hardy's associates spent on the criminal cases anyway, and if the civil cases made any money, the firm could expect reasonable compensation. And it was, again, an opportunity to do a small good deed for a judge, and that was never a bad idea.

"You could probably get them all assigned out or closed in the next couple of months."

"I'm sold, Your Honor. I'd be happy to help you out."

"Thanks, Diz. I appreciate it. I know it's not very sexy. I'll have it all delivered to your office within the week."

"How much stuff is it?"

Thomasino paused. "About sixty boxes." In other words, a lot. "But here's the silver lining. It's only half as much as it appears, since half the boxes are one client."

"Tell me it's Microsoft."

A soft chuckle. "No such luck. It's Evan Scholler."

"Why is that name familiar?"

"Because you've read all about it. The two guys who'd been over in Iraq together?"

"Ah, it comes flooding back," Hardy said. "They had the same girlfriend or something, too, didn't they?"

"I believe so. There's a bunch of juicy stuff, but you'll find that out soon enough, I guess. But in any event, Diz, I really appreciate you doing this."

"I live to serve the court, Your Honor."

"You're already up on points, Counselor. Don't lay it on too thick. Have a nice night."

Hardy hung up and stood for a moment, musing. The judge's line played back in his mind: "There's a bunch of juicy stuff" in the Scholler case. Hardy thought he could use some juicy stuff in his life about now. If his memory served, and it always did, Scholler's situation was even more compelling than the bare bones of the murder case, because of its genesis in chaos and violence.

In Iraq.

PART ONE
[2003]

[1]

A BURNT-ORANGE SUN KISSED the horizon to the west as twenty-six-year-old Second Lieutenant Evan Scholler led his three-pack of converted gun-truck support Humvees through the gates of the Allstrong Compound in the middle of an area surrounded by palm trees, canals, and green farmland. The landscape here was nothing like the sandy, flat, brown terrain that Evan had grown used to since he'd arrived in Kuwait. The enclosure was about the size of three football fields, protected, like every other "safe" area, by Bremer walls—twelve-foot-tall concrete barriers topped with concertina wiring. Ahead of him squatted three double-wide motor home trailers that Allstrong Security, an American contracting company, had provided for its local employees.

Pulling up to the central temporary building, over which flew an American flag, Evan stepped out of his car onto the gravel that extended as far as he could see in all directions. A fit-looking American military type stood in the open doorway and now came down the three steps, his hand extended. Evan snapped a salute and the man laughed.

"You don't need to salute me, Lieutenant," he said. "Jack Allstrong. Welcome to BIAP." Calling Baghdad International Airport by its nickname. "You must be Scholler."

"Yes, sir. If you're expecting me, that's a nice change of pace."

"Gotten the runaround, have you?"

"A little bit. I've got eight men here with me and Colonel . . . I'm sorry, the commander here?"

"Calliston."

"That's it. He wasn't expecting us. Calliston said you had some beds we could use."

"Yeah, he called. But all we've got are cots really."

"We've got our own on board," Evan said. "We're okay with cots."

Allstrong's face showed something like sympathy. "You all been on the road awhile?"

"Three days driving up from Kuwait with a Halliburton convoy, four days wandering around between here and Baghdad, watching out for looters and getting passed off around the brass. Now here we are. If you don't mind, sir, none of my men have seen a bed or a regular meal or a shower since we landed. You mind if we get 'em settled in first?"

Allstrong squinted through the wind at Evan, then looked over to the small line of Humvees, with their M60 Vietnam-era machine guns mounted on their roofs, exhausted-looking and dirty men standing behind them. Coming back to Evan, he nodded and pointed to the trailer on his right. "Bring 'em on up and park over there. It's dorm style. Find an empty spot and claim it. Showers are all yours. Dinner's at eighteen hundred hours, forty minutes from now. Think your men can make it?"

Evan tamped down a smile. "Nobody better stand in their way, sir."

"Nobody's gonna." Allstrong cocked his head. "Well, get 'em started, then."

IT HAD COME TO DARKNESS outside through the windows, but even inside, the noise never seemed to end. Planes took off and landed at all times. Beyond that constant barrage of white noise, Evan was aware of the hum of generators and the barking of dogs.

He'd gotten his men fed and settled and now he sat in a canvas-backed director's chair in the spacious double-wide room at the end of a trailer that served as one of Allstrong's personal offices. His gaze went to the walls, one of which was filled with a large map. On the other, commendation and service plaques, along with half a dozen photographs with recognizable politicians, attested to what must have been Allstrong's illustrious military career—his host had been Delta Force, finally mustering out as a full-bird colonel in the Army. He'd received two Purple Hearts and the Distinguished Service Cross. No sign of marriage or family.

Evan, taking Allstrong's measure as he pulled a bottle of Glenfiddich from what appeared to be a full case of the stuff behind his desk, put his age as late thirties. He had an open face and smiled easily, although the mouth and eyes didn't seem in perfect sync with one another. The eyes tended to dart, as though Allstrong was assessing his surroundings at all times. Which, now that Evan thought of it, probably made sense after a lifetime in theaters of war. Allstrong wore what he'd been wearing when they'd met outside—combat boots, camo pants, a black turtleneck. He free-poured a stiff shot into a clear plastic cup, handed it over to Evan, and splashed a couple of inches into a cup of his own. Pulling another director's chair over, he sat down. "Don't bullshit a bullshitter," he said.

"It's not bullshit," Evan said. "They weren't expecting us."

"Two hundred and ninety-seven men and they didn't know you were coming?"

"That's correct."

"So what did you do? What did they do?"

"They had us camp just about on the tarmac at a holding station in Kuwait. We had all our gear with us. They put us on the ground until they figured out what we were here for."

Allstrong shook his head, either in admiration or disbelief. "I love this glorious Army," he said. "Who's the commander down there? Still Bingham?"

"That was the name."

"So you're telling me they had you weekend warriors running your asses off stateside—hustling you out of your day jobs, rushing you through training—then packed you up in a 737, flew nonstop for twenty-two hours, Travis to Kuwait—and it's all hurry up! move it! we need you over here!—and you get here and nobody knows you're coming?"

"That's right."

"So what'd they do?"

"You know Camp Victory?" This was a sand-swept safe zone five miles north of Kuwait City where the Army had erected five enormous tents to hold overflow troops.

"Camp Victory!" Allstrong barked a laugh. "That kills me!" He drank off some scotch, coughed, shook his head. "And I thought I'd heard it all. How long before they found out who you were?"

"We camped there for a week."

"Christ. A week. So how'd you wind up here? What happened to the rest of your unit?"

Evan took a good hit of his own drink. For a few months after he'd graduated from college, he'd put away a lot of beer, but since joining the police force a few years ago, he'd been at most a light social drinker. Here and now, though, his first sip of real alcohol, though technically forbidden while he was on duty (always), seemed appropriate and even earned. "I don't know," he said. "Most of 'em are probably still back in Kuwait, working on the HETs they eventually found." These were the heavy-equipment transporters that hauled 2½- to 5-ton cargo trucks and other massive ordnance and equipment from the Iraqi or Kuwaiti air bases where they'd been delivered to where they were supposed to get used in the field. Evan's National Guard unit, the 2632d Transportation Company out of San Bruno, California, was actually a medium transportation unit that had been trained to move troops and equipment.

"So what happened to you guys? The nine of you."

The drink was kicking in quickly. Evan felt his body relaxing and leaned back into his chair, crossing one leg over the other. "Well, that was just dumb or bad luck, one of the two. Once Bingham found the fleet of HETs, it turned out most of 'em didn't work. Heat, sand, four months without maintenance, you name it. So about half the guys got assigned to repair-and-rebuild work, and Bingham farmed out the rest of us wherever he needed somebody. I was a cop back home, and prior service enlisted with the infantry, plus I was the only guy with any crew-served-weapons experience, so Bingham had a convoy going to Baghdad and me and my men got assigned gun-truck support."

"So your other guys, they're cops too?"

"No. I'm the only cop, and the only one trained on the M60, if you don't count the forty-five minutes of instruction we all got before they sent us out."

"Now you are shitting me."

Evan held up three fingers. "Scout's honor."

"Jesus," Allstrong said. "So where do you guys stand now?"

"What do you mean?"

"I mean, what's your mission? What are you doing tomorrow, for example?"

Evan sipped his scotch, shrugged his shoulders. "No clue. I check in with Colonel Calliston tomorrow morning at oh eight hundred and find out, I suppose. I don't see him sending us back to our unit, although that's what I'm going to request. The men aren't too hot on this convoy duty, maybe wind up getting shot at. That wasn't in the original plan."

A small knowing chuckle came from Allstrong's throat. "Well, Lieutenant, welcome to the war. Plans are what you work with before you get there. They give you the illusion you've got some control, and you don't."

"I'm getting a sense of that," Evan replied. "So the short answer is I don't know what's happening tomorrow, or next week, or anything. We seem to be the lost company."

Allstrong stood up with his drink and walked over to the map. Staring at it for a few seconds, he spoke back over his shoulder. "Maybe I can talk to Bill. Calliston. Get you and your men assigned to us. How'd you like that?"

"Staying on here?"

"Yeah."

"Doing what?"

Allstrong turned. "Well, that's the bad news. We'd want you to support our own convoy trucks, but there's a lot fewer of them and we're not afraid to drive faster if we need to."

"Where to?"

"Mostly Baghdad and back, but we're hoping to open offices at other bases near Fallujah and Mosul too. Wherever we can get work and beat damn Custer Battles to the punch."

"Custer Battles?"

"New guys. Contractors like us and kicking ass at it. They got the other half of this airport gig and they're going for everything else we are. I'm thinking of having their people killed." Evan nearly choked on his drink as Allstrong came forward with a laugh. "That's a joke, Lieutenant, or mostly a joke. Anyway, as you might have noticed, we're staffing up here. In a couple of months, this place will be hopping. Calliston's going to want to assign us some protection in any event. I figured you guys are already here. It's a good fit. Besides, over time, it's only going to get safer here, I mean the road between Baghdad and BIAP."

"You mean, the one known as RPG Alley?"

Allstrong smiled. "You heard that one already, huh?"

"Rocket-propelled-grenade alley just doesn't sound all that safe."

"It's going to get better."

Evan wasn't about to argue with his host. "You guys don't do your own security?" he asked. "I thought guys like you were guarding Bremer." This was L. Paul "Jerry" Bremer, head of the Coalition Provisional Authority, or CPA, who had set up headquarters to administrate infrastructure and the economy and all nonmilitary aspects of the occupation in Hussein's Republican Palace in Baghdad a couple of weeks before.

Allstrong chortled again. "Yeah. True. Another absurd moment. Guys like us protect civilians and admin staff, but we're not supposed to carry heavy arms, so the military needs to guard our convoys."

"That's beautiful."

"Isn't it? Anyway, if you're interested, I could put in a call to Bill. At least get you guys attached here. Call it a short-term home."

"That might be a start to belonging somewhere," Evan said. "Sure. Call him."

[2]

"ROUTE IRISH" FROM THE AIRPORT to Baghdad proper was a thoroughly modern freeway, three well-maintained lanes in each direction. From Evan's perspective, the main difference between it and an American freeway, aside from the apparently near-standard practice of driving the wrong way on any given lane, was that from many places cars could enter it anywhere from either side—the asphalt ended on a sand shoulder that usually proceeded without a demarcating fence or barrier of any kind out across an expanse of flat, marginal farmland. So once you got away from Baghdad, where on- and off-ramps and bridges were more common, traffic could and did enter the roadway willy-nilly and not necessarily at designated entrances and exits.

This became a major problem because of suicide car-bombers. In the four days since Colonel Calliston had attached Evan's unit to Allstrong, they hadn't gotten approached by any of these yet, but the threat was real and ubiquitous. On his way through Baghdad this morning, Evan had counted four burnt-out hulks of twisted metal, one of them still smoldering as he drove by after an hour's delay while the powers that be stopped all traffic and cleared the road.

Today his assignment was to pass through Baghdad and proceed up to Balad Air Base, nicknamed Anaconda, about forty miles north of the capital city, and pick up a man named Ron Nolan, a senior official with Allstrong who'd been scouting potential air bases to the north and west for the past week, assessing contracting opportunities. After collecting Nolan, they were to proceed back to downtown Baghdad and make a stop at the CPA headquarters for some unspecified business, then return to BIAP by nightfall.

The round-trip distance was give or take a hundred miles and they had about twelve hours of daylight, but Evan wasn't taking any chances. Movement Control had signed off on his convoy clearance and he had his full package—the three Humvees—out and rolling at oh dark thirty hours. Each of his Humvees had a driver and an assistant driver, who was also in charge of feeding ammunition to the gunner, whose body remained half-exposed through the hole in the car's roof. The heavily armed men alternated roles on successive trips. Evan could have claimed rank and never taken a turn as gunner—as a lieutenant his official role was to be convoy commander, or radio operator—but he made it a point to ride in each car and take a turn at the crew-serve weapon as the opportunity arose.

Today he rode as a passenger in the lead vehicle, in one of the two back seats. Because of the traffic delay, the package didn't pass Baghdad until eight o'clock and didn't make it the forty farther miles to the outer periphery of the enormous Anaconda base—soon to be named "Mortari-taville"—until eleven-fifteen. Even without car bombs, traffic on the road to the main logistics supply area close to Baghdad crept at a near stand-still, not too surprising considering the sixteen thousand flights per month that Anaconda was handling.

When they got through the gate, Evan's driver and the second-in-command of their unit, Sergeant Marshawn Whitman, drove for a half mile or so through a city of tents and trailers before they came to an inter-section with a sign indicating that the camp headquarters was a mile far-ther on their right. But Whitman didn't turn the car immediately. Instead, his window down, he stared out to his left at two of the corner tents, one sporting a logo for Burger King and the other for Pizza Hut. "Am I really seeing this, sir? Aren't we in a war here? Didn't we just make it into Bagh-dad, like, two months ago? Can I get out and grab a quick Whopper?"

WHEN EVAN SHOOK Ron Nolan's hand just outside the headquarters tent, he had an immediate impression of great strength held in check. He went about five ten and came across as solid muscle, shoulders down to hips. Square jaw under brush-cut light hair. Today he wore a sidearm at his belt and a regular Army camo vest with Kevlar inserts over his khaki shirt.

"Leff-tenant," Nolan boomed, pronouncing the word in the British manner and smiling wide as he fell in next to Evan, "I sure do appreciate the punctuality. Time is money, after all, and never more than right here and right now. I trust the limo's got good air-conditioning."

Evan slowed, jerked his head sideways. "Uh, sir . . ."

But with another booming laugh, Nolan slapped him on the back. "Joking with you, son. No worries. Ain't no part of a Humvee don't feel like home to me. You know we're planning to stop off in Baghdad?"

"Those are my orders, yes, sir."

Nolan stopped, reaching out a hand, laying it on Evan's arm. "At ease, Lieutenant," he said. "You a little nervous?"

"I'm fine, sir. But I'd be lying if I said Baghdad was my favorite place."

"Well, we won't be there for long if I can help it, and I think I can. Jack Allstrong's a master at keeping doors open." He paused for a second. "So. You regular Army?"

"No, sir. California National Guard."

"Yeah. I heard they were doing that. How big's your convoy?"

"Three Humvees, sir." They were approaching it now, parked just off the pavement. "Here they are."

Nolan stopped, hands on hips, and looked over the vehicles, bristling with weaponry. "Damn," he said to Evan, "that's a good-looking hunk of machinery." Nodding at Corporal Alan Reese, a former seventh-grade teacher now manning the machine gun on the closest Humvee, he called up to him. "How you doing, son?"

"Good, sir."

"Where you from back home?"

"San Carlos, California, sir."

"San Carlos!" Nolan's voice thundered. "I grew up right next door in Redwood City!" He slapped the bumper of the vehicle. "You believe this small world, Lieutenant? This guy and me, we're neighbors back home."

"We all are," Evan said, sharing the enthusiasm although he couldn't exactly say why. "Our unit's out of San Bruno. The nine of us, we're all Peninsula guys."

"Son of a bitch!" Nolan crowed. "I got hooked up with the right people here, that's for damn sure. How long have you guys been over here?"

"Going on three weeks," Evan said.

"Get shot at yet?"

"Not yet."

"Don't worry about it," Nolan said with a grin, "you will."

FOR AN OBSCURE and possibly impenetrable reason, they got routed through the mixed neighborhood of Mansour by Haifa Street rather than through the military-only secure road they normally took when coming in to CPA headquarters from BIAP. Ron Nolan's destination was Saddam Hussein's old Republican Palace in central Baghdad, and the line of traffic on Haifa waiting outside the checkpoint to get into the Green Zone—bumper to bumper with weapons off-safe, ready to react—stopped them cold. Nolan extricated himself from his seat and opened his door, stepping out into the street and stretching. Evan, loath to let his passenger out of his sight, overcame his own reluctance—Iraqi civilians were all over the street, any one of them possibly an armed insurgent—and got out as well.

It was late afternoon by now, sweltering hot with nary a freshening breeze. The air was heavy with the smells of roasting meat and fish, manure, oil, and garbage. Haifa Street was wide and lined with three- and four-story concrete buildings, most with at least some of their windows blown out. From the crowd on the sidewalks, including women and children, no one would conclude that they were in a war zone, though. Merchants had lined up where most of the traffic into the Green Zone had to pass, and the street had the air of a bazaar—makeshift stands sold everything from clothing to batteries, toilet paper to money to candy.

Nolan, taking it in, seemed to be enjoying it all. Finally, he caught Evan's eye and grinned over the hood of the car. "We can make it in half the time if we walk. You up for it?"

Evan, reluctant to leave his troops, would have much preferred the relative security of his Humvee, but he also had a responsibility to protect Ron Nolan and get him back to Allstrong, and if that meant braving the streets of Baghdad, this was something different he should do as well. The mutually exclusive options played across his features.

Nolan noticed the hesitation. "Come on, Lieutenant. No guts, no glory."

"Just thinking about my men, Mr. Nolan," Evan covered.

"Hey. If they get to the gate before we're done, have 'em pull over and we'll meet 'em there. But at this rate they won't even be there by the time we're through. And I'd like to make it back to BIAP before dark."

Their Humvee moved forward about six feet and stopped again.

"Either way," Nolan said, "I'm going. You with me?"

"Sure." Evan leaned inside the passenger window and told Marshawn what he was doing.

"I don't like being out of contact," his driver replied.

"I don't either, Marsh. This is all new to me too." He indicated their passenger with a toss of his chin. "But he's going. And things here look pretty calm."

"Yeah," Marshawn said, "the 'before' shot."

They both knew that he meant "before the bomb exploded in the crowded marketplace."

"Let's hope not," Evan said. "And the sooner we get done and leave Baghdad, the sooner we're back home."

"I'm not arguing, sir. If you got to go, you got to go. But what if you're not at the gate? What are we supposed to do? Where will you be?"

For an answer, Evan shrugged and held up his portable Motorola radio, which was good for about a mile. Nolan, who'd heard the exchange, leaned back to Marshawn. "Budget office, down in the basement of the headquarters building. You can't miss it. But a hundred bucks says we beat you back to the gate."

The traffic gave and Marshawn crept forward another five or six feet before stopping again. The line of cars stretched for at least a quarter mile in front of him. "That's a bad bet for me, sir," he said, "even if I had the hundred bucks."

"I think so, too, Sergeant. That's why we're walking." Nolan snapped his fingers, remembering something, and reopened his back door. Reaching in, he emerged a second later with his backpack, apparently empty. "Can't forget this," he said with another grin, and strapped it onto his back, over the Kevlar vest.

* * *

RON NOLAN WAITED for Evan to fall in next to him, then said, "And by the way, my name's Ron, okay? Mr. Nolan's my dad. You okay with Evan?"

"That's my name."

"Yeah, well, Evan, I didn't mean to put you on the spot back there with your men, and I apologize. But you can't afford to be tentative here. You've got to make decisions and run on 'em. That's the main thing about this place."

"I just made my decision. But I'm not sure that leaving my convoy was the right one. We've had it drilled into us that procedures are crucial to maintain order."

They were walking shoulder to shoulder at the curb. Nolan shook his head, disagreeing. "My experience says it's more important to trust your gut. And I'm not talking just about deciding in a split second who's a Muj and who's a Hajj"—these were the Mujahideen and the Hajji, the bad guys and the good guys, respectively—"which is life and death and I mean right now. But the business environment here . . . Christ, what a gold mine! But you've got to see the opportunity and jump, and I'm talking like yesterday, or it all goes away. Did you get a chance to talk to Jack Allstrong at all back at BIAP?"

"A little bit."

"He tell you how he got the airport gig? The one that got us on the boards?"

"No. He never mentioned it."

"Well, it's a perfect example of what I'm talking about. You know what our half of that contract's worth? If you guess sixteen million dollars, you're on it."

"To do what? I saw the trailers, but it wasn't clear what you guys were doing there."

"We're guarding the airport, that's what."

"What about us?"

"What do you mean, us?"

"I mean the military, the Army, the Marines. What about us? We're not guarding the airport?"

"No. You're fighting the insurgents—most of the regular units, anyway. Jerry Bremer, God love him, in his wisdom fired all the Iraqi police and disbanded the military, so nobody's left over here except us contractors to provide security for the people who are coming in droves to do oversight and infrastructure, which is, like, everybody else."

Evan had his hand on the weapon in the holster on his hip. Most of the local people in the street and on the sidewalk were simply stepping out of the way as the two Americans passed by, but many of the children were smiling and jogging along with them—Evan had already learned, along with the Iraqi kids, that U.S. servicemen were a common source of candy from their MRE kits. But Evan had no candy on him and he wanted to get inside the Green Zone as fast as he could, so he kept pressing through the crowd.

Meanwhile, Ron Nolan kept up the patter. "Jack really hadn't been doing too good after he cashiered out. He'd been trying to set up a security business in San Fran, looking into water supply issues and the whole domestic terrorist thing, but it wasn't going very well. So then Baghdad falls, and what did Jack do? Same thing as Mike Battles with Custer Battles. He hopped on a plane with his last couple hundred bucks and flew over here to suss the place out for business opportunities." Nolan spread his arms theatrically. "*Et voilà!* Couple of months later, sixteen million smackeroos."

"Just like that?"

"Almost. Jack still knew a few guys from when he'd been in, and they turned him on to the airport gig and talked the guy in charge into letting Jack bid on it."

"But how'd he get it?" In spite of himself, Evan found himself taken by the narrative, and by Nolan's enthusiasm. "I mean, I'm assuming he's bidding against the giants, right? Halliburton, Blackwater, KBR." KBR was Kellogg, Brown, and Root. Unbeknownst to Evan, KBR was itself a subsidiary of Halliburton, not truly a separate entity.

"Yep. And don't forget DynCorp and ArmorGroup International. The big boys. To say nothing of Custer Battles—actually, they gave us the toughest run for it. But Jack wrestled 'em down and pulled out half the gig." Even in the madness of Baghdad's afternoon market, Nolan beamed at the memory.

"So what did he offer?"

"Well, first, a low bid, but that was basically because he was clueless and didn't know what it was worth. But the main thing was time. He promised to have almost a hundred and fifty men on the ground out here within two weeks."

"Two weeks?"

"Two weeks."

They walked on for a few more steps, before Evan couldn't help himself. "How was he going to do that? What was he going to pay them with? In fact, who was he going to hire? Did you guys have a hundred and fifty employees in San Francisco you could fly out here?"

Nolan howled out a laugh. "Are you kidding? He had three employees in San Francisco. And he'd paid them off of his credit cards in June. It was the end of the road for him if this didn't work. But it did."

"How'd that happen?"

They'd come almost to the checkpoint while the traffic hadn't budged, and Nolan stopped and faced Evan. "That's the great part. Jack didn't have any more credit. Nobody would lend him any more money back home, so he flew back here and convinced the CPA that they needed to lend him two million dollars against his first payment on the contract."

"Two million dollars?"

"In cash," Nolan said. "In new hundred dollar bills. So Jack packed 'em all up in a suitcase and flew to Jerusalem, where he deposited it all in the bank, then called me and told me to get my ass over here. He was in business."

At the gate, in spite of the crowd pressing up to get admitted, Nolan flashed his creds and the two men breezed their way through the CPA checkpoint—even the grunt guards seemed to know who he was. He and Evan crossed an enormous, open, tank-studded courtyard—at least a couple of hundred yards on a side—that fronted a grandiose white palacelike structure that, up close, bore silent witness to the bombardment that had rained upon the city in the past months—windows still blown out, the walls pocked with craters from shells, bullets, and shrapnel.

Inside the main building, in the enormous open lobby, pandemonium reigned. In a Babel of tongues, military uniforms mingled with business suits and *dishdashas* as half a thousand men jostled and shoved for position in one of the lines. Each line wended its way to one of the makeshift folding tables that apparently controlled access to the inner sanctum of Bremer and his senior staff. The noise, the intensity, the hundred-plus temperature, and the general stench of humanity assaulted Evan's senses as soon as he passed through the front door.

To all appearances, Nolan was immune to all of it. He hadn't gone three steps into the lobby when he plucked Evan's sleeve and pointed to their right. So they hugged the back wall, skirting most of the madness and making progress toward a wide marble staircase that led down. The crowd on the stairs was far less dense here than in the room behind them.

"What's all that about?" Evan asked as soon as he could be heard.

Nolan stopped at the bottom step. "Those folks," he said, "are basically the ones who got here a day late and a dollar short. I'd say they're Jack's competitors, except most of 'em are angling for subcontracts with the big boys. Basically, the entire country's for sale and Bremer's trying to administer all the deals from this building, from those tables, each of which represents a different ministry, if you can believe that. Seventeen, twenty of 'em. I don't know. And with, as maybe you can see, mixed results. Everybody wants a piece. Thank Christ we're beyond that stage. Fucking bedlam, isn't it?"

But he didn't wait for an answer. Turning, Nolan continued along the wall, Evan tagging behind him, the crowd gradually thinning around them the farther they went along the hallway. After thirty yards or so, finally, they turned a corner. Another long corridor stretched out before them, startlingly untraveled. A man in a military uniform sat at a lone table a little more than midway along, and three other men, apparently civilians, stood in front of him. But otherwise the hallway was empty. The noise and craziness behind them still echoed, but suddenly Evan felt psychically removed from it in spite of the fact that there was still a terrible odor of human waste and—even with holes where the windows should have been—no ventilation.

Nolan never slowed down. If anything, checking his watch, he glanced up at the window openings high in the wall and speeded up. But as they approached the desk, he put out a hand to stop their progress and swore.

"What's up?" Evan asked.

Nolan swore again and came to a dead stop. "It would be Charlie Tucker when we're in a hurry. Maybe your sergeant should've taken my hundred-dollar bet."

"Who is he?"

"He's a twerp. Senior Auditor for Aviation Issues. I think back home he was a librarian. Here, he's a bean counter, but mostly he's a pain in the ass for people like Jack and me who are actually trying to do some good and make things happen." But Evan was starting to understand that Nolan wasn't the type of guy to brood about stuff like Charlie Tucker or anything else. He pasted on a brave smile. "But hey," he said, "that's why they pay us the big bucks, right? We get it done."

In the short time it took them to walk to the desk, Major Tucker had processed one of the three men who'd been standing in front of his desk. As Nolan got closer, the man in the back of the line turned and took a step toward them and bowed slightly. "Mr. Nolan," he said in accented English, "how are you, sir?"

"Kuvan!" From the apparently genuine enthusiasm, Kuvan might have been Nolan's best friend from childhood. Kuvan seemed to be in his early thirties. The face was light-skinned, bisected by a prominent hooked nose, and featured the usual Iraqi mustache. Nolan came up to him, arms extended, grabbed him by both shoulders, and the two men seemed to rub noses with one another. They then exchanged what Evan had already come to recognize as the standard Muslim praises to the Prophet, after which Nolan continued. "Kuvan Krekar, this here is Second Lieutenant Evan Scholler, California Army National Guard. He's only been here a few weeks and I'm trying to make him feel at home." Then, to Evan: "Kuvan helped us with some of our Filipino personnel down at BIAP. He's a genius at finding people who want to work."

As Krekar put out a hand and offered Evan a firm and powerful grip, he smiled and said, "All people treasure the nobility of work. If everyone had a job, there would be no war."

"Then *I'd* be out of a job," Evan said, surprising himself.

Krekar took the comment in stride, his smile never wavering. "But not for long, I'd wager. Even my friend Mr. Nolan here, a professional soldier of some renown, has found meaningful work in the private sector. In any event, welcome to my country, Lieutenant. You're in good hands with Mr. Nolan."

"I'm getting that impression," Evan said.

Krekar brought his smile back to Nolan. "One hears rumors that Mr. Allstrong is going to be bidding on the currency project."

This was the contract to replace Iraq's old currency, thirteen thousand tons of paper that featured the face of Saddam Hussein on every bill, with one of a new design. Twenty-four hundred tons of new dinars would have to be distributed in under three months. This would involve hundreds of Iraqis in all parts of the country, all of whom would need to be housed and fed in new camps with new infrastructure and Internet services at Mosul, Basra, and many other sites—exactly the kind of work Allstrong was doing now at Baghdad Airport. It would also involve supplying a fleet of five-ton trucks to carry the people and the money.

"It's entirely possible," Nolan said. "Although I haven't talked to Jack in a couple of weeks. And you know, here a couple of weeks the world can change."

"Well, when you do see him," Krekar said, "please mention my name to him. The paper and pressing plants as well as the design elements and the banking issues—I know some people with these skills and perhaps Jack and I could reach an arrangement, if Allah is willing."

"I'll be sure to let him know, Kuvan. If he's bidding at all, that is."

Behind them, Tucker cleared his throat. Krekar bowed a hasty goodbye to Nolan and Evan and then stepped up to the desk.

Backing up a couple of feet, bringing Evan with him, Nolan spoke sotto voce, "Talk about getting it done. If Kuvan's with us on this currency thing, we're going to lock it up. Taking nothing away from Jack's accomplishment, without Kuvan we don't have the airport, and that's no exaggeration."

"What'd he do?"

"Well, you know I told you it was all about getting a lot of feet on the ground here in a couple of weeks. Jack promised he could do it, and the CPA believed him—he's a persuasive guy. But still, push came to shove and Custer Battles was beating us getting guys to work for them at every turn. Jack had no idea where he was going to find guards and cooks and all the other bodies he was going to need. So, it turns out that one of Jack's old Delta buddies does security for KBR, and he turns him on to Kuvan, who's connected to this endless string of mules—Nepalese, Jordanians, Turks, Filipinos, you name it. You give these guys a buck an hour, they'll do anything for you—cook, clean, kill somebody . . ."

"A buck an hour? Is that what they're making?"

"Give or take, for the cooks and staff. Guards maybe two hundred a month." Nolan lowered his voice even further, gestured toward the desk. "But don't let Tucker hear that. Jack bid it out at around twenty an hour per man, but as I say, Kuvan's a genius. His fee is two bucks an hour, which takes our cost up to three an hour, so we're hauling in seventeen. That's per hour, twenty-four seven, times a hundred and sixty guys so far, with another two hundred in the pipeline. And the more we bring on, the more we make. Like I told you, you play it right, this place is a gold mine. How much they paying you, Evan, two grand a month?"

"Close. Plus hazard duty . . ."

Nolan cut him off with a laugh. "Hazard duty, what's that, a hundred fifty a month? That's what our cooks make."

"Yeah, you mentioned that." The news disturbed Evan—a hundred and fifty dollars extra per month and he faced death every day.

After a little pause, Nolan looked at him sideways. "You know what I'm making?"

"No idea."

"You want to know?"

A nod. "Sure."

"Twenty thousand a month. That's tax-free, by the way. Of course, I've got lots of experience and there's a premium on guys like me. But still, guys like you can finish up here, then turn around and come back a month later with any of us contractors, and you're looking at ten grand minimum a month. A six-month tour and you're back home, loaded. This thing lasts long enough, the smart-money bet by the way, and I go home a millionaire."

UP AT THE DESK, Major Charles Tucker looked like he could use some time in the sun. He'd sweated through his shirt. He sported rimless glasses, had a high forehead, and nearly invisible blond eyebrows—a caricature of the harried accountant. And he made no secret of his disdain for Nolan. "Let's see your paperwork. Who signed off on it this time?"

"Colonel Ramsdale, sir. Air-base Security Services Coordinator."

"Another one of Mr. Allstrong's friends?"

"A comrade-in-arms. Yes, sir. They were in Desert Storm together."

"I'm happy for them." Tucker looked down at the sheets of paper Nolan had handed him. He flipped the first page, studied the second, went back to the first.

"Everything in order, sir?" Nolan asked with an ironic obsequiousness.

"This is a lot of money to take away in cash, Nolan." He gestured to Evan. "Who's this guy?"

"Convoy support, sir. Protection back to the base."

Tucker went back to the papers. "Okay, I can see the payroll, but what's this sixty-thousand-dollar add-on for"—he squinted down at the paper—"does this say dogs?"

"Yes, sir. Bomb-sniffing dogs, which we need to feed and build kennels for, along with their trainers and handlers."

"And Ramsdale approved this?"

"Apparently so, sir." Nolan leaned down and pretended to be looking for Ramsdale's signature. Evan stifled a smile. Nolan, punctiliously polite, somehow managed to put a bit of the needle into every exchange.

"I'm going to have somebody in audit verify this."

Nolan shrugged. "Of course, sir."

"Sixty thousand dollars for a bunch of dogs!"

"Bomb-sniffing dogs, sir." Nolan remained mild. "And the infrastructure associated with them."

But apparently there was nothing Tucker could do about it. Nolan had his form in order and it was signed by one of the Army's sanctioned paymasters. He scribbled something on the bottom of the form. Then he looked up. Behind Nolan, the line had grown again to four or five other customers. "Specie?" Tucker said.

"I beg your pardon," Nolan replied.

"Don't fuck with me, Nolan. Dollars or dinars?"

"I think dollars."

"Yes. I thought you would think that. You're paying your people in dollars?"

"That's all they'll take, sir. The old dinar's a little shaky right now."

Tucker made another note, tore off his duplicate copy, and put it in his top right-hand drawer. "This is going to audit," he repeated, then looked around Nolan and said, "Next!"

[3]

THAT NIGHT IN HIS TRAILER'S OFFICE, Jack Allstrong sipped scotch with Ron Nolan while they tossed a plastic-wrapped bundle of five hundred hundred-dollar bills—fifty thousand dollars—back and forth, playing catch. Allstrong's office, nice at it was, remained a sore point with him. This was because the main office of his chief competitor, Custer Battles ("CB"), was in one of the newly reburbished terminals. When Mike Battles had first gotten here two months before, he found that he'd inherited several empty shells of airport terminal buildings, littered with glass, concrete, rebar, garbage, and human waste. He had cleaned the place up, carpeted the floors, wallpapered (all of his supplies bought and shipped from the United States), put showers in the bathrooms, and hooked the place up to a wireless Internet connection.

At about the same time, Jack Allstrong had had to start work on his trailer park to house his guards and cooks, although he still couldn't compete with such CB amenities as a swimming pool and a rec room with a pool table. Allstrong knew that these types of cosmetics would be important to help convince his clients that he was serious and committed to the long-term success of the mission, but he was initially hampered by lack of infrastructure and simple good help.

But then that genius Kuvan Krekar had come up with the idea of dog kennels as another income source, and that was already working. Allstrong now had a decent number of the ministry people starting to believe that IED- and bomb-sniffing dogs would be an essential part of the rebuilding process in bases all over the country.

So all in all, Jack was in high spirits for a variety of reasons: Kuvan was in fact interested in going in with them on their currency-exchange bid,

which gave it immediate credibility and might make them the front run-
ners over CB; the CPA was still paying them in dollars (which meant
Allstrong could buy his own dinars to pay his local workers at the deeply
discounted black-market exchange rate); the bomb-sniffing-dog revenue
wasn't going to be stopped, at least in the short term, by bureaucrats like
Charlie Tucker.

The bottom line was that the two million dollars in cash that Nolan
had retrieved today and carried here in his backpack covered approximately four hundred thousand dollars in the company's actual current
expenses, including tips to Colonel Ramsdale and several other middle-
men. Everyone was too busy and/or too afraid and the times were too
chaotic for anyone to bother keeping close tabs on exactly what the money
was used for, or exactly where it went. There was plenty of it, in cash, and
the mandate was to get Iraq up and running again. Subtext: whatever it
cost.

For example, in the first month of the contract, Allstrong's trailer park
had run out of drinking water within a week, a true crisis. Jack had gone
to Ramsdale and told him he desperately needed to buy more water immediately, but that he was out of money, what with payroll, housing costs,
legitimate security equipment, weapons, and vehicles such as armored
Mercedes-Benz sedans, and all other daily supplies for his now close to
150-man staff. Without a personal look at the situation and apparently
without a qualm, Ramsdale signed off on an authorization for Allstrong
to add six hundred thousand dollars to the original sixteen-million-dollar
contract over its six-month life—peanuts considering the fact that the
contract as written already was paying Allstrong a little bit more than
eighty-eight thousand dollars a day, all of it in cash.

Allstrong had requested a total of a hundred thousand dollars from
Ramsdale for the water, but the colonel had been so used to thinking in
one-month units that he'd okayed six times the requested price, and Allstrong had seen no reason to correct him. And after all, the truth was that
they were all working in an extremely hostile environment, where the
danger of death was real and omnipresent. In Allstrong's view, that risk
should not go without significant reward, even if much of it turned out to
be under the table. It wasn't as though people like Ramsdale didn't know

what was happening. In fact, Ramsdale was planning to retire from the active military before the year was out, and he'd already made a commitment to stay on in Iraq as one of Allstrong's senior security analysts at a salary of $240,000 per year.

Standing over by his wall map, Allstrong caught the latest toss of the packet of bills from Nolan and turned it over in his hands. "So." It wasn't a question. It wasn't an answer. The tone seemed to say, *I'm holding on to fifty thousand dollars in cash, when last year I was flat broke.* He smiled. "How sweet is this, huh, Ron?"

"Yes, sir." Nolan tipped up his scotch. "It's turning out to be a good year."

"Yes, it is." Allstrong crossed over to his desk, casually flipping the wrapped bills package over to Nolan. "And I think it could be even better, but I'm leery of burning out my best assets, which are men like you. No, no, no, don't give me any of that false modesty bullshit. I send you out to do a job and you get the job done. It's not every guy in the world can walk around with two million dollars and not be tempted to disappear with it."

This was more than just idle chatter. That exact temptation, though for far less money—a quarter of a million dollars—had proven too strong for at least one of Allstrong's other senior employees in the past two months. Beyond that, almost two dozen of his first crew of guard hires— from pre-Kuvan sources—had disappeared with guns and credentials almost as soon as they'd been issued them.

But Ron Nolan merely shrugged. "You pay me well, Jack. I like the work. It's nice to get a regular paycheck. Beyond which"—he broke his own smile—"I disappear with two million of your money, I'm pretty sure you'd hunt me down and kill me."

Allstrong pointed a finger at him. "You're not all wrong there. Nothing personal."

"No, of course not."

Allstrong put a haunch on the corner of his desk. "What I'm getting at is whether you're starting to feel stretched a little thin."

"No, I'm good."

"I ask because another opportunity has come up—I know, they're growing on trees nowadays, but if I don't pick 'em somebody else will. Anyway, I wanted to run it by you, see if you wanted to take point on it. I should tell you, I consider it pretty high risk, even for here."

"Taking a walk over here is high risk, Jack."

"Yes, it is. But this is in the Sunni Triangle."

Nolan tossed the package up and caught it. He shrugged. "What's the gig?"

"Pacific Safety—Rick Slocum's outfit, he's tight with Rumsfeld—just pulled in a contract through the Corps of Engineers to rewire the whole goddamn Triangle in three months. High-voltage wiring and all the towers to hold it. You ready for this? He's going to need seven hundred guards for his people."

Nolan whistled. "Seven hundred?"

"I know. A shitload. But I'm sure Kuvan can get 'em."

"I'm sure he can too. You gotta love them Kurds."

"Who doesn't? So . . . you want to hear the numbers?"

"Sure," Nolan said. "I haven't had a good hard-on in a couple of days." With the wrapped bills in one hand and his tumbler of scotch in the other, he got up and crossed over to Allstrong's desk.

His boss pulled over the adding machine and started punching and talking. "Let's assume two hundred a month for the guards, what we're paying now. Good? We've got seven hundred guys working for ninety days, that's four hundred twenty thousand. Plus food and ammo and other incidentals. Let's go wild and call that twenty bucks a man per day, so forty-two grand. Shooting high, call our whole expense five hundred grand. Slocum told me off the record that because of the high risk in the area, he expects the winning bid to come in at no less than twelve mil. Which is exactly what I'm going to bid it at and which, if you're doing your math"—he hit the calculator—"is a three-month profit of eleven million five hundred thousand dollars."

"I've definitely got wood," Nolan said.

"So you're in if we get it?"

"All the way, Jack. We'd be crazy not to."

"I agree. But I'm not sugarcoating it. I'm thinking we might lose a dozen guys. I'm talking dead, not deserted or disappeared."

"Okay."

"There'd be a significant bonus in it for you. Twenty a month sound good?"

"When do I start?"

"First, let's get the gig. But remember, I want you to be sure you're good with it. You'll have your bare ass hanging out there."

"And seven hundred guys guarding it, Jack. Can I bring my escorts? I like that guy Scholler. He runs a tight ship."

"I'll talk to Calliston, but I can't imagine there'd be any problem. He doesn't even know who those guys are."

"Poor bastards."

"Hey," Allstrong said, "they enlisted. What'd they expect?" He went around his desk and stood looking out the window at the airport outside. An enormous C-17 Globemaster III transport plane coasted by on the tarmac—several hundred more tons of supplies and equipment direct from the United States. Without turning around, he said, "So between now and then, what's your schedule look like?"

"When exactly?"

"Next couple of weeks."

"Pretty free. I got the message out up at Anaconda and Tikrit. We've definitely got friends trying to hook us up in both places, but they've got to clear their own brass first. We might have to sub under KBR, but I got the sense they're generally open to us doing what we've done here. Whatever happens, it's going to take a little time. Why?"

Now Allstrong did turn. "I'd like to send you back to the States for a week or two. Clean up some problems in the home office. I'd go myself, but I don't feel like I can leave here just now if we want to pick up these jobs we're talking about. You'd be back in plenty of time for the Triangle thing if that comes about. And after today, payroll's covered until next time."

"What kind of problems?"

"Well." Allstrong tipped up the last of his scotch. "I hired a private eye and he's found Arnold Zwick. The idiot went back home to Frisco." Zwick was the company's senior executive who'd disappeared with a quarter million dollars of Allstrong's money about six weeks before. "I'd kind of like to get my money back. I was hoping you could talk some sense into him. After that, take a little well-deserved R and R wherever you want to go. Sound good?"

"When do you want me to leave?"

"I can get you on a plane to Travis tomorrow morning."

"Done."

Allstrong broke a smile. "You know, Ron, I hate it when you take so long to make your decisions."

"I know," Nolan said. "It's a flaw. I'm working on it."

At his desk, Allstrong picked up a manila envelope and handed it across to Nolan. "If what's in that doesn't answer all your questions, I'll brief you further in the morning. Now you'd better go do some packing."

"I'm gone."

Nolan executed a brisk salute and whirled around. His hand was on the doorknob when Allstrong spoke behind him.

"Aren't you forgetting something?"

Nolan straightened up and turned around as he pulled the packet of bills out from under his jacket. He was smiling. "Oh, you mean this old thing?" He tossed it back to his boss. "Just seeing if you're paying attention, Jack, keeping you on your toes."

"Pretty much always," Allstrong said.

"I can see that. Catch you in the morning."

Dear Tara –

So today I got to walk through some of the mean streets of scenic Baghdad with this crazy guy, Ron Nolan, who didn't seem to know or care that we were in hostile territory. He's one of the security guys for Allstrong, which, you may remember from my last letter, if you're reading them, is the contracting firm that we've somehow gotten semipermanently attached to. I find it ironic, to say the least, that I'm supposed to be out protecting him. This guy needs protection like a duck needs a raincoat.

It was too surreal. He's there to collect the company's payroll for this month. So I'm thinking we're going to go in someplace like a bank and get a check from Bremer's people that Allstrong can then go deposit in their bank. Wrong. They've got barbed wire and cement blocks set up in the hallway in front of this door. Nolan shows his ID to the Marine sergeant on duty with his whole platoon. The place is a fortress.

Anyway, we pass the ID check—everybody knows Nolan—and they walk us into this tiny internal room—no windows out to the hall, even. Stucco is still all over the floors from when the building was bombed in April. No drywall either. After Saddam left town, the looters came in and took everything, and I mean everything. Rebar out of the walls. Internal wiring. You wouldn't believe it. There's not a desk in the whole ministry building—everybody uses folding tables like you get at Wal-Mart. I wouldn't be surprised if we bought 'em from Wal-Mart and had 'em shipped over.

Anyway, so we're in this small, dim, dirty room. Four lightbulbs. It's roughly a hundred and fifty degrees in there. And there's these two guys who take Nolan's papers, check 'em over, then disappear into what looks like a warehouse behind them. Ten minutes later, they're back with a shopping cart full of packages of hundred-dollar bills.

I'm standing there thinking, They're kidding me, right? But they count out these forty wrapped bags of fifty thousand dollars each and— you won't believe this—Nolan signs off on the amount and together, counting them a second time, we load 'em all up into his backpack!

Picture this. Nolan's got two million American dollars in cash in a backpack he's wearing, and we're walking out through this mob of not very friendly people in the lobby of the Republican Palace, and then we're back outside the Green Zone, strolling through the impoverished Baghdad streets that are crawling with citizens who make less than a hundred dollars a month and who really don't like us. Was I a little nervous? Is this guy out of his mind, or what? And I got the sense he was loving it.

Long story short, a couple of blocks along through this really really crowded marketplace and finally we hooked back up with my guys in the convoy and made it out of town and back to the base here, where Jack Allstrong has supposedly got a huge safe—flown in from America, of course—bolted into the cement foundation under his office.

Anyway, lots more to tell about some of the other insane elements of the economics of this place—all the cooks here at the base are Filipinos, and the actual guards out at the airport are from Nepal. We met a guy named Kuvan today who evidently supplies Allstrong with all these workers. Nolan tells me none of them make more than a hundred and fifty bucks a month, where he makes twenty thousand! He tells me that when I get done with my service here, I should volunteer to come back and work for Allstrong. Ex–American military guys make out like bandits here. You'd love it if I went that way, huh?

Okay, enough about this place. You hear about Iraq enough anyway, I'm sure. What I'd really like to know is if you're reading any of these, if I'm at least communicating with you a little. It's hard you not answering, Tara. If you've gotten this far on this letter, and you don't want me to write to you anymore, just tell me somehow and I promise I'll stop. If you've made up your mind and it's completely over. But some part of me holds on to the hope that you might be willing to give us another try when I come home.

I know, as you said a hundred times, IF I get home. Well, here's the deal. I'm coming home.

I'm just having a hard time accepting that our slightly different politics have really broken us up. It's true that I think sometimes it's okay to fight for something, either because you believe in the cause or because you've signed on to fight. You've given your word. It's as simple as that. Maybe you don't think that, and we can argue about it more someday, I hope.

If you could just write me back, one way or the other, Tara, I'd love to hear from you. I love you. Still.

"Hey! Evan."

He looked up to see Ron Nolan standing in the doorway that led back to the dormitory where his men slept. He had written his letter sitting in muted light at a table in the otherwise empty mess hall. Now he'd just finished addressing his envelope and put his pen down, nodding in acknowledgment. "Sir."

Nolan stepped into the room. "Hey, haven't we already been over this? You're Evan, I'm Ron. What are you, twenty-five?"

"Twenty-seven."

"Well, I'm thirty-eight. Give me a break. You call me 'sir,' I feel old. I feel old, I get mean. I get mean, I kill people. Then you'd be to blame. It's a vicious circle and it would all be your fault."

The last words he'd written to Tara still with him, Evan had to force his face into a tolerant smile. "You'd just kill somebody at random?"

Nolan was up to the table by now, grinning. "It's been known to happen. It's not pretty. You want a beer?"

Evan had a nagging feeling that this recreational drinking could become a slippery slope. It would make the second time he'd had alcohol since his arrival over here. But then really, he thought, what the fuck. With everything else that was going on over here, who really cared? Nevertheless, he took a half-swing at reluctance. "We're not supposed to drink," he said.

"Oh, right, I forgot." Nolan cocked his head. "Are you fucking kidding me? Somebody here gonna bust you? You're in charge here, dude."

"I know. I'm thinking about my men."

"What's that, like a mantra with you? You see that in a movie or something? I don't see any of your guys around who are going to be scandalized. They won't even see. Don't be a dweeb. I'll get you a beer."

"One." Evan was talking to his back as he turned.

"Okay. For starters." Nolan walked back into the kitchen, opened an enormous double-doored refrigerator, and returned carrying two bottles of Budweiser. Twisting off the top of one, he slid it down the length of the table to where Evan stopped it and brought it to his lips. When he finished his first sip, Nolan was sitting across from him. "There's e-mail out here, you know." He pointed at the envelope. "Mom or girlfriend?"

"Ex-girlfriend. I e-mailed her all during training and she never answered. It's too goddamn easy to hit Delete. Or change your address. So now I write letters." He shrugged. "Stupid, but maybe some kind of physical connection."

"If she's your ex-girlfriend, why are you writing her?"

"I don't know. It's probably a waste of time. I'm an idiot." He took another pull at his beer. "I'd just like to know if she's even getting these damn letters."

"So that's not the first one?"

"It's like, the tenth."

"And she hasn't written back? Not even once?"

"It was a pretty bad fight. We disagreed about the war."

"People don't break up over that."

"We did." He looked across the table. "But then sometimes I think maybe something's happened to her. I can't believe she won't write me back. Maybe she's not getting them. If she's read 'em, I know she'd . . . maybe she died, or something happened and she can't . . ."

"Can't what?"

"I don't know."

Nolan spun his bottle slowly. "Dude," he said. "No offense, but you're sounding a little pathetic. Here you are laying your life on the line every day. You got bigger fish to fry."

"Yeah. I know." He slugged down a mouthful. "I know."

"You want to just give it up."

"If I heard from her, maybe it'd be easier."

"You *are* hearing from her. Think about it."

"Yeah, you're right. I know you're right." He tipped up his bottle and drained it.

Nolan got up and went back into the kitchen, returned with another round, twisted off Evan's cap, and passed it across to him as he sat down. "So where'd you go to school?"

"Santa Clara."

"College boy, huh?" At Evan's shrug, Nolan went on. "Hey, no crime in that. I went two years to Berkeley. Couldn't stand the place, though, so I went out and enlisted. Made the SEALs and life got good. You finish?"

"Yep."

"What'd you do after?"

"Became a cop."

Nolan cracked a grin and nodded. "I had a feeling you were a cop."

"Why's that?"

"You look like a cop."

"I know a lot of cops who don't look like me."

"You know what you're looking for, I bet they do." Nolan drank, his grin in place. "It's how you walk, how you carry yourself. You're a big guy. You keep yourself in good shape. I would have guessed a cop. Here's to good cops everywhere."

Nolan straightened up, raised a flat palm, and Evan reached up and slapped it hard enough that the clap rang in the empty room. Back down on his seat, Nolan raised his bottle and the two men clinked them together and drank them down in one long gulp.

When Nolan got back with the next round and they'd clinked again, he pointed down at the letter, still on the table between them. "You in touch with anybody else back home who can talk to her, find out what's happening?"

"Not really. This place isn't the best for communication, maybe you've noticed."

"You got family?"

"Yeah, but . . . what am I supposed to do? Ask my brother or my mother to go see if Tara's okay? That'd just be weird. She'd think I was stalking her or something."

"Well." Nolan tipped up his beer again. "Here's the deal. I'm flying back to San Fran tomorrow. You give me that letter, I'll go put the damn thing right in her hand, ask her if she's read the other ones. Find out the story. Be back here in two weeks."

"You're going home. What for?"

He waved away the question. "Just some logistics stupidity for Jack. Office problems. Show a presence and make sure the staff is on board with the big picture. We get either one of these new contracts, we're going to need a new building back at home." He shrugged. "Business stuff. But the point is I'll have plenty of time to drive down to Redwood City. Suss out what's going on with your babe."

"Ex-babe."

"Whatever." He reached out and turned the envelope around, looked down, and read, "Tara Wheatley. Cute name anyway."

"Cute girl," Evan said.

"I believe you."

"You really wouldn't mind going down and giving her the envelope?"

Nolan spread his hands expansively. "Hey! Dude. Please. Forget about it. It's done."

[4]

RON NOLAN SAT ON THE TOP STEP of the shaded outdoor stairway that led to the second landing at the Edgewood Apartments in Redwood City, California. The shade came courtesy of a brace of giant magnolia trees that stood sentinel over the entrance to the apartment complex.

An hour ago, at about five o'clock, he'd climbed the steps and rung the doorbell at 2C, but no one had answered. He could have called first and made an appointment—Tara Wheatley was listed in the phone book—but he thought it would be better if he just showed up and delivered the letter in person. He didn't want to give her the option of saying she wouldn't see him, didn't care if she ever got another letter from Evan. That would have complicated the whole thing. It was better to simply show up and complete the mission.

He wasn't in any hurry. He'd give it an hour or two and if she didn't come home in that time, he'd come back either later tonight or tomorrow. Evan had told him that this time of the summer, she was probably spending most days in her classroom, preparing it for the start of the school year. Tara taught sixth grade at St. Charles, a Catholic school in the next town. Evan assumed that she wasn't dating anybody else, at least not yet, so he was reasonably sure she'd be around by dinnertime most nights, if everything was still okay with her—if she wasn't hurt or sick, or dead.

So Nolan waited, comfortable on the hard stone step. The weather was really ideal, an afternoon floral scent from the gardenia hedge overlying the auto exhaust from the busy street, the fresh-cut-grass smell from the lawn below him, a faint whiff of chlorine from the complex's pool, a corner of which was visible off to his left. If he closed his eyes, Nolan could almost fool himself that he was back for a moment in high school. People were laughing and splashing down at the pool, and the disembodied sounds combined with the softness of the air to lull him after a while, carrying him away from what had become his real world of dust and duty, danger and death.

Like the trained animal he was, he came back to immediate full consciousness as a new vibration from the steps registered with his psyche. He looked down and saw a woman in a simple two-piece blue bathing suit stopped now on the third step, turned away from him, exchanging some banter with other friends who'd obviously just left the pool too. From the shade of her wet hair, he imagined it would be blond when it dried. A thick fall of it hung down her back to a little below the halter strap. She'd hooked a finger through her beach towel and thrown it carelessly over one shoulder. Nolan's eyes swept over the length of her body and he saw nothing about it he didn't like. Her skin was the color of honey.

He shifted on his step to get a better look just as she turned and glanced up at him. Catching him in the act, she shot him a brief complicitous smile that was neither embarrassed nor inviting, then quickly went back to the good-bye to her friends. One of them left her with some parting remark that Nolan didn't quite hear, but her spike of carefree laughter carried up to him. He hadn't heard a sound like that in a while.

Then she was coming up the stairs toward him.

Nolan stood up. He was wearing black shoes, pressed khakis, and a tucked-in camo shirt. He was holding Evan's letter in his hand. Suddenly she stopped halfway up, all trace of humor suddenly washed from her face. As tears welled in her eyes, she brought her hand up to her mouth. "Oh, my God," she said. "It's not Evan, is it? Tell me it's not Evan."

Realizing what she must be thinking—that he was the Army's messenger sent to inform her of Evan's death in Iraq—Nolan held out a reassuring hand and said, "Evan's fine. Completely fine. I'm sorry if I startled you. You must be Tara."

Still knocked out of her equilibrium, she nodded. "Yes. But . . . this is about Evan?"

Down below, one of her male friends called up to her. "Tara? Everything okay?"

It gave her an instant to collect herself. Turning, she waved. "I'm fine.

It's okay." Coming back to Nolan, her voice had firmed up. "Who are you, then? What are you doing here? You had me thinking Evan had been killed."

"I'm sorry. My name's Ron Nolan. I'm a friend of Evan's over there. I should have realized what I'd look like waiting here for you to show up. I'm sorry."

"Okay, you're sorry." She pointed at the envelope he held. "What's that, then?"

"It's a letter that Evan asked me to hand-deliver to you. He was worried about you."

"Why would he worry about me? He's the one in the war zone."

"Well, he hasn't received any letters back from you."

"That's right. That's because I haven't written any. We broke up. Maybe he didn't tell you that. What does he want me to say?"

"I don't know." Nolan held the envelope out to her. "I'm just the messenger here. My job is to give you this last letter and then to tell Evan that you're all right."

"I'm fine."

"Yes, I can see that. You want to take this?"

She didn't move.

He waited, the envelope in his outstretched hand, looking at her, taken by her remarkable face. Her hair was pulled back; it revealed a clear, wide forehead. She'd just come from swimming, so there was no makeup to cover the landscape of pale freckles under her widely spaced glacier-blue eyes that spilled over onto well-defined cheekbones. Even without lipstick, her mouth looked slightly bruised.

Nolan forced himself to look away. It took a serious effort.

Tara looked down at the envelope. "Does he think I haven't gotten his other letters?" she asked. Her shoulders settled as something seemed to give in her. "I don't want to start again with him. Doesn't he see that? It's never going to work."

"Because you disagree about the war?"

"It's not just that."

"No?"

"No. Why do you ask that?"

"Because he seems to think it is. Just about the war, I mean. Although

I told him, and I'll tell you the same thing, people who love each other don't break up over that."

"Over agreeing about whether or not killing people is the way to solve the world's problems? Oh yes, they do, I think."

Neither of them moved.

"And I didn't say that I loved him," she said.

Cocking his head, he said, "When you thought I was here to tell you he was dead, it seemed like you cared about him more than a little bit."

"You can care about someone without either loving them or wanting them to die. Don't you think that's possible?"

"Sure." The woman was beautiful, but Nolan thought that a little attitude check wouldn't hurt her. "Anything's possible," he said. "For example, it's possible that you might even change your mind someday about the people who are risking their lives to guarantee your freedom."

He'd clearly hit a nerve. Her whole face went dark. "That's not fair," she said. "I have nothing but respect for the military."

His mouth smiled, but his eyes didn't follow. "Sure you do," he said. "You just wouldn't want to marry one."

"Besides," she went on, "this war isn't about guaranteeing anyone's freedom. It's just about oil."

Nolan shook his head. As though fighting for oil or anything you needed was wrong. He looked down at his hand and held it out. "Are you going to take this letter or not?"

Her mouth set in a hard line, she stared at the thing as though it were alive and could bite her. And perhaps in some sense it could. At last, she shook her head. "I don't think so. I haven't even opened any of the others. I'm not going to start reading them now."

He nodded again as though she'd verified something for him.

"What does that look mean?"

"Nothing. There was no look."

"Yes, there was. And it meant something."

"Okay. You said you weren't going to start reading Evan's letters now. I guess the look meant, 'Spoken like someone who's afraid that if she gets some facts about what she's already decided on, she might change her mind.'"

Perhaps suddenly aware that she was standing arguing with a man while she was wearing less than her everyday underwear, she pulled the towel up over her shoulders and held both ends of it closed over her breasts. Her voice went soft and low in anger. "I'm not afraid of getting facts, Mister . . . what is it again?"

"Nolan. Ron Nolan."

"All right, Mr. Nolan . . ."

"Ron, okay?" Again, he grinned, taunting her.

"Okay, Ron." He'd gotten her heated up, which was his intention. "For your information, as a matter of fact I do have all the facts I need about Evan and about this stupid war in Iraq. And I don't need his letters to make me feel sorry for him. He made the decision to go over there. He decided to leave me and do that. Now I've moved on and he can't just think he's going to explain his way out of it and if I'd just understand how hard it was for him, then somehow we'd get back together. I'm not going to do that."

"No. I can see that." Nolan held out the letter again. "Last chance." When she didn't move to take it, Nolan slipped it into the pocket of his shirt and said, "I'll tell Evan you're in fine health. Excuse me. Nice to have met you." Moving past her, he started down the steps.

When he got to the bottom, she spoke. "Mr. Nolan. Ron."

Turning, he looked up at her. "I'm not against the military," she said. "I'm against Evan being in this war. There's a difference."

Nolan raised his hand in a salute. "Yes, ma'am," he said. "If you say so."

At SEVEN-THIRTY, he rang her doorbell again.

She answered the door in tennis shoes, a pair of running shorts, and a black Nike tank top. Her hair back in a ponytail. She still hadn't put on any makeup and it looked as though she'd been crying.

"I'm not going to read that letter," she said first thing. "I already told you."

"Yes, you did. I'm not here for that."

"Well . . . what?"

"Well, pretty clearly you're not with Evan anymore. I thought maybe you'd like to go get a drink somewhere."

She crossed her arms. "You're asking me on a date?"

"I'm asking if you'd like to go get a drink or something. Not that big a commitment."

"I thought I made it clear how I feel about getting involved with military people."

"You did, which would break my heart if I were a military person. Which, fortunately, I'm not."

"But you said you were with Evan over there?"

"I am. But I'm a civilian. I work for Allstrong Security. Evan's based with our headquarters group. I'm back home on assignment here for a couple of weeks and tonight I'm looking at dinner all by myself, which isn't my favorite."

"So, as a last resort . . ."

"Not exactly that, but we had a couple of issues we could have fun talking about if we left Evan out of it." He looked around behind her into her apartment. "It doesn't look like you've got much of a party going here anyway."

"No." She sighed.

Sensing that she was weakening, he asked, "Have you eaten?"

"No."

"You can pick the place," he said. "Anywhere you want, sky's the limit."

Sighing again, she broke a weak smile and nodded. "That's a nice offer. Eating by myself isn't my favorite, either, and I've been doing a lot of that." She met his eyes, then looked away, wrestling with the decision.

"I don't want to have another fight about this war or about Evan."

"I don't want to fight either. I just want to put myself on the outside of some good food and drink."

"That does sound good." She gave it another second or two, then stepped back a bit, holding the door open for him. "You want to come in and sit down a minute, I'll go put on some clothes."

SHE PICKED AN UNDERSTATED and very good Italian place on Laurel Street in San Carlos, maybe a mile from her apartment, a car ride short enough to preclude much in the way of conversation. Nolan, usually voluble in any situation, found himself somewhat tongue-tied from the minute she walked out of her hallway in low heels and the classic simple black spaghetti-strap dress. She wore a gold necklace that held a single black pearl, and matching earrings. She'd put her hair up, revealing a graceful neck, showcasing the face in relief.

Neither the bathing suit she'd been wearing when he'd met her nor the tank top, tennis shoes, and running shorts when she'd opened the door tonight had prepared him for the sophistication that she now exhibited. Before, of course, she'd been pretty enough to attract him—good-looking California-girl cheerleader—but now something in her style bespoke a worldliness and maturity that, frankly, intimidated him. Nolan's style, and his plan for that matter, had been to tease her about her political leanings and beliefs, wear her down, get her laughing and eventually tipsy, bed her, and report back to Evan that he was lucky she hadn't read his letters or written back—she wasn't worth the trouble.

Now, ten minutes of silence on the drive over pretty much shattered that plan. Try as he might, and as much as he might have wanted, he wasn't going to be able to take her that lightly. It wasn't just the bare fact of her substantial beauty, but a seriousness, a gravitas, that he couldn't remember ever having encountered before in the women he'd known.

Handing his keys to the valet in front of the restaurant, Nolan noticed that Tara remained seated, her hands clasped in her lap. A test? Would he be a chivalrous gentleman if he opened the door, or would that make him a chauvinist pig? He hadn't worried about a social nicety like that in ten years, and now suddenly he badly wanted to make the right decision, to look good in her eyes. But his only option was to be who he was, and his parents had raised him to have old-fashioned manners, so he came around and got her door for her. She rewarded him with a small smile in which, inordinately pleased, he read approval.

The tuxedoed maître d' knew who she was, at least by looks. He greeted her familiarly, kissed her hand, nodded at Nolan with respect and perhaps a soupçon of envy, and led them to a private banquette in the back. Lighting in the place was dim, with pinpoint lights onto the tables to facilitate reading the menu. Tara ordered an Italian-sounding white wine he'd never heard of and he asked for a Beefeater martini up.

The waiter left. Tara sipped her water. "I said I didn't want to fight, but we're allowed to talk if you want. If we don't, it might get to be a long night."

"I've been trying to avoid sensitive subjects."

"Okay, but you haven't said two words since my apartment."

"That's because everything I thought of seemed risky."

"Like what?"

Nolan hesitated, came out with it. "Like how lovely you look. See? I've offended you already."

"I'm not offended."

"I think you are. You frowned."

"I did?"

"Definitely."

"I didn't mean to frown. I'm not offended. It wasn't an offended frown. I'm even flattered. Thank you." She scratched at the napkin next to her plate. "I'm just not very comfortable with compliments, I suppose. Plus, I'm a little nervous. This might have been a mistake."

"What?"

"You and me. Going out for dinner. It just sounded so good to go out and . . ." Sighing, she killed a moment with another sip of water. "I don't want to give you the wrong impression."

"About what?"

"About if this is a date. Like a boy/girl date."

"Okay, I'll try not to get the wrong impression. What would be the right one?"

"That it's just dinner. Two people out at a restaurant together."

He smiled across at her. "As opposed to what? A romantic dinner?"

"I guess. I wasn't thinking this was going to be a romantic dinner. That's probably why I frowned."

"Back to that, huh? You frowned because I said you were lovely, which means I'm romantically interested."

"Something like that, I suppose."

The waiter arrived with their drinks, and Nolan waited until he'd moved out of earshot, then sipped at his martini and picked up where they'd left off. "Okay," he said, "I promise I'm trying not to be romantically interested. You're the girlfriend of a pal of mine, so that would be awkward, except you said that you're done with him."

"I think."

"Ah. A change in the story."

"No, not really. I just wasn't thinking that I was going to go out with anybody else so soon. I mean on a date."

"I've got an idea. How about we don't call this a date or anything else? Just let it be what it is. Do you have to decide that right away?"

"Maybe not. I just don't want to send you any mixed signals. I'm not really with Evan anymore, but I'm . . ."

"You still care about him."

She raised her shoulders. "I don't know. Not answering his letters is a decision. Not having feelings about him isn't something you just decide. I can't say I'm there yet. And now here we are, you and me. You asked me out and I said yes. I don't know why I did that."

"You were hungry?"

"We could have gone to McDonald's. I didn't have to get dressed up. This feels . . . different."

"Than McDonald's? I'd hope so." Nolan leaned in across the table, caught and held her gaze. "Look, Tara, it's not that complicated. I don't know you, and the only two things I know *about* you are, one, that we probably disagree about the military, which we're not allowed to talk about. And two, you're very pretty. That's just an observation, and risky because you might think I was coming on to you, which would put this more in the line of a date, I admit. So let's get that off the table right now." He straightened back up. "This is not a date. I'm way too old, and what are you, twenty-two?"

"Try twenty-six."

"Well, I'm thirty-eight, that's too much right there. I could be your father."

Around a small smile, she sipped wine. "Only if you were a very precocious eleven-year-old."

"I was," he said, and held out his stem glass. "Here's to precocious children."

She stopped, her glass halfway to his. "I don't know if I can drink to that. I teach eleven-year-olds. If they were any more precocious, we'd need bars on the windows."

Nolan kept his glass where it was. "All right," he said, "here's to peace, then. Is peace okay to drink to?"

She clinked his glass. "Peace is good," she said. "Peace would be very good."

NOLAN PULLED INTO A SPACE in the parking lot by her apartment. He killed the engine and his lights and reached for his door handle.

"You don't have to get out," she said.

"No, I do. A gentleman walks a woman to her door on a dark night."

"That's all right. I'll be fine."

He sat back in his seat, then turned to look at her. "You're trying to avoid that awkward here-we-are-at-the-door moment. Understood. You don't have to ask me in for a nightcap. I won't try to kiss you good-night. Even if I am finding you marginally more attractive than before we'd had such a good time. That was a great meal."

"It was." But she spoke without much enthusiasm. Her hands clasped in her lap, she sat facing forward, stiff and unyielding.

"What is it?" he asked. "Are you all right?"

She exhaled. "Do you still have Evan's letter?"

"Yes, ma'am."

She didn't move. "I think I should read it. I should read the other ones."

"All right. It's in the glovebox, right in front of you. Help yourself." He opened the car door and stepped out. The night smells of gardenia, jasmine, magnolia—he'd forgotten how beautiful it could be here in California in the summertime. Walking around the car, he opened the passenger door.

Tara sat still another second, then opened the glove compartment, picked out the envelope, swung her legs, and got out. She said, "Really, Ron, I'm okay. That's my place, right up there, you can see it from here."

"Yes, you can, but it's against my religion to let you walk up there alone."

She sighed. "Okay."

"And no funny stuff," he said. "From you, I mean."

Amused in spite of herself, she looked up at him and shook her head. "I'll try to keep myself under control." Holding up the letter so he could see she had it, she turned and he fell in beside her—across the parking lot, up the outside stairs. Unlocking her door, she pushed it open and turned on the inside light. "Safe," she said. "Thank you."

"You're very welcome." He executed a small bow. "I had a great time," he said. "You sleep tight."

[5]

SATURDAY HE TOOK HER up to San Francisco. This one was a non-date, he told her, because it was in the daytime and a real date by definition had to be at night. He picked her up at ten-thirty in the morning and with the top down on his Corvette, they took Highway 280 up to the city, the beautiful green back way, Crystal Springs reservoir on their left, and then, farther on, the great expanse of the glittering Bay down to their right.

She didn't know the city as well as he did. She'd told him that at dinner, and he'd used it as his excuse to ask her out again: She couldn't live as close as she did to one of the world's great cities and not know very much about it. It was morally wrong.

So they hit the Palace of the Legion of Honor, then swung back through Golden Gate Park, stopping for tea at the Japanese Tea Garden after an hour inside the De Young Museum. The fine August weather was holding up, and parking at Ghirardelli Square, they walked back up Polk Street and ate baguettes and pâté and drank red wine at one of the outdoor tables of a French bistro. Taking a walk afterward, idly sightseeing, they essayed the descent of Lombard, the "crookedest street in the world"—although it wasn't in fact even the crookedest street in the city, Nolan told her. That distinction belonged to Vermont Street down in Potrero Hill. Nevertheless, Lombard was crooked and steep enough, and he told her that she might want to put her hand on his arm for balance, and she did.

In North Beach, at Caffe Trieste, Nolan brought their cappuccinos over and put them down on the tiny table in front of her. "Okay," he said, "risky-question time again."

This time, more comfortable with him by now, she smiled and said, "Uh-oh."

"Think you can handle it?"

"You never know, but I'll try."

"Evan's letters."

"What about them?"

"Have you read them?"

She looked down at her coffee, lifted the cup and took a sip, then put it down carefully. "Why don't you just tell me I'm pretty again and we'll run with that instead?"

"Okay. You're pretty again. After that ugly time you had back there for a while."

"Yeah, that was terrible." But the gag wasn't working. Her mouth went tight and she closed her eyes, sighing, then opened them and looked him full in the face. "Not yet. I tried starting to read them the other night, but I'm still too emotional about him. I haven't changed my mind about what he's doing, so there's really nothing he can say . . ."

Nolan took a long moment before he sipped his coffee, another one before he spoke. "You don't see anything noble or glorious or even good in the warrior, do you?"

She briefly met his eyes. "The *warrior*," she said in a derisive tone.

"The warrior, that's right."

She shook her head. "Evan's not a warrior, Ron. Evan's a simple soldier, a grunt who's taking orders from men he doesn't respect, fighting in a country that doesn't want us there, risking his life for a cause he doesn't believe in. I have a hard time with words like *noble* and *glorious* and *good* coming into that equation when I keep seeing waste and stupidity and ignorance."

"Okay," Nolan said. "We could maybe get in a good fight about this particular war. But that's not what I'm talking about. I'm talking about the philosophical concept of the warrior."

Her face was still set in stone. "I never think about the warrior, Ron. War is what's wrong with the world, and always has been."

Again, Nolan let a silence accumulate. "With all respect, Tara," he said quietly, "you owe it to yourself to think about this."

"To myself?"

"If you're dumping the guy you're in love with over it, then yes. To yourself."

"I've told you, I don't know if I'm in love with him anymore."

"Because he went to fight?"

She slowly turned her coffee cup around. "I told him we could go to Canada, or anywhere else."

"And what happens when Canada or wherever feels threatened and needs soldiers?"

"But that's the point, Ron. There was no threat. Iraq was no threat. It was preemptive, like Germany invading Poland. America doesn't do that, that's the point. There are no WMDs, you wait and see. The whole thing's a sham. It's about oil profits and that's all. Halliburton and those people. Can't you see that?"

"Defense contractors, you mean?"

"Yes. Defense contractors. Big business. Cheney and his buddies."

"Well, of course I see what you're saying, but I'm in a little bit of a bind here, because a defense contractor is who I work for. But from my perspective, we're the guys who are protecting the Army and the civilian admin guys over there. We're the ones feeding our troops, moving water and supplies, doing good work, saving lives, trying to rebuild the country."

"That we destroyed in the first place."

Nolan took a breath. "Look, Tara, war may be hell but that doesn't mean everybody involved in it is evil. I've seen evil, and believe me, it's a whole different animal than what you're thinking of. So let's not talk about this war. I grant you it's got some issues. Let's talk about the warrior."

"The warrior, the warrior. I don't want the warrior in my life, that's all. I don't want the warrior in the world."

"Ah, but there's the crux of it. Of course it would be wonderful if there didn't need to be warriors. Just like it would be great if there were no evil in the world. But here's the thing—there is evil. And without warriors, evil would triumph."

"How 'bout this, Ron: Without warriors, evil couldn't attack."

"So it's chicken and egg, is that it? Which came first? No"—he put his hand on hers, took it away as though it burned him—"listen. My point is this: There is always going to be evil and, yes, it will attract evil warriors. You buy that so far?"

She managed a small nod.

"Okay," he went on. "So evil and its minions are a given, right? Right. Come on, you admit that. You've just admitted it. And, P.S., it's true."

She hesitated, then said, "Okay. Yes. So?"

"So once evil's on the march, what's going to stop it except a greater force for good?"

She sat back and folded her arms. "The greater force doesn't always have to be physical. It can be spiritual. Look at Gandhi, or Martin Luther King. Fighting should be a last resort. I think a lot of so-called warriors are really warmongers picking fights to justify their own existence."

"Sometimes they are, yeah. And Gandhi and King, great men, both of them, no question. And both assassinated, I might point out. And neither used their nonviolence in an actual war. Okay, they fought evil, but it wasn't on the march. It wasn't to the warrior stage yet. But even so, for every King or Gandhi, you've got a Neville Chamberlain or somebody who doesn't want to fight. It's not till you get yourself a warrior—like, say, Churchill—that you really can stop active evil. You think Hitler would have stopped by himself? Ever? Or Saddam Hussein, for that matter?"

"We did stop him, Hussein," she said. "He wasn't a threat."

Nolan let his shoulders relax. His face took on a peaceful neutrality. His voice went soft. "Tara, please, you've got it backward. If he wasn't a threat, it was because we did already stop him once. Our warriors stopped him in Kuwait. That's the only thing he understood."

Tara was twirling her cup around in its saucer, biting on her lower lip. Eventually she raised her eyes. "I don't like to think about this, Ron. About evil's place in the world."

He kept his voice low, met her eyes, again put his hand over hers and this time left it there. "I don't blame you, Tara. Nobody likes to think about it. And some places, like here in the U.S., and on a gorgeous afternoon in this great city, it can seem so far away as to be nonexistent. Thank God. I mean, thank God there are islands where the beast is kept mostly at bay. It's in its cage. But the thing to remember is that somebody, sometime, had to put the beast in there, and has to keep it there. And that's why we need—we all need, the world needs—warriors. How did you feel about Evan being a cop?"

Her frown deepened, her head moving from side to side. "I don't think I was exactly thrilled, but that was different."

"How?"

She worried her lip for another moment. "Soldiers, their job is to kill. Cops, they mostly protect."

"And sometimes to protect, don't they have to kill?"

"But it's not the main job."

"Could that be because individual bad guys don't need an army to defeat them?" He took his hand away from hers and sat up straighter, lifted his cup to his mouth, put it back down. Looking at her, he saw that her eyes had gone glassy and tears hung in their corners. "I'm sorry. I don't mean to ruin your day and make you cry. We can stop talking about this."

One tear fell, leaving its streak on her face. "I don't know what I'm going to do. It's so hard."

"It is," he said. "I know."

"I'm trying to do the right thing."

"I can see that."

"I should at least read his letters."

"That might be nice."

"But I'm still . . ." She stopped, looked at him, shook her head again. "I don't have any answers. I don't know what I should do."

"You don't have to decide anything today. How's that?"

She gave him a grateful smile. "Better."

"Okay, then," he said. "I think that's about enough philosophy for one day. Why don't we blow this pop stand?"

ONE OF THE LANDMARKS of old San Francisco was Trader Vic's, the restaurant where the mai tai was purportedly invented and a favorite hangout for the famous columnist Herb Caen and his pals. The original Vic's had gone out of business decades ago, but a couple of years back, they'd opened a new one near City Hall. It had a great buzz and was the same kind of place—a Pacific-island-themed destination spot serving enormous "pu-pu" platters of vaguely Asian appetizers that could be washed down with mai tais or any other number of generous rum drinks, many of them served for two out of hollowed coconut shells.

Nolan and Tara had ordered one of these when they sat down and then had another with their dinner. Their relaxed sightseeing and later the intense conversations had drawn them closer somehow and blurred the distinction between date and nondate, and by the time the waiter cleared the dinner trays and left them the check, Nolan was beginning to let himself consider the possibility that this incredible woman might like something in him after all. Clearly, Tara had an ambiguous commitment, at best, to Evan Scholler, and she seemed to be enjoying his company—laughing, teasing, drinking. Not quite outright flirting, certainly not coming on to him overtly, but giving him a lot of her time and attention, her foot nowhere near the brakes. His personal code of honor regarding a fellow warrior wouldn't permit him to pursue her if she claimed any sort of allegiance to Evan, but she'd rather definitively avoided that, and if she responded to one of his overtures later, then that would be a clear answer in itself.

Nolan had known that they had valet parking at Trader Vic's, but as a general rule he wasn't too comfortable letting valet attendants get behind the wheel of his Corvette. So, keeping his eyes open, a few blocks before they'd reached the restaurant, he had spied a miraculous section of free curb and he'd pulled into it without much thought. It had still been warm, with a certain softness to the dusk light, and walking a few extra blocks with Tara had seemed both natural and appealing.

Now, outside, it had grown dark. In typical San Francisco summer fashion, the temperature had dropped twenty degrees in the past two hours and a chill, biting wind off the Pacific was scouring the dust off the streets and making the very air gritty. They were on Golden Gate Avenue, an east-west street that funneled the blow and intensified the unpleasantness.

Tara said, "How'd it get this nasty this fast?"

"The city got the patent on this weather back in the Forty-Niner days. It was supposed to keep out the riffraff. I don't think it's worked too well, but they've kept it up. Why don't you go back inside and I'll get the car and come back for you?"

"We don't have to do that. It's not that far. I can take it."

"You're not too cold?" Tara was wearing sandals and shorts and a T-shirt with the midriff showing—California summer gear. Now ridiculously inappropriate.

But she just laughed. "It's only a few blocks. It's invigorating, don't you think?"

Nolan, in civilian shoes, khaki-colored Dockers, and a Tommy Bahama silk shirt, nodded and said, "Invigorating. Good word. You sure?"

"Let's go."

At the first corner they hit, Polk Street, they stopped at the curb for the light. He noticed that her teeth were beginning to chatter. "It's closer going back to Trader Vic's than it is to the car. You're sure you don't want to do that?"

"You think I'm that much of a wimp?"

"I never said that. But you do seem cold."

"I'll be fine. Promise."

"Okay, then." He put his arm around her. "This is for warmth only," he told her. "Don't get any ideas."

Perhaps a little tipsy, she folded her arms across her chest and leaned slightly into him. "Warmth is good," she said, then added, "Come on, light, come on."

But just then, before the light changed, a break in the traffic opened up, and taking her hand, he squeezed it. "¡Vámonos!" And they darted out into the street. In the next block, and the one after that, the streetlights weren't working. Even though they were only a few blocks from City Hall, Nolan realized that they were entering the Tenderloin District, one of the city's worst neighborhoods, where services tended to need upkeep. They walked quickly, still holding hands, their footfalls echoing, and, at the next crosswalk—Larkin—had to stop again for traffic and the light. Behind them, a prostitute in a black minidress and fishnet top stepped out from the lee of a building. "Are you two looking to party?" From the voice, Nolan realized that the woman was a man. "I've got a place right here behind us."

"Thanks, but we're good." Nolan stepped between Tara and the prostitute. "Just going to our car."

"Isn't this the street, up to the left?" Tara whispered to him.

"One more."

They jumped the light again and moved into the next darkened block. Suddenly the glittering city they'd been enjoying all day had disappeared. The breeze carried on it the acrid smells of garbage and urine. In the passing cars' headlights, Nolan could see that nearly every doorway they passed held a person lying down, bundled up in cloth or newspaper. At a break in the traffic, they crossed over in midblock, all but running now with cold and adrenaline. They turned up Leavenworth toward Eddy, into the heart of the Tenderloin. But—the good news—they were now only a bit more than a half block from where they'd parked.

As it turned out, though, that distance wasn't going to be short enough.

THE THREE YOUNG AFRICAN-AMERICAN MEN appeared out of nowhere and blocked their way. Tara whispered, "Oh God," and moved in a step behind Nolan. All of the men wore heavy, hooded jackets and as they fanned to surround the couple, the one in front of them flashed the blade of a knife. "Where y'all hurryin' up to?" he asked.

Nolan, following the flow as the men moved into position, one to the side into the street, and the other behind them, let go of Tara's hand and put an arm protectively around her waist. "Our car's just up the street there," he said, pointing.

"The 'Vette, I'm guessing?"

"That's right."

"Nice ride?"

"Yes, it is. I'm hoping that it's still in good shape."

The leader spoke to his troops. "He hopin' it still in good shape. You hear that? Man worried about his wheels." Coming back to Nolan, he moved the knife to his other hand. "Thing is, we been watchin' it, make sure nobody mess wid it, you know what I'm saying?"

"I appreciate that," Nolan said. He turned now, placed the position of his other two assailants clearly in his mind, then moved sideways a bit with Tara so that he could see any movement from the man behind him in case he was getting ready to strike. Looking now directly at the three men, one at a time, he said, "But my girlfriend's cold and she really needs to get inside the car right away." He reached behind him, as though reaching for his wallet. "How much can I pay you gentlemen for watching over my car for me?"

"Ron . . ." Tara began.

"Just stay cool," he whispered, tightening his grip on her waist, holding her to him. Somehow he'd taken the keys from his pocket, and now he found one of her hands and pressed them into it. "When it starts," he whispered directly into her ear, "get to the car and get it running."

"When what starts? Ron, you can't . . ."

Nolan started to reply when, with no warning beyond a guttural obscenity, the leader suddenly lunged forward, leading with the knife. Nolan pushed Tara back out of the way, then ducked away from the attack, deflecting the knife, and kicked out behind him, hitting the trailing man in the knee. The man screamed and went down. Nolan whirled, kicked again, and caught the leader in the hip, knocking him into the third guy coming in from the street. It was only a temporary holding action, but it gave the couple an instant's reprieve and, for Tara, a clear run to the car. "Go!" he yelled to her.

She ran.

Nolan saw the shadow looming up in his periphery, and he ducked away and slashed backward as he turned. Seeing the glint of the knife, he came down with a chop on the wrist above it, and it clattered away on the sidewalk. He no longer knew whether he was fighting the leader or the second guy, but it didn't matter. Close enough to smell him now, he lifted a knee into the man's groin and when he doubled over, followed it with a rabbit punch to the man's neck. Knowing that he'd killed him, as much by the way he fell as anything, he saw that there was still another knife in the equation. The other man swung a wide broadside at him and Nolan stepped back, let it pass harmlessly in front of him, then stepped inside and delivered a flat-hand uppercut to the base of man's nose, driving the cartilage back into the brain. The body straightened for an instant before crumpling back to the street.

Looking back at the first man whose knee he'd shattered, Nolan realized that while he was no longer a threat, he was a witness. And witnesses, Nolan firmly believed, were bad luck. A brief scan of his surroundings confirmed that there were no others—none of the homeless were huddling in doorways on this block. The man was still down, moving on the ground, pushing himself in a crablike fashion back and away from the fight. It took Nolan only a few steps, a couple of seconds, to get back next to him.

"Dude," he said. He was breathing hard, but his voice was almost apologetic, devoid of any emotion. "This was a bad idea. You got to stop this shit. Your leg okay? Can you get up? You ought to get that looked at. Here, let me help you."

The young man hesitated for a minute, but then took Nolan's outstretched hand and allowed himself to begin to be lifted. But as soon as he had the leverage he needed, Nolan reached his other hand around the man's neck, found his chin, and gave it a vicious snap back and sideways. Letting this last body fall back to the sidewalk, Nolan looked down at the carnage he'd wreaked. Satisfied, he broke back up the street at a jog, jumped over the fallen leader, and in a couple of dozen steps was where Tara had started the car and already maneuvered it out from the curb, ready to make a getaway. He knocked on the car's trunk as he was going around the back of it and then opened the passenger door and jumped in, breathless. "Are you okay?" he asked her. "Can you drive?"

She was holding the wheel, shivering, and managed a nod.

"Hit it, then. Now!"

TARA DROVE IN SILENCE for about six blocks before she pulled over and stopped the car. "I don't think I can drive anymore," she said.

"I'll take it."

She looked over at him for the first time since he'd gotten in with her. "Are you hurt?"

"No."

"What happened to them?"

"I don't know. They got tangled up in each other and that must have slowed them down enough to give me a minute to come running."

After a minute, she said, "We could have been killed, couldn't we?"

"I don't know about that. I think maybe they were trying to feel us out, that's all. They didn't have guns. They probably would have just taken our money and other stuff if we would have let them."

She sat still and allowed the silence to gather there in the confined space. Then, letting out a staggered breath, she opened the car door and got out. Nolan took the cue and did the same on his side, waiting for her to get in the passenger seat before he closed the door behind her. Behind the wheel, he belted up and got back into traffic.

"God," she said after a while. "You're sure you're all right? I can't believe that just happened. It was so fast. Just suddenly they were there."

"Yeah. That's how it happens." He glanced across at her. "I shouldn't have parked there. I should have known better. I wasn't thinking. I'm so sorry."

"You don't need to be sorry. It wasn't your fault. In fact, if you hadn't been there . . ."

But he shook his head. "Then *you* wouldn't have been there. You would have parked at the valet station like any other thinking human being."

"Well, still . . ." She hugged her arms to herself. "God, I just can't stop shaking."

"It's okay," he said. "It's just adrenaline." He took his right hand off the wheel and held it out. "If it'll help," he said, "here's a hand you can hold."

It took her a moment to decide. She took in a breath and let it out, then reached over and put her hand in his, bringing both hands over the gearshift and into her lap, then covering them with her other hand. "Thank you," she said. "That helps."

THERE WAS NO ARGUMENT about whether he should walk with her to her door. She opened it, flicked on the inside light, and turned back toward him, her face reflecting her turmoil. Breaking a weak, somehow apologetic smile, she started to raise her hand then let it fall. "I was going to say, 'Thank you, I had a good time,' but"—she met his eyes—"I'm a little confused right now. Is that all right?"

"That's fine," Nolan said.

"I'm going to read Evan's letters."

"As well you should."

"I don't want you to think I'm being ungrateful."

"Why would I think that?"

"Well, for saving my life and everything. For being a warrior."

That brought the trace of a smile. "I wondered if that had occurred to you. But you don't owe me anything, Tara, and certainly nothing for that." He gently chucked her chin with his index finger. "Don't you worry about me. I'm fine. You've just had a trauma you're going to need to process. It's okay. You're home now. Have a good night." And with that, he came forward, quickly kissed her cheek, and backed away. "Close the door," he said. "That's an order."

UNABLE TO SLEEP, she finally got to the letters.

They were from Evan's heart and soul. The way she remembered him came through loud and clear in every one—mostly chatty and irreverent, but then always there with the real stuff at the end. He missed her. He loved her and wanted them to try again when he got home.

When.

But it wasn't when, she knew. It was *if.* There was no certainty that he'd come back alive or in one piece. She couldn't shake the idea that even as she was reading his words, he might already be dead. She wasn't about to commit to him again and then have him die over there. There would be no commitment, she knew, until they were back together in person, until these philosophical issues had been resolved one way or the other. To give him hope before that would just be counterproductive and stupid.

Tara was reading in her bed with blankets over her, wearing pajamas and her warmest bathrobe against her continued shivering, even though it was a balmy night in Redwood City. Finally, she put down the latest letter—it was the fifth or sixth one she'd read—and closed her eyes, trying to picture the Evan she had known in her mind, trying to dredge up a feeling from the time when she'd thought they were the perfect couple, that they'd marry and have a family and a wonderful life together. It wasn't coming easy.

Part of her, perhaps most of her, still believed that she loved him, that he would come home from this war and they'd start over and work out all the issues. But he'd been gone now for several months and she'd spent the time putting him behind her. When he came back—if he came back—they'd see where they were. She thought that if she and Evan were in fact the perfect couple, if they were meant to be together, then nothing could keep them apart. But in the meanwhile she had her life and her principles. She wasn't going to remain in a relationship where those principles were compromised from the beginning.

But tonight's object lesson with Ron Nolan had shaken some of those core beliefs. They had been set upon by bad people who wished them harm, and without Nolan to defend her, she might very well . . .

Suddenly the memory of the assault came over her again—the men surrounding them with knives glinting in their fists. The utter lack of warning when the unexpected first thrust came at them. If Ron hadn't been there . . . or, no, more than that . . . if he hadn't been who he was, it could have ended so badly. It could have been not just a robbery, but the end of her life, of everything.

A fresh wave of adrenaline straightened her up in the bed.

Throwing off her covers, she went to the window in the bedroom and pulled aside the drapes a couple of inches, just enough so that she could see out. The blue-lit water in the pool down below was still. No shadows moved on the lawn, in the surrounding hedges. All was peace and suburban serenity. Letting the drapes fall, she crossed her bedroom and, turning on lights as she walked, she went out into the living room. She opened the closet in that room, the other one by the front door, then she turned and went into the kitchen. The window over the sink looked down on the parking lot and she turned out the kitchen lights so that she could more clearly see outside.

In the puddle of one of the streetlights, Ron Nolan's Corvette faced away from her apartment, toward the entrance to the driveway that led into the parking lot. The top was down, and it was close enough that she could easily see Ron himself still in the front seat, his elbow resting on the windowsill. She looked at the clock—he'd left her at the door nearly forty-five minutes before.

"Ron?"

He'd heard the footsteps coming up and had forced himself to remain still, facing forward, until she'd come abreast of him. Now he looked over at her, in her T-shirt, jeans, and sandals. "Hey." Low-key.

"What are you doing?"

"Just sitting here. Enjoying the night." She seemed to need more explanation and he gave it to her. "I was a little wound up earlier. I thought I'd decompress a little before braving the roads again. I thought you'd be asleep by now."

"No," she said. "I was wound up too." Pausing, she let out a small breath. "I read Evan's letters. I think he's still confused. I know I am."

"About what?"

"Us. Me and him. What I'm going to do."

"What do you want to do about Evan?"

"If I knew that, I wouldn't be confused, would I? I haven't been fair to him either. I should write and tell him what I've been feeling."

"And what is that?"

"That maybe we still have a chance if he's willing to try to get through all this stuff. But that has to be in the future, when he gets back, if he does get back. I can't commit again until then, till we see what we've got. Does that sound fair to you?"

"I'm not an unbiased source," he said. "It sounds to me like you just said you weren't committed to him."

"We broke up five months ago, Ron." She took in a breath. "What were you really doing out here?" she asked.

"I was enjoying the night, the smells, the absence of gunfire." He looked up at her. "I was also hoping you might not be able to sleep and you'd see me down here, and that you'd come down and that I'd see you again. Maybe walk you back to your door."

After a second, she said, "You could do that."

[6]

IN SAN FRANCISCO, Deputy Chief of Inspectors Abe Glitsky entered the homicide detail at nine-thirty on the following Monday morning. Darrel Bracco, one of Glitsky's early protégés, looked up from the report he was writing and almost spilled his coffee standing up to attention, saluting, yelling, "Ten-hut!"

Glitsky felt the scar through his lips straining against the rare urge to smile. In the end, as usual, the smile never appeared. Some inspectors in the room looked up, of course, though nobody else went military on him. But Bracco was still on his feet, expectantly. He evidently had some knowledge of why the head of homicide, Lieutenant Marcel Lanier, had summoned the deputy chief. "Marcel told me to keep an eye out for you, sir. I was just warning him that you're here."

Glitsky stopped. "On the off chance that he's misbehaving in some way?"

"You never know," Bracco said. He fell in beside Glitsky, then nodded at another inspector, a woman named Debra Schiff, who looked up and was getting to her feet while Bracco went on. "Schiff was in there with him with the door closed for an hour already this morning. To look at her, you'd never know she was a screamer."

Schiff, gathering some stuff from her desk, nodded at Abe and replied in a conversational tone, "Bite me, Darrel."

Glitsky kept walking, Bracco and Schiff behind him. At Lanier's open door, he knocked. The lieutenant was on the phone, feet up on his desk, and waved everybody in. His new office upstairs was at least twice as large as the cubicle he (and Glitsky before him) had inhabited one floor below. There was room for as many as half a dozen people in front of his desk, with four chairs folded up against the back wall with its "Active Homicides" blackboard. Glitsky unfolded one of the chairs and let the other two inspectors grab theirs.

"I understand," Lanier was saying into the phone. "Yes, sir. That's why I've asked Abe to come down and get briefed. No"—he rolled his eyes with the tedium of it all—"I realize we don't want to . . ." He moved the telephone away from his ear and Glitsky could hear a voice he recognized as Frank Batiste's, the chief of police. So whatever this was about, it had some profile already. "Yes, sir," Lanier repeated in the next pause, "that's the idea. I will. Yes, sir." Finally, he hung up, got his feet back down on the ground, and brought his upper body in close to the desk, elbows on it. "That was the chief."

"I got that impression," Glitsky said. "How's Frank doing this fine morning?"

"Frank's concerned about our citizenry, lest they panic."

"And why would they do that?"

"Well, that's what I asked you down to talk about, since the media's going to be all over this if it gets out, and I know how much you cherish all things that give you face time in front of cameras." Everyone appreciated the irony of Lanier's statement. Within the department, Glitsky was notorious for two things: He didn't tolerate or use profanity, and he hated interactions with any form of media. Unfortunately, this latter made up about eighty-five percent of his job.

Now, a tight look of resigned patience firmly in place, Abe sat back and crossed one leg over the other one, ankle on knee. "Okay. What do we got?"

Lanier glanced at his two inspectors, came back to Glitsky. "We've got the possibility of a serial killer."

"Ah," Glitsky said. "And we haven't had one of those for a while."

"Hence the panic," Lanier said, "which Frank would so like to avoid. Anyway, I thought I'd let Darrel and Debra get you up to speed and you can decide where we are exactly and how we handle things if it gets hot." He nodded at his female inspector, whose pretty face she tried to make invisible, with limited success, by wearing a tough expression most of the time. "Debra, you want to start?"

"Sure." Bent over slightly in her chair, she had her elbows on her knees, her hands clasped in front of her. Raising her chin, she shifted a little to face Glitsky. "It's not much of a story by itself, but last Wednesday, I got a late call down in the Mish, early a.m. There's a body in an alley down there around the corner from the Makeout Room. White male, decently dressed, his wallet's still in his back pocket. Turns out he's a thirty-six-year-old ex–Navy SEAL named Arnold Zwick. No criminal record, unmarried and unconnected, currently unemployed. But he'd evidently come back from Iraq recently where he'd done some work for Allstrong Security, which is based here in town."

"What kind of work?" Glitsky asked.

"Whatever they do over there with former military guys. I went back to Allstrong and they told me that their main contract right now is protecting Baghdad Airport. But they didn't know where Zwick had gone to. The manager of the office told me they thought that he might have been killed over there. One day he just disappeared. Except that we now know he came back here. And some witnesses I talked to—neighbors he'd made friends with—seemed to have had the impression that he had a lot of money. But it's not in a bank account that I've been able to find, and there wasn't any cash in his apartment, so robbery might still be a motive, either that or he had the stuff hidden pretty well."

Glitsky asked, "Do you think it's possible he stole money from Allstrong over there?"

Debra nodded, apparently pleased at the question. "That was my assumption, too, sir. Especially given the way he died."

"And how was that?"

"Somebody snapped his neck."

"Close work," Glitsky said. "Not that easy."

"It's even harder when you factor in Zwick's training and that there was no sign of struggle or a weapon from his attacker. And Zwick was heavily armed. He had a knife in a sheath on his leg and a forty-five carried loose in his coat pocket. Both still on him when I got to him."

"So his killer," Glitsky said, "was another commando. You were thinking probably with Allstrong, somehow, getting back their money."

Debra nodded. "That is kind of where I was going until Marcel called me yesterday and told me about Darrel's latest."

Glitsky shifted his interest over to Bracco. "Talk to me," he said.

"Three street thugs, all with sheets. All of 'em young, strong, and armed, out for a good time on Saturday night in the Tenderloin. All of 'em killed by hand. Maybe they just decided to mug the wrong guy, the same guy who killed Zwick, but that's a stretch, don't you think?"

"The stretch is why he would have stayed around," Glitsky said, "if he's one of the Allstrong people."

"There aren't any Allstrong people, though," Debra said. "The whole staff is over in Iraq. They've got a woman manager over here in a tiny office by Candlestick and a couple of clerks. None of 'em had ever met Zwick personally. And I believe them."

"On the other hand," Lanier interjected, "maybe we got a bona fide wacko who's getting off on killing people with his hands. These Tenderloin meatballs, we got two broken necks and a septum jabbed up into the brain. But there's no connection we can come up with between Zwick and these dirtbags. None of the victims had anything stolen off them."

Glitsky scratched at his cheek. "How many broken-neck murders have you seen in the past twenty years, Marcel?"

The lieutenant nodded. "I know what you're saying, Abe. And every one of the very few was in the course of some kind of a fight. These guys, there was hardly a sign of a struggle. The problem is that we got reporters already onto the story—I got a call at home this morning, and so did Frank—and they're salivating over this serial killer possibility."

Glitsky chewed the inside of his cheek for a minute. "And Allstrong hires Navy SEALs and guys like that for their security work over in Iraq?"

"That's what I gather," Debra said. "They've got nice brochures, but really, as I said, no people."

"But let's not lose sight of the main question," Lanier said. "We don't want to spin this toward a serial killer loose in the city. Frank would have my balls. Excuse me, Debra."

But Glitsky was standing up. "I'm doing my very favorite Monday-morning press briefing in fifteen, Marcel. I'll put that fire out at least until we get another broken neck."

"What are you going to tell 'em?" Lanier asked.

"I'll say I can't comment on ongoing investigations, except to say that it would be irresponsible to print or run rumors of a serial killer when there is no evidence to support it. And none of these victims are high profile. We got three dead brothers in the hood and one dead unemployed white guy in the Mish. This stuff is unfortunate but it happens. And the story goes away."

"Even if this guy's the same guy," Bracco said, "who did all of them?"

"If it was," Glitsky said, "I've got to believe he's long gone by now and never coming back."

[7]

MAJOR CHARLES TUCKER, the Senior Auditor for Aviation Issues, didn't like to leave the Green Zone any more than anyone else did. But in the past ten days, since Ron Nolan had shown up downstairs at the Republican Palace with his $2 million requisition, he had signed off on another $3.3 million in cash to Allstrong Security—all of it approved by Airbase Security Services Coordinator Colonel Kevin Ramsdale.

Jack Allstrong himself had shown up at his desk four times, patiently explaining to Tucker that obviously, if he continued to question the need for money, he was unaware of the sheer vastness of the task that Allstrong Security had contracted to undertake. The airport itself, BIAP, was enormous—thirty-two thousand acres. Securing even half of all that land alone in a hostile country was a monumental job. Besides that, Allstrong needed immediate money to buy the cars and trucks that would deliver the new dinar cash all over the country on his latest contract. He also needed more money for the bomb-sniffing dogs, for his enormous payroll, for food for his constantly growing influx of employees.

In spite of the danger inherent in every trip outside of the Green Zone, Tucker decided he had to see for himself what was going on out at BIAP. Leaving the Republican Palace in the early afternoon, and in uniform, he was chaffeured through the city and out to the airport by a three-Mercedes convoy of KBR security people who carried only sidearms—the irony wasn't lost on him. Nevertheless, by the time they arrived at the first airport checkpoint, it was nearly four o'clock in the afternoon.

There was, as always, a long line of cars ahead of his convoy, all of them waiting to be searched and to have their papers inspected. At this rate, Tucker's convoy wasn't going to get inside for at least another hour.

So to save himself the time, he decided to get out of his vehicle and enter the compound on foot. With any luck, he could complete his informal inspection and start back to Baghdad before his convoy even made it as far as the gate anyway. They could U-turn away and be gone with that much less of a hassle.

But no sooner had he gotten out of his car than he became aware of the sound of gunfire. Not distant gunfire, which was so common in Baghdad and often relatively harmless, but nearby gunfire that seemed to be coming from the neighborhood just to his left, adjacent to the eastern border of BIAP. In contrast to the airport's western edge, which bordered the Euphrates River and opened into a plain of flat and formless ditch-crossed farmland that gradually degraded into desert, this eastern no-man's-land was a densely populated area of the ubiquitous low-lying, dung-brown structures that seemed to make up so many of Baghdad's suburbs, and that Tucker knew to be home to hundreds of Saddam Hussein's former officers. Gunfire in this area wouldn't be good news. But still, if it was confined to the neighborhood, he knew that it needn't necessarily concern him here.

Squatting, moving along the safe side of the line of vehicles, Tucker had almost made it to the gate when he realized that the gunfire was in fact close by. Stopping, he saw a handful of men scurrying along just outside the compound, by the barricades that had sprung up along the perimeter's fence. All of the black-clad men had camo'd their faces—Tucker knew that they weren't regular Army. They all carried rifles and belts of ammunition, and they were firing out into the suburbs.

Still keeping low, he sprinted to the gate, where four men—also heavily armed, in matching dark fatigues—were manning the entrance, seemingly unconcerned with the firing going on behind them. Tucker walked up to the nearest of them. "Hey!" Holding up his hand. "Major Charles Tucker. What the hell's going on over there?"

The man, who was not American, looked over his shoulder, then back at Tucker. He shrugged and spoke in a stiltedly correct British accent. "We were taking some fire from over there. Jack Allstrong ordered our men to put them down."

"You're attacking them?"

"It appears so, yes."

"*You can't do that.* That's against policy."

Again, the man shrugged. "Mr. Allstrong called them out."

"Well, let's get Mr. Allstrong here so he can call them off. You can't conduct an offensive with nonmilitary personnel."

Another man, with the same accent as the first, broke away from his inspecting comrades and got in front of Tucker. "Is there a problem, sir?"

"You bet there's a problem." He pointed to the shooters. "I'm assuming those men are working with Allstrong. Who's in charge here?"

"I am."

"What's your name?"

"Khadka Gurung."

"Where are you from?"

"Nepal."

"Well, Mr. Gurung, I'm a major in the U.S. Army. Private military forces are not allowed to attack insurgent groups."

"But we were fired upon first. From over there." He pointed vaguely to the general neighborhood.

"You were fired upon?"

"Yes, sir."

Tucker pointed. "Was anyone in this line of cars hit?"

"I don't believe so. No, sir."

"But the cars were just sitting here, like they are now?"

"That's correct."

"And none of them were hit?"

"I don't believe so."

"And nobody's firing from over there now?"

"No. We must have driven them off."

"Either that, Mr. Gurung, or there wasn't much of a concerted attack, if they couldn't manage to hit stationary vehicles at less than a hundred yards. Maybe the attack was just celebratory gunfire, which we hear all the time in Baghdad. How about that?"

"That's not impossible."

At that moment, several of the group of commandos broke into a run across an open area toward the Iraqi buildings. "They're attacking, for Christ's sake! That's blatantly illegal. Where's Jack Allstrong now? He's got to call this off. I need to talk to him right away. Do you think you could manage to arrange that?"

Gurung, nonplussed by Tucker's apparent anger, said, "Of course. Please to wait here and I'll try to reach him." In no great hurry, he walked over to a small stucco building that looked as though it had recently been constructed just inside the gate. He picked up a telephone.

Tucker, meanwhile, whirled back to face the first man he'd talked to. "Who are you?" he snapped.

"I am Ramesh Bishta."

"Well, Mr. Bishta, while we're waiting for Mr. Allstrong, can you tell me what's holding things up so badly here? Why can't you get this line moving?"

"The drivers," he explained. "So many do not speak English. It is difficult."

"Of course they don't speak English. They're mostly Iraqis. They're delivering Iraqi goods, doing Iraqi business. Don't you have people here at the gate who speak Arabic?"

"No, sir. I'm sorry, but no."

"How about translators?"

"Again. No. Maybe someday."

Tucker brought his hands to his head and squeezed his temples. He'd personally overseen the transfer of nearly six million dollars to Allstrong Security in the past two weeks and apparently Jack Allstrong couldn't find one local worker to speak Arabic to the Iraqis who needed to get into his airport? To say nothing of the fact that against all regulations he was paying his private commandos to lead offensive military strikes against the civilian population. Tucker had come to believe that Allstrong was playing fast and loose with the chaos that was Iraq, but now he was starting to believe that he didn't understand the half of it.

Gurung returned and informed Tucker than Mr. Allstrong was on the way. The next car at the gate finally got approval and moved on into the compound. The raiding party seemed to have stopped for the moment at the back line of the neighborhood buildings. Tucker took the opportunity to ask Gurung about the dogs.

"I'm sorry?" The unfailingly polite guard shrugged.

"The bomb-sniffing dogs. I would assume they would be here at the gate, checking the cars. The trunks."

"No. I haven't seen these dogs yet. Perhaps soon." Still smiling, the soul of cooperation, Gurung asked to be excused for a moment. He went over to Bishta, and after a short conversation, the two men went and had a few words with their other two colleagues. Almost immediately, they stepped away from the next car in the line and waved it through the gate. And then the next. And the next. The line was starting to move.

Tucker watched for a minute, then stepped in front of the next car up, holding up his hand to stop it. The driver laid on his horn, but Tucker kept his hand up where it was, holding him back. "Mr. Gurung!" he yelled out. "What's happening now? You've kept these people sitting here for hours and now you're just letting them in?"

This finally brought a disturbed frown to Gurung's face. "Mr. Bishta said you told him the line should be moving faster."

"Yes, but, well . . . you don't just wave 'em in now, for Christ's sake! You still gotta get their papers and check the cars. Maybe you get some Iraqis down here, at least a translator, somebody who can speak Arabic. You get your bomb-sniffing dogs . . ."

Gurung's expression changed in the middle of the tirade. His focus went to someplace out over Tucker's shoulder and then suddenly he was walking away across the parade ground to intercept Jack Allstrong, who was jogging up. The two men stopped maybe twenty yards from where Tucker stood. After a short exchange of words, Allstrong put a quick, reassuring hand on Gurung's shoulder and then went past him as he strode toward the gate.

At this moment, Tucker, still in the middle of the road, holding up the flow of traffic, got another blast from the horn of the car in front of him. By now truly enraged, he put his hand onto his sidearm and pointed the index finger of his other hand at the car's driver—the warning explicit and eloquent.

Behind him, he heard Allstrong's relaxed voice. "Maybe you want to step out of the way and let my men do their job, Major."

Tucker whirled on him. "How can they do their job and question these people when they don't speak the language?" he said. Without pause, he went on, pointing to the commando team, now hard up against the back of one of the buildings. "But before anything else, you've got to call those men off. They can't conduct an offensive sweep."

Allstrong glanced over to them. "We were being fired on, Major. It's defensive. We have to protect ourselves, and we have every right to."

"Your men here tell me that nothing's been hit. Which makes me doubt there was much of an attack."

Allstrong pulled himself up to his full height, his usually affable expression suddenly harsh. "Maybe you missed the mortar attacks last month, Major, that punched holes as big as Volkswagens into the runways out here and killed four of my workers and wounded twenty more. Or the rifle fire that shot my office up and, oh yeah, killed another two of my guys." It was Allstrong's turn to point to the low-lying buildings. "That neighborhood over there is a breeding ground for attacks on this airport, and it's my job to stop them."

Tucker stuck his chin out. "There's no attack going on now, Allstrong. You either call your men back or I swear to God I'll personally intervene with Calliston and even your buddy Ramsdale to cut your funding off. We don't need wildcat contractors playing cowboys out here. You play by the rules or you don't play at all."

By this time, Gurung had come up near them. Allstrong glanced again at his commandos, then nodded to his employee. "Radio them to come on back in," he said. "Fight's over for today." Then, back to Tucker, "But that isn't why you came out here."

"No, it's not. I came here to inspect what our money's being used for. You realize that your gate guards here don't speak Arabic? How are they supposed to get information from these drivers when they don't speak the language?"

Allstrong shook his head. "These men are British-trained Gurkha guards, Major, the pride of Nepal. They're completely capable of handling this mission. I've tried hiring locals a few times and you know what happens? They either steal my shit or they don't show up, or both. They're afraid if they take a job with me, their families will get killed, and they're not all wrong. My guys are thorough and they get the job done. If it's a little slower than American standards, well, excuse me all to hell, but we're in a war here."

"What about the dogs? The bomb-sniffing dogs?"

"What about them? We're still training them. I've got sixty trainers and a hundred dogs working full-time out behind the terminals. When they're ready, I'll put 'em all to work. Meanwhile, again, I go with my guys."

"I'm going to want to see your kennels. And your fleet of trucks and cars that we've coughed up the money for. In fact, you can just look on my visit here today as an unannounced, informal audit to see if we've got to come back with a full-on inspection. I've got preapproval both from Calliston and the Inspector General of the Army."

"Good for you." Allstrong backed away a step and crossed his arms over his chest. "But I'm afraid I can't allow you inside the compound."

"The hell you can't."

"You watch me, Major. You're forgetting that I don't work for the Army. My contract is with the Coalition Provisional Authority. Jerry Bremer, through Kevin Ramsdale. I don't hear a Calliston in there, do you? Or a Tucker. And my bosses are happy enough with the job I'm doing that I'm getting almost more work than I can keep up with. So, look. You want to check up on me, clear it with Ramsdale. I've got nothing to hide, but I'm not showing my books to anybody who doesn't have permission to see them. So thanks all to hell for your interest, Major, but I'm afraid this trip's going to turn out to be a waste of your time." He turned to his worker. "Mr. Gurung, Major Tucker is not to enter the compound today or any other day without my permission. Is that clear?"

Gurung nodded. "Yes, sir."

Tucker glared at Allstrong. "I'm going to go to Ramsdale, and even Bremer if I have to," he said. "If I were you, Allstrong, I'd get my books in order. I'm going to be back with all the authority I need. You just wait."

"I'll look forward to it. Meanwhile, you have a nice drive back to Baghdad, Major. And keep your head down." Allstrong broke his trademark smile. "You never know."

RON NOLAN HAD ARRIVED back in the compound earlier that same day, and now he and Evan Scholler sat on the steps to the chow trailer. A few minutes of natural sunlight remained in the hot August evening. Dust from the afternoon winds hung in the air, smearing it yellowish-brown.

"Dude," Nolan said. "I'm telling you. She's moved on. You ought to do the same."

Evan didn't argue with Nolan this time about whether or not he'd have another Budweiser. He'd already had three—cans this time, not bottles. He popped the top and lifted the next cold one to his lips. He wiped foam from his lips. "Was there anybody else?"

"What? You mean with her? Did I see anybody? Haven't we been through this already? No." Nolan took a pull from his can. "But we're talking about a total time in her presence of about three minutes, all of it at the door to her apartment trying to get her to just take the damn letter. If there was some guy inside with her, I didn't see him."

"So maybe—"

But Nolan cut him off. "Maybe nothing, Evan, don't do this to yourself. You had to see her face—great face, by the way, so I know where you're coming from and you've got my sympathy—but if you'd seen her face you wouldn't have any doubts. She didn't want anything to do with you or that letter. You want to hear it again? She says, 'I'm not going to read it.' And I go, 'You don't have to read it, but I promised Evan I'd get you to take it from my hands. You can do that, can't you?' So she goes, 'I'm just going to throw it away.' And I go, 'That's your call, but I've got to give this to you.' So she takes it, says thanks, and looking straight into my eyes, she rips the envelope in half."

Evan sipped beer and blew out a breath. "Fuckin'-A."

"Right. I agree, it's a bitch. But, hey, the good news is you don't have to wonder anymore." Nolan hesitated, sipped his beer, shot a sideways glance across the steps. "I don't know if you want to hear this, my friend, but I've got to tell you or you'll never know. She put a move on me too." Holding out a restraining hand, Nolan hurried on. "Nothing I couldn't handle and I very reluctantly gave her a pass, but if you needed any more certainty . . ."

"No, that ought to cover it."

"I hear you. But you know, give me certainty anytime. I can deal with that any day over not knowing."

"Maybe you're right."

"Damn straight I am."

Evan looked over at him. "She really came on to you?"

Nolan nodded, solemn. "And I didn't get the impression it was the only time since you've been gone. The girl's a stone fox, Ev. You think she's sitting home alone nights watching TV? Come on, she's human, life's short, and she's got a life back there. This isn't rocket science. You guys broke up before you came here. It's over. Accept it."

Evan hung his head. He couldn't seem to muster the strength to lift it up.

SHIT, NOLAN WAS THINKING. *Maybe the guy's not going to get over her.* That possibility hadn't occurred to him. Nolan had told the small lie about Tara ripping up the envelope because he thought it made for a convincing story, brought the finality of Evan and Tara's breakup a bit closer to home. But now he saw that Evan might not accept it. He might keep trying to reach her again, might find out what had gone on in Redwood City, might even manage to snag Tara back away from him.

Nolan couldn't let that happen. He wanted Tara. He'd gotten her and he intended to keep her until he didn't want her anymore, which might be a very long time. However, Evan's reaction caught him off balance; now he'd simply have to adjust. Fine-tune the mission. Keep him away from her.

All was fair in warfare anyway. And the old saying was right: in love, the same thing. You needed to be willing and able to adjust to the unexpected.

Evan Scholler was stationed in a dangerous place, after all, where anything might happen to him. Nolan could tweak the odds just a bit, give Evan a little something else to deal with instead of Tara Wheatley.

He reached over and hit Evan's arm, hard but friendly. "You know what you need, dude? You need something to take your mind off all this, that's all."

"And that's always an easy call here at party central."

"Hey, there's things to do here. You just got to know where to look."

"Right."

"You doubt me?"

For an answer, Evan drank beer.

"The man doubts me." Nolan shook his head in disbelief. "Dude," he said. "Put your beer down. Come with me."

Evan took a beat, then tipped his can up, emptying the contents into his mouth. When he finished, he got to his feet. "Where we goin'?"

"Smoke-check party," Nolan said.

"What's that?"

"Smoke-check the Muj. You'll love it."

THE SPY FOR JACK ALLSTRONG in the airport's adjoining neighborhood was an educated ex–Republican Guard officer, a Sunni named Ahmad Jassim Mohammed. No one knew the exact game he was playing, and this was no doubt the way Ahmad preferred things, but the pretense was that he had accepted the new, post-Saddam status quo and wanted to work with America and its allies to help rebuild his country. He'd gotten connected to Allstrong during the July mortar attacks on the airport, when under the guise of offering his services as an interpreter, he'd instead provided five thousand dollars' worth of information that had proved valuable in identifying several target houses in the airport's neighboring slum that had contained large caches of weapons, mortars, and other explosives.

Though no one, least of all Jack Allstrong, ruled out the possibility that Ahmad might in fact be a spy checking out airport conditions for the insurgents, and though the consensus among Nolan and the other executives at Allstrong was that Ahmad was using the American military presence to settle vendettas with his personal enemies among his former Republican Guard colleagues, the fact remained that his information tended to be correct. When the targets he'd provided were eliminated, the mortar attacks on the airport had abruptly come to an end. That was about as far as Allstrong or Calliston needed to take it. Allstrong had paid Ahmad for similar information several times now, and counted on the intelligence he supplied to keep a step ahead of the insurgency just outside his perimeter. And so far it was working.

No one had expected today's attack, but Ahmad had arrived at the compound in its aftermath. Now, in the sultry early night, he sat in the front seat of one of Allstrong's convoy vehicles. Ron Nolan was driving. Evan Scholler, in black fatigues, his Kevlar vest, and with four beers in his bloodstream, stood uncomfortably manning the machine-gun platform on the vehicle's roof. Behind him in the seats, two other black-clad Gurkha commandos checked their weapons.

The party rolled out of the main gate. Off to their right, they could sense, more than see, the slumlike contours of the mud-caked domiciles of the residents. A quarter mile or so outside of the compound, the Humvee veered suddenly right and began bouncing across the no-man's-land that separated the airport from the homes. Nolan killed the regular beams, leaving only the car's running lights on.

Evan squinted ahead into the night, unable to make out many details either to the sides or ahead of them. He wished he hadn't had those beers. He wasn't drunk, but he could feel the alcohol, and though Nolan had assured him that they faced little or no danger, just an awesome adrenaline rush, he'd also insisted that Evan wear his bulletproof vest, as all the others had done.

Evan thought he might in fact wind up needing all of his faculties, and couldn't shake a keen awareness that his reflexes might not be there for him in a pinch. So his mouth was dry, his palms sweaty, his head light. He was alone up here, half-exposed. Behind him in the car, he heard nothing—and that didn't help his nerves either.

What the hell was he doing?

In another minute, they'd entered the town itself. As they'd approached, Evan thought for an instant that the car might just try to crash through one of the yards, but evidently Ahmad knew where he was directing them. Suddenly they were in a street so narrow it barely fit them. It was lit only by the lights from within the houses, but the place wasn't dead by any means. The locals were outside smoking, talking—their Humvee picked up some kids, running along beside the car, whistling, calling out for food or candy.

The foot traffic forced them to slow down. Nolan honked from time to time, never stopping, forcing his way ahead, making the populace move out of his way. Evan, sweating heavily now, kept his hands gripped tightly on the handles of his machine gun, even as he heard Nolan call up to him. "Stay cool, dude. Nothing happening here. We're not there yet."

They turned left, then right, then left again, now down unmarked and unremarkable streets, into more of what looked like a marketplace area, closed up for the night, with few if any pedestrians. Nolan accelerated through the space and entered another quarter of the suburb. People still milled about, but less of them, and with far fewer children. Nolan made another turn and pulled up to a stop at a large open space in front of what appeared to be a mosque. Here the foot traffic had all but disappeared. The only light or sound—television and music—came from a two-story dwelling at the next corner down on their left.

The passenger door opened and Ahmad got out of the car, closed the door gently, then leaned back in the window and said something to Nolan. Then he turned and ran, disappearing into another of the side streets. Nolan killed even the running lights next, and then immediately they were moving, only to stop again sixty yards along, after they'd passed the house Ahmad had pointed out to them.

This time the engine went quiet. The radio music from the house was louder down here, providing cover for whatever noise they made as Nolan and his two commandos opened their doors and got themselves and their weapons out into the street.

They all gathered now down under and just to the side of Evan's position. They'd blackened their faces and hung grenades on their vests since they'd gotten into the Humvee and these two details chilled Evan, who could barely make out anything but Nolan's teeth in the darkness. He seemed to be smiling. "I'm leaving the keys in the car," he said to Evan, "in case you need 'em. You remember how we got here, right?" A joke, even in this setting. Nolan went right on. "If you need to, hop in the driver's seat and get out any way you can. But this shouldn't be long. And, hey, remember, we're in black, but we're the good guys, for when we come out."

Then he illuminated the light on the helmet he wore, as did the other men. All of these were clearly well-rehearsed maneuvers. At a nod from Nolan, the men broke into a trot toward their target. In an instant, one stood on each side of the door of the house. Nolan took a position in front of the door and, without any warning or fanfare, opened fire with his submachine gun. This knocked the door open and Nolan kicked it and led his men in.

Immediately, bedlam ensued. Screams and yelling, shots and sporadic bursts of automatic weapons fire, then the three men assembling outside again—Evan thinking it was already over—when the night was split by a shattering explosion out of the lower window. And the men rushed in again, this time into pure darkness.

Evan's knuckles tightened on the handles of his machine gun. Behind him, he heard a sound and whirled. He couldn't make the gun turn a full one-eighty, and he suddenly realized that if anyone were to come up behind him, he had no defense. Drawing his sidearm, he ducked down for a second below the backseat and peered back behind him, but there was nothing in the street. In the house across the way, the yelling and the gunfire continued—again individual shots followed by bursts of automatic weapons. Another explosion ripped through the night, this one blowing out the upstairs windows, and then suddenly all went quiet.

A few seconds later, the three men in black fatigues appeared outside the front door again. Two of them bolted back toward the car, while the third reentered the building, then emerged on a dead run just as his two colleagues got to the car. Behind him, in the house, two nearly simultaneous explosions blew out any remaining glass in the downstairs windows and halfway knocked him to the ground, but he kept running until he, too, reached the car.

By this time, Nolan was back in the driver's seat, breathing hard, starting the thing up. Over his shoulder, he yelled up at Evan. "That was the place all right. That Ahmad is okay. Must have been a dozen Muj in there, dude, maybe two hundred AKs. RPGs, you name it. But nothing that a few frag grenades couldn't cure. God, I love this work. How 'bout you? Was that fun or what? Hang on, we're rolling."

Behind him, fire and smoke were beginning to billow out of the building's windows. Evan couldn't take his eyes off the spectacle. He was vaguely aware of doors opening on the street around him, people pouring out into the night, more shouts, the screams of women. Behind them now, he heard the crack of what he imagined must be gunfire, but he saw nothing distinctly enough to consider it a target.

But then they had turned the corner and were headed back through the space in front of the mosque, then the marketplace. Evan swallowed against the dryness in his throat, his stomach knotted up inside him, his knuckles burning white on the handles of his machine gun.

[8]

A WHILE AFTER MIDNIGHT, Evan tried to carefully and quietly navigate the three steps up to the dorm trailer. Between the news from home about Tara and his involvement in the raid, he figured he had every excuse in the world to split most of a bottle of Allstrong's Glenfiddich with Nolan after they returned to BIAP, and now the ground was shifting pretty well under him. He was looking forward to lying down on his cot. Tomorrow he'd try to process most or all of what he'd been through tonight, the aftermath.

He and his reservists had worked it out with the Filipino cooks and clerical staff and now had a dorm section of their own, eight cots in a double-wide bedroom. When he pushed open the door, the greeting was like a surprise party without anybody yelling surprise.

Suddenly all the lights went on, and these nearly blinded him, especially in his inebriated state. Stumbling backward against the brightness, his hands up in front of his eyes, he might have tripped on the steps and fallen back out of the trailer if one of his guys, Alan Reese, hadn't been waiting there to grab him.

As the glare faded, Evan blinked himself into some recognition. Facing him, some sitting on their cots, some standing, was his squadron. Marshawn Whitman, his sergeant and second-in-command, much to Evan's surprise, was standing at attention and even offered a legitimate salute before he began with a formality he'd never used before. "Lieutenant," he said, "we all need to have a talk."

Evan tried to focus so that he only saw one Marshawn, instead of two, looming there in front of him. He put a hand out against the doorjamb to hold himself steady. His tongue, too big for his mouth in any case, could only manage the word "Now?"

"Now would be best," Whitman said. "We need to get out of here."

"Where to?"

"Back to our unit."

"Our unit? How we gonna do that?"

"We don't know, Lieutenant. But being here just isn't right."

Evan, stalling for time, looked over first at Reese standing next to him, then around to Levy and Jefferson and Onofrio sitting forward on their cots, identical triplets—elbows on their thighs, hands clasped in front of them—and finally to Pisoni and Koshi and Fields, who were standing with their arms crossed, leaning against the wall. Whatever this was about, these guys were a unit, all of them in it together. And from the looks of them, all of them angry.

"Guys," Evan said, "it's not like we got a choice. They sent us here."

"Well, not really. They sent us up to Baghdad, then we wound up here."

"I'm not sure I see the difference, Marsh."

Corporal Gene Pisoni, a sandy-haired, sweet-tempered mechanic for a Honda dealership in Burlingame, and the youngest member of the squad, cleared his throat. "We could get shot at doing what we're doing here, is the difference, sir. They shot up this base today. We've just been lucky out in the streets up until now."

Next to Evan, Reese piped in. "The casualty figures posted today list a hundred and sixteen dead this last week in Baghdad alone. Our luck can't hold much longer."

Lance Corporal Ben Levy, a law student at Santa Clara, added to the refrain. "We've been here almost a month, sir. This was supposed to be a temporary assignment, wasn't it?"

Evan still felt the room swaying under him, but part of him was sobering up. "Well, first, our luck can hold, guys, if we just stay careful. But I'm not arguing with you. This isn't what we got sent over here for, I agree. I just don't know what we can do about it."

"Talk to Calliston." Nao Koshi was Japanese-American, a software engineer who'd been pulled out of what he'd thought was the world's best job at Google. "He assigned us here. He can assign us out."

"We shouldn't be doing this." A thick-necked Caltrans employee from Half Moon Bay, Anthony Onofrio was thirty-three years old. He had two young children and a pregnant wife at home. He was perennially the saddest guy in the group, but rarely spoke up to complain. Now, though, he continued. "This really is all fucked up, sir. They've got to have the trucks we're trained to fix at least down in Kuwait by now. We ought to be down there doing what we're trained to do, not standing up behind machine guns."

"I agree with you, Tony. You think I want to be here? But I thought you guys were happy to have regular quarters, regular meals."

"The guys we came over with," Marshawn said, "they've probably got that by now, too, wherever they are. Maybe better than we got it here. We're all willing to risk it. Huh, guys?"

A general hum of affirmation went around the room.

"Bottom line, Ev," Whitman continued, "is what Tony said. Us going out in these packages every day is just bullshit. We don't want to die driving Jack Allstrong or Ron Nolan around to pick up money."

"Nobody does, Marsh. I don't either."

"Well, the way it's going now," Whitman said, "it's only a matter of time."

Evan shook his head in an effort to clear it, then wiped a palm down the front of his face. "You guys are right. I'm sorry. I'll talk to Calliston, see what I can do. At least get things moving, if I can."

"Sooner would be better," Pisoni said. "I got a bad feeling about this. Things over here are heating up too fast. It's only going to get worse."

"I'm on it, Gene," Evan said. "Promise. First chance I get. Tomorrow, if he's around."

"Oh, and sir," Whitman added. "It might be better, when you get to see Calliston, if you were sober. He'll take the request more seriously. No offense."

"No," Evan said. "Of course. None taken. You guys are right."

As it turned out, Colonel Calliston did not have a free seventeen seconds, much less fifteen minutes, that he felt obligated to devote to the problems of a reserve lieutenant whose squadron was gainfully employed doing meaningful work for one of the CPA's major contractors. Finally, Evan took the guys' beef to Nolan, who listened with apparent sympathy to the men's position and promised to bring the matter up with Allstrong, who in turn would try to make a pitch to Calliston. But, like everything else in Iraq, it was going to be a time-consuming, lengthy process that might never show results anyway. Nolan suggested that, in the meanwhile, Evan's squadron might want to write to the commander of their reserve unit, or to some of their colleagues in that unit, wherever they happened to be in the war theater.

In the few days while these discussions and negotiations were transpiring, things in Baghdad—bad enough to begin with—became substantially worse, especially for the convoys. One of the KBR convoys delivering several tons of dinars in cash from Baghdad to BIAP was ambushed just outside of the city and barely limped into the compound with one dead and four wounded. The lead vehicle's passenger-side window was blown out, and the doors and bumpers sported dozens of bullet holes. The attack had been a coordinated effort between a suicide-vehicle-borne explosive device—an SV-BED—and insurgents firing from rooftops. The consensus was that the damage could have been much worse, but the Marines in the convoy had shot up the suicide vehicle and killed its driver before he had gotten close enough to do more significant damage.

Earlier in the week, another convoy manned by DynaCorp contract personnel had shot out the windshield of the Humvee carrying the Canadian ambassador as a passenger, when his car hadn't responded to a warning to stay back. Luckily, in that incident, because the contractors had used rubber bullets, no one was badly hurt. But nerves were frayed everywhere, tempers short, traffic still insanely dense.

By now, most of the routes in and out of the city had been barricaded off and access to those thoroughfares was nominally under the control of the CPA and Iraqi police/military units. All vehicles had to pass at least one and often several checkpoints to be admitted to these streets. Unfortunately, the inner city was a cobweb of smaller streets that fed into the larger main roads, and access to these was much more difficult to control. A convoy like Scholler's would be sitting in traffic downtown, essentially stationary, and a car with four Iraqis in it would suddenly appear out of one of these alleys and begin crowding the convoys in the slowly moving endless line of traffic.

Since many of these cars were in fact SV-BEDs, they, too, ignored escalation of the hand and audio signals in their efforts to get close enough to destroy the convoys they'd targeted. And of course, in these cases, the machine gunners standing through the roofs of the Humvees in the convoys had little option, if they wanted to save their own lives, but to open fire on the approaching vehicle.

Tragically, though, all too often the approaching car held innocent Arabic-speaking Iraqi civilians who simply didn't understand the English commands to back off, or the simple Arabic commands soldiers had been taught to give to help with the confusion. Or they failed to appreciate the urgency of the hand signals. In the first months after the occupation of Baghdad, these shooting "mistakes" had come to account for ninety-seven percent of the civilian deaths in the city—far more than the deaths caused by all the insurgents, IEDs, sniper fire, and suicide bombers combined. If a car got too close to a convoy, it was going to get shot up. That was the reality.

NOLAN, scheduled for the rear car this Tuesday with Evan, picked right up on the bad vibe that had been riding along with Scholler's squadron for the past few days. Now, as he walked up to the convoy, he was somewhat surprised to see Evan outside his vehicle, having some words with one of his men, Greg Fields. Tony Onofrio, another of the guys, was standing by listening, obviously uncomfortable.

"Because I say so," Evan was saying, "that's why."

"That ain't cutting it, Lieutenant. I've been up there three days in a row. How about we put Tony on the gun today?" Fields was obviously talking about the machine gunner's spot, the main target popping out of the roof of their Humvee.

"Tony's a better driver than you are, Greg, and you're better on the gun, so that's not happening. Mount up."

But Fields didn't move.

Nolan had been aware that the unit's respect for Evan's leadership had declined over their recreational drinking coupled with Evan's inability to get them transferred, and now it looked as though Fields might flatly refuse his lieutenant's direct order. So he stepped into the fray. "Hey, hey, guys. No sweat. I'll take the gun. Greg, you hop in the back seat and chill a while."

Nolan knew that the men might also be mad about his own role in Evan's drinking, plus driving him all over to hell and gone, but figured that neither as a group nor individually could they resent him if he took a turn in the roof. Although this was technically forbidden.

Caught in the middle, Evan felt that he had to assert his authority. "I can't let you do that, Ron."

"Sure you can." He gestured toward the machine gun. "I'm a master on that mother."

"I'm sure you are," Evan said, "but you're only allowed to use a sidearm."

Flashing the smile he used to disarm, Nolan stepped up and whispered into Evan's face. "Dude, the other night ring a bell? That's not your rule. That's the recommendation for contractors. Nothing to do with you. I'm betting Fields has no objection." He turned. "That right, son?"

The young man didn't hesitate for an instant. "Absolutely."

"Fields isn't the issue," Evan said, even as the guys from the other Humvees were moving down in their direction, wondering what the beef was about.

"I'm the issue to me, Lieutenant," Fields said. "It ain't right, me being up there every day. If Mr. Nolan wants a turn, I say tell him thanks and let's roll out of here."

Evan didn't want this to escalate in front of his other men. Nolan was throwing him a lifeline that could save his authority and preserve some respect in front of his squad. And maybe what he said was true. Maybe it was a rule for contractors, and none of the Army's business.

"All right," Evan said at last, lifting a finger at Fields. "This one time, Greg."

NOW EVAN and his very disgruntled guys were in a Baghdad neighborhood called Masbah, where Nolan was to meet up and conduct some business with a tribal chief who was a friend of Kuvan. They'd already passed the checkpoint into the wide main thoroughfare that was now choked with traffic. On either side, storefronts gave way to tall buildings. Pedestrians skirted sidewalk vendors who spilled over into the roadway on both sides of the road.

But in contrast to many of their other trips through the city, today they'd encountered quite a bit of low-level hostility. Kids who, even a week before, had run along beside the convoy begging for candy, today hung back and in a few cases pelted the cars with rocks and invective as they drove by. Older "kids," indistinguishable in many ways from the armed and very dangerous enemy, tended to gather in small groups and watch the passage of the cars in surly silence. The large and ever-growing civilian death toll from quick-triggered convoy machine gunners—in Evan's view, often justifiable, if tragic—was infecting the general populace. And in a tribal society such as Iraq's, where the death of a family member must be avenged by the whole tribe, Evan felt that at any time the concentric circles of retribution might extend to them—all politics and military exigencies aside.

Riding along with Nolan on the big gun above him, Evan was more than nervous. He honestly didn't know his duty. He hadn't been briefed on this exact situation and had no ranking officer above him to tell him the rules. Should he have stood up to Nolan and forbade him to man the machine gun, alienating himself from his men even more? Could he just continue to let him ride up there and hope the problem would go away? But playing into all of his ruminations was the fact that since the unauthorized raid into the BIAP neighborhood, everything about Nolan had him on edge.

The more Evan reflected on it, the less defensible that attack seemed, the more like some variant of murder. Evan had been a cop long enough in civilian life that he was sensitive to the nuances of homicide, and the raid had certainly been at the very least in a dark gray area. If the house that Nolan and his Gurkhas had trashed had in fact been identified as a legitimate military target, shouldn't it have been a military unit that took care of it? Though it was possible that the house full of AK-47s and other ordnance could have been an insurgent stronghold, Evan couldn't shake the thought that the attack might have been more in the line of a personal reprisal—payback to one of Ahmad's (or Kuvan's) enemies, or even to a business competitor.

Now, stuck in traffic in the passenger seat on a sweltering morning in Masbah, and still hung over from the previous night's beers, Evan tried to get his thoughts in order. He had to figure out a way to get his troops out of this assignment; he had to stop drinking every night with Nolan; he had to accept that it was over with Tara; he had to get a plan for his life when he got out of here.

He closed his eyes against the constant dull awful throbbing. In the driver's seat, Tony Onofrio must have caught his moment of weakness, because he turned the music way up to a painful decibel level—Toby Keith's new hit "Courtesy of the Red, White, and Blue (The Angry American)." This was Tony's not-so-subtle punishment for the fact that Evan hadn't succeeded in getting them transferred yet. The other beautiful aspect of the earsplitting volume was that Evan couldn't acknowledge that it bothered him—to do so would be admitting to his hangover. Tony, of course, knew he had the hangover. The message was clear enough—if Evan could jeopardize all of their safety putting more priority on drinking than on getting them out of here, then Tony could play his goddamned music as loud as he fucking wanted.

But suddenly, all the cogitations became moot. They were moving along at about ten miles per hour and they had just passed a side street when Nolan slapped three times rapidly onto the hood of their vehicle. "Heads up," he yelled down with real urgency, "bogey at ten o'clock. Ten o'clock."

Instantly jarred alert—this was a situation Evan had been trained for—Evan hit his radio and passed the word up to the rest of his squadron. "Pisoni! Gene, any way to speed up?" Then he yelled at Nolan. "Hand-signals first, Ron. Back 'em off. Back 'em off!"

From the radio, he heard, "Negative, sir. We're stuck up here."

Nolan shouted, "Comin' on."

"Don't fire! Repeat, do not fire."

He knew that he had to see how serious the threat was before he could formulate his response. If nothing else, he needed to make sure that this encounter went by the rules of engagement, the escalated warning process. But on the other hand if it was a suicide bomber who had targeted them, it would happen quickly and he couldn't be afraid to pull the trigger. He drew his own sidearm, the 9mm Baretta M9, and, turning half-around in his seat, stuck his head out the window. Behind them, just out of the alley and pulling out ahead of the backed-up traffic in the space behind them, was a beat-up white sedan with no license plates. The rear car in all of the convoys already sported relatively large signs, written in English and Arabic, warning following vehicles to leave at least one hundred feet of space, and experienced drivers in Baghdad tended to err on the side of caution. And yet this car had entered the roadway at about seventy-five feet and was advancing.

Looking up, Evan saw that Nolan had drawn himself up to full height and was standing with both arms extended, palms out—the classic "stay-back" signal in any language. Trying to get a better glimpse of the car behind them, Evan stuck his body out even farther. With the sun beating down on the windshield, the view inside the vehicle was generally obscured, but Evan was fairly certain that he could make out two people in the front seats. The back window on his side was down as well, and he caught a glimpse of forearm for a moment, instantly retracted.

"There's three of 'em in there at least," he called up to Nolan. Then, into the radio again, "Gene, can you get to the side and go around? The sidewalk, even?"

"Clogged up, sir. Negative. In fact, slowing."

"Shit." Evan knew that they had a megawatt flashlight in the backseat for just this situation. He pulled himself back in and told Greg Fields, behind the driver's seat—who should have been up where Nolan was—to find it and shine it at the approaching driver's face. It was supposed to be for nighttime use, but it might do some good during the day as well.

Digging in his duty bag on the floor at his feet, Evan pulled out the airhorn klaxon they carried for just such a moment. Amazingly enough, it seemed that even this many months into the occupation, some people—even whole families—would simply take to the streets in their cars to go shopping or run an errand. They'd get to talking or arguing and never see the warning hand signals until it was too late.

Coming out the window again, airhorn in his hand, Evan looked quickly to the roof. Nolan had gotten down out of his extended position and now his palms were gripped around the handles of the machine gun. "Hold off, Nolan! Hold off! Wait for my order!"

The car had closed to under forty feet in ten seconds, and seemed to be accelerating. Like everywhere else in the civilized world, Iraq seemed to raise drivers who abhorred a vacuum between vehicles. Even in the bright sunshine, even with the glare off the windshield, Evan could see that Fields had trained his blinding light on the driver. From his own side, he held out the airhorn and let out a blast.

The radio squawked out. "Deadlock up here, sir. Slowing down."

Evan checked the position of the approaching car—was it, too, slowing down at last? Good, it had stopped in time, thank God. This crisis would pass. He reckoned that he had time for a quick look ahead of them. Turning, he was about to order Pisoni onto the sidewalk—the pedestrians would have to scatter and that was just too damn bad. Onofrio hit the brakes and they came to a complete stop.

All was still. Evan breathed a sigh of great relief.

And then, with a maniacal war whoop, right above him, Ron Nolan opened fire.

THE CAR DID NOT EXPLODE.

That alone was enough to cause Evan grave concern. That and the fact that in the seconds before Nolan had started shooting, the car had finally gotten the frantic message from the lights and airhorns and without a doubt had come to a complete halt. Only after the first hail of bullets had slammed into it had it started moving again—the dead driver's foot letting up its pressure on the brakes?—coming on, actually faster now, with Nolan continually pouring rounds into it, until it rammed into the back of Evan's car and shuddered to a stop.

"Don't leave the cars unattended!" Evan tried to keep his rising panic out of his voice. "Stay at the wheel! Man your guns! Who's riding shotgun in your car, Gene? Well, get Reese back here with us. Fields," he yelled at his assistant driver, "out with me!"

The street had first seemed to go eerily silent, but already now as he all but fell out of the car, Evan became aware of the upswell of volume that was growing around them. Back behind them, on the sidewalk, a man was screaming, keening, and there appeared to be a form down on the sidewalk next to him—one or more of Nolan's bullets had apparently hit a bystander as he or she was walking down the street. This was perhaps unavoidable once the shooting started, but it aggravated the situation terribly.

A man on the curb was yelling at him in English. "He was stopping! He was stopping!" Back at the shot-up sedan, Fields and Reese on the other side, Evan approached with great caution. Although the windshield was blown out and red streaks tinted the inside of the other windows, someone might still be armed and alive inside, or there might still be an unexploded bomb.

Evan came up to the passenger door, gingerly pulled it open, then spoke into the radio to Pisoni. "Gene. Get through to somebody somewhere and tell them about this. Give 'em our location and tell 'em we need support yesterday. Anything they can get to us."

Behind him, he became aware of more shouts, randomly laced with fury. He turned his attention to the body—a woman, judging by the bloodied shreds of the *niqab*, or veil, that now stuck to what had been her face. Now she sprawled partially out of the front seat, her upper body bleeding into the street. On the other side of the car, Fields had opened the back door and stepped back in disgust and horror. "Holy shit, Ev, there's kids back here."

A minute later, the first of the rocks hit his Humvee.

FOR PERHAPS TEN MINUTES, though it seemed more like an hour, Evan tried to direct events, even through the bombardment of projectiles that the entire convoy was beginning to endure. He gave his machine gunners, including and especially Nolan, strict orders not to fire into the crowd. He hoped that the reinforcements that Pisoni had called for would arrive in something like a timely manner, and he entertained the hope that this wouldn't escalate further, at least until the cavalry showed up.

But he couldn't keep the crowd from closing in around the white sedan, some members of it clearly recognizing the family that Nolan had just slaughtered. As Evan and his men retreated back to their own bunched-up vehicles, they heard from Pisoni that Iraqi police units, stationed nearby, were on their way.

Meanwhile, though, some of the crowd members had laid down blankets in the street and begun the process of removing the bodies from the car. First the woman, then her husband, who'd been behind the wheel, finally the three children—by the size of them, none older than six or seven. All of them were badly bloodied, but one was apparently still breathing, and someone grabbed that child and disappeared with it into the crowd.

Nolan, still up behind his gun, now had his eyes on the street in front of them, which had cleared as the forward traffic had begun to move. "Evan," he said, and when Scholler looked up, he pointed. "Check it out."

Evan turned. "What?"

"We're good to go, dude."

"What are you talking about? We're not going anywhere. We've got a multiple fatality incident here, Ron. We stay till we're cleared."

"Bad idea, Lieutenant. We go while we can. These people will take care of their own, but we'd best be gone by the time word gets out around here."

"We *can't* be gone. We've got to report—"

"Report? To the local cops? And then what? No, man, what we've got to do is get out of here now, while we can, before it gets ugly and personal."

"Personal with us?"

"We killed 'em, Lieutenant."

"We didn't kill 'em, Nolan. You killed 'em."

"So split a straw. They're not gonna care. We're on the same side, is all that matters. This is a clan culture, so everybody in these poor fuckers' clan is honor bound to kill us. It's going to get personal in about two minutes, I promise."

Evan looked off down the street at the still-receding line of traffic that had been blocking their way all morning. Behind them, the horns of a hundred other cars urged him to drive off, clear the road, get out of the way. He didn't know how he could in any kind of conscience leave the scene of an incident such as this one—all his police training went against it. There would have to be an investigation, photographs, testimony taken. They couldn't just see an opportunity to get away and run from all this, could they?

From across the car, Fields said, "I think Mr. Nolan's right, sir. We've got to get out of here. We get back to an FOB someplace." Fields was picking up the jargon. An FOB was a secure troop area, or forward operating base, with Bremer walls, crew-served weapons, and security checkpoints. "We make our report out of there."

Evan didn't respond and instead went to his radio. "Gene," he said, "what's it look like for getting out of here?"

"When?"

"Right now."

"Decent. There's an off-road to a barricade point another quarter mile up, and I can—"

At that moment, a low hum filled the torpid air around them. Nolan yelled out, "RPG. Down!" And sixty feet from where Evan stood, the first Humvee suddenly exploded in a ball of flame, knocking him, Fields, and Reese to the pavement. Nearly deafened, Evan still registered that Nolan had come up out of his crouch and turned his machine gun to the building from which he believed the rocket-propelled grenade had been fired.

Gene Pisoni and Marshawn Whitman had just taken a direct hit that they couldn't have survived. Across the hood of Evan's own Humvee, Reese stood back into his view, the left half of his face awash in blood. He was trying to say something, motioning to Evan, but either he wasn't saying any words or Evan couldn't hear them through the deafening roar in his head. Fields, too, finally got to his feet, apparently unharmed, and pointed to the Humvee, then to the empty street yawning open before them, in an unambiguous gesture. It was past time for talking about it. They had to get out of there.

He was right. Now the second and third Humvees were open targets— possibly saved, Evan later realized, by their proximity to the white sedan or to the crowd that had initially gathered around it. But that wasn't any part of his consideration as he pointed Reese to the second Humvee and hopped into the third one just as a spray of bullets pinged off the street in front of them all, cutting across the hood of his vehicle. Nolan wheeled and fired into the buildings again.

Onofrio had his vehicle in gear and started forward. In the second Humvee just in front of them, Reese reached the open passenger door and half jumped, half fell inside, joining Levy, Koshi, and Davy Jefferson—a twenty-four-year-old In-N-Out manager from Sunnyvale—who was stationed on the machine gun. And perhaps because of fear, or maybe an understood complicity among the locals, Evan noticed the crowd had suddenly fallen back from around them, isolating them as targets even further. Up out of the roof of the Humvee in front of them, Davy Jefferson had opened fire at some rooflines as well.

Another spray of bullets kicked at the street between the two vehicles. Over Evan's head, Nolan fired another burst, which was followed closely by a terrifyingly close low humming vibration as another RPG somehow missed them and exploded into a storefront over on their left. Glass and stucco dust rained down over them.

Evan hit his driver's arm and pointed to the burned-out, still smoking remains of their #1 vehicle. He still could barely hear himself, although he was yelling. "Gene and Marsh! Gene and Marsh!" Telling Onofrio he wasn't going to leave his dead men behind to be mutilated by the mob, which was the way this scenario looked like it was starting to develop.

They pulled around next to their #2 Humvee and at Evan's signal, he and Fields jumped out into the street again. Evan motioned to Nolan and Jefferson, on the two still-working guns, to cover them as they ran to the destroyed, still smoking #1 Humvee. Whitman's charred and bloodied body had been blown clear out of his hole by the machine gun and now lay sprawled over the roof. Evan and Fields grabbed their fallen comrade by the arms and pulled him down, then began dragging him as fast as they could back to their vehicle.

For a few seconds, the firing ceased. Evan and Fields managed to load Whitman's body into the back of their car, then they turned and went to join Alan Reese, who had come out of the #2 Humvee and was trying to open the front doors to the first car and get Pisoni out. But the doors were still too hot to touch, as well as sealed shut. The windows, of course, had all been destroyed by the blast as well, so Fields leaned in on the driver's side and tried to get some purchase on Pisoni's lifeless body, but couldn't get it to budge.

"He's still got his seat belt on!" he called back.

The force of the grenade had all but knocked the back door on the driver's side off its hinges, and Evan was able to force it further open with a few kicks. They could get Pisoni out that way. Evan got Fields over next to him, put his shoulder to it, and had just started to push when more rounds of automatic weapons fire exploded from the roofs around them. Fields, at his elbow, made a sickening guttural sound, then spun around and collapsed to the ground in a sitting position.

On the other side of the car, Reese fired off a few useless rounds with his sidearm just as heavy automatic weapons fire began coming from the roofs of buildings on Reese's side of the street as well. Somewhere behind them, Nolan was firing continuously now, back and forth, side to side, from the roof of his vehicle, but when Evan looked over, hoping he might be able to direct some covering fire from the other Humvee, he saw that Davy Jefferson had disappeared and that bullet holes had pocked across the #2 windshield as well. If Levy and Koshi hadn't been hit in their front seats, it was a miracle.

"Alan!" Evan yelled to Reese. "Get around here on this side!"

Reese looked at him over the Humvee's hood and nodded. Turning, still firing his sidearm at the rooftops on his side, he made it nearly to the back side of the car before several more automatic rounds straightened him up, threw him up against the car's body, and dropped him out of Evan's sight.

His own gun drawn, Evan sat next to Fields's crumpled body on the pavement in the partial cover of the Humvee. Up to his left, he could make out a couple of running figures at the edges of the roofline, but Nolan was doing a decent job of keeping them down, stippling the fronts of the buildings they occupied, holding their fire to a minimum. But Nolan was the only machine gunner left and at his firing rate, he would soon be out of ammunition.

Evan nudged at Fields. "C'mon, buddy, we've got to move." He pushed at Fields's shoulder again and the man's body slumped all the way to the side on the ground, the front of his shirt soaked in red. Another burst of machine-gun fire shattered the air directly behind him, and Evan turned and saw that it was his own #3 Humvee, Nolan on the roof, coming around in the street and running its own screen between the buildings to cover him.

But he had three men down here at the #1 Humvee, and three more in #2. He could only guess at Reese's condition. Perhaps he'd only been wounded. He'd have to get around the Humvee here to check that out. And then still there were Koshi, Jefferson, and Levy, over in #2. He'd have to order Nolan and Onofrio to help him load the dead and wounded into the backseat and cargo area of the one working Humvee. He couldn't leave his men out here in the street.

It wasn't possible that he'd lost so many of them in so short a time.

And then his own Humvee pulled up, the back door open, Onofrio behind the wheel, frantically gesturing that he should jump aboard, screaming at him although Evan could barely hear him. It was his only chance, their only chance.

But here was Fields right at his side, bleeding to death if not already dead. There was no option but to try to get him in the car first.

"There's no time!" Nolan yelled down from the roof at Onofrio. "Keep driving! Go! Go! Go!" He fired a short volley up into the rooflines. "Move!"

It seemed like Nolan was urging—ordering!—Onofrio to save themselves and abandon Evan with the rest of the men. But his driver slowed the vehicle as it came abreast of Evan, looked over in panic and desperation, reached out a hand across the seat.

Nolan yelled from the roof. "Leave 'em, leave 'em, there's no time! They're gone!"

The Humvee stopped now, and Onofrio leaned over further and pushed open the passenger door, his hand outstretched. Evan reached around, trying to get ahold of Fields to pull him along. Getting a purchase on his squadmate's sleeve, Evan was halfway to his feet, his own free hand out to Onofrio's, when, deep in his bowels, he felt again the low hum of another incoming RPG.

It was the last thing he felt for eleven days.

PART TWO
[2003-2004]

PART TWO

[9]

FROM RON NOLAN'S PERSPECTIVE, there was just no benefit to staying in Iraq and talking about it.

The inquiry into the incident looked like it was going to be a tricky thing. Onofrio was the only witness left in the immediate aftermath, and Nolan believed that his testimony wouldn't be harmful. Onofrio had been busy driving and wouldn't have had a clue about whether the following car was in fact stationary when Nolan had opened fire on it. But the word from the street, the result of Jack Allstrong's reaching out to the local Iraqi and U.S. military cops, had already filtered back about what had actually happened, and there was a reasonable chance that Nolan would be arrested.

The good news was that the Abu Ghraib scandal had just surfaced, and every American remotely connected to law enforcement in Iraq had been assigned to that investigation. Even Major Charles Tucker, that pain-in-the-ass bean-counter who'd been constantly in their shit about money, found himself reassigned to that scandal.

But in spite of that, and though he knew that jurisdictional issues were problematic at best in Iraq, especially when they involved contractors accused of criminal activity such as, in this case, murder, Nolan was unwilling to risk his own arrest. You never knew what could happen then. The CPA might decide to use him as an example for other trigger-happy contractors, or give him to the Iraqi prosecutors, both nonstarters from Nolan's point of view.

In fact, Nolan didn't feel particularly bad about what he'd actually done—hey, you're in a war, shit happens. The dumbasses should've stopped sooner, or better yet, stayed off the street entirely. What the hell were they thinking? If he had it to do over again, he'd do the very same thing, rules of engagement or no. And although he did very much regret the loss of life among his own convoy, again this was just another turd in the gigantic shitpile that was this war. Who could have predicted such a massive local retaliation for such a small, localized event? And then again, how was he supposed to know that this particular Mohammed Raghead, the father who'd stupidly driven his whole family into the killing radius of Nolan's Humvee, was in fact Jahlil al-Palawi, a major tribal leader and the most influential Shiite in the Masbah neighborhood?

Anyway, clearly the intelligent thing to do was for Nolan to blow Dodge until this incident blended into the chaos of all the other ones that were happening somewhere in the country just about every day. In a few months, Nolan could always come back with Allstrong or with another security outfit and pick up where he'd left off. In the meanwhile, Jack Allstrong certainly didn't want an army of investigators coming into BIAP without his say-so. Who knows what they'd see that they didn't like, and report back to the CPA?

So within a week of the incident, Nolan was back in Redwood City. After negotiations with Jack Allstrong that consisted of a couple of glasses of Glenfiddich each, the company chose to construe his departure as caused by an act of God, which meant it would honor his contract for a six-month hitch at full pay. And with some of this apparently inexhaustible supply of money, Nolan put a down payment on a modern and elegant furnished townhouse near the sylvan border between Redwood City and Woodside. Still employed by Allstrong, he was the company's chief Bay Area recruiter of ex-military personnel. He knew the kind of people Jack Allstrong needed over in Iraq and he generally knew where to find them.

TARA WHEATLEY WAS SURPRISED to see Nolan back so soon. She'd spent the weeks he was gone coming to grips with her nagging sense of guilt. Which was, she told herself, ridiculous. She was an adult who could make her own decisions, and she and Evan had been broken up for months. She hadn't betrayed anybody. She was moving on in her life. She'd finally gotten around to reading the last four of Evan's letters, but after the night when she had invited Nolan back to her apartment, she couldn't make herself get around to writing back to him.

What was she supposed to say?

Oh, and under local news I slept with your friend Ron who came to give me your letter. I didn't really mean to, but I was confused and lonely, really lonely, and scared to be alone, he'd just more or less saved my life that particular night and I never thought you and I would ever work out our problems anyway. It was just time to act on us being finally apart, okay? We weren't together anymore and weren't going to be together, so I could sleep with another man if I wanted and you had no say over it. Okay, okay, there could have been some element where I was punishing you for going off the way you did—if you can leave me, then this is exactly what you're risking. And now— you see, you dummy?—it's happened.

No. She wasn't going to write that letter, not now, not ever.

And Evan, of course, never wrote to her again either.

Ron Nolan was a strong, powerful, attractive older guy and if her life wasn't going to work out with Evan, and it clearly wasn't, then with his charm, experience, confidence, and—admit it—money, Nolan would at the very least be able to help her get over her first love. She could use a simple, uncomplicated relationship until the next real one came along.

As if there'd ever be another one as real as Evan.

NOLAN NEVER SAW the need to tell her about the ambush at Masbah, what had happened to Evan, or the role that Nolan himself had played in it all. As far as Tara knew, Nolan had voluntarily made the decision to come home, possibly even as a result of some of their discussions about the morality of the war. Explaining it to her, he had kept it all, as his old English teacher used to say, vague enough to be true.

And in fact, all Nolan knew about Evan Scholler was that he'd sustained a serious head wound from the last grenade they had taken and, by the time Nolan had flown out of Baghdad, still hadn't been expected to live. He might in fact already have died, although Nolan suspected that if that had happened, Tara would have heard about it from somebody.

But whatever had happened to Evan, nearly three months had passed.

Tara had moved on. For Ron Nolan, there just didn't seem to be any benefit to talking any more about it.

SHE WAS STANDING in front of the artichokes in the vegetable aisle of the grocery store, two days after the start of her school's Christmas vacation. The canned music coming in to keep everybody merry and bright had just changed from the ridiculous to the sublime—the Chipmunks' version of "Rockin' Around the Christmas Tree" segueing rather inharmoniously into Aaron Neville singing "O Holy Night." The latter had been her and Evan's favorite recording of any Christmas song, and suddenly, hearing the first notes, Tara's mind had gone blank. Looking down at the bins of produce arrayed in front of her, she suddenly had no idea why she was here, or what she wanted to buy.

Unconsciously, her hand came up to cover her mouth, and she sighed deeply through her fingers, her eyes welling beyond all reason. "God," she whispered to herself.

"Tara? Is that you?"

Letting out another breath, she started out of her reverie. "Eileen?"

Evan's mother was still quite attractive, and Tara had always thought it was not so much about her trim body or her pleasant, vaguely Nordic facial features, but because she exuded kindness. In Eileen Scholler's world, everybody was equal and everybody was good, even if the rest of humanity didn't think so, and she was going to like you and treat you fairly and gently no matter what. Now, her head cocked birdlike to one side, she frowned with concern. "Are you all right? You look like you're about to faint."

"That's what I feel like." Tara tried to put on a smile but knew it must look forced. "Wow. I don't know what just happened." Bracing herself against her shopping cart, she again forced an unfelt brightness. "Stress, I'm sure. The season. But how are you? You don't shop here normally, do you? But it's so good to see you."

"I was on my way home from work and remembered I needed some veggies. But I'm glad I stopped here now. It's so good to see you too." Her expression grew wistful. "We've missed you, you know."

Tara nodded, sober. "I've missed you too. I really have."

"Yes, well, I don't think you children realize what you put us poor parents through when you break up with each other. Here we were, considering you all but the daughter we never had, and the next thing you know, you're not in our lives anymore. It's the saddest thing."

"I know," Tara said. "I'm so sorry. I never meant that to be part of it."

"I know, dear, it's nobody's fault. It's just one of life's little heartbreaks. Or as Jim says, it's just another FOG." Lowering her voice, she came closer. "Fucking opportunity for growth. Pardon my French."

"It's pardoned. How is Evan, by the way?"

"Well, we still worry, of course, but he seems all right. There are still some issues, but we're going out to see him for Christmas, so we'll have a better idea how he's doing after that."

"You're going to see him for Christmas?"

"Yes. We're flying over next week."

"To Iraq?"

For an instant, Eileen Scholler went completely still. "No, dear." Her eyes narrowed—was Tara kidding her?—although the kindness remained in them. "To Walter Reed."

"Walter . . ."

"You didn't hear? I was sure you must have heard. In fact, I was a little bit annoyed, to be honest, that you never called us. If I'd have known you didn't know, I would have—"

Tara waved her off. "That doesn't matter, Eileen. Heard what? Did something happen to Evan over there?"

"He was wounded," she said, "this past summer. Badly, in the head. He was nearly killed."

"Oh, my God." Suddenly her legs felt as though they weren't going to support her. She tightened her grip on the shopping cart, looked plaintively at Eileen. "What happened?"

"They got attacked someplace in Baghdad. Most of his squadron was killed. They were all from the Peninsula. It was everywhere in the papers and on the news. Didn't you see anything about it?"

"I stopped reading all of those articles, Eileen, and watching the news on TV. It says Iraq and I tune out. I just can't stand it. I figured if anything happened to Evan, I'd hear about it. I couldn't face the news every day."

"Well, fortunately, he wasn't killed, and that's all they seem to report. It's like the wounded don't count. So you might never have seen his name anyway. But his squad . . . those poor boys."

"All of them died?"

"All but one, I believe. Two, counting Evan."

"Oh, God, Eileen, I am so sorry. How is he now?"

"Getting better every day. He's making more sense when he talks on the phone. The doctors won't say for sure, of course, but his lead neurologist predicts that Evan might be one of the very, very few to recover almost completely. Though it's probably going to be a while."

"He's what, doing therapy?"

"Every day. Physical and mental. But as I say, he's really coming along now. For a few weeks there, after he first arrived, we didn't even dare hope for that, so this is all really good news. Once they decided he was eligible for therapy, it's been better."

"Why wouldn't he have been eligible?"

Eileen pursed her lips. "There was some question about whether he'd had something to drink before he went out on his last convoy. Nobody said he was drunk, but . . . anyway, they had to clear that up first. If he was in fact under the influence, he might not have been eligible for benefits."

"Even though he was shot?"

Eileen took a calming breath. "He wasn't shot, Tara. It was a grenade."

That news stopped her briefly. "Okay, but even so, they weren't going to treat him?"

"If he'd been drunk, maybe not. Or not right away, anyway. And we've learned time is everything with his kind of injuries, believe me."

But Tara was still reeling from the revelation. "I can't believe they really might not have treated him. How could he not be eligible for benefits if he got wounded in a war zone?"

"It's one of the great mysteries, dear, but don't get me started on how they're treating some of those other poor wounded boys at Walter Reed. It's atrocious. But—you'll really love this—even after they ruled that he was eligible for benefits, the Army made it one of the conditions of Evan's treatment that he wouldn't complain about conditions at Walter Reed to the media or anybody else." She laid a hand on Tara's arm, forced a tepid smile. "So the thing to do now is be grateful that they're finally helping him, and we are."

"You are a way better person than I'd be, Eileen."

"I don't know about that. It's the only way I know how to be. Of course it's frustrating and terrible, but at least Evan's getting better now. I don't see how making a stink at this point would do anybody any good."

Closing her eyes, Tara blew out her frustration. She didn't believe Eileen was right—she thought that making a stink might in fact help things improve. But suddenly the country's culture seemed to have shifted to where everybody was afraid to make a stink about anything—it meant they weren't patriotic. It meant they supported the terrorists. And this whole mentality was, to her mind, just stupid.

But she wasn't going to get in yet another argument about this ongoing and disastrous war—not with Eileen, not with Ron Nolan, not with anybody else. At least it appeared that, bad though it might have been, the worst medical part of Evan's ordeal was over. "So he's been there how long now?" she asked.

"About three months. We hope he'll be coming home in a couple more, but we're afraid to move him too quickly. At least he's got quality care now, and we don't want to rush his recovery. When he comes back, we want him all the way back, you know?" Eileen's serene gaze settled on her might-have-been daughter-in-law. "And how about you, Tara? How have you been?"

"Mostly good, I think."

"Mostly good, you think? That's not the most enthusiastic response I've ever heard."

"No. I guess not. I'm just . . . kind of at a loss somehow. I don't really feel whole in some way. It's like I'm waiting for something, but I'm not sure what it is, or even if I'll recognize it when it comes along. Does that make any sense?"

"More than you think. Are you seeing anybody?"

"More or less. I'm a little conflicted about him too. In fact . . ." She stopped.

Eileen's head fell off angling to one side in her trademark gesture. "Yes?"

Tara sighed. This close to Eileen's physical presence, now, she almost imagined she could feel emanations of her son in the air around them. And it affected her still, this sense of some deep-rooted connection between them that she'd never approached with anyone else. Certainly not with Ron Nolan.

So why, then, was she still seeing Ron? Was it only because she'd given up on Evan after he'd clearly stopped caring about her? Or was there something simply easier about Ron? Love didn't have to be all-encompassing and overpowering, did it? True, deep, abiding love was a fairy tale, a myth. She'd found that out the hard way. Now she'd moved on into an adult, reality-based relationship that could never hurt her the way she'd been hurt with Evan. And that was smart. She was in a better place, all in all. She had to believe that.

Besides, Evan would never take her back now. Not after what she'd done. She knew that, and she didn't blame him.

"Tara?" Eileen stepped closer to her. "What?"

She tried to smile, mostly failing in the effort. "Nothing really. Just what I said, being conflicted about this guy."

"Well, if you'll take some advice from an old woman who loves you, don't do anything irrevocable unless you're sure."

"Oh, don't worry. I'm a long way from either of those—irrevocable, or sure. I keep thinking it's the Christmas season, those old high expectations that don't seem to pan out." She swallowed against a surge of emotion that suddenly had come upon her. "Maybe Evan and I shouldn't have had such good times with you and the family back in the day. I keep waiting for it to feel that way again at Christmastime."

"It still can, you know."

"Well, maybe. I can keep hoping, at least." Putting on a smile now, Tara reached for some vegetables. "Anyway, I don't mean to sound so negative. Next to what you're going through, my life's great."

"Ours is, too, dear," Eileen said. "Evan's alive and we pray he'll be fine someday. It's been a bit of a challenge, but the worst is definitely behind us. Having gotten through the worst of it, I don't know if we could be happier."

"Well, that's the best news I could hear. You deserve it."

"Everybody deserves happiness, dear."

"Good people deserve it more."

"I don't know about that." Eileen laid a hand on Tara's arm. "But either way, you do. You're a good person."

"Not as good as you think." Not even close, she thought. She could not shake the feeling that somehow she had cheated on Evan, even though they'd broken up, even though they weren't a couple any longer, even though she hadn't written him one letter since he'd gone overseas. "I shouldn't have been so pigheaded with Evan," she said. "I should have written him and . . ."

"Hey, hey, hey." Eileen moved up closer to her. "You two had a disagreement. You did what you thought was right and so did he. That's not either of you being a bad person. You're both good people." She rubbed Tara's arm reassuringly. "Maybe you could write him now, just a friendly little note. I'm sure he'd like to hear from you."

"No, I couldn't do that. Besides, it's too late for that now. He's better off without me."

"Don't you think he should be the judge of that? Maybe I'll just tell him I saw you and you said to tell him hello. I know he'd be glad to hear that. Would that be too much?"

"I don't know, Eileen. It might be."

"If he wrote you, do you think you could write back?"

Tara's head tracked a pathetic little arc. She bit at her lip. "I don't even know if I could promise that." She put her own hand over the other woman's. "We tried, Eileen, we really did. But now it's just"—she shrugged—"it's just behind us."

Eileen, ever serene, nodded. "And that's all right too. If you change your mind and want to see him when he gets back, you've got our numbers still, I'm sure. Or even if you'd like to drop by and see us before that, you're welcome anytime. You know that, I hope."

"I know that. Thank you." She leaned over and planted a kiss on Eileen's cheek. "You're great. I love you."

Eileen held herself against Tara for a moment, then pulled away. "I love you, too, girl, and you're also pretty great. Us pretty greats have to stick together. And try not to be so hard on ourselves."

"I'll try," she said. Tara's vision had suddenly misted over. "I'll really try."

"I know you will. It was wonderful seeing you, dear. Be happy." With a quick last little kiss on the cheek and a smile, Eileen pushed her shopping cart by behind Tara, turned the corner at the end of the aisle, and was gone.

NOLAN ARRIVED AT TARA'S PLACE within twenty minutes of getting her call. Now Tara sat in her big chair, drinking her second glass of wine. It was nearly dark inside, the only light in the living room coming from the kitchen. With his own drink of scotch in hand, Nolan sat with his elbows on his knees, way forward on the couch, intent. "You've got to be kidding me. It must have happened within a week or two after I left."

"You didn't know anything about it?"

"Nothing. Why would I know anything about it?"

"Don't get defensive, Ron. You were there, that's why."

"I'm sorry, but no. It must have been after I left. Evan was trying to get himself and his guys transferred out of the airport and back to their regular unit the last couple of weeks I was there. It sounds like that's what must have happened. If they were still with us, Jack Allstrong would have mentioned it to me, I'm sure." Pushing himself back into the cushions, he sat back and crossed his legs. "His mom says he's at Walter Reed now?"

"For the last few months."

"Jesus," he said, "that's unbelievable." But if Nolan's pose was relaxed, he felt far from it—his assumption had all along been that Evan was dead, or at least permanently rendered mentally incompetent. After the RPG hit at Masbah, Onofrio had insisted that they pile Evan into the Humvee. Nolan had field-assessed the damage to Evan's head, and it didn't look like the kind of wound from which people recovered, so he'd let himself be persuaded.

Now Nolan drummed his fingers on the arm of the couch. "But his mother said they expect him to get better?"

"Completely, though maybe not soon."

"Well, that's good news, at least. And she told you all of the other troops were killed?"

"All but one, that's what Eileen said. And then Evan."

Nolan raked his palm down the side of his face. "God, those guys.

They were good kids. I can't believe . . . I mean, they shouldn't have even been there. They should have been fixing big trucks." He looked across at her, so lovely and vulnerable in the dim December night. Her tears had begun again and now glistened on her cheeks. "How are you doing with this, T? You want to go see him?"

"No!" The word came out in a rush. Then, more reflectively, she said, "I don't know what good that would do. I just didn't really expect anything like this, that's all. Maybe I should have, you know, but it just . . . when it's someone you know, who you loved . . ." She let out a weary sigh. "I don't know what to do with it. I want him to be okay, but Eileen asked me if I wanted to get back in touch with him, and I couldn't say I did. Although sometimes I think . . ."

"What?"

"No, it just would sound bad. For us, I mean."

"I can take it."

"I know that, Ron. You can take anything. But maybe sometimes a person doesn't need to say everything. You've just got to get through stuff."

He sipped his drink. "Sometimes you think you would want to go see him, or talk to him, if it wasn't for us. Is that it? Because if it is, I won't stand in your way. I really won't, T." He came forward. "But let me ask you this: Were you thinking a lot about him before you ran into his mother and found out he'd been hurt?"

"Not a lot, no. Sometimes."

"So maybe—just a thought here—maybe it's guilt. Maybe on some level you feel like you need his permission."

"To do what?"

"Move on. Have a life of your own."

She sat on the edge of her big chair, biting her lip, holding her forgotten wineglass in both hands between her knees. Eventually, slowly, she began to shake her head. "No," she said. "I don't think that's it."

"Okay," Nolan said. "I've been wrong before. Twice, I think." A quick smile, trying to break the tension. It didn't work. "What's your theory?"

"It's not a theory so much as it's a change in the facts I was living with. I thought he stopped writing to me because he'd stopped . . . loving me."

"Maybe he stopped writing to you because you didn't write back."

"Okay, maybe some of that too. But that wasn't really him, I don't think. He's a stubborn guy. I mean, he wrote me ten letters and I didn't answer any of them, so why would he stop at number ten? I think he would have kept on until I told him to stop. Except he got shot and he couldn't."

"So he's still carrying a torch for you?"

"He might be."

"And that would make a difference?"

She blew out the breath she was holding. "I'd gotten comfortable thinking it was over, that's all. Mutually over. Thinking he was okay with it. It made it easier for me."

"With me, you mean?"

She nodded. "Which is really why I didn't write back to him. You know that."

"Yes, I do." He sat back, let out his own long breath, and took a drink. "Do you regret that? Us?"

Tara's head kept moving slowly from side to side. "I don't know, Ron. I just don't know. You're a good guy and we've had a lot of good times . . ."

"But?"

She raised her eyes and looked at him, her lovely face drawn with indecision and regret. "But I think I might need some time to sort this out a little." Her eyes widened. "God, I don't even know where those words came from. I'm not saying I want to stop seeing you. I don't know what I'm saying."

Nolan pushed the ice around in his glass with his index finger. Sitting back now, an ankle on its opposite knee, he let the silence hang for a few beats. "Here's the deal," he said at last. "You take all the time you need, do everything you think you need to do. The downside is I might not be around anymore if the deciding goes on too long. That's just reality. I don't want to lose you, but I don't want half of you either. Just so it's clear where I stand."

"It's always clear where you stand. That's one of the great things about you."

He leveled his gaze at her. "You're going to call him?"

"I don't know. I shouldn't, at least not right now. His mother made it sound like he still wasn't all the way back to normal. I don't want to hear him or see him and start to feel sorry for him. That wouldn't be good."

"No, it wouldn't. It's easy to confuse pity and love, but it's bad luck."

"But I've still got to figure out where to put him. For my own peace of mind. And to be fair to us."

"I get it," Nolan said. "Truly." He drained his drink and got to his feet. "But as I say, T, don't be too long. I want for you what makes you happy, but I'd be lying if I said I didn't hope that that was me."

"It might be, Ron, but I'm just all confused by this right now. Please don't hate me."

"I couldn't hate you, T. You get this settled, maybe we can start over."

"That'd be good."

"I hope it would." He offered her a cold smile. "Well, listen. You've got all my numbers. I'll wait for you to call." Nodding, he placed his empty glass carefully on the coffee table, crossed over to the front door, opened it, and stepped out into the night.

[10]

EVAN SCHOLLER WAS the enemy. Sometimes it was a split-second evaluation, and sometimes a long-considered one, but once you made the decision that an enemy had to be eliminated, it came down to tactics— how to do it. And in this case, there was no more time to be lost. Tara remained undecided about getting in touch with Evan, but that could change in the blink of an eye. For all of Tara's apparent reluctance, at some point she'd need to see or talk to him. And any contact between the two of them would be a disaster.

Nolan had lied to Evan about what Tara had done with his letter; he'd lied to her about the incident in Masbah and many other things. Those lies and all the other ones would come out and he'd lose her.

He couldn't let that happen.

So Evan was the enemy.

Nolan left Tara's, went home and packed a bag with a heavy jacket in it, and made it to the Oakland Airport by ten o'clock. In the mobbed waiting room at the JetBlue terminal, he found a likely looking college kid, chatted him up, and ended up giving him three thousand dollars in cash to cancel his own ticket so that Nolan could get his own last-minute ticket on the otherwise sold-out red-eye flight to Washington. He caught four hours of solid sleep on the five-hour flight.

The sky was deeply overcast, a light snow was falling, and the temperature hovered at twenty-six degrees at ten twenty-five when he arrived by cab from National Airport at the main entrance to the enormous complex that was the Walter Reed Army Medical Center. The place brought him up a little short. Though he had some general understanding of the numbers of injured service personnel being treated at the center, he had more or less assumed that the place was in essence just a big hospital—a building with a bunch of patients and doctors.

It was more like its own city. The main reception area throbbed with humanity. It reminded him in some ways of the main hall of Baghdad's Republican Palace. By the information board, he checked out a rendering of the facility and saw that there were nearly six thousand rooms—he figured probably fifteen to twenty thousand beds—spread out on twenty-eight acres of floor space.

Turning back to the mob, he scanned the cavernous lobby, hoping to get his bearings somehow. A large information booth commanded a good portion of the reception area's counter space, but Nolan was here to neutralize one of the hospital's patients. It wouldn't be a good idea to call any attention to himself. Returning to the rendering, he found a building labeled Neurology and decided to start there. Grabbing the map from its slot, he started out across the huge campus.

The snow had begun to dump more heavily by the time he reached his destination, and he stopped inside the door to shake out his jacket and stamp his feet. The lobby here wasn't nearly as crowded as the main reception lobby, but it still was far from deserted.

He was surprised to see four gurneys lined up against one of the walls, each of them featuring hanging drips and holding a draped body. The line for surgery? For a room? He didn't know and wasn't going to ask, but it struck him as out of place and terribly wrong. These guys had no doubt been wounded in the line of duty—the least the Army could do, he thought, was get them some rooms.

But he wasn't here to critique conditions at Walter Reed. The Army he knew was so fucked up in so many ways that he'd given up thinking about it. Besides that, he had been running on a mixture of adrenaline and low-level rage ever since he'd left Tara's apartment last night, and now, suddenly, the logistics of carrying out this particular mission demanded his complete attention.

As the tide of humanity continued to flow past him in both directions, Nolan experienced a rare moment of indecision: Why did he assume that Evan Scholler would be here anyway? The front door of the building identified it as the Neurology Surgery Center, but Evan's surgery had possibly been months before, and he was now probably somewhere among these fifteen thousand beds, recovering or in rehab.

How did Nolan propose to find Evan without asking directions, and without calling attention to himself? And then, once found, how did he propose to kill him, especially if—as seemed likely if overflow gurneys here in Neurology were any indication—he was in a room with other patients?

Of course, he could eliminate them all. Collateral damage was inevitably part of the equation in any military strike. But this wasn't Iraq, where he could simply disappear without a trace. Here, potential witnesses would have to inform him of Evan's location. Staff members or nurses might be mandated to accompany him if he visited any of the patients.

Beyond that, and perhaps most significantly, Nolan had to consider that Lieutenant Evan Scholler wasn't some raghead nobody shop owner in Baghdad. If he were the victim of a murder here at Walter Reed, every aspect of Evan's life would come under the microscope, including the incident in Masbah, the scrutiny for which Nolan had thus far managed to evade. The authorities would find a reason to talk to Tara, and that would eventually, inevitably, lead back to him.

Bottom line: it was mission impossible.

Fuck that, Nolan thought. *The guy is going down.*

"EXCUSE ME." A young woman in a pressed khaki uniform smiled up at him. "You look a little lost. Can I help direct you somewhere?"

Nolan's face relaxed into a smile. "I'm afraid I'm having some trouble finding a friend of mine, one of your patients."

"You're not the first person that's happened to," she said. "I've got a directory over at the reception desk that is marginally up to date, if you'd like to come follow me."

He started walking next to her. "Only marginally up to date?"

Rueful, she nodded. "I know, but we're so slammed lately, sometimes it takes the computer a while to catch up."

"That darned computer," Nolan said.

"I know. But we're trying. The good news is if he's not where the computer says he is, at least there they'll probably know where he went."

"That would be good news."

"You're being sarcastic," she said, "and I don't really blame you. But believe me, good news around here is scarce enough. You take it where you can get it." They arrived at the reception desk. "Now, your friend," she said. "What's his name?"

"Smith," Nolan said. "First initial *J*. We called him 'J' but he might have been Jim or John. I know," he added, with a what-can-you-do look, "it's a guy thing."

EVAN SCHOLLER STARED OUT at the falling snow.

He had either been asleep or didn't remember when it happened, but somebody had tacked up some Christmas decorations on the wall. There was a tree and those animals that flew and pulled Santa's sled—he couldn't remember what they were called, but he was sure the name would come to him someday. Then there was Frosty the Snowman—he remembered Frosty and even the song about him, sung by that guy with the big nose. They'd also hung up by the door one of those round things made out of evergreen branches and ornaments.

It was making him crazy. He knew what objects were. He just often couldn't remember what they were called.

What he did recognize as a real memory was that he was in his third room since he'd arrived at Walter Reed. His first stop for about ten days had been the Intensive Care Unit, where he'd mostly been unconscious, and about which he had little recollection except that while he was there, he was unwilling to believe that he wasn't still in Baghdad. It didn't seem possible that he could have gone from squatting next to his Humvee in Masbah directly to the ICU here.

Of course, that wasn't what had happened. His speech and language therapist, Stephan Ray, had made his physical and mental journey a kind of a recognition game that he'd memorized as part of his therapy. His first stop after Masbah had been to a combat support hospital in Balad, which was where they took out a piece of his skull. The operation, which gave his brain room to swell, was called a craniectomy—remembering that word had been one of Evan's first major successes in therapy. When he'd gotten it right, repeating it back to Stephan the day after he'd learned it, Stephan had punched his fist in the air and predicted that he was going to recover.

What the doctors did next, still in Balad, was pretty cool. They'd taken the piece of his skull that they'd cut out and put it into a kind of a pouch they cut into his abdomen. He could still feel it in there, a little bigger than the size of a silver dollar—they were going to put it back where it belonged in his head in the next month or so, when his brain had healed sufficiently.

From Balad, they'd evidently flown him to Landstuhl in Germany, where after a quick evaluation they decided to get him here to Walter Reed.

His second room here was in Ward 58, the Neuroscience Unit. His mom and dad told him that for his first days there, the doctors more or less left him alone while the Army decided if he was eligible for benefits. He didn't understand that—eventually they had worked it out—but nevertheless he had nothing but good memories of the ward because this is where he had met Stephan. Though Evan hadn't had a clear sense of where he was or what had happened to him, in fact his therapist was there to explain things and pull him through some of the tougher, disorienting times.

Basically, what they did in those first days was play games, do flash cards and puzzles and simple math exercises. Neither Stephan nor his doctors seemed to understand exactly why, but Evan's progress was surprisingly rapid, far better than that of most of the other soldiers who were in here for head wounds. After only about a week in the ward, they moved him again to the room he currently occupied, on the fourth floor above the Pediatric ICU.

THERE WERE NINETEEN J. SMITHS at Walter Reed, but only one with traumatic brain injury similar to Evan's. The nice nurse/receptionist at Neurological Surgery checked her monitor at the desk and told Nolan that his friend was listed as being in Ward 58, the post-op Neuroscience Unit, but that if he was still under observation there—it was only one step removed from the ICU—she didn't think he would be allowed to see visitors.

"That can't be right," Nolan said. "I know his mom and dad have already been in to see him." He gave her a warm smile. "Why do I sense computer issues again?"

"I'm sorry," she said. "I told you it might take a little patience."

He kept smiling, relaxed. "Patience is my middle name. Is there someplace they send brain injury patients when they're starting to get a little better, after this Ward Fifty-eight?"

She screwed her lips in frustration. "I don't really know. But wait." Picking up the telephone, she leaned down to read something from the computer monitor, then punched in some numbers. "Hi. This is Iris Simms at Neurosurgery reception. I've got a guest here to visit one of your patients, Jarrod Smith, and the computer's still got him in your unit, and the guest doesn't think he could still be there. In which case, where would he be?"

She covered the phone and conveyed the message to Nolan. "There's a lot of overflow, but they're saying maybe you could check the upper floors of the Pediatric ICU building, but wait . . ."

She raised a finger, went back to listening. "He is? Oh, I see. But I understand his parents were able to see him." She waited for the reply. "Okay, thank you. I'll let him know."

Hanging up, shaking her head in continued frustration, she came back to Nolan. "I'm afraid Jarrod is still in Ward Fifty-eight, but they say he's still pretty incoherent. And they don't allow nonfamily guests in that unit. I'm sorry."

"Nothing to be sorry about," Nolan said. "You gave it a good try. I'll call first before I come next time. Thanks for all your help."

"No problem," she said, "anytime."

EVAN MIGHT BE RECOVERING FASTER than most, but to him it was still agonizingly slow going. This morning, he'd tried to get once through all of his flash cards—he had six hundred of them now in a shoe box next to his bed—but by about number two hundred his head felt as though it was going to explode, so he'd closed his eyes just for a minute.

And opened them more than two hours later. All of his three roommates were gone, out with their rehab or other therapies. Outside, the snow was falling in heavy clumps, which he found depressing—so depressing, in fact, along with his failure to succeed earlier with his flash cards, that for a moment he succumbed to the blind hopelessness of his situation here. He was never going to recover, in spite of what they said. He'd never really be normal again. People would notice the dent in his head, even after they put his skull back together. He'd never again talk like a regular person. He'd never have another relationship like the one he had had with Tara. He wished the shrapnel had just cut a little deeper and had killed him, the way it had his troops.

So many of them gone now. So many gone. Regular guys. And he'd been leading them. To their deaths.

Sitting up in his bed, he closed his eyes against the unexpected sting of unwelcome tears. Bringing both hands to his face, he pressed hard against his eyelids, willing himself to stop. In an instant, before he was even aware of it, the self-flagellation and depression had turned, as it often did, to fury. He was goddamned if he was going to cry. But why had this happened to him? Why wouldn't they let him out of here? Why were we having this fucking stupid war anyway? Who cared if he ever learned his fucking flash cards? He turned his head, ready to slap the damn box of the things to the ground, when his eyes grazed the wall again, stopped for a second at the new decorations. Santa and . . .

Reindeer!

Those flying animals pulling the sled were reindeer. That was the word.

He started to laugh. At first it was just a small chuckle emanating from his throat, but it soon swelled to something completely out of his control, paroxysms that violently shook him until he could no longer catch his breath. His shoulders heaved and heaved some more as he tried to grab air into his lungs and now suddenly he was crying again, crying for real. Exhausted, his body shaking with the release of so much that he'd kept pent up, he collapsed back into his pillows, tears flowing unabated in a steady stream down his face.

STEPHAN WAS WIPING his face with a warm towel. "What happened here?"

"Nothing. What do you mean?"

"I mean, your face is wet. Are you all right?"

"I got frustrated. Then the reindeer."

"Right." Stephan, perhaps more attuned to absurdist dialogue than most people, nodded as if he understood the meaning of what Evan had just said. "But you're all right now?"

"Fine."

"You're sure?"

"Sure."

"Because I've got a staff meeting in ten minutes, but I'll bail on it if you need me here. Even just to talk."

"No. I'm good. Really, Stephan. Everything's okay."

NOLAN WAS THINKING that this was why you didn't waste too much thought on what could go wrong. You just kept moving forward, you kept your goal in your sights, you pushed the niggling doubts out of your mind.

Walter Reed wasn't wallowing in chaos by any means, but clearly it was an understaffed and overburdened institution. In theory, maybe somebody was supposed to inquire whom he had come to visit, somebody should have checked his ID—he had almost hoped for that, since he had a Canadian passport in his pocket that identified him as Trevor Lennon— but no one had. Beyond those oversights, the crowding had become so serious that in many areas, and specifically on the upper floors of the Pediatric ICU building that had been pressed into service for recovering brain trauma patients, there was no video surveillance.

He was invisible.

There was no need to be impatient. The building had six stories and he'd covered floors two and three already, walking the hallways with a purposeful stride, as though he knew exactly where he was going. He stepped into each room on both floors, checking for Evan. As he walked the halls between rooms, he nodded to patients lying on their gurneys, or shuffling with their walkers; gave a brisk hello to anyone who looked like a doctor or nurse or staffer. He even had a name, Jarrod Smith, if anyone asked him who he was coming to visit, but he didn't think that was going to prove necessary.

Turning into the third door down on the fourth floor, he saw Evan in the bed across the room, over by the window. The three other beds in the room were all unoccupied. He walked into the room and closed the door behind him, checking the terrain, thinking on his feet that the best way to do it would be out the window.

Depressed brain-injured guy, left alone by a high window. An obvious suicide.

"DUDE."

For some reason, Evan found himself tempted to laugh. Inappropriate laughter, Stephan called it, a normal symptom of his kind of brain injury—this time he was able to resist the impulse. "I know you," he said after a moment.

"Of course you know me. I'm Ron Nolan."

Evan nodded. "That's it. Ron. How you doin', Ron?"

"I'm good. The question is, how are you doing?"

"They tell me I'm a miracle in progress, but I don't much feel like it. What are you doing here?"

"I was in town and found out you were too. I thought I'd come by and say hi."

"What town?" Evan asked.

"Washington, D.C., or close enough. They don't tell you where you are?"

"No, they probably do." He smiled. "I don't remember everything the way I should yet."

"Well," Nolan said, "wait a second." He walked around the bed and over to the window. Looking left outside, then right, he suddenly threw up the bottom half of the double-hung window and stuck his head out. Bringing his body back in, he asked. "Can you get up out of bed?"

"Slow but steady."

"Well, check it out. Come on over here. Next time you forget where you are, look out here—you can read the Walter Reed logo out there on the—"

"What's a logo?" Evan had thrown off his covers and was sitting on the edge of the bed. "I told you," he explained, "some words—"

Nolan reached out a hand, ostensibly to stop his talking. "Hey, a picture's worth a thousand of 'em. Come here." Taking him by the wrist, he pulled him gently off the bed to a standing position, then backed away from the window to let Evan look out.

Three steps and then . . .

Nolan put a hand on the center of Evan's back. A slight pressure, moving him forward.

Two steps.

"WHAT'S THAT WINDOW DOING open?" Stephan Ray yelled from the doorway. "You're going to freeze yourself and the rest of the room to death." Then, pointing at Nolan, "And who the hell is this?"

Nolan recovered without missing a beat. Pasted the smile back on as he turned. "Ron Nolan," he said. "I was with Evan over in Iraq."

"He was with me in Iraq," Evan repeated.

"Glad to hear it, but let's close that window, what do you say? And, Evan, you shouldn't be walking around too much without the walker, right?" He softened his tone, spoke to both of them. "Falling would not be a good thing right now."

"No. I hear you. My fault," Nolan said. "Sorry."

The door was still open to the hallway, and now another man came in with his therapist and the two started to get the patient arranged on his bed.

The moment had passed.

PLAN B WASN'T GOING to be nearly as satisfying, final, or effective. In fact, it might not do any kind of a job at all, but at least it would give Nolan time. And keep Evan and Tara apart. But he had to work his way into it—besides, it was about the only possibility left, with the other witnesses remaining doing their therapy on the other side of the room. And with Nolan identified for who he really was. "Your nurse seemed a little upset," he said when Stephan had left them.

"He's not a nurse. He's a . . . ." The word *therapist* suddenly wasn't there. Evan searched the corners of the ceiling for an instant and couldn't find it up there either. So he regrouped, came out with, "He's a . . . helper. He's here to help me. And sometimes I get upset. TBI will do that to you."

"TBI?"

"Traumatic brain injury. That's what I've got. Or had. They tell me I'm getting better. I'm not sure I believe them." Evan picked up the sheet that covered him, he wiped some sweat off his brow. It was, if anything, still cold on his bed, but something about this man Nolan's presence stoked him up, made him sweat with nerves. "What are you really doing here, Ron?"

"I told you. I had some business in D.C. and thought I'd drop by and see how they're treating you."

"They're treating me fine." The snow out the window held his attention for a beat, then he came back to Nolan. "And you're not here from Baghdad?"

"No. I left about a week after you did."

"What for? Were you hurt?"

Nolan's cheek ticked. "No. Me and Onofrio, we picked you up, then made a run for it and got out clean. It was a lucky thing."

"You got me out?"

"Yeah."

"I don't remember any of that."

"No, I don't suppose you would. I didn't expect you to live. Nobody did."

"I should thank you."

Nolan shrugged. "Line of duty, dude. We couldn't have left you behind."

"What about the other guys? What happened to them?"

Nolan took a breath. "They were all killed, Evan."

"No, I know that. But what happened to them, their bodies? If we didn't get them out? Nobody will tell me anything about that."

"You don't want to know, dude. Really." He paused. "And that ought to tell you everything you need."

His jaw set, Evan looked over again at the snow, then came back to Nolan. "So why'd you leave? If you weren't hurt . . . ?"

"Politics. They were going to offer me up, maybe to the CPA, maybe to the locals. Either way, I lose. So I'm out of there, for a while, at least.

Until it blows over or all the other shit that happens every day over there covers it up."

"What do you mean, exactly? What are they accusing you of?"

"Some lying witnesses over in Masbah said I fired too soon. That the car we hit had already stopped. Which is bullshit, since it kept coming and slammed into us way after I blew out the whole front windshield. But they were going to lay it all off on me. I didn't see any point in sticking around."

The nebulous memory in Evan's gut began to coalesce around Nolan's words, the all-but-forgotten moments just preceding the attack coming back to him with a sickening urgency. It wasn't some lying witnesses in Iraq—it was people who had seen what had happened and were coming forth with the truth. And the truth was that this trigger-happy son of a bitch was responsible for everything that had happened in Masbah, for all of Evan's men's deaths, for all of his own suffering.

Nolan, oblivious to Evan's growing awareness, continued. "Anyhow, this way, I'm home for Christmas, doing business development over here for Jack Allstrong. You wouldn't believe how many soldiers like me want back in on the private side. The contractors' market is going through the roof over there and we get the pick of the litter."

Evan's blood pounded in his brain. Pinpricks of bright light danced in the periphery of his vision. The pain forced him to close his eyes, to bring his hands up to cover them.

"But you know," Nolan went on, his voice suddenly taking on a confiding familiarity, "what I'm really here for is to talk about Tara."

Evan opened his eyes. The throbbing inside his head squeezed itself down to a tiny pulsing silent ball of focus. Bringing his hands down slowly to avoid drawing attention to the internal violence of his reaction, he forced a curious expression to gather in his facial muscles. "Tara? What about her? Is she all right?"

"She's fine. She's terrific, in fact." Nolan cleared his throat. "The thing is, though, the main reason I wanted to see you in person, I thought I owed it to you . . ."

"What?"

"To tell you to your face that Tara and me, we're kind of an item. We're going out together. I thought the right thing would be to let you know."

Evan felt his hands tighten into fists again under the sheets, but he couldn't find a response in words right away. Until at last he said, "All right. Now I know."

"I don't blame you for being pissed off," Nolan said.

Evan's nostrils flared and his breath seemed to be coming in ragged chunks. But he said, "I'm not pissed off. It's none of my business. We were broken up."

"Yeah, sure, but I met her doing an errand for you. That's got an odor on it. You being hurt makes it worse."

"So? You want some kind of forgiveness? You're barking up the wrong tree, *dude*."

"I don't think so. And I don't have a guilty conscience. I just wanted you to know how it happened, so you'd know it wasn't me. I didn't start it."

"I don't care how it happened."

"No. You'd want to know. It was when I came to tell her you'd been hit."

"You did that? What for?"

"I thought I owed it to both of you." Nolan raised his right hand. "I swear to God, I went over to her place as your comrade-in-arms. I told her the whole story, that you'd been talking about her the night before the attack, that you knew she'd ripped up your last letter and were still going to try to work things out with her."

Beyond the bare truth of Tara and Ron's involvement with each other, a far more important fact leapt out at Evan, and he wanted to make sure of it. "You're saying she knew I was hit from before I even got here to Walter Reed?"

Nolan nodded. "Within a week of it anyway. All she said was that this is what she assumed was going to happen when you went over in the first place. When you actually left, she was done. That's why she never wrote. It's why she never contacted you here. It was over, dude. When she knew I was coming out here this trip, I told her I was going to come see you and at least try to explain my side of it . . ."

"There's nothing to explain. Who wouldn't want her? You think I blame you for that? I barely knew you for a few weeks in Iraq. You didn't owe me squat, Ron. And, okay, you got her. Good luck. I mean it. Now get out of here, would you? Get out of here."

"I'm going," Nolan said. "But there's one last thing. I asked if there was anything she wanted me to say to you. You need to hear this. You know what she said?"

"I can't imagine."

"Here's the quote: 'I'm sad he got hurt, and I hope he's okay. But I've really got nothing to say to him. He made his bed, he can lie in it.'"

IT TOOK TARA three days to work up the nerve to call Evan. Still uncertain exactly about what she was going to say, even once she'd made up her mind to call, she actually wrote some ideas down so she'd hit all the notes—she didn't know he'd been injured, she missed him. Mostly—she wrote it five separate times—she was going to say she was sorry. She was going to tell him that when she'd found out what had happened to him, she was resolved to reach out and try to connect with him again. In spite of how badly she'd treated him by not answering his letters, she hoped he could forgive her. She had been wrong, and she was sorry, sorry, sorry. Now she had to know where she stood with him before she could go on with her life anymore. In spite of their philosophical differences, they'd had something rare and special. He knew that. She was sure they'd both changed since he'd left, and possibly it could never work between them, but maybe they could at least start talking again and see where that led.

Sitting in the big chair in her living room, she listened to the ring at the other end of the line, three thousand miles away. Her mouth was dry, her heart pumping wildly. She realized that she was holding her breath and let that go with an audible sigh, reminding herself to breathe again.

"Hello."

"Hello. Evan, is that you?"

"No. This is Stephan Ray. Do you want Evan Scholler? I'm his therapist."

"Yes, please, if he's there."

"Just a second. Can I tell him who's calling?"

"Tara Wheatley."

Stephan repeated her name away from the phone and then she heard Evan's voice, unnaturally harsh and unyielding. "Tara Wheatley? I don't want to talk to any Tara Wheatley. I've got nothing to say to her."

Stephan must have covered the mouthpiece with his hand, because his next words were muffled, but even through the muffling, there was no mistaking what Evan said next. It was loud enough they probably heard it at the Pentagon. "Didn't you hear me? I said I'm not talking to Tara Wheatley. Get it? I'm not talking to her! Tell her to get out of my life and stay out! I mean it." Next she heard what sounded like a heavy object being thrown against a wall, or knocked onto the floor. And swearing, Evan insane with rage.

Or just insane from what he'd been through.

Back in Redwood City, Tara stared at the mouthpiece that she held in her shaking right hand, then slowly, as though the violence she'd heard in it might escape and hurt her further, she lowered it into its cradle.

[11]

FIVE MONTHS LATER, at the main Redwood City police station, Evan Scholler sat waiting in a hard chair just outside the room to which he had been summoned, the small wire-glass-enclosed cage that was the office of his boss, Lieutenant James Lochland. Evan's shift had ended twenty minutes ago, at five o'clock. The summons had been taped to his locker downstairs. Now, as he sat, he could see Lochland at his desk, moving paperwork from a pile in the center of it to one of the trays at the far right corner. When the surface of the desk was clear, the lieutenant drew a deep breath, looked through his wired glass, met Evan's eyes and, in his no-nonsense style, crooked an index finger at him, indicating he should come on in.

Lochland was a young forty and considered a good guy by most of his troops, who, as patrolmen, were by and large, like Evan, young themselves. The scars from a severe case of teenage acne marred what would have been an otherwise handsome face, so that now he came across as approachable. He wore his brown hair a little long by cop standards, and cultivated a mustache that could use a trim. Now he told Evan to shut the door behind him, to take one of the two seats that faced his desk. He had his hands clasped loosely in front of him on the pale green blotter and waited while his visitor was seated.

"What's up, sir? You wanted to see me?"

"Yeah, that's why I sent the note. I thought maybe it'd be a good idea if we had a little informal chat and maybe nip a couple of habits, or tendencies, in the bud before they get you in trouble. But before we go into any detail on those things, I wanted to ask you how you think things are going in a general way. In your life, I mean."

"Pretty good, sir, I think. But, listen, if there've been complaints—"

Lochland held up a restraining hand. "If there have, we'll get to 'em, promise. But we're not there yet. Meanwhile, what I'm really asking about is your state of mind. How you feel about being back here, in the job."

"Pretty good. I feel okay about it. I'm glad to be back."

Lochland nodded, put on a tolerant look. "You sleeping?"

Evan let out a breath, started a smile that went nowhere. "Most nights. Whenever I can."

"You need help with it?"

"What's that?"

"Getting to sleep?"

"Sometimes I'll have a drink or two, yes, sir. When I can't get my mind turned off."

"What are you thinking about?"

Evan shrugged.

"Iraq?"

He let out a long sigh, lifted his shoulders again. "I can't seem to get it out from inside me. The guys I lost. My girlfriend. The whole thing."

"You talking to somebody?"

"A shrink, you mean?"

"Anybody."

"I talked to some woman at the Palo Alto VA until my discharge came through."

"And that was just before you started here, right?"

"April nineteeth. Not that I'll have a party on that date for the rest of my life or anything. So, yeah, a couple of weeks before I started here."

"And you're not talking to anybody since then? They didn't give you any referrals for when you were done with them?"

This brought a snort. "Uh, no. I'm reading between the lines here, but you're saying you think I've still got issues."

"I'm asking, that's all. I'm asking if maybe it's a little too soon. If you feel like you're under too much stress."

"You mean post-traumatic stress?"

Lochland shrugged. "Any kind of stress. Stress you don't need if you're trying to do a good job as a cop. What I'm saying is that there are programs we've got here, and people we could recommend if you think you need it."

"I don't want to go down that road."

"What road?"

"PTSD. You get that label, you're damaged goods. The Army says I'm good. Physically and mentally I'm the miracle child. Now, if one of our own shrinks says I've got PTSD, I'm done."

"That's not exactly accurate."

Evan shook his head. "It's close enough. Post. Traumatic. Stress. Disorder. *Disorder*, Lieutenant. That's a mental illness. I'm not copping to that, period. That's not what I'm dealing with. I'm fine, sir. Maybe I just need to let a little more time go by." Again, Evan let a long breath escape.

"There!" Lochland said. "That's what I'm talking about."

"What?"

"You don't feel that when you do it? You're sighing like a bellows, Evan. Every time you open your mouth, it's like you're lifting this burden and dropping it on the side before you can say anything."

After a second, Evan hung his head. He came close to whispering, "That's the way I feel." Raising his eyes, he looked across the top of the desk. "So how am I screwing up? On the job, I mean."

In spite of military guidelines supposedly guaranteeing that police officers who got deployed to active duty from the reserves or the National Guard would be returned to their civilian work without demotion or loss of time served, Evan's assignment since he'd come back to work as a Redwood City patrolman was roving grammar school officer for the Drug Abuse Resistance Education (DARE) program. In that role, he visited classrooms of fourth-, fifth-, and sixth-graders all over the city, spreading the doctrine of clean and sober living. Though it wasn't a technical demotion and paid what he was making when he'd been called up, it still was not a job normally held by someone with three full years on the force. But it was the only opening they'd had when he was discharged and ready to go back to work, and he had taken it.

Now Lochland reached out and took a small stack of papers from his top tray. Removing the paper clip from the top, he leafed through them quickly—there were perhaps a dozen pages—then put them all down on his desk. "I don't think we have to go over these one by one, Ev. They're pretty much the same."

Evan sat stiffly, his back pushed up tight against the chair. He had little doubt as to what the complaints had been about. "I just can't stand to see these kids who've got everything—I mean *everything*, Lieutenant— iPods, two-hundred-dollar shoes, designer clothes—I can't stand to see how spoiled they are. How they don't take anything seriously. I mean, this whole DARE thing, it's a joke to them. And when I think of the kids I saw over there in Iraq, with *nothing*, no shoes, no food, begging for MRE handouts . . ." He shook his head, the rave worn down by its own momentum.

Lochland sat forward, elbows on the desk, hands templed in front of his mouth. "You're not there to yell at them, Evan. You can't let yourself lose your temper."

"They don't listen, Lieutenant! They don't listen to a word I say. They've got everything going for them in the whole world and they don't give a good goddamn!"

"Still . . ." Lochland pushed the papers around in front of him. "The point is, school's out soon enough anyway. Anywhere you get assigned next, I solemnly promise you'll have more aggravation than these kids could give you on their best day. Serious aggravation. You can't go out there on the streets half-cocked and ready to explode. That just can't be any part of the job." He pulled himself up in his chair, lowered his voice. "Look, Evan, we're all proud as hell of you, of what you've done, of the fact that you've come back at all. You're our poster boy too. But you've got to get yourself under control. You've got to let this stuff go."

"Yes, sir. I know I do. I'm sorry."

"Sorry's a good start, but I'm thinking maybe you want to think about anger management, maybe take a class, maybe talk to somebody, some professional. I'm afraid that if I get any more complaints after this little talk, it won't be a request. And next time we'll have an HR person in here with us. Understand?"

"Yes, sir."

"You think you can do this?"

"Yes, sir."

"I think you can, too, Evan. But get some help. And some sleep."
"Yes, sir. Thank you, sir. I'll try."

HE WASN'T SUPPOSED to engage in any sports that had a physical risk or contact element for at least another year and, depending on his follow-up neurological examinations, maybe forever. This left out his favorites, softball and basketball—he'd been active at least a couple of nights every week on a city-league men's team in both sports before he'd been deployed. But the police department had a bowling league and while it wasn't much in the way of exercise, it was something to do to get out of the apartment at night and mix with some of his colleagues, even if they were generally from a somewhat different subset—heavier, slower, and older—from the softball and basketball guys.

The positive aspect of this population was that it included men who had attained seniority or rank—Evan's three teammates included two sergeant detectives and a lieutenant. All of whom were more than happy to have recruited a returning young war hero with an average of 191—they all thought the kid had a chance to seriously turn pro. He was a natural. Tonight his three-game score of 621 was fifty points better than any of them individually, and more than enough to ensure the Totems' victory over their opponents, the Waterdogs.

"So here's to the Totems," intoned robbery-division sergeant Stan Paganini, hoisting a gin and tonic in the Trinity Lanes bar after the games, "and their upcoming undefeated season."

Lieutenant Fred Spinoza raised his glass of bourbon on the rocks. "And to our own uncontested rookie of the year, *Doctor* Evan Scholler!" Spinoza often bestowed random honorifics, such as "Doctor," on his colleagues when he got enthusiastic or excited. "Six twenty-one! That's got to be close to the record set. I know I've never heard of a higher one. Three two-hundred games in a row! That just doesn't happen in this league. In any non-pro league."

"They ought to write you up, Ev. Get your name in the sports page." This was white-collar-division sergeant Taylor Blades, drinking a Brandy Alexander.

"Thanks anyway, guys." Evan had acquired a taste for scotch but couldn't afford any of the single malts, so he was drinking a Cutty Sark and soda on the rocks. "But I've been in the paper enough to last me for a while."

"Yeah, but not as a sports hero," Paganini said. "You get known as a sports hero, you become a babe magnet. It's a known fact."

"He's got a point," Spinoza acknowledged. "Your teammates could benefit too. We could pick off stragglers from the swarm around you. Think about that, what it could mean to us and our happiness."

"Yeah, but you guys are all married anyway," Evan said. "You'd just get in trouble. And besides which I think the whole babe-magnet question in an amateur bowling league, even if it's a really good article, is going to be more or less underwhelming."

"No!" Blades said. "There's got to be bowling groupies. In fact, I think I see a bunch of 'em coming in right now. Maybe the word got out about your set already." He snapped his fingers. "YouTube. Somebody was filming you on their cell phone, and they posted it right up, and all these chicks . . ."

But Spinoza was holding out a hand, stopping Blades midrant. "Ev?" he said. "Is everything all right?"

IN THE BATHROOM, Evan threw water in his face a few times, checking his reflection in the mirror to make sure nothing showed in his expression. When he went back to the guys, he told them that he'd just gotten whacked by a wave of dizziness—an occasionally recurring symptom from his head wound. He excused himself, apologizing for raining on the postgame parade, saying he thought he'd better go home early, like now, and lie down, if he was going to be any good for work the next day.

Instead, he went outside and moved his car to the back of the parking lot so they wouldn't see it when they left. A half hour later, after he'd seen them all leave, he got out of the car and walked back into the alley, where he took a stool at the bar and ordered another Cutty Sark, a double this time, on the rocks.

Tara's lane wasn't fifty feet from where he sat. She was with three girl-friends, all of them acting animated and happy. She wore a short white polka-dotted red skirt that showed off her shapely legs, and on top, a red spaghetti-strap silk blouse that he fancied he could see shimmering to the beat of her heart.

Drinking off his scotch in a couple of swallows, he ordered another double and watched the group of young men from the next alley strike up, if not a conversation, then from the body language a running, flirtatious banter. At least, Evan thought, she wasn't here with Ron Nolan. That would have been very hard to take, far harder than seeing her alone, which was difficult enough. Was she still seeing him, he wondered, or could she in fact be unattached again? And if she was unattached . . . ?

But what was he thinking? This was the woman who hadn't even cared about his near-death in Iraq. Whose self-righteousness made her write him off forever when he was simply trying to do his duty. Who never even wrote him one letter or returned one e-mail from the minute he left.

Looking at her now, so carefree, it suddenly seemed impossible to him that the person he'd known and loved for two years had changed so much. She had always had strong opinions, but one of her best traits, and what his mother had always loved about her the most, was her innate kindness. Tara had always been a good person. What had happened that had changed her so very much?

Well, he was going to find out.

Putting a twenty-dollar bill in the bar's gutter, he again emptied his glass like a man dying of thirst. When he stood up, the dizziness he'd invented for his teammates came and whopped him upside the head for real. He stood leaning against the bar for a few seconds, getting his bearings, surprised at how tipsy he'd become—he'd only had four or five beers during his games and then the five shots of scotch in the bar. Or were they all doubles? He took a step or two and had to grab the back of a nearby chair at one of the tables for support.

This wouldn't do.

He wasn't about to approach Tara as a stumbling and slurring drunk. He didn't want to make it easy for her to dismiss him out of hand as a common nuisance. He would pick another time, when he was sober. Looking down at her and her friends one last time, he concentrated on his walking and made it to the front door without mishap, then down the steps and out to his CR-V in the darkness at the back of the lot.

Settling into the front seat, he locked the car doors and fastened his seat belt, lowered the backrest nearly to horizontal, leaned all the way back, and closed his eyes.

EVAN HEARD THE REPORTS from heavy rifles, bullets pinging now off the asphalt all around him. He was screaming at Alan and Marshawn. "Get down! Get down! Take cover!"

The barrage continued, a steady staccato as the car was hit and hit again. He turned to look and the second car behind him now was a twisted wreck, the bodies of two more of his men bleeding out onto the street where they'd been thrown from the force of the blast. And then suddenly he was aware that it was dark and that the beam from Nolan's headlamp was on him, blinding him as he tried to get his Humvee moving from his position up on the roof of it. His hands up in front of his face, he yelled down to the driver. "Kill that light! Now!"

More bullets raked the car, but as the muffled sound filtered into his consciousness, it became more of a repeated thudding, a knocking. When he opened his eyes, the light was still in his face, but this time he recognized it for what it was—a flashlight outside the car. Still shaking from the fear and immediacy of the dream, he took another second or two before he knocked on his own driver's window, then held his hand up to block the light. He could see enough in the pool of the streetlight above them to make out a couple of uniforms.

Cops. His brethren.

He rolled down the window halfway. "Hey, guys, what's going on?" He shot a glance at his watch. It was three thirty-five.

The officer with the flashlight moved back a step or two. "Could you please show us your driver's license and registration, sir?"

"Well, sure. I, uh . . ." He reached for the door handle and pulled it to open the door.

But the near officer outside slammed it back closed, spoke through the half-open window. "Please stay in your vehicle. License and registration, please. Where've you been, buddy?"

Evan stopped digging for his wallet for a moment and sat back, closed his eyes, tried to remember. "Trinity Lanes," he said at last. The view of a suburban street out his car's windshield had him disoriented. "I was bowling."

"And drinking."

"It would appear so."

"Which leads to the question of how you got *here*." But as he opened Evan's wallet, the officer would have had a hard time missing the badge. "Holy Christ," he said with disgust, and flashed it at his partner, handing him the ID. Then, back to the car, he said, "You know how you got here from the lanes? Somebody must have driven you, right?"

Evan just looked at him.

"'Cause you wouldn't have tried to drive in the state you're in, would you?"

But then the second cop butted in. "You're Evan Scholler?"

This one he could answer. "Yeah."

Number two said to his partner. "The guy from Iraq." Then, to Evan, "Am I right, pal?"

"Right."

"You don't have your gun on you, do you?"

"Nope. In the glovebox."

The first cop shook his head in frustration, then said, "You want to get out now, you can." He pulled open the door. "Smells like a distillery in there, pal."

"Not surprised," Evan replied.

"You might want to open the windows, let it air out for the next time you're driving," the first cop said. "So, for the record," he continued, "do you remember who drove you over here?"

By now, Evan knew where he'd gotten to and where he'd parked, although the piece of the puzzle concerning the actual drive over was a complete blank. "My girlfriend." He pointed to the apartment building across the way. "She lives right up there. We had a fight and she left me in the car to sleep it off."

"That's a good story," the first cop said. "You want to lock up here and go up there now, we'll stick around till you get in."

Evan leaned back against his car. He swayed slightly from side to side. "We're not living together. She won't let me in. I've got to get back to my place."

The second cop handed the wallet back to Evan. "How you gonna do that?"

Evan took a beat deciding whether or not he should laugh; he decided against it. "Good question," he said. "*Excellent* question." He looked from one of them to the other. "I guess I'll walk. It's not that far. Thanks, guys. Sorry for the hassle."

He'd gone about five steps, none of them very steady, when one of them spoke from behind him. "Scholler. Maybe you want to lock up your car."

Stopping, he turned back to them.

The first cop said, "It'd be a bad idea to pretend to walk until we pulled out and then come back and try to drive."

"Yeah," Evan said. "That'd be dumb."

"Where's your place?" the second cop asked.

"Just up by the college," Evan said.

The second cop said to his partner, "Not that far. Only about four miles, all uphill."

The one with the flashlight said, "Get in the squad car with me and he'll follow us to your place in your wheels. You barf in my car, you clean it up."

"Got it," Evan said.

[12]

EVAN WAS AT HIS PARENTS' HOME for a Sunday dinner that had become a more or less regular event since he had come back out to California. Once Daylight Saving Time arrived every year, Jim Scholler barbecued almost every night, and on this warm evening in late May he'd grilled chicken, which they'd eaten with fresh spring asparagus, a loaf of sourdough bread, and Eileen's "famous" tomato-potato salad with cilantro and red onions. Now, still long before true dusk, they were sitting outside, in the Schollers' large backyard in the long shadows cast by their mini-orchard of plum, fig, lemon, orange, and apricot trees.

Over their last glasses of cheap white wine, and with Evan now reemployed with the police department, ensconced in his new apartment, and with the immediate physical danger from his head wound behind them, at long last Eileen had mustered the courage to ask Evan about his love life.

He dredged up a chuckle. "What love life?"

"You're not seeing anybody at all?"

"That's not been at the top of my priorities, Mom. I'm not really looking."

His father cleared his throat. "What about Tara?"

"What about her?" The answer came out more harshly than he'd intended. "Didn't I mention that she never answered one of my letters—not one, Dad!—and I wrote about a dozen of them? That said it all clear enough. Plus, last I heard, she had another boyfriend."

"When did you hear that?" Eileen asked.

"At Walter Reed. In fact, the guy came to see me."

"Who did?" Jim asked. "Tara's new boyfriend? Why'd he do that?"

"I don't know. Guilt, probably."

"Over dating Tara?" Jim asked.

"Over stealing my girlfriend after I sent him over with one of my last letters to hand deliver to her? And instead he snags her away while I'm half-dead in the hospital? Could a person feel guilt about that? Or maybe if you were the reason a whole squad got wiped out?"

"You mean your boys?" Eileen asked. "Are you saying that Tara's new boyfriend is the man in your convoy who shot too soon?"

"You got it, Mom. Ron Nolan. I believe I've mentioned him once or twice."

"Never nicely," Jim said.

Evan slugged some wine. "What's nice to say?"

"Evan." Eileen frowned and threw him a quizzical glance. "I don't think I'd heard before that he was seeing Tara."

"But wait a minute," Jim said. "I thought you and Tara broke up over the war. Wasn't this guy Nolan over there too?"

"Yeah," Evan said. "Funny, huh? So I guess maybe it wasn't the war with me and Tara after all. Maybe she just wanted out and that was a good excuse."

"No." Eileen's voice was firm. "That's not who Tara is. She would have just told you the truth."

He shook his head. "I don't think we know who the real Tara is, Mom. Not anymore, anyway."

But Jim came back with his original question. "So this guy Nolan came to Walter Reed to apologize, or what?"

"That was the spin he put on it. But you ask me, it was to rub it in."

"Why would he do that?" Eileen asked.

"Because that's who he is, Mom. He's a mercenary who shot up that Iraqi car because he wanted to, period. Because he could. And if you want my opinion, he came to Walter Reed, among other reasons, to show me he'd gotten clean away with it. And while he was at it, he stole my girlfriend. This is not a good guy, believe me."

"Then what does Tara see in him?"

"That's what I've been getting at, Mom. She's not who you think she is."

"I still don't see how you can say that."

Facing his mother's implacable calm, her hard-wired refusal to think ill of anybody, Evan suddenly felt his temper snap. He slapped a palm flat down on the table, his voice breaking. "Okay, how about this, Mom? When Nolan told her I'd been wounded, you know what she said? She said I made my bed, I could sleep in it. Her exact words." His eyes had become glassy, but the tears shimmering in them were of rage, not sorrow. "She just didn't care, Mom. That's who she is now."

For a few seconds, the only sound in the backyard was the susurrus of the breeze through the leaves of the fruit trees.

"I can't believe that," Eileen said finally. "That just can't be true."

Evan drew a deep breath and raised his head to look straight at his mother. Exhausted and angry, he nevertheless had his voice under control. "No offense, Mom, but how can you know that? That's what she said."

Eileen reached out across the picnic table and put a reassuring hand on her son's arm. "And when was this?" she asked.

"When was what?"

"When she heard that you'd been wounded and said you'd made your own bed and you could sleep in it."

"I don't know exactly. Sometime in early September, right after Nolan got back home, about the time I got to Walter Reed."

"No, that's not possible." She told him about meeting Tara just before Christmas in the supermarket. "I may be terminally predisposed to seeing the good in people," she said, "and I know that sometimes I'm wrong. But there is no possible way that she had heard about your being wounded before I told her. And that was in December."

"If that's true, why didn't she call me then? Just to see how I was doing? Wish me luck? Some—?" He stopped abruptly, suddenly remembering the reindeer on the wall across from his bed, and that her call to him at Walter Reed—when *he'd* refused to speak to her—had been just before Christmas.

Or, if his mother was right, within a few days of when Tara had heard for the first time that he'd been injured.

Eileen patted Evan's arm. "She didn't call you because maybe she was already going out with this Nolan man by then. Maybe she felt guilty about that, or maybe she just thought it would be too awkward. But my point is, she certainly didn't know back in September that you'd been hurt. And it really doesn't sound like her to say you'd made your own bed."

"But then why would—?"

Jim, who'd been listening carefully to the debate, suddenly couldn't keep the enthusiasm from his voice. He knew the answer before Evan finished asking the question. "Why would Nolan come all the way to Walter Reed to tell you a lie? Could it be so that you'd get to hate Tara so much that you wouldn't be tempted to call her when you got back?"

Evan's flat gaze went from his father, over to his mother, back to his father again. "You know, Dad," he said, "you've gotten pretty smart in your old age."

THE SUN WAS JUST SETTLING in behind the foothills as Evan ascended the outside steps at Tara's apartment building and rang her doorbell. When there was no answer, he walked down to the kitchen window and peered inside, where the lights were off and nothing moved. He should have called first and made sure she was home, but the determination to go directly from his parents' house and talk to her had come as an impulse, and acting on the impulse—he was mostly sober, well-rested, recently showered and shaved, there'd never be a better time—he'd told his parents good-night, jumped in his car, and driven down.

Since she hadn't been with Nolan at the bowling alley, Evan had more than halfway convinced himself that her relationship with him was over. And if that were the case, he'd talk to her and see once and for all if there was any trace of a spark left to what they'd had, in spite of everything. At least they'd be dealing with the truth.

He'd parked not in the building's parking lot, but out in the street, in the same space his unconscious had apparently picked the other night. Now he went back to the car and got in. Taking out his cell phone, he began to scroll down to her numbers, both cell and home, but then stopped. If she was still going out with Nolan, or worse, if she was out with him at this moment, the timing would be disastrous.

He turned on the car's engine for a minute so he could roll down the driver's window, and saw that the clock on the dash read nine-fifteen. One of the inviolable rules of Tara's life while they'd been going out was that she wouldn't stay out too late, or party too hard, on a school night. And Sunday was a school night. Setting his seat back down a couple of notches, but to where he could still see above the ledge of the window, he turned the engine off and settled down to wait.

It didn't take long.

There was still a trace of natural light left in the day when a yellow Corvette, top down, turned into the lot. Tara was in the passenger seat and still with Nolan, all right. He got out and came around and opened her door and they walked, casually familiar, hand in hand, across the parking lot and up the stairs. She opened the door and they both went inside and Evan felt the blood pulsing in his temples. He put his hand gently over the area when he'd been wounded and imagined that it felt hotter than it had been.

In the apartment, the kitchen lights went on in the front window. A shadow passed into the frame, occupied it for a moment or two, then moved out. The room—and the entire apartment—darkened again.

Evan placed his shaking hands on the steeering wheel and tried to get some physical control back into his body. Swallowing was difficult. Sweat had broken on his brow and down his back.

What was he going to do?

"C'mon, c'mon, c'mon, c'mon, c'mon," he said to himself. But it was an empty imperative with no meaning. Seeing them together, knowing that they were in fact a couple, rendered unimportant the day's discovery that perhaps Tara hadn't cruelly ignored his injuries. What did that matter if she was sleeping with Nolan? If he was in her life, and Evan wasn't.

Suddenly, rocked with self-loathing and hatred, he allowed a steely calm to wash over him. Like most off-duty cops, he kept his weapon available for emergencies. His .40 semiautomatic was locked in his glove compartment, and now he took it out. Checking the chamber and the safety, he took a breath and then opened his car door, tucking the gun under his Hawaiian shirt into his belt.

He stepped out into the street.

EVAN SAT AT ONE of the computers at police headquarters. There wasn't much call for accessing the Department of Motor Vehicles database with his work in the DARE program, and this was the first time he'd actually had occasion to use the department's software. So far, it hadn't gone as quickly as he would have liked. In a perfect world, he could have already been in and out and nobody would have seen him, which would have been his preference.

But his world hadn't been perfect for a long time.

And sure enough, suddenly, at nine-thirty on a Sunday night, when the whole station should have been all but deserted, somebody called out his name from the doorway. Straightening his back, he hit the "ESC" button and jerked his head to the side so quickly he felt a crick in his neck as he looked over to see Lieutenant Spinoza from the Totems now coming toward him. Breaking a casual smile, he said, "Hey, Fred, what's going on?"

"People keep killing each other, that's what. So we poor public servants have to burn the midnight oil and then some." He gripped Evan's shoulder. "But, hey, how are you feeling?" he said. "I didn't like the way that dizziness came up on you all of a sudden the other night."

"No, I'm fine. I don't know what that was. My brain whacking out on me again."

"Well, whatever it was, you looked like you got hit by a train, and I mean that in the most flattering possible way." He pulled around the chair next to Evan and straddled it backward. "You're aware, I hope, that when you're not feeling good, you can call in sick. Everybody knows what you've been through. You don't have to push it. Nobody's going to bust your chops if you need a little time off. Plus, the major issue, just to keep life in perspective, we need you sharp for the game next Tuesday, rather than frittering away your energies trying to convince kids not to smoke dope."

"I'm all right, Fred. Really. I don't need to take time off."

"Obviously, if you're down here now. What's so important on a Sunday night?"

Evan gestured vaguely at the screen in front of him. "Honing up on my computer skills." He crossed his arms over his chest, all nonchalance. "But why are you here?"

"I'd say the usual, but it's not." Spinoza had clearly put in a long day already. "Does the name Ibrahim Khalil mean anything to you?"

"Should it? Is that an Iraq question?"

The response slowed Spinoza down. "No," he said, "but where you're coming from, I can see that's how it would hit you. But no. Mr. Khalil lives—lived—in this mansion in Menlo Park. He owns about half the 7-Elevens on the Peninsula. Owned. He and his wife don't own anything anymore, though. If it is him and his wife. . . ."

"What do you mean? You don't know?"

Spinoza shook his head. "Well, we know it was their house. And we know there were two bodies in it. But it's going to be a while before we can put the pieces back together."

"The pieces of what?"

"Their bodies."

Evan digested that for a second, then asked, "Did somebody cut 'em up?"

"No. Somebody *blew* 'em up, like with a bomb or something. Which of course set the house on fire and burned half of it down around them. So we won't for sure know much of the details for a while. But the neighbors all heard an explosion and then the fire."

"Somebody trying to get rid of the evidence."

Spinoza broke a small weary smile of approval. "Not only does he bowl," he said, "he also thinks. I think I see a detective badge in your future, my son."

"Let's get me out of DARE first."

"That's a good idea. How much longer you on that?"

"Well, after school's out." Evan let out a tired breath. "I can handle it if I can just keep from strangling any of the kids."

"Yeah, don't do that. Parents get all upset." Suddenly Spinoza's gaze went to the computer and he clucked in a schoolmarm fashion a couple of times. "This, boys and girls, is a bozo no-no."

"What is?"

" 'What is?' he asks. I'm sure. You think I'm an idiot?" He spoke in an exaggerated stage whisper. "We—and by 'we' I mean the department—we officially frown upon this method of meeting pretty young women." He lowered his voice further. "But really, privacy issues, don't go there. If you got busted, it wouldn't be pretty."

"I'm not trying to find a girl, Fred."

Spinoza nodded. "Of course you're not. Perish the thought. I just thought, on the off chance that you were, that I'd point out to you the department's policy. So whose address are you looking for, then?"

"Just this guy."

Spinoza raised his eyebrows. "Same rules go for cute guys," he said. "I know we're not supposed to ask about sexual orientation, but—"

"I'm not gay, Fred. Some of my DARE kids say this guy's selling dope."

"So why don't you just kick it over to vice?"

"'Cause they'd just put it on a back burner, and if I find out this guy is really selling drugs to my kids, I'm going to hunt him down and kill him."

"That's different, then. Why didn't you just say so?" Spinoza moved in closer to the keyboard. "So you got a plate number?"

FOR THE FIRST TIME since he'd left Walter Reed, Evan felt he needed to talk to his therapist, Stephan Ray. He didn't know if there was a technical term for what he was experiencing, but subjectively it felt somewhat similar to his inability to recall the names for things in the first months after his surgery. Except that now, and several other times in the past few days, he had found himself in the middle of some activity, or in the grip of some emotional reaction, and didn't seem to have a memory of how he'd come to be there. Or any control over his actions.

Earlier tonight by the Corvette with the gun, for example.

What did he think he was going to do with the gun? What did he *want* to do with the gun? He didn't know, didn't recall any moment of actual decision. First he was sitting in his car, waiting for Tara to come home so he could have a reasonable discussion with her. And the next thing he knew—the next thing he *remembered*—he was standing by the Corvette in the parking lot with his gun in his hand. *Wondering* why his gun was in his hand.

Surely he wasn't planning to shoot Nolan. Or Tara. Or, God forbid, both of them. Maybe he'd decided to shoot out one or more of Nolan's fancy-rimmed tires. In the dim light of early evening, that at least seemed like a semibaked idea. But his sentient mind realized that this would produce a loud noise and the very likely possibility that he'd at least be seen and possibly be recognized. It would also—perhaps—announce himself as interested in Nolan's activities in a way that he'd rather keep to himself, until he made some rational decisions about what he wanted to do with the rest of his life.

With Tara.

The stop at the police station had been a rational decision. He knew what he wanted there, though he wasn't sure *why* he wanted it, and he knew how to get it.

But now, having learned where Nolan lived and having driven up there, he found himself sitting in his car, parked curbside, again with his gun in his hand. If Nolan came home alone, it wouldn't be the same situation at all as it had been when Tara was with him. This was a quiet street, far less traveled than Tara's, lined with mature trees.

The address was a nice-looking, stand-alone townhome with attached garage amid a cluster of similar units. Separate, yet somewhat isolated. Perfect for . . .

For what? he asked himself.

And suddenly, again, the awareness of where he was, of what he was doing, flooded back. He was doing something here—figuratively staring at a drawing of a reindeer and wondering what the name of it was—but the exact nature of what he hoped to accomplish continued to elude him.

Looking down at the gun, he reached over and placed it back into the still-open glove compartment, then closed the door behind it, turned the key to lock it up. Then, the keys in his hand, he realized that he had to get out of here before he did something stupid. Something that he couldn't even explain to himself.

So he hit the ignition. The dashboard clock read ten forty-two.

Putting the car into gear, he pulled out from the curb and hadn't gone twenty feet when he jammed his foot on the brakes enough to make the tires squeal. His windows were down, he hadn't turned his headlights on, and running dark with a warm breeze over him sparked a jolt of familiarity.

In the months since he'd been injured, it had left the forefront of his memory, but now, suddenly, all the elements of this night rekindled a vision of the episode with Nolan when they'd raided the insurgents' lair in the neighborhood close to BIAP. The bright light and the terrific explosion blowing out the windows; the flames licking into the night as gunfire erupted behind him.

A mercenary mission to kill.

An explosion and then a fire.

A dog barked somewhere in the neighborhood.

Evan let out the breath he'd been holding, turned on his headlights, and eased his foot off the brake.

[13]

"WELL, MY SON, the latest theory, which might still be wrong," Spinoza said, "is that it was a thing called a fragmentation grenade. You ought to know about them. They're evidently using 'em in Iraq right now. Blow the shit out of everything so you need a snow shovel to pick up the pieces. Which pretty much fits what happened here, by the way." He sat back in his chair and picked up his sandwich. Putting his feet up on the desk, he took a bite. "So why do you want to know? You teaching execution techniques in DARE to the little fuckers?"

"No reason, really," Evan said. "I just thought it was interesting. I don't think I've ever heard of somebody being killed that way. At least not here in the States."

"Yeah, well." The lieutenant chewed thoughtfully. "It's not the norm, I'll give you that. Somebody wanted these people completely dead, in a big loud way. It wasn't some gangbanger taking potshots at a residence and hoping somebody gets hit."

"Could the guy, the victim, have done it himself?"

Spinoza shrugged. "Not impossible, I guess. There's no evidence pointing to anybody else. But also there's absolutely no sign so far of why Mr. Khalil would want to do that. The businesses were going great. He apparently loved the wife. No health problems. At least that's what we got from the rest of the family. And, believe me, there's a lot of the rest of the family. So I'm betting against murder/suicide, which leaves a pro. 'Cause I'll tell you one thing. Whoever did this did it right. At this moment, the only evidence we've got is—maybe—the bits of the frag grenade. And just between you and me, I'm kind of hoping we don't have that."

"Why not?"

"Because as we stand now, we've got a local murder of a businessman. At least we can get away with calling it that, since Ibrahim was a naturalized citizen."

"Where'd he come from?"

"I thought I told you that last night. Iraq. Half his family, evidently, still lives there. The other half has the 7-Eleven concession for the Bay Area wrapped up here."

"So what's the issue if you've got a frag grenade?"

"You can't own a frag grenade. It's a federal offense. Which means the ATF's involved. Which, in turn, sucks."

"So how do you find out if it was a frag grenade?"

Spinoza came down in his chair, brought his feet to the floor. "Fear not, my son. The ATF has already picked up samples from the scene. They'll have it analyzed by tonight and soon we'll all know for sure. If it is what it is, the FBI's in before morning. The preliminary call is yep, frags. So it's gonna be their case."

"Why's that so bad, Fred? Don't they have a lot more resources than we do?"

"Oh, no question," Spinoza said. "More resources, more money, more access to data, the whole nine yards. The thing is, though—they don't share. So we wind up spending a week finding stuff they already have. It's kind of a race to see who can get there fastest, but we've got one leg tied behind our backs."

"I don't think that's exactly the expression."

"No?" Spinoza popped his last bite of sandwich. "Well, that's what it feels like."

HE KNEW THE LOCKSMITH from Ace Hardware both from his high school class and from his men's softball team. Now, at a few minutes before two o'clock on an afternoon after Evan had told *his* lieutenant, James Lochland, that he was suffering from a migraine and needed to go lie down in his dark bedroom, Dave Saldar pulled up outside of Nolan's townhouse and parked in back of Evan's CR-V.

Evan, in his police uniform to reinforce his legitimacy, got out of his car and they high-fived each other on the sidewalk. After a couple of minutes of catching up—Saldar had heard some of Evan's story from guys on the team—they got around to what Evan had called Dave up here for.

"You didn't hide a spare under a rock or something?" Saldar asked.

"No. I didn't think I'd ever forget my keys. Who forgets their keys?"

"My wife does every time she leaves the house."

"Yeah, well, I don't. I never have before."

"I would love one thin dime for every time I'd heard those exact words. Why do you think the world invented locksmiths?"

"I never could figure that out."

"Well, now you know." Saldar inclined his head toward the town-homes. "Okay, which one's yours?"

They went down to Nolan's doorway, partially enclosed and blocked from the street by an L-shaped, glass-block privacy screen. Saldar got out his tools and went to work. Evan found that his legs were weak enough that he had to lean against the screen for support. With each passing second, the enormity of the implications of what he was doing worked on his system. He felt as lightheaded as he'd been on Nolan's night raid outside of BIAP. A jackhammer pulse pounded where they'd cut open his skull. The migraine he'd invented for Lieutenant Lochland threatened to become a reality—pinpoints of light exploded at the outer edges of his vision. He kept looking to the street, nearly passing out when a yellow Miata convertible crested the incline and drove by.

Saldar, noticing something in his reaction, glanced up at him. "You all right?"

"Good," he said. In fact, he could feel the sweat breaking on his forehead. Summoning all the control he could muster, he brought his hand up and dragged it across his brow.

At last, Saldar turned the knob and pushed the door open. "There you go, a minute and fifteen seconds. This could be a new record."

"I'm sure it is, Dave. That's awesome."

Saldar was holding open the front door. "Hey, are you okay, Ev? You really don't look so good."

"I'm all right. The head's acting up a little, that's all." He reached back for his wallet, thinking, *I've got to get him out of here! What if Nolan shows up?* But keeping it casual, he said, "So what's the damage?"

"Let's call it thirty, since we're friends. You want, you can go grab your set of keys and I can make you a couple of quick copies right out of the truck, five bucks each."

"That's all right." Evan fished out two twenties. "I know I've got some dupes inside. I've just got to remember to put 'em out here somewhere for next time. But right now I think I'd better get in there and lie down a minute."

"Sure, okay. But let me run and get you your change."

"No, keep it."

"I can't take tips from teammates, Ev. It's one of my rules. I've got some cash back in the truck. Won't take me thirty seconds."

He put a firm hand on his friend's shoulder. "Dave, really, I'm hurting a little here. Thanks for your help, but I've got to get horizontal pretty quick or I'm going to get sick. Seriously. Take care of yourself. I'll see you around."

"You need a doctor?"

The effort for even half a smile was almost too much to bear. "You don't let me get inside pretty quick, you're gonna need a doctor. You hear me?"

"All right, all right. But stop by the field sometime. We're still playing Tuesdays and Thursdays."

"I will. Promise."

"I'll buy you some beers with your tip money."

"Deal," Evan said, stepping inside the door. "Later."

HE STOOD IN THE LIVING ROOM. Part of him had a hard time believing that he was truly here, illegally inside another man's home. It felt surreal. This wasn't who he was. It wasn't the kind of thing he'd ever done, or even thought about doing.

But now, once inside, he couldn't let those considerations slow him down. There was no telling when Nolan might return. Evan had no idea what hours he worked, or what he did on a day-to-day basis, or even if he had any regular schedule at all. If there was something incriminating to be found in this place, and Evan's guts told him there was, he had to find it and then get out fast. It wasn't a matter of finding evidence that could be used in court—he simply wanted the knowledge.

Or at least that's what he let himself believe. He would decide then how to use what he knew at his leisure.

The room he was in was Spartan, furnished with a leather couch and matching twin leather chairs in front of built-in, mostly empty, book-shelves on either side of the fireplace. A large mirror over the mantel gave an impression of space, but the room probably wasn't more than ten feet wide. Half of the back wall was a glass doorway that opened onto a small brick patio, shaded by large oak trees. A potted plant squatted in the cor-ner. The first glance told him that there would be nothing of interest here, but he forced himself to slow down and make sure.

When he was done, he parted the blinds in the front window, saw nothing out in the street, and crossed the tiled entry area that led into the kitchen, which didn't have much more personality than the living room. It was, however, quite a bit more exposed, since the double-wide window over the sink looked out over the small lawn to the street beyond.

It didn't appear that Nolan did a lot of cooking for himself—the re-frigerator had eggs, beer, a pack of American cheese, and milk, with toma-toes and lettuce in the vegetable bin, and some condiments, while the freezer held three boxes of frozen spinach, a carton of ice cream, and a few packages of chicken breasts and ground beef.

A door next to the refrigerator led out to the small single-car garage, where Nolan had hung his empty duffel bag and two empty backpacks on hooks on the far wall. An uncluttered workbench obviously hadn't seen much use, and neither had the drawers under it.

Back in the kitchen, Evan finally got his nerves under control as he scoped out the street again and then ducked under the window passing through. Just off the living room in the back of the house, he entered a decent-sized den with a desk and a computer. The wall featured a tacked-up map of Iraq with several color-coded pins stuck in various spots—Baghdad, Mosul, Kirkuk, Abu Ghraib, Anaconda. Evan tried the mouse first to see if the monitor screen came on, and when it didn't, he hit the button on the CPU. While it booted up, he went through the next door into the bedroom and stopped in his tracks.

Drawing a heavy breath, he crossed over to the bureau next to his ene-my's perfectly made bed and picked up the photograph of Nolan and Tara in a heavy silver frame. They were hugging each other for the picture, obviously from the deck of a boat out on the Bay, both smiling out at him on a lovely day. He held the picture long enough that the urge to smash it against the wall came and went. Then, replacing it carefully in its original position, he went back to his searching in earnest. Dresser drawers, bathroom drawers, cupboards, and closets.

The headboard of the bed yielded up the first weapon, another M9 Beretta, the same weapon that Evan had carried in Iraq. He smelled the barrel and picked up no odor, then removed the clip and verified that it was full. But a pro like Nolan, if he had used the gun, would have cleaned it and reloaded immediately afterward.

The bedroom closet, neat like the rest of the house, contained another backpack on the top shelf. This one he emptied out on the bed piece by piece. It held another Beretta 9mm, ten clips of ammunition, and six hand grenades. Evan didn't know for sure if they were fragmentation grenades or the so-called flash/bangs, which were nowhere near as lethal. But either way, he was willing to bet that they were illegal in the hands of private citizens. Evan was sure that they would be of interest to the police, once he figured out a way to get some law enforcement person interested in Nolan as a suspect in the Khalil murders.

Replacing the backpack, he went back into the den and sat in front of the computer. Clicking on the icon labeled "Allstrong," he scanned through a few documents—mostly what appeared to be copies of or amendments to government contracts or work orders that the company had secured overseas. There were also a significant number of e-mail files, and several résumés of people who had served in the military, which attested to the kind of work Nolan was probably doing over here Stateside. Evan entered a few more of the documents and searched for the name Khalil, but came up empty.

Lacking a password, though he tried several obvious ones, he couldn't get into Nolan's regular e-mail file. The icon named "My Pictures," by contrast, came right up. Immobilized by what he feared he might see there—more photos of Nolan and Tara in much more intimate settings than the deck of a boat—he finally clicked on the first folder and, finding not even one picture of Tara, sighed in relief.

These appeared to be shots Nolan might have taken when he was shopping for a house. Here was a tree-lined street just like the one he lived on, cars parked along the curb. Then different angles, in different lights, on another house, large and grandiose. In fact, on closer inspection, on the clearest picture from directly in front of the building, the place was actually a pink-hued monstrosity. What in the world, Evan wondered, could Nolan have seen in the place that would have prompted such a detailed study?

Suddenly recognition straightened him upright. In the paper that morning, Evan had seen a black-and-white picture of the remains of Mr. Khalil's house, which of course no longer looked very much like the residence in this picture. But in the article, hadn't he read something about the house being pink?

Hurriedly he started pulling open the drawers to the desk. There was a digital camera in the middle drawer and for a second he considered looking at what it contained. But he couldn't take the time. He checked his watch—two forty-five. He'd been in here too long already. In the lower right drawer, he found an open ten-pack of floppy disks. Four remained in the box, and with his hands shaking now, he took one out, inserted it into the A-disk slot, and copied the file from the "My Pictures" photo onto the disk.

Ejecting the disk, he put it in his breast pocket, then sat back, took a breath, and walked himself through turning the computer off the careful way, through the "Start" menu.

Keenly listening for the sound of the garage door opening, or of a car pulling up out in the street, he forced himself to wait until the terminal screen went black. Then he got out of the chair and replaced it where he hoped and thought it had been. He pushed all the desk drawers flush against their inserts. Checking one last time to make sure that he still had the disk in his pocket, he walked back up through the living room, locked the front door from the inside, looked out through the window, saw that it was safe, and let himself out.

[14]

THE LAST CHILD HAD GONE home two hours ago; the sounds from the hallway were small and distant. The occasional whirrings of the Xerox machine way down in the office barely registered on Tara's consciousness as she looked out at the view from her classroom window. She'd always considered it a particularly fine view, with the small grove of scrub oak hugging the hilltop just across the street. She could imagine that the hilltop was far from anything mundane or suburban—say, in Tuscany, where she'd never been. Sometimes in the late afternoon like this, with the springtime scents of lilac and jasmine coming up on the breeze mingling with the closer smells of pencil and chalk, this classroom was her favorite place in the world.

She felt that she could count on her fingers the times when she'd been the absolute happiest and most content, and many of them had been right here. Some of the long-timers here at St. Charles had gotten perhaps a little cynical over the years, but either Tara hadn't been here long enough yet, or she didn't have the genes for cynicism; she wasn't that kind of a person. She still loved her kids. Every year a new batch, and every year with fresh challenges—oh yes, thank you, challenges—but also with something new to learn, to connect with, to love. New clay. That was how she always thought of her classes when the year began. New clay.

Sitting back in her desk chair, she daydreamed, her face relaxed in contented repose, an almost infinitesimal upturn to her lips. It had been a day almost exactly like this one, soft and scented—had it been three years now? She remembered that the whole day she'd felt almost sick with herself since she'd been so easy on the first date with this new guy, Evan. Too easy. She'd been too attracted and let him know it and wasn't really inclined to fight herself. Not against that kind of heat.

But what if it turned out to be that old cliché and he didn't respect her and never called again? Hell, she was an intelligent woman with a fine career and knew that she would never build her world around some man, but the thought of never again seeing this man she'd met only one time just suddenly didn't seem bearable.

And she had gotten up from her desk, sick at herself, and went to smell the outdoor smells by the window, which always helped when she was worried or depressed, and she looked down and there Evan was, getting out of his car with a bouquet in his hand. The happiest single moment of her life.

Sighing, she opened her eyes, surprised at how quickly the contented daydream had retrieved enough emotion to nearly bring her to tears. Breathing deeply, she dabbed at her eyes and pushed back from her desk, thinking that, oh, well, it was time to go home. No need to dwell on the past. It was still a beautiful day, with the incredible floral perfume outside on the breeze.

She crossed over to the window to smell the day one last time. And then she looked down.

In the street, Evan was getting out of his car. No flowers. But it was him nevertheless, coming to see her at last.

Tears welled again, and her hand went to her mouth. Then, after a moment, she brought it down to rest over her heart.

"Hi."

"Hi."

"I thought you might be here."

"You were right. It's a beautiful afternoon. My favorite time."

"I remember."

A silence. She'd been standing when he got to the classroom door, and now she boosted herself back onto her desk. "So how are you?" she finally asked. "You look good."

"I'm okay. I still get headaches, but basically I'm Mr. Lucky."

"That's what I've heard. I'm glad for you. Glad you're alive."

"Me too." He moved a step closer to her. "Are you all right? You look like you've been crying."

She shook her head, smiled with a false brightness. "Allergies. The downside of all these blooming flowers." She sucked in a quick breath and let it out, then tried another smile that died on the vine. "I tried to call you."

"I know. I was a shit. I could say I was still recovering and don't remember anything about it, but that'd be a lie. I'm sorry."

She shrugged. "I was a shit too. Too inflexible. Too stupid."

"Okay," he said, "we're a couple of shits."

"Stupid shits," she corrected him. And finally a small smile took.

"Better," he said. He looked away, over at the window to the oak-studded hillside. Coming back to her, his jaw somehow had a harder line. He drew a breath and blew it out sharply. "You still seeing Ron Nolan?"

Biting at her lower lip, she nodded, answered in a very small voice. "Sometimes."

"Love him?"

She shrugged, shook her head, shrugged again. "I don't know, Evan. We've had some good times, but I don't know. *Love's* a big word."

"Yes, it is. What are we going to do about it?"

"What do you mean, we?"

"You and me. We. The usual meaning. The fact that I love you."

"Oh, God, Evan." She shook her head from side to side. "Don't say that."

"Why not? It's true."

"Well . . ." She slipped herself off the desk and walked over to the windows again, stood still a moment, then turned back to him. "Please don't say that," she repeated. "I don't know what to do with that."

"You don't have to do anything. Although that's one of the reasons I came here. To tell you that. Just so that if you were wondering, you'd know."

Her gaze settled on his eyes. "Okay," she said softly. "Okay, now I know." Bringing her hand up to her forehead, she pushed until her fingers went white, then pulled her hand away. "Were there other reasons?"

"Other reasons for what?"

"For why you came here. You said one reason was to tell me you loved me. What was another one?"

Evan's brow clouded over—he couldn't remember. For an awful moment, he thought he might have forever lost the real reason he'd come to see Tara today. He hadn't come to tell her he loved her. He hadn't been sure of that until he was with her. But then they'd started talking and that had come out and now he was unable to retrieve the real purpose of his trip here. "I'm trying to remember," he said. "Can you give me a couple of seconds?"

This was the first time she was seeing an effect of his injury, and he was acutely aware that this moment might change everything forever between them. He might, in her eyes, now be damaged, challenged, handicapped— somehow not as sharp as he'd been, not quite exactly the same person. Not quite her equal.

He couldn't let that happen.

Closing his eyes, concentrating, he thought, *"Come on, brain, come on. Retrieve it."* Then he opened his eyes as the answer found its way to his tongue. "The other reason I came here," he said, "is I wanted to ask you a simple factual question."

At once, she was all the way with him again. Her expression now relaxed, she moved a few steps toward him, her arms crossed over her chest. "I can do simple factual," she said. A smile played around her mouth.

"Okay. Do you remember when you first heard about me getting hurt?"

Her quizzical look stayed on him for a long moment, as though she were surprised that he would have to ask that question at all. "Sure," she said. "I ran into your mom at the grocery store one night. I think it was a few days before Christmas. I know it was a few days before I called you."

"You mean called me at Walter Reed? When I didn't talk to you?"

"Right."

"You're sure of that? The time, I mean. Just before Christmas."

"Of course. That's when it was. When else would I have heard?"

"How about back when it happened? Say, September?"

"No way, Evan. How could I have known then?"

He shrugged. "Well, when did you start seeing Ron Nolan?"

"What does Ron have to do with that?"

"I would have thought he'd have mentioned it, that's all."

"He never knew about it, Evan. You guys all got transferred out of his base the week he got back."

Evan canted his head a bit to one side. Studying her expression, he read only sincerity, openness, perhaps a bit of confusion. But one thing was clear—she was telling him the truth as she knew it.

"We got transferred?"

"That's what Ron said."

"Where'd we get tranferred to, Tara? Did he tell you that?"

"No. I don't think he knew."

"Right. He didn't know. You know why? Because we weren't transferred. We ran our last mission out of Baghdad Airport, where we'd been with Ron all along. You can look it up."

The germ of confusion spread like a plague over her features. Mouth tightened, brow furrowed, eyes darting, seeking a place to land. "But . . ." The word hung in the room between them. Her arms hung down, inanimate at her side. "I don't get this."

"Ron was with us in the convoy, Tara. He was in my Humvee. He was next to me when I got hit."

"No. That can't be true."

"Why would I make it up, Tara?"

"I'm not saying you're making it up, Evan. Although I could see a reason why you might. But I don't think you'd do that."

"I wouldn't. I'm not making it up," he said. "It's what happened."

She held his gaze for a minute, and then, her voice barely audible, grabbed at the next straw. "Maybe . . . I mean, I'm just thinking, could it be with what happened to your head . . . maybe you don't remember it all exactly?"

He nodded—sober, patient, restrained. "That's a legitimate question. I have forgotten some stuff. I don't remember whole days and weeks from when I woke up. But Ron was with us in that convoy. I remember everything about that. If you still don't believe it, you can look it all up on the Web. Just Google Masbah." He spelled the name of the neighborhood in

Baghdad. "It's all there. He's the reason it all went down. And that's the reason he had to get out of Iraq so fast. They were starting the investigation, and he knew it led straight to him."

The color had drained from her face. Her eyes flitted to the corners of the room as though she hoped to find some answer there. She brushed a strand of hair from her forehead. Placing her hand flat on one of the students' desktops for support, she lowered herself into the connected chair. "He told me he had no idea you'd been hurt," she said, "that he found out about it from me after I ran into your mom that night and she told me."

"Christmastime."

She nodded. "Definitely."

"And he told you he knew nothing about it before?"

"Nothing. I swear, Evan. No, he swore. He'd never heard a thing about it."

"He didn't have to hear about it, Tara," Evan said. "He was there. He fired the first shots."

SPINOZA POURED THEM both a cup of coffee and took Evan out into the backyard so they wouldn't interrupt the movie Leesa and their four young kids were watching in the family room. The day, with at least another half hour of light in it, continued warm and fragrant. The two men sat down at a picnic table under a vine-covered trellis. "So," Spinoza began, "did you get your dope dealer yet?"

"Not yet," he said. "He's out of town."

"Timing's everything," Spinoza said.

"I don't know," Evan replied. "Timing's important, but I'd give points for location too. A quarter inch either way and my story's different. That's been pretty good nightmare material."

"I'd imagine so." Then, going back to his original subject, Spinoza said, "You know he's out of town?"

Evan shrugged. "His car's gone. Nobody answers the door."

"Don't do anything stupid, Ev," the lieutenant said. "If you think there's really something to this guy, send him to the narcs." Spinoza blew on his coffee and took a sip. "And in other news, you know Mr. Khalil, who we talked about at lunchtime? As of a couple of hours ago, Mr. Khalil is officially a joint-jurisdiction case. You remember the frag grenade issue we talked about? Well, the feds have conclusively determined that that's what blew up the room and started the fire. So they're in the case, in spite of the fact that it also looks like Mr. Khalil and his wife were first shot in the head with a nine millimeter bullet."

Evan's face must have betrayed something. Spinoza abruptly put his coffee cup down on the table. "What?"

"Nothing," Evan said.

EVAN LEFT SPINOZA'S HOME in great frustration. He'd planned—hoped—somehow to get the picture from Nolan's computer in front of Spinoza, but there was no way he could tell his lieutenant how he'd gotten it—that he'd broken into someone's home—and that rendered hopeless his entire ill-conceived plan. But cruising down to the Khalils' ruined house, Evan had satisfied himself that the house in the picture was in fact theirs, then decided that the thing to do would be simply to send the disk to the FBI. The Bureau would have Nolan in their database and know all about his history. The advantage to his new idea was that both the ATF and the FBI were known to play fast and loose with due process and probable cause. If they came to think that Nolan had killed the Khalils, especially if there was an Iraqi or terrorist connection, they would find a way to question him and perhaps even get inside his house, where they would discover the grenades, the other pictures, the guns. In any event, after they got the disk, Nolan would be on their radar. After that, it would only be a matter of time before they could take him down.

Now night had fallen. In his kitchen, Evan's head throbbed and again the pinpricks of bright light at the edges of his vision presaged the onset of a migraine. He'd already taken a couple of Vicodin, and as soon as he finished the last of his business, he had to get to bed if he was going to work tomorrow.

Wearing blue latex gloves, he pulled the self-adhesive manila envelope over closer to him. It had taken a while, left-handed, to write down both Nolan's address on a piece of notepaper and the FBI's address on the envelope. But now he was satisfied—the writing was legible yet unidentifiable as his own. He slid the slip of paper with Nolan's address into the envelope along with the disk, then pulled the paper strip from the adhesive and closed the top. He peeled off ten self-adhesive stamps from the roll he'd bought and stuck them on. Tomorrow he would stop off in another neighborhood and drop the envelope into a mailbox.

Now he set the thing on his table and gave it a quick once-over. Satisfied that it couldn't be traced back to him, he walked back through his apartment to his bedroom, turning off the lights as he went. Lying down on the bed, his clothes still on, he pulled a blanket up over his shoulders, turned on his side, and closed his eyes.

A LITTLE WHILE after it was truly dark, Tara called Evan's mother, Eileen, and got his address. She waited and thought and second-guessed herself and eventually left her place sometime after eleven o'clock and drove. Parking out in the dark street across from his apartment, she sat for another five minutes or so with her car windows down, her hands in a prayerful attitude in front of her mouth.

By the time she got to the door, she barely heard her own timid knocking over the beating of her heart. After a minute, she knocked again, harder. And waited.

A light came on inside and hearing his footsteps, she held her breath.

The door opened. He'd been sleeping in his clothes. His hair was tousled, his eyes still with that sleepy look she remembered so well. She looked up at him, realizing that she loved having to look up, had missed that; loving the size of him, so different from looking across at Ron Nolan. Everything was so different and so much better with Evan. How could she have forgotten that?

She couldn't get her face to go into a smile. She was too afraid, the blood now pulsing in her ears, her hands unsteady at her sides.

He just looked at her.

"Is it too late?" she asked. "Tonight, I mean."

"No."

"I needed to talk to you some more. Would that be all right?"

"Everything's all right, Tara. You can do whatever you want. You want to come in?" Stepping back away from the door, he gave her room to pass and then closed the door quietly behind her as she kept walking through his living room, stopping by the counter that delineated the kitchen and turning back to face him. Her shoulders rose and fell.

From over by the door, he said, "I can't guarantee talking too well. I've been having some trouble sleeping, so I'm a little doped up. Plus I've had a couple of drinks. I'm drinking too much. I need to stop."

"Are you in such pain?"

He managed a small shrug. "Sometimes, but that's not it really." He took a second to continue. "I know that whatever they say, I'm not all the way back. Maybe I'll never be. To tell you the truth, it freaks me out sometimes. When I'm alone mostly. But I don't want to have anybody feel like they have to be with me all the time either."

"Your mom?"

"For one example, yeah. Anybody, really. But it's"—he shrugged again—"it's just what I'm doing now, Tara. Holding on. Getting better, I hope. Getting over what happened."

Evan still stood by the door, making no effort to close the space between them. She felt the distance tugging at her, causing a pain of its own, and took a step toward him, then another.

"But that's all just me," Evan said. "What did you want to talk about?"

"Ron. I never . . . I wanted to tell you that it was never like it was with us. It was just a completely different thing."

"Was? Past tense?"

She let out a heavy breath. "Yes. After what you told me today."

"Okay. And how was it with us that was so different?"

Tara put her hands together at her waist. She deserved that question. And he deserved the real answer. "Because we connected, Evan. So basically."

He nodded. "I know."

"I don't think that ever goes away."

"No. Me neither."

She looked across the living room into his eyes. "Why are you staying over there? It's almost like you're afraid of me."

"I am. As much as I need to be."

"How much is that?"

"That depends on how much being done with Ron means you're back with me."

She waited another few seconds and then closed the space between them. Looking up at him again, now the smell of him so close. "Does it hurt you to touch the scar?" she asked.

"It's just a scar." But he inclined his head so that she could see it. Almost a perfect circle, slightly indented.

Slowly, she reached out her hand and brought it up to his head. As soon as she touched it, she felt something give in her legs. As she traced the shape of the scar, tears sprang into her eyes and she made no effort to stop them. Evan brought his head down, leaning into her.

Bringing her other hand up into his hair, she cradled his head in both her hands.

Holding on to her, his arms behind her, he went to his knees in front of her, his face first pressed to one side against her thigh. But then, her hands on his head now directing him, she turned him to be up against her, his hands gripping her from behind, pulling her into him, while she pressed herself against him. She pulled him gently away for an instant, only long enough to let her step out of her clothes, and then brought him back to where he'd been.

Beyond any time, then, she was on the floor with her legs around his neck, until the surge of blood and heat she'd only known with him took her and then there was the taste of her on his mouth and his own cry as everything between them came back and came again and left them both flung out on the floor, wasted and sated, and connected in every part.

[15]

THE RELEVANT PORTION of the e-mail from Jack Allstrong that had put Nolan on the road had read: "When the CPA hands over the government to the Iraqis, Uncle Sam is going to be shipping over $2.4 billion—that's right, *billion*—in shrink-wrapped 100s. That's twenty-eight *tons* of greenbacks, Ron, almost all of it earmarked for infrastructure and rebuilding, which means us. My standing directive to you is to recruit as many qualified personnel as you can find. Starting now."

Now Nolan was just getting back home from a productive couple of days. Frequenting the bars around some of California's military bases—Pendleton, Ord, Travis—he'd recruited four men for Allstrong's ongoing and growing operations in Iraq. Though Allstrong's security work was dangerous and demanding, ex-officers who were bored or broke or both in civilian life often jumped at the chance to resurrect their careers, their self-esteem, and their bank accounts, and to once again utilize the special skills that had served them well in the military.

And nowhere were they needed more than in Anbar. As Jack Allstrong had predicted in August, the rebuilding of the electrical tower infrastructure in that province was turning out to be a gold mine for the company, albeit a costly one in terms of human life. Allstrong had by now put more than five hundred men to work on this latest contract, which initially bid out at forty million dollars, although it had grown to more than one hundred million in the past seven months. Allstrong Security, Jack liked to point out, was in 2003 the fastest-growing company in the world, outstripping Google, compliments of U.S. largesse and Jack's ability to surf the chaos of the reconstruction.

But in Anbar, the company also had already lost thirty-six of Kuvan

Krekar's men, and Kuvan's supply chain of bodies was growing thin and dispirited. Beyond that, Kuvan had been facing severe competition from another broker named Mahmoud al-Khalil, who was not only supplying cheaper workers but was perhaps terrorizing and even killing Kuvan's people to discourage others from signing on. Why? So that Mahmoud and not Kuvan could pocket the extremely lucrative cash commissions. Well, with the recent untimely demise of his paterfamilias in Menlo Park, Mahmoud would hopefully soon conclude that competing directly with Allstrong's chosen subcontractor was not a sound business decision.

Hefting his duffel bag, Nolan let himself into his townhome through the garage door to the kitchen. He walked through the living room, stopped in his office and turned on his computer, then went into his bedroom, where he dropped the duffel bag on his bed, then returned to his desk and checked his e-mail and—first things first—made sure he'd been paid. He had.

With that taken care of, Nolan went back into his bedroom and started to unpack. Grabbing a pair of pants, he turned and opened the closet, and stopped short.

Something was not right.

Nolan didn't spend much time thinking about his military-ingrained penchant for order, but when he woke up in the mornings, he automatically made his bed with hospital corners so that the covers were tight enough to bounce a coin off them. The spare shoes were always shined and perfectly aligned on the floor of the closet. He hung his shirts and pants in order from light to dark, the hangers spaced with an automatic and practiced precision.

Now he stared at the row of hangers. He didn't specifically remember taking down the shirts and pants that he'd packed for his trip, but could not imagine that he would have taken down his clothes and left the hangers spaced unevenly as they were now. His eyes went to the backpack on the top shelf. He had lined it up exactly with the break in the hangers between his shirts and his pants, and now it was clearly centered over the shirts. Reaching up, he pulled it toward him, relieved by the familiar weight. He opened it and saw that nothing—not the grenades, the gun, or the ammo—was gone.

Which was weird.

Maybe he'd imagined that the hangers had been moved. It didn't seem possible that someone would have broken in here and not taken the grenades and the gun.

But it wouldn't be smart to take chances. Reaching into the backpack, he removed the Beretta and slammed one of the clips into place, then racked a bullet into the chamber. He dropped the backpack next to the duffel bag on his bed and went to check the bathroom, where an intruder might still be lurking. Finding no one there, he went back out into the living room to the front door, where the piece of Scotch tape that he'd laid over the connection between the door and its jamb was now stuck under the jamb.

Somebody had definitely been here.

Methodically now, he went back out to the garage, where he patted down the empty backpacks hanging against the wall. He was about to start opening the drawers when he straightened up, stopping himself.

He didn't see how it could be remotely possible, but it occurred to him that if one of the members of Khalil's extended family could have somehow traced the patriarch's execution back to him, their method of retribution might include a bomb—open a drawer and it goes off. By the same token, his experience with IEDs in Iraq told him that if there was a bomb, someone would have been hiding somewhere outside, seen him drive up, and sent an electrical pulse to detonate the device after he was inside. Alternatively, Nolan could trigger the bomb himself by switching on any one of a dozen electrical connections in the house. But any of those scenarios contemplated the possibility that someone had identified him as the Khalils' killer.

Which from Nolan's perspective was flatly not possible. He'd made no mistakes. Therefore, there was no bomb. He'd also already turned on his computer, and several lights. Walking back out to the garage, this time he opened all the drawers. Back in the kitchen, he did the same. Opened the refrigerator. He had no idea what, if anything, he was looking for, but someone had been in his house in his absence, and if it hadn't been to take something, what did that leave?

He just didn't know.

Back in his office, he sat at his desk, laid the gun on it, and stared for a minute again at his computer. Picking up his telephone, he got the pulsing dial tone that meant he had messages, and entered his password.

The first message was from an obviously very distraught, though composed, Tara, who had called him on Monday night. "Ron. Evan Scholler came by to visit me today at the school. We had a long talk with one another and he told me some things that shocked me—you probably have a good idea what they were.

"I don't know what to say to you, other than that I just want you to know how completely violated I feel. And how used. I don't know how you could have lied to me so much. I'm leaving this message on your machine on purpose because I don't want to talk to you, or even see you anymore. I can't believe you've done this. It just doesn't seem possible that anyone could be so cruel and so selfish. I'm so sorry for who you are, Ron, but not for what I'm saying. Good-bye. Don't call me. Don't come by. Just stay away. I mean it."

The phone still at his ear, he hadn't let up his grip yet on the receiver when the next message began. The call had come this morning, about six hours ago. "Mr. Nolan. My name is Jacob Freed. I'm a special agent with the Federal Bureau of Investigation, and I wondered if we might be able to take a few minutes of your time to talk to you about a routine matter involving national security that's come to our attention. I don't mean to be unnecessarily vague, but I'm sure you understand that these days some things are best left unsaid over the telephone. If you could call me for an appointment at your earliest convenience when you get in, or alternatively, I'll try to get back to you in the next day or two. My number is . . ."

When Nolan finally hung up, he sat unmoving with his right arm outstretched and his hand covering the Beretta. After a minute or two, he let go of the gun and moved his hand over to the mouse. As soon as he saw the "My Pictures" icon, he realized that he'd made an error by not erasing that file before he'd gone away. Opening it now, intending to close the barn door after the horse had escaped, he checked the access record and saw that someone had, indeed, looked at the file two days before—the same Monday that Tara had spoken to Evan Scholler.

Though it might be too late, he still thought it would be better to delete the file now, so that if the FBI came and looked . . .

Except he knew that there wasn't really any such thing anymore as truly deleting something. Experts could always retrieve whatever it was from the hard disk.

Still, his finger hovered over the mouse as he stared at one of the many pictures he'd taken of Mr. Khalil's house while he was working on access and egress. One click and all of that would at least be gone for now.

Sitting back, his eyes narrowing, he took his hand abruptly off the mouse. Suddenly, he decided that he did not want to delete the picture file after all. Although he would have to remove the memory chip from the digital camera in the desk drawer and get rid of it. Tapping his index fingernail against his front teeth, he sat as if in a trance for a full minute, and then another one.

The idea looked perfect from every angle.

He reached again for the telephone.

"AGENT FREED, please."

"This is he."

"Agent Freed. My name is Ron Nolan. You left me a message about a national security matter and asked me to call for an appointment."

"Yes, sir, I did. Thanks for getting back to me."

"I think maybe I should be the one thanking you, sir. I've just returned from a business trip. While I've been gone, somebody let themselves into my house. I was going to call the regular police, but then I got your message. I don't know if you know it, but I do some sensitive work with Allstrong Security, a government contractor in Iraq, and I thought what you wanted to talk about might have something to do with that."

"Well, as I mentioned, perhaps it would be better to meet in person to talk about the issue that's come up with us, although if you're reporting a robbery or burglary, you should probably call the regular police. That's not really our jurisdiction."

"Agent Freed, this wasn't a robbery. Whoever it was didn't take anything. They left something. Plus, they messed with my computer. I don't know what it's all about, but it's almost like somebody's trying to plant something on me."

"Like what?"

"Well, I just found one thing, but there might be more. I'm afraid to look in case he's planted a bomb someplace."

"Who's he?"

"I don't know. I mean the person who broke in."

"Okay. So what's the one thing?"

"This is what's so weird. It's a backpack full of ammunition and, you're not going to believe this, it looks like about a half dozen hand grenades."

"Hand grenades?"

"Yes, sir. As you may know, I've been over to Iraq several times. I know the ordnance. And these look like fragmentation grenades to me."

FREED AND HIS PARTNER, a middle-aged fireplug named Marcia Riggio, sat with Nolan on the small, oak-shaded back patio. Inside the townhouse, a three-man team of forensics specialists, having already confiscated the backpack with its contents, were fingerprinting every clean surface and cataloging anything that might be of interest—Nolan's other gun from the bed's headboard, the digital camera in the desk drawer, downloading his hard disk.

Nolan didn't want to rush anything with these federal cops. He didn't want to appear to point them in any specific direction. But now, as Agent Riggio looked up from her notepad, Nolan decided that it was getting to be the time. "Let me ask you something," he said. "Is there any scenario you can think of that makes any sense of this to you?"

The two agents exchanged a glance. Riggio got the nod from Freed and took point. "Do you have any enemies?" she asked.

Nolan frowned. "Even if I did," he said, "what does this do to hurt me? Unless I pulled the pin on one of those grenades, which anybody who knows me knows I'm not going to do."

"Maybe it's not about hurting you," Riggio went on. "Maybe it's about framing you."

"For what?"

But Freed stepped in. "Before we get to that," he said, "let's go back to your enemies."

This time, Nolan broke a grin. "I don't see it, really. I like people. I really do, and they tend to like me. My boss thinks it's a flaw in my character." He shrugged. "So I'd have to say no. No enemies."

"Okay," Riggio said. "How about rivals?"

"In business?"

"Business, pleasure, whatever."

He took his sweet time, savoring the anticipation. "The only even remotely . . ." He shook his head. "No, never mind."

Freed jumped on it. "What?"

"Nothing, really. Just a guy I knew in Iraq who used to date my girlfriend. But that was a long time ago."

"If he's in Iraq," Freed said, "he's out of this."

"Well, he's home now. Here."

"And he's not over her? Your girlfriend?" Riggio asked.

"I don't know. He had a hard time with it at first, but now I haven't seen the guy in months. But, look, this is a dead end. He's a good guy. In fact, he's a cop. He'd never—"

Freed interrupted. "He's a cop?"

"Yeah, here in Redwood City. His name's Evan Scholler. He got hurt over there and they let him out early."

"So he would have had access to these types of grenades over there?"

"Yeah, but he wouldn't have taken any home. He did a few months at Walter Reed before he came out here."

"Soldiers have been known to send illegal ordnance and contraband stateside as souvenirs on the slow boat," Riggio said. "It's a problem. It happens all the time."

"Well, I don't know what Evan would have . . . I mean, what's the point of putting hand grenades in my closet? I'm not going to blow myself up with them. It's not like they're going to get rid of me as his rival."

Riggio and Freed again shared a glance, and again exchanged the imperceptible nod. Riggio came forward, elbows on her knees. "Do you know a man named Ibrahim Khalil?"

"No," Nolan said. "Should I?"

"He was a local businessman with ties to Iraq. He and his wife were killed last weekend."

"Well, I'm sorry to hear that, but I've been out of town. I haven't heard about it."

"Would Evan Scholler have known you were gone?"

Nolan shrugged. "If he knew where I lived, he could have just checked to see if my car was in the garage. If it is, I'm home."

"Has he ever, to your knowledge, been up here?" Riggio asked.

"No. As I say, we're not exactly pals anymore." As though it had just occurred to him, Nolan added, "But he's a cop. He could find out where I live easy enough, couldn't he? That's what it looks like he's done."

Freed picked it up. "So Sunday morning early you were with this same girlfriend that this Evan Scholler likes?"

"Tara," Nolan said. "Tara Wheatley. And, yes, she's the one. So what's this all about?"

"Those pictures you couldn't identify on your computer?" Riggio said. "They were pictures of Mr. Khalil's house before somebody killed them and hit it with a fragmentation grenade, and before it burned down."

"A frag grenade . . ." Nolan didn't want to overplay his apparent naïveté. Both Freed and Riggio knew that he had seen combat, and they might even know more than that. This was about the moment in the interview that, against his own deep-seated reluctance to believe ill of a fellow soldier, he might finally come to accept the apparent truth. So he nodded somberly and met both of their gazes in turn. "He's trying to set me up. Christ, he killed them, didn't he?"

[16]

THE EARLY EVENING SUN BAKED the parking lot and the landing outside Tara's apartment. She could feel its warmth in her hand through the closed and locked front door as she stood behind it. "I told you, I won't see you. I don't want to talk to you."

"I need to talk to you, though, T. Please. I need to explain."

"There's nothing you can say to me. Nothing I'd believe. I can't believe you'd even come by here and try this. You *lied* to me, Ron. You've been living a lie for all these months."

"No. I've been living the truth. And the truth is that I love you."

"You don't lie to someone you love."

"You're right. That was a mistake. I shouldn't have done that. I am so sorry."

"Sorry's not enough. I don't want to talk about this. I need you to go away now."

"I can't, T. I can't leave it like this. Could you please open up? Just so I could see you." When she didn't answer, he went on, talking at the door. "Listen, I knew you were confused about Evan, especially the timing about how we started. I thought that if you heard he'd been wounded . . . that you'd feel sorry for him, or like you owed him another chance . . . and that whatever happened, somehow I'd lose you."

"And now that's what's happened."

"I can't accept that, Tara. I didn't think he was going to live. I didn't think it would matter."

"That's not the question, Ron. You lied to me. Everything we did was false, don't you understand that? If you couldn't stand to have Evan in the picture on any level, even if he was dying, how were we—you and me—ever going to amount to anything anyway?"

"We did amount to something."

"No, we didn't. That's the worst part. We supposedly trusted each other. Now that can't ever happen again. Don't you see that?"

"Because of one mistake?"

"You really don't see it, do you?"

"I see somebody who was terrified he was going to lose the woman he loved, who wanted to make sure they had some time together without the distraction of a wounded ex-boyfriend, who might never be coming home alive anyway."

"That's all you thought Evan was to me, a distraction?" The chain lock rattled and the door opened the couple of inches that the chain allowed. "I'm not going to yell at you through the door anymore. I just need you to go. You're actually scaring me now, all right?"

"How can I be scaring you, T? I'm here begging you just to listen to me, to give me another chance." He shifted his weight. "Is it because of him?"

"Do I still love him, you mean? I don't know about that. I lost track of who he was, and now I don't know what I feel. But I know you're scaring me now. And why? Because you lied. And lied and lied."

"I lied once, T. Once to try to protect what we were starting to have, that's all."

"No, it isn't, Ron. What about Masbah?"

"What about it?"

"You firing on that innocent family. I Googled you and read all about it. You started that whole thing."

Ron hung his head, wiped his brow against the glaring heat. "I was trying to protect the convoy. I thought the car was on a suicide mission. You had to have been there, but I can't apologize for what I did."

"The report said they'd stopped way back."

"You can't believe everything you read. It was a damn close call and if I waited another two seconds, we all could have been dead."

"Most of you died anyway. How about that?"

"Not my fault. The point is that if I fired too soon, and I'm not saying I did, it was on the side of caution."

"Ron. You killed an entire innocent family! Doesn't that bother you at all?"

"It bothers me a lot, T. It makes me sick to think about it. But I can't say, given the circumstances, that I wouldn't do the same thing again. It was a split-second, life-or-death decision, and I decided I had to try to save my men."

"That's not what Evan says, Ron. And he was there too."

"I guess he doesn't mention the part about me pulling him out of the line of fire and getting him out of there alive."

"So now you're the hero?"

"I'm not saying that. I'm saying Evan's memory maybe isn't the most reliable thing in the universe right now. I'm also saying that he's got a reason to make me look bad."

"He didn't make you lie."

"How many times do I have to apologize for that? However many it takes, I'll do it."

"And what about the other lies?"

"What other lies? There were no other lies."

"How about me ripping up that last letter that you delivered to me?"

"You didn't rip it up."

"Right. But you told Evan I did."

"No, I didn't. Did he tell you that?"

"Yes."

"Then he's lying."

"I don't believe that, Ron. And what about when you visited him at Walter Reed, when you told him I said he'd made his own bed and he could sleep in it?"

Nolan looked down and shook his head.

"What?" she asked him.

"That's not true, either, T. Why would I say that? I went to see him to see how he was doing, if he was going to be all right. That's all. He's the one who didn't want to hear anything about you."

"That's not what he told me."

"No, I guess not. And why, do you think, would that be?"

Through the crack in the opening, he saw her close her eyes, lean her head up against the wall next to the door. He was wearing her down, getting to her. "Do you want to hear something else?" he asked. "Something truly scary, especially if you think your friend Evan is so innocent and so nice. You want to hear what he left in my house after he broke into it last weekend?

AFTER TARA WATCHED Nolan finally drive away, she went into her living room, sat down, and put her feet up on the coffee table. Templing her fingers over her lips, she closed her eyes and tried to get herself to breathe deeply. A whirlwind of conflicting possibilities and emotions was literally causing her body to shake.

Ron Nolan had maintained a sustained falsehood, but did that mean that every word out of his mouth was a lie? She hadn't expected him to show up here, or to own up to the lies upon which he'd based their relationship. Perhaps the truth was that he loved her and had made a mistake. A terrible mistake, yes, and one he sincerely regretted.

Just like killing the Iraqi family.

What was the truth in that story? Had he been justified shooting when he did? And in fact, had he pulled Evan to safety and saved his life? They'd been outnumbered and surrounded. If there had been a bomb in the car, none of them would have survived. Might she have made the same decision to fire under the same circumstances?

It struck her forcefully that maybe it was she who was being unfair. Ron Nolan had always treated her well, better than well. He'd literally saved her life that time in San Francisco. And surely his appearance today to beg her forgiveness—even while admitting he'd done the unforgivable—spoke to a depth of character she'd never given him credit for.

People grew, people changed, people learned from their mistakes. And if what Ron had told her about Evan were true? He might himself be in danger.

No. She could not believe that. That was more of Ron's poison, trying to get inside her.

After seeing Evan in her classroom, and then the intimacy last night, she knew what she felt—not just the still-powerful physical bond, but a connection that went down to the bottom of her soul. It was irrational, chemical, fundamental, and she knew that she would never feel it with anyone else.

But now, according to Ron, Evan had lied to her too. A known liar accusing another of lying. It was like game theory, where "A" always told the truth, and "B" always lied, but you didn't know which was the truth-teller and which the liar. Who did you believe?

Could Evan have made up the story about Ron saying she'd ripped up his letter? Or the Walter Reed moment? Evan admitted that his memory had been faulty, especially early on. Could he have lied to her and not even known he was lying? Finally, could Evan have broken into Ron's house and tried to frame him for a murder? A murder that he himself had committed?

Tara could not believe any part of that. She knew who Evan was. Even after all this time and all of their problems, she knew his heart.

He was not a liar. He was not a murderer.

And this meant that Ron Nolan was lying to her again. And lying to the FBI. And possibly to the local police.

Liars deal in lies.

Suddenly she opened her eyes and sat up.

She needed to get to Evan. She needed to warn him.

[17]

THOUGH IT WASN'T really a hangout for cops, the Old Town Traven wasn't far from the police station downtown, and it served a decent-tasting though nutritionally suspect happy-hour spread of chicken wings, peanuts in the shell, tiny meatballs in gravy, and popcorn. Even though happy hour had officially ended more than two hours before, there was still plenty of food available. The Traven didn't exactly pack 'em in, and now Evan, who'd changed out of his uniform at the station, and his bowling partner Stan Paganini, also in street clothes, held down one end of the bar all by themselves.

Between his low-watt nervousness over the envelope he'd mailed to the FBI and his need to keep himself occupied so that he wouldn't do something stupid and try to get in touch with Tara until she'd dumped Nolan, if she actually was going to dump him after all, Evan felt that a drink or ten wouldn't be amiss. Pass the difficult night in a haze and see what tomorrow brings.

Now it was half past nine and he and Paganini were on to the name of the place. Due either to the marginal intelligence of its owners, a drunken mistake, a simple typo, or all of the above, the neon sign above the door read "Old Town Traven." The place's business cards also had *tavern* spelled incorrectly, so Evan decided it was probably that the proprietors just weren't too bright and certainly had not been the San Mateo County Spelling Bee champions, as he had been when he'd been in eighth grade.

"No, you weren't." Paganini stabbed the last meatball on his plate with a toothpick and washed it down with a good swig of his gin and tonic.

"Was too. I won on *hygiene,* which is almost unfair, it's such an easy word."

"Wait! Don't tell me." Paganini took in a little more of his drink. "H, Y," he began.

"Good so far."

"G." He paused, glanced at Evan.

"I before E." Evan tipped his vodka rocks all the way up. "Except after C. "

"Don't tell me!"

"I just did. 'Or when sounded like *a* as in *neighbor* or *weigh.*'"

"Okay, trying the old head-fake double reverse. I get it. But I'm on to you, boy. So here goes, again. H, Y, G, E . . ."

"*Buzz!* You're out." Evan shook his head. "I just told you, *i* before *e*, Stan. I told you the whole damn poem. You think I was making that up?"

"I thought you were trying to trick me. And then *g* is close to *c* sound-wise, so it was the exception."

"Nope. It's the rule." Evan spelled the word out.

"That doesn't sound right. I'm going to look it up at home."

"You want to bet?"

"No, I don't want to bet. But you're right, that's a pretty simple word to win the whole county spelling bee on."

"Well, harder than *tavern*, anyway. And they got that one wrong here. Twice. Three times? Who knows, maybe more. They might have it on the matchbooks."

"Yeah, well . . ." Paganini shifted his bulk and cried out. "Hey!"

"What?"

"Sat on something." Paganini slid himself off his stool and was digging in his pants pockets. Plopping down a large set of keys in the bar's gutter, he reached in again and produced a heavy item that he plunked onto the bar. "Knucks," he said.

At one of their bowling league nights, the cops had gotten into a discussion about various common enhancements to a man's natural defensive arsenal. Brass knuckles had featured large in Paganini's experience, and Evan said he'd never actually encountered them.

Now he picked up the hunk of fitted metal. "Heavy sucker."

"Get hit with it, you're clocked," Paganini said. "Although who fights with their fists anymore, huh? Nowadays, you know you're going to be in a fight, you pack heat, am I right?"

"Maybe you don't want to kill who you're fighting?"

Paganini chuckled. "Yeah, like that happens anymore. Go ahead, put 'em on. Keep 'em if you want. I collect the ones I get off perps. I got a half dozen like these at home."

As Evan was pocketing the brass knuckles, the bartender, a midthirties slacker with a wispy effort at a beard, suddenly appeared in front of them. Paganini looked down at his glass. "We empty again?"

"Seem to be," Evan said. "Let's double us up here, would you, Jeff?"

Jeff looked from one of them to the other. "You guys walking home from here? You pull a DUI, they can come back and get us."

"We're not going to get any DUI," Paganini said. He reached around into the back of his pants and pulled out his wallet, opened it to the badge. "Pour us a couple more, would you, please, and I won't report the obvious health violation keeping those meatballs out so long. Awesome meatballs, by the way. Remind me of my mom's." He cocked his head over toward Evan. "I believe the gentleman requested a couple of doubles."

Jeff took a beat, nodded, and then turned to get fresh glasses and ice.

Evan lowered his voice, leaned into Stan. "Am I slurring?"

"Nope. You're as eloquent as Cicero. How about me?"

"How about you what?"

"Am I slurring?"

"No."

"You keeping track of where we are?"

"The Traven," Paganini replied.

"Drinkwise, Stan. Drinkwise. I know where we physically are."

"Four, I think, maybe. Couple of doubles is six, and we've been here"— he checked his watch—"three hours. So I figure we're blowing point oh five, six, max, which means we're totally cool to drive and will be for the foreseeable future."

But Evan—all too familiar with the average cop's rationalization genius when drinking—was doing his own math. He was fairly certain they'd had more than four drinks already, maybe as many as six or seven, and if they had a couple of doubles on top of that, two doubles each, that would take him up to eleven generous pours. He was just about to say that maybe he'd better stick with singles to give them a better chance to metabolize off, when the bar's door opened. Glancing up at the mirror behind the bar, he put a hand on Paganini's arm and without a word stood up and turned around.

"YOUR MOM SAID this was where she might look for you." From their table in the back, where they couldn't be heard by anyone else, Tara looked around the seedy bar. "Nice place. You come here often?"

"Sometimes. Nights get long, and I go crazy at home. Some nights I bowl. Or read or something. Two days ago I was at Mom and Dad's. I've got a life."

"Of course you do. I didn't mean that."

"Yeah, you do." He sat back and folded his arms. "You disapprove of me being here." He looked at her, flat affect. "You come down here to bust my chops?"

"No," she said. "No. I don't mean to do that. I came down here to . . . well, just to talk to you again."

Jeff showed up with two drinks and put them down at their table. "And for the lady?"

"Maybe I'll just have one of his. And some cranberry juice."

When Jeff left, Tara pulled her chair up, reached out across the table, and touched Evan's hand. "I'm really not here to criticize you, Evan. It's just that the other night you said you'd been drinking too much and were trying to slow down a little."

"Yeah, well, I guess I'm not succeeding tonight. What's that look? You don't think a couple of drinks is a good idea?"

"I didn't say that. If you need it, you need it." She pulled his hand from his glass and covered it with hers. "Look," she whispered, "I don't know even any small part of what you've been through. You're the one who said it would be better if you didn't need so much alcohol."

"That would be better. I agree." Defiantly, he picked up his glass and took a long drink. "But that doesn't seem to be what I'm doing right now, which is trying to keep things together."

"What things?"

"My job, for one. What happened with my guys in Iraq. Why I'm still alive. Anger. Guilt. You name it." He brought his eyes up, unfocused, heavy-lidded. "And all those are before we even get to you."

Jeff showed up with Tara's cranberry juice, placed it on the table in front of her, turned, and left. A silence settled. Evan again lifted his glass, then put it back down. "You want to tell me about you and Ron?"

"There isn't any me and Ron. Not anymore. How can you even ask that after . . . ?" She swallowed. "I called him after I saw you at school on Monday. It's over." Sighing, she went on. "But then this afternoon he came by."

"Didn't take the hint, huh? How did that go?"

"I never let him in. He told me he never said I'd ripped up your letter."

Evan took that in with a solemn nod. "The guy's a congenital liar."

"Evan, look at me." Her eyes bored into his. "You're swearing to me that he said that? You didn't make that up to make him look bad? I know it's awful of me to ask, but I've got to ask you straight out. I've got to know for absolute certain."

Evan covered Tara's hand with both of his. "I swear to God," he said. "I swear on the memory of the lives of my men, I have never lied to you."

Tara let out a long, shuddering breath, as though something that had been squeezing her had suddenly let go. "He also denied what he told you I said in the hospital, about making your own bed and you could lie in it."

Evan shook his head, almost in admiration. "Old Ron was on a roll." Lifting his glass, he finished his drink, reached across, and took the second one from in front of Tara. "He said it, all right."

"He said something else today too."

"I can't wait to hear it. What? Did I kill somebody now?"

But Tara had straightened up. "God, Evan, why do you say that?"

"What?"

"That you'd killed somebody."

"I didn't. I was kidding. What?"

She started to talk and stopped herself, then started again. "Ron told me you broke into his house last weekend and left stuff that you'd somehow smuggled out of Iraq to make it look like Ron had killed this man and his wife, when in fact it was you who'd killed them."

Evan's shoulders sagged. He slumped in his chair. He lifted his drink and put himself on the outside of it in one gulp.

"Evan?"

"That fucker. That *motherfucker.*"

She went on. "He said you'd brought over hand grenades and guns to his place that you'd smuggled out of Iraq. And planted incriminating pictures on his computer."

Evan's body molded itself back into his hard chair. He spoke slowly, with great caution lest his thick tongue betray him. "This guy who got killed, Khalil. He was Iraqi. Think about it. Think about Ron's real job over here . . ."

"What do you mean? Ron's a recruiter mostly. He's . . ."

"No, listen. He's a mercenary mostly. Those were his weapons, his grenades, his pictures."

Tara sat back and crossed her arms. "You mean you *do* know about this? How could you know about this? Or about Ron?"

He just looked at her, opened his mouth, closed it again.

She came forward now. "Are you telling me he wasn't lying about you breaking into his house? Did you do that, Evan? Tell me you didn't do that."

"No, I . . ." Evan shook his head, hard, trying to clear away the fog of alcohol. "I mean, okay, I went in."

"You broke into Ron's house? And did what?"

"Nothing. I didn't do anything. No," he said, "that's not true. I got on his computer and got pictures of this guy's house before it burned down."

"Why did you do that?"

"'Cause Ron's a murderer, Tara. He killed this guy and this was the evidence . . ."

"So what did you do with it?"

"Mailed it to somebody."

"The FBI, you mean?" She hit the table with her palm. "Did you send your diskette to the FBI, Evan? Because Ron had the FBI over at his house today, and he told them you'd planted all that stuff there. And now you tell me you were actually inside, so they'll find your hair or fingerprints or something, don't you see that? He's trying to have you framed for this." She ran both of her hands through her hair, over her scalp, down to her neck. "God, God, God, how can this be happening? They may be at your apartment right now, wanting to talk to you, do you realize that? And then what are you going to do? What are you going to tell them?"

He stared blankly at her for a long minute, then brought his hand up and chewed at the knuckle of his index finger. "Enough of this shit." His words starting to slur.

"Evan." She gripped at his hands. "He's already got the FBI in on it, don't you understand? It's already happening."

"Can't be. I've got to stop him."

"No. Don't you do anything. Get a lawyer or talk to one of your bosses. Maybe they can deliver a message, get something through to Ron. But you stay out of it personally. Ron's dangerous, Evan. And he's out to get you. You've got to be smart. Get sober and get a plan."

Evan slammed a heavy hand on the table. "What do you mean, get sober? Is that what everything's about, whether I'm sober or not? I'm sober right now, enough for fucking Ron Nolan."

"Evan," she pleaded, "you're not. Listen to yourself. You don't swear when you're sober. You don't slur when you're sober." She stood up, reached out and touched his arm. "Look, why don't you come home now with me. I could drive us."

"And then what?" Evan's thick voice trembled with rage. "And then the FBI finds me there? Or at work tomorrow? What do I do then?"

"Come home with me. We can talk about it and work something out." She let her arm fall along his sleeve and took his hand. "Come on. Really."

"No!" He pulled his hand from hers, turned away. His shoulders rose and fell and then he turned back to her. "I am not fucking dealing with him anymore! This has got to end. It can't go on."

"You're right, but it can't end tonight, Evan."

"Yes, it damn well can."

Tara kept her voice low, conciliatory, restrained. "Evan, come on. There's no way you can do anything the way you are now, so don't be crazy. You're just really mad—"

"Way more than that, Tara. I'm going to kill the son of a bitch."

"Shh, shh, shh." She moved up and put her fingers to his lips. "Don't talk like that. That's just crazy drink talk. Let's just the two of us get out of here and—"

"Hey!" Taking her hand down, roughly, away from his mouth. "Listen to me!" Low and deadly earnest. "It's got to stop! It can't go on! It's not about fucking drinking. Are you hearing me? It's about honor. Who I am. What he's done to us! Don't you see that?"

"Yes, I do see that. You're right. You're completely right. But this isn't the time to fix all that." She moved in close and stood straight before him, arms at her side. "Please, Evan. I'm going to ask you one more time. Please come home with me. Whatever it is, we'll work it out together. I promise."

But the glaze in his eyes was all that answered her. Standing, weaving slightly, he gripped the back of his chair. "Enough's enough," he said.

She looked him in the face one last time. "I'm begging you," she said. "Please."

If he heard her at all, he didn't show it. He stared blankly ahead at her, shaking his head, shaking his head. Then he started walking toward the door.

"Evan, please," she called after him. "Wait."

He stopped, and for a second she thought that she'd convinced him. He turned back to her. "Leave me alone," he said. "I know what I've got to do and I'm gonna do it."

And then he turned and again started walking unsteadily toward the door.

PART THREE
[2005]

[18]

TARA HAD NEVER FELT so grateful for her job.

It was getting to the end of the year, and her kids were handing in their big reports and concluding their projects on the ancient world in preparation for the school's open house on Friday night, when all the work would be displayed in the classrooms. In Tara's room, they had rearranged all the desks to make room for the papier mâché pyramids, the dioramas of the growing cycle along the Nile, the plumbing schemes for the residences of the pharaohs. Hieroglyphics, the early domestic cat, the library at Alexandria, Moses and the Exodus.

So all day and much of the nights of Thursday and Friday, Tara was busy organizing and tending to last-minute crises among her students and, often, their families. She had no time to contact Evan to find out what, if anything, had happened after he'd stormed out on her on Wednesday night. And, truth to tell, she wasn't too inclined to call him anyway. She thought she would let him take a few days to sober up and get over his embarrassment about how he'd acted. Then, after he'd called her and apologized, they'd see where they were. But in the meanwhile, she had her job and her kids. She thought that a couple of days' respite from the emotional turmoil and upheaval surrounding Ron and Evan might do everybody involved a world of good.

Saturday, she slept in until nearly ten o'clock, then went down to the pool and swam a hundred laps. Coming back upstairs to her apartment, she showered and threw on some shorts and a T-shirt, made a salad for lunch, and after that dozed off watching a tennis match on TV. When she woke up, she graded the last of the written reports for another hour or so. At a little after four, she was just finishing up the last one when her doorbell rang. Checking the peephole, she saw Eileen Scholler, her face blotched from crying.

LIMPING, SCABBED, AND BRUISED in his orange jail jumpsuit, Evan entered his side of the visiting room chained to twenty other men. Watching the line enter, Tara stood among a loose knot of mostly women in a kind of bullpen waiting area on their side of the Plexiglas screen that separated the visitors from the inmates. A row of facing pairs of talking stations bisected the room from one end to the other.

Tara had to fight to hold back her tears as they unfastened Evan from the chain of men to whom he'd been attached. He saw her and started to raise a welcoming hand, but his wrists were still attached to the chain around his waist. The guard directed him to one of the desks and Tara excused herself through the now-pressing crowd of visitors and sat herself at last facing him. There was a hole in the Plexiglas through which they were supposed to talk.

It was Wednesday, his fourth day in custody, and the first day that his injuries had healed enough to allow him to walk unaided and to see visitors. In the first moment, neither could find anything to say. They looked at each other, then away, and back again.

How could either of them be here? How could it have come to this?

Finally, Evan leaned forward, shrugged, manufactured some kind of brave face. "I guess I should have gone home with you after all."

Tara didn't trust herself to say anything.

"I am so sorry," he said.

Tara opened her mouth, but again no words came. Now, unexpectedly, tears began to overflow onto her cheeks. She didn't try to stop them.

"Oh, babe," he said. Then, "I don't think . . ." He shook his head and looked at her. His shoulders rose and fell. "I don't believe I killed him."

Tara was still reeling from the bare fact that Ron Nolan was dead. Putting Evan together with that on any level wasn't yet possible for her; the idea couldn't bear any scrutiny. Instead, she found herself fighting a sense of unreality that permeated her waking hours as though she were living within a bad dream from which she couldn't will herself awake.

"I wouldn't have killed him," he said, then waited for her until he couldn't take it any longer. "Can you say something, please?"

"What am I supposed to say? What do you want me to say? I'm here. That says something, doesn't it?"

"I hope it does."

"I hope so too. But I'm not sure. Are you hurt?"

"I'll be all right."

"Will you? When will that be? What does that mean?"

He just looked at her.

TEN WEEKS PASSED before they saw each other again.

In that time, Evan was charged with the murder of Ron Nolan, but no charges were brought against him for the Khalil slayings—the district attorney, Doug Falbrock, decided that the evidence tying Evan to those murders wasn't strong enough to convict. As almost always in a murder case, bail was denied.

Tara had cleaned up her classroom and then hung around her apartment for the first couple of weeks of summer. On the Fourth of July, she went up to her parents' condominium to spend the holiday near Homewood on Lake Tahoe and decided on more or less the spur of the moment that she wasn't going to go back home. She couldn't bear reading about Evan every day in the newspapers down there. She needed to be away from the whole thing—the requests for interviews with reporters, her proximity to the jail, the expectations and/or accusations of people who didn't know her. She wound up staying alone at Homewood until late August—reading, running at altitude, dead sober, swimming in the cold lake.

Finally, it was time to come and get her classroom ready for the new year. She drove down on a Thursday morning, cleaned up the dust that had gathered in her apartment, stopped by the school, and started in again on the familiar yearly routine. And somewhere in the middle of it, she realized that she'd come to her decision. Finishing for the day at a little after three o'clock, she drove directly to the house Evan had grown up in, parked out front in the street, and knocked at the door.

Eileen greeted her as she always did—effusively, sincerely—with a welcoming smile, a hug, a kiss on both cheeks. They went together into the airy, modern kitchen and made catch-up small talk until Eileen had poured them both iced teas and they were sitting across from each other at the table in the nook that looked out at the Eden that was the Schollers' backyard. At last, Eileen cocked her head in her trademark fashion. "So what brings you around today?"

"I wanted to ask you if you think Evan would want to see me again."

"I think he'd want that more than anything."

"I wasn't too good the one time, you know? Did he tell you about that?"

"He didn't give me too many details. He said it wasn't very easy between you two. But he didn't blame you. Nobody blames you—I mean we don't—you know that, don't you?"

Tara nodded. "I just didn't know where to put any of it. Everything happened so fast. Finding out about all the lies Ron told me, and then thinking Evan and I, we might get another chance. Then that last night in the bar . . . where I thought . . ." She stopped, swallowed, shrugged.

Eileen reached over and patted her hand. "It's all right. If it means anything, and I think it does, Evan has no memory of what happened over there. He doesn't believe he killed Ron. He says that's just not who he is. He never would have done that."

"I believe him."

"So do I."

"But somebody did."

"Maybe somebody connected to these Khalils. That's what Everett says he believes."

"Everett?"

"Everett Washburn. His lawyer." A rueful smile. "His *expensive* lawyer." She waved away the comment. "But that's all right. We've got enough savings, thank God. I can't think of anything better to spend it on."

Tara hesitated, then came out with it. "They want me to testify about that last night. Against him."

"Everett said they would. I think it'll be all right if you just tell the truth."

"The truth wasn't too pretty, Eileen."

"No, I understand. But you can't do anything about that."

Tara twirled the iced tea in its little ring of condensation. "I could marry him," she said.

Sitting back and straightening in her chair, Eileen drew in a big breath and let it out. "Well . . . and here I've been thinking these old bones would never be surprised by anything again. But I don't think you'll have to take it that far."

"Not just to keep from testifying, Eileen. I've had all summer to think about how I feel about all this stuff. And over the weeks, it's just gotten clearer and clearer. Whatever happens, I'm on Evan's side. If he still wants me. If he'll see me."

Again, Eileen patted Tara's hand. "Oh, I wouldn't worry about that at all, dear. Not in the least little bit. I'm going down there to visit him in the next fifteen minutes if you'd like to come along."

When Evan saw Tara standing next to his mother on the other side of the room, he turned his face upward and closed his eyes. His body seemed to heave in relief. Tara came to the window—Eileen waiting in the back—and sat down across from him.

"Hi," she said.

"Hi."

"You look a lot better than last time."

"I feel a lot better too. How have you been?"

"Good. Gone. I'm sorry it's been so long."

He shrugged.

"I was trying to figure things out," she said.

"Any luck?"

"Pretty much. I finally got so I could see what ought to have been obvious all along."

"Which is what?"

"That if I'd have just gotten down off my high horse when this all started, when you deployed . . . I was just afraid I was going to lose you, that you'd be killed. I couldn't believe you'd be willing to sacrifice everything we had. I was so mad—"

He raised his palm. "Hey, hey, hey. We've been through that enough, haven't we?"

She nodded, almost letting a smile break. "Way enough. You're right."

Now he reached his hand out and put it against the Plexiglas separating them. "It's so incredibly good to see you. Do you know that?"

"You too." She leaned in toward him. "I came down here to tell you that I love you, you know, Evan Scholler. I've always loved you. All that other stuff, not answering your letters, everything with Ron, I was just young and stupid."

"No, the stupid award goes to me. Walking away from you that night at the Traven."

This time, a smile broke. "Okay, maybe we're tied on that one. But I'm not going to be stupid anymore."

He sat back, then came forward again, his voice raw. "You realize people might say that this is stupid, visiting me, getting involved again with me on any level. If you're going to be doing that."

"I am. And it's not stupid, it's right. This is what I need to be doing. This is who I am, who we are. I'm just sorry it took me so long to figure it out."

"You don't have to be sorry for anything," he said.

But she shook her head. "No, you're wrong. I'm sorry for everything that's got us to here. I'm just so, so sorry, Evan. I really am."

His eyes met hers. "I am, too, Tara," he said at last. "I am, too."

[19]

ON TUESDAY MORNING, the second week of September 2005, an assistant district attorney with the impossible name of Mary Patricia Whelan-Miille looked at her wristwatch in Department 21 of the San Mateo County Courthouse in Redwood City. It was nine forty-two A.M. This meant that court was starting a few minutes late, but the tardiness didn't bother her.

Mary Patricia's law-school friends had given her the nickname of Mills almost before she'd gotten her full name out for the first time, and now Mills, with excitement and some trepidation, took in the scene around her. She was exactly where she wanted to be at this moment—in a courtroom as a prosecutor about to begin the trial of her life, and one that had a chance to become a defining moment in her career.

Oh, there would undoubtedly be pitfalls ahead, as in fact there had already been. Her boss Doug Falbrock's decision to abandon the charges against Evan Scholler in the murders of Ibrahim and Shatha Khalil for lack of evidence, for example, had been a bitter pill for her to swallow in the early innings. Pulling Tollson, a multidecorated Vietnam combat veteran who'd lost a foot to an antipersonnel bomb in that war, as the trial judge perhaps wasn't the greatest bit of good fortune imaginable either. Probably fewer than two or three years from retirement, Tollson, as the prototypical éminence grise, had earned the sobriquet "His Griseness" from Mills's paralegal, Felice Brinkley, and it fit perfectly.

Outside of the courtroom, in the building's halls, Tollson limped along exuding a nearly boyish enthusiasm. He came across as preppy, favoring casual menswear instead of coat and tie. He wore blue contact lenses, his perfectly combed, silver-tipped, Grecian Formula hair nearly luxuriant in a man his age. But on the bench he wore the black robe and thick black eyeglasses that magnified a pair of rheumy, depthless black pupils. His hair remained permanently in disarray, as though he spent his time in chambers running his hands through it in constant despair at the human condition. Add the permanent scowl, which emphasized heavy brows, a prominent and aggressive nose, and the thin-lipped set of his mouth, and His Griseness was a formidable and vaguely menacing force that attorneys in court crossed at their own peril.

Nor was Mills entirely sanguine about the defense attorney who was now standing behind his desk fifteen feet to her left. Everett Washburn, somewhere north of seventy, white-haired, and in rimless glasses, wore a light tan suit that was at least one size too large. His shirt had had all of its wash-'n'-wear washed out of it. The tie was an orange-and-tan paisley design, three inches wide. His florid face was a creased dried apple, and his voice combined equal parts honey and whiskey. He had the teeth of a horse, yellowed with age, cigars, strong coffee, and wine.

Washburn, reportedly, had lost a murder trial once, but nobody remembered when. Mills herself had come down to court just to watch him perform several times and considered him tenacious, brilliant, ruthless, and unpredictable. A dangerous combination.

Plus, and this made it worse, he was a famous nice guy, a favorite of all the judges, bailiffs, clerks, and even prosecuting attorneys such as herself. He knew every birthday and anniversary in the building and reportedly spent in excess of fifty thousand dollars a year on political fund-raisers, charity events, and lunches.

And that didn't include his bar tabs.

But all of that being said, Mills liked her chances. Greater forces were at work here, the first of which was the fact that some benign karma had delivered her to San Mateo County. Her first seven years as a prosecutor had been in San Francisco and in spite of always being prepared beyond reason and never seeing a suspect who hadn't committed the crime of which he or she had been accused, she had only managed four jury trials—the rest had been pled out by her superiors for far less than any sentence they would have received in a fair world—and her record in those trials had been three hung juries and an acquittal. San Francisco juries, she believed because it was true, just didn't convict.

But San Mateo County!

She loved San Mateo County as it in turn hated its criminals—its vandals, gang-bangers, burglars, petty thieves, and murderers all alike. San Mateo County wanted these people dealt with and trusted the system to deal with them. As did Mills, whose parents she'd loved in spite of the mouthful of moniker they'd laid on her at birth, and who'd been murdered in a carjacking when she was sixteen.

So there was San Mateo County, essentially on her side. It was a miracle, given her record, that they'd hired her here. The interview had come on the particularly bad afternoon when the big fourth of her four losses had come in and she'd been in a quiet and reasonable fury in her interview with Falbrock—a real I-don't-give-a-fuck-what-happens mood. Karma again. She'd found herself launched into her take-no-prisoners tirade before she could stop herself, and much to her surprise and delight, after she gave her exceptions about people the state should put to death, Falbrock had smiled and said, "I don't know. I'm not so sure we shouldn't execute shoplifters. It's a gateway crime." And he'd hired her on the spot.

There was, next, her victim, Ron Nolan—a young, wealthy, clean-cut, handsome, and charismatic ex–Navy SEAL, recipient of three Purple Hearts, the Afghanistan and Iraq Campaign Medals, the Liberation of Kuwait Medal, the Global War on Terrorism Expeditionary Medal, the Meritorious Service Medal, and the Bronze Star. Mills, learning about the extraordinary life of Ron Nolan as she had investigated his death, had wondered more than once why she hadn't had the good fortune to have met him in her real life before he'd been murdered. She hadn't quite fallen in love with his memory, but she felt a fascination bordering on infatuation that she couldn't deny, and if she could avenge his senseless death in any way, she would consider it her privilege and duty.

Which brought her to her suspect.

She stole a glance over to where Evan Scholler stood. To her, he was the definition of scumbag, and it still galled her to see him in the courtroom now all cleaned up, with a dress shirt and tie and nice jacket. But she was convinced that by the time she was done, the jury would see beyond the façade that Washburn was so adept at creating, beyond the injured war veteran with the pretty and supportive girlfriend and the loyal parents, to the alcoholic and Vicodin addict whose incompetent leadership had led his squad of San Mateo County boys into their fatal ambush in Iraq.

As she waited for the judge to enter the courtroom, her heart was beating hard in anticipation. She was particularly keen to face some of the issues that were to be adjudicated before jury selection was to begin, the most important of which was going to be up first today. Mills had prepared a 402 motion requesting a foundational hearing to determine the admissibility of evidence related to post-traumatic stress disorder.

From the outset, it had been clear that Everett Washburn intended to use PTSD as an integral part of his defense of Evan Scholler. After all, the young man had endured exactly the kind of severe personal trauma during wartime that had produced volumes of literature on the subject. He'd also exhibited, to a host of witnesses over a substantial period of time, some, if not all, of the classic symptoms of PTSD.

So for a while early on, Mills had let herself get lulled into a grudging acceptance that PTSD, with its expert-witness madness, media appeal, and the emotional overtones it created, particularly in the context of the increasingly unpopular war, was going to be part of the trial.

And then one day it came to her that Washburn couldn't have it both ways. Either he could argue that Scholler had killed Ron Nolan but that PTSD was an extenuating circumstance or even a defense; or he could maintain that Scholler hadn't killed Ron Nolan at all, in which case he wouldn't, strictly speaking, need any other defense. If Scholler didn't do it, then it wasn't PTSD or self-defense or anything at all that had made him do it. So, believing that she had logic on her side—not that it always mattered—Mills had written her 402 motion. She wanted a full-blown hearing on the issue and was prepared to argue heatedly for it.

"All rise. Hear ye! Hear ye! The Superior Court, State of California, in and for the County of San Mateo, is now in session, Judge Theodore Tollson presiding."

Now she stood up and brought her eyes forward. Tollson had ascended to the bench. The clerk said, "You may be seated." After fifteen months, interviews filling thirty-seven binders, twelve pretrial written motions, three boyfriends, and the hint that the proper outcome would garner a six-figure book-deal offer, they were about to get on the boards at last.

Tollson glared down from the bench to both attorneys' tables, back over the small bullpen partition, and across the packed gallery. He looked in no way amiable. He straightened his back and pushed his glasses up to the ridge of his nose. "Mr. Washburn," he began. "Ms. Miille. Are you ready to begin?"

Both intoned, "Yes, Your Honor."

"All right, then, before we get down to it, let's spend a few moments in my chambers." And with that, he was up again, off the bench, and through the side door. To Mills, there was an absurd quality to the judge's formal entrance minutes before, followed by his near-immediate retreat back to his private office, but it was far from the only absurd moment she'd spent in and around courtrooms.

By the time she'd gathered her papers, Everett Washburn had come over to her table and, like the cultured gentleman that he was, waited for her to come around. She almost expected him to hold out his arm as a courtier might, for her to take it. But he merely bowed and let her precede him across the courtroom and to the back door, where the bailiff was waiting.

IN TOLLSON'S CHAMBERS, a faded green-and-gold pennant from the University of San Francisco took pride of place on the wall behind the large oak desk. A trophy case held more than a dozen ancient baseball and football trophies. A golf bag sat up against the bookshelf wall. A credenza sported a dozen or more framed photos of family members. Someone had arranged his diplomas, honors, and ceremonial pictures in a large rectangular pattern that covered the last empty wall.

The bailiff stayed until they were seated, then disappeared, leaving only the two lawyers and the judge. Tollson, in his robe and glasses behind his desk, nevertheless was his casual, out-of-the-courtroom self as he began. "So, I take it you two haven't reached a last-minute settlement, Mr. Washburn?"

The old lawyer sat back with his legs crossed—bemused, tolerant, good-natured. "That's correct, Your Honor."

"So what are we looking at for time?"

The question was asked of both of them, but Mills spoke up first. "The People's case, Your Honor, maybe four weeks, depending on cross. I've never worked with Mr. Washburn before, so I don't know how long he takes. I'll let him give you the estimate for the defense. I don't know about rebuttal." She paused, decided to hedge her estimate. "A lot will depend," she said, "on what you let in."

"We'll be getting to that here," Tollson said. "Jury selection?"

"Probably a couple of weeks, Your Honor. I would suggest a week of hardship, based on the length." She was suggesting that they first screen prospective jurors to see who could be with them, basically without pay, for what looked like a couple of months. The idea was that it was wise to eliminate the vast majority of prospective jurors whose employers would not pay for that length of jury service, or who could not otherwise handle the commitment. Only those who survived the initial screening would undergo the more complex and time-consuming questioning that would decide who would sit on the jury.

She went on, "So we've got twenty peremptory challenges each, and some hot-button issues such as the Iraq War and maybe some psych stuff, depending on your rulings. We use questionnaires, we should get our hardships done in three days or so, and the regular jury picked a couple days after that, give or take."

Tollson nodded. "Mr. Washburn? Sound about right to you?"

"Pretty close," he intoned. "I agree we should hardship first, and have the jury fill out questionnaires." He reached into his inside pocket and extracted a handful of paper, folded the long way. "And I just happen to have a proposed questionnaire for this case with me." Handing a copy to Mills and the judge, he added, "I'll need about a week for the defense, Your Honor."

Tollson, perusing the questionnaire, didn't look up, but said, "Motions?"

This time Washburn went first. "Limit the use of autopsy photos, Your Honor. They don't need a bunch of gory photos to prove this guy is dead."

"Your Honor," Mills said. "This *guy*, the victim, was in superb health. Somebody beat him to a bloody pulp. Not a robber or a burglar, but someone who hated him. The jury will need to see the savagery of the attack to appreciate that this was a personal killing."

Washburn shot back, "Too many autopsy photos might unduly prejudice the jury."

Tollson held up a hand. "Show me the photos you want to have admitted. I'll let you know which ones you can use before we start jury
selection. Anything else?"

This was the moment. Mills produced copies of her 402 motion for
Washburn and Tollson and said, "Mr. Washburn has discovered some
stuff on PTSD, Your Honor, and has expert witnesses on his list. We
would like a full-blown hearing on what you're going to admit before we
get near a jury."

She wanted the judge to require Washburn to call his witnesses outside
of the presence of the jury and have them testify under oath. Then the
two sides could argue over whether such testimony was admissible, and
the Court could rule on it. If the evidence was admitted, the same witnesses would have to give exactly the same testimony later in front of the
jury.

If the Court refused to hold the hearing, testimony got heard for the
first time with the jury present. In this case, if the Court then ruled that
the testimony should not have been admitted, the only remedy was to
instruct the jury to pretend they had never heard it. Popularly known as
"unringing the bell," this was a notoriously ineffective way to deal with
the problem.

Mills went into her pitch. "The defendant claims PTSD, Your Honor,
but the defense here is that he didn't do it. If he didn't do it, then his state
of mind is irrelevant. All this is going to do is put his war record and injuries in front of the jury to excite sympathy."

Washburn, leaning back with his legs crossed, ran a finger around in
his ear. "My client was blacked out during the period where it appears Mr.
Nolan was killed, Your Honor. First, evidence of PTSD will support his
claim that he can't remember anything about this period. Second, if he
did kill someone and there is a doubt about his mental state because he
might have been in a PTSD episode, then he is entitled to that doubt. The
crime would certainly be less than premeditated murder, maybe voluntary
or even involuntary manslaughter."

This brought the first sign of Tollson's courtroom testiness. "I believe

I understand the issues, Counselor." He spent a few more seconds looking over Mills's pages, then squared them and put them down with Washburn's questionnaire. "I'm going to allow two weeks for motions. Until we know what the jury will hear, we can't tell them how long the case will be, so jury selection starts two weeks from today. Sound good?"

It sounded good to Mills. She'd gotten her hearing. A good omen.

Tollson continued. "My staff will have the jury commissioner start to put panels together. Six court days for jury selection, including three days of hardship. Six weeks of trial or so if you get into PTSD, probably four at the outside if you don't. Let's get outside on the record and get to work."

[20]

EVERETT WASHBURN STOOD in the center of the courtroom, addressing his first witness in the hearing on PTSD. Dr. Sandra Overton was a frizzy-haired, earnest psychiatrist in her mid-forties. She wore a dark blue business suit with low heels. She had already recited her credentials and experience as a psychiatrist—i.e., a medical doctor—specializing in veterans returning from active combat. "In your experience with these veterans, Doctor," Washburn asked her, "have you run across a condition known as post-traumatic stress disorder, or PTSD?"

She almost laughed at the question. "It's pretty much all I work with."

"Can you tell the Court exactly what it is, then?"

"Certainly." She looked across at the prosecution table, where Mills sat with her hands folded in front of her, then around and up to where the judge sat on the bench. "It's pretty much what the name says. It's a psychiatric disorder that occurs after an episode of traumatic stress."

"A psychiatric disorder? Do you mean it's a mental illness?"

She shook her head. "That's not really a descriptive term. Legally it would qualify as a disease, defect, or disorder. Medically it is more a range of continuing symptoms and reactions experienced by someone who's endured a traumatic event. The key word being *continuing*."

"In what way?"

"Well, almost everyone who experiences a traumatic event has a reaction to it. Shock, or depression, or insomnia. But with PTSD, the reaction first tends to be more serious and second, it persists for a lengthy period of time, sometimes forever. It becomes a disorder, not a reaction."

"And what is a traumatic event, Doctor?"

Again, Overton shook her head. "There's no one definition. What's traumatic for one person might be relatively innocuous to another. But certainly traumatic events would tend to include military combat, serious accidents, crimes such as rape, natural disasters, terrorist incidents, and the like."

"Military combat?"

"Yes. Very commonly. Although the disorder wasn't much studied until after the Vietnam War. Before then, when people talked about it at all, it was usually called Da Costa's syndrome. But since Vietnam, estimates of soldiers with combat experience suffering from PTSD have run as high as thirty percent."

"And what are some symptoms commonly associated with PTSD?"

"One of the main symptoms is a reliving of the original traumatic experience through either flashbacks, or in nightmares. Beyond that, there's insomnia, of course, and a sense of disconnect with life. Then depression, memory and cognition issues, abusive and self-destructive behavior. A huge range of personal and societal problems, actually."

"Doctor, you referred to abusive and self-destructive behavior. Could this include alcohol abuse?"

"Yes, of course."

"And memory issues? Do you mean blackouts?"

"Yes. Blackouts are not uncommon, especially if coupled with excessive drinking or drug use or both."

"I see." Washburn acted as though he were hearing all of this for the very first time in his life. Now he moved a step closer to his witness. "Doctor, is there a physical component to PTSD? Or is it simply what a layman might just call a mental problem?"

As Washburn intended, this question kept Overton from becoming lulled in her relatively straightforward recounting. This hearing hadn't been his idea, but since he was in it, he was dry-running her to play to the jury's sensibilities when and if she testified at trial. She sat up stiffly, her expression defiant. "Absolutely not! In the first place, a mental problem is a real problem. It's as real as a broken leg. Secondly, with PTSD there is measurable altered brain-wave activity, decreased volume of the hippocampus and abnormal activation of the amygdala, both of the latter having have to do with memory. The thyroid's affected, as is production of epinephrine and cortisol. I could go on, but suffice it to say that there are many, many physical and neurological changes and reactions associated with PTSD."

"I see, Doctor. Thank you," Washburn said. "Now, have you had an opportunity to interview and examine my client, Evan Scholler, with regard to PTSD?"

"I have."

"What were your findings?"

"I found that Mr. Scholler clearly suffers from the disorder. His memory, particularly, seems to be compromised, and this symptom has been aggravated by a traumatic brain injury he suffered in Iraq in August of two thousand three. He suffers from frequent migraine headaches. Beyond that, he has reported the experience of blackouts and episodes of rage, shame, guilt, and depression. Sleeping has been a consistent problem. Finally, he has spoken to me about a tendency to abuse alcohol and other painkilling drugs, such as Vicodin. All of these symptoms are not only consistent with PTSD, they are diagnostic of it."

"And what about the physical changes you've described—to the amygdala and hippocampus and so forth? Did you test Mr. Scholler for these?"

"Yes, I did."

"What were your findings?"

"I found decreased cortisol with increased epinephrine and norepinephrine levels. Together, these hormone levels impact the body's fear response and the startle reflex, both of which I found to be in the abnormal range with Mr. Scholler."

"And your conclusions as a medical professional? Does Mr. Scholler suffer from PTSD?"

Dr. Overton looked over at the defense table where Evan sat. "Yes. Unremitting and severe PTSD. Without a doubt, in my professional opinion."

"Without a doubt. Thank you, Doctor." Washburn inclined his head in a courteous bow. Facing Mills, he turned his palm up. "Your witness, Counsel."

* * *

"DR. OVERTON," the assistant district attorney began, "you've testified that blackouts were not uncommon among people with PTSD. Were you saying that PTSD causes blackouts?"

"Not exactly. I believe I said that blackouts were common, especially when drugs or alcohol were part of the picture."

"Oh, so PTSD does not in itself cause these blackouts, is that true?"

"Well, in a sense you can say that—"

"Doctor, I'm sorry. It's a yes or no question. Does PTSD cause blackouts?"

Overton frowned, glanced over at Washburn. "They are commonly associated with PTSD, yes."

"Again, Doctor, not my question. Does PTSD cause blackouts?"

Washburn cleared his throat and spoke from his table. "Objection. Badgering."

Tollson didn't take two seconds to make up his mind. "Overruled." He leaned over to speak to the witness. "Please answer the question, Doctor."

Mills jumped right in. "Would you like me to repeat it?"

Tollson transferred his scowl down to her. "Can the sarcasm, Counselor. Doctor, answer the question, does PTSD cause blackouts?"

"Yes, there are some reports of that."

"Some? How many of these reports are you personally familiar with?"

"I'm not sure. To the best of my recollection, a few."

"A few. All right. And do any of these few reports with which you're familiar speak to the duration of any of these rare PTSD blackouts?"

From behind her, Everett Washburn rumbled forth again. "Objection. Assumes facts not in evidence. The doctor's awareness of only a few reports on blackouts doesn't mean that the blackouts themselves are rare."

"Sustained."

But Mills came right back at Overton. "Doctor," she said, "do any of these few reports with which you're familiar speak to the duration of any of these PTSD blackouts?"

"Yes, they do."

Mills had her own expert witness on this topic, although she wasn't sure she was going to use him. In any event, she'd done her homework and knew her facts. "Doctor," she said, "isn't it true that these PTSD blackouts tend to be of very short duration?"

"Yes."

"Along the line of forgetting where you put your keys, for example?"

"I'm not sure I understand what you mean."

"You put your keys on your kitchen counter, for example, then are struck with a vivid post-traumatic flashback. When it's over, you can't remember where you placed your keys. That's the kind of PTSD blackout discussed in the literature, is it not? In other words, a memory lapse of relatively short duration?"

"I think so. Yes."

Mills walked back to her table, took a drink of water. Turning around to the witness, she asked, "Doctor, are you aware of any PTSD blackouts that extended for more than a day?"

"No. I've never heard of that."

"How about an hour?"

"No, I don't think so."

"Ten minutes?"

"Somewhere in that realm, I believe. The flashback, usually, tends to be intense but short-lived."

The gallery might not have understood exactly what Mills was getting at with this questioning, but the doctor's answer of ten minutes sent a buzz through the room. Galvanized by it, the prosecutor moved in closer to the witness. "Doctor, you've also testified about blackouts that are coupled with excessive alcohol and drug use, or both. Would you characterize these blackouts as caused by PTSD, or by the alcohol and/or drug use?"

"Well, they're related. The PTSD exacerbates the abusive behavior."

"But it is the drinking or the drug use that causes the actual blackouts, is it not?"

"I don't think we can say that."

"Well, Doctor, alcohol and drug use by themselves can cause blackouts, correct?"

"Yes."

"And this is a fairly common and well-documented phenomenon, is it not?"

"Yes."

"But blackouts associated with PTSD are both rare and of short duration, isn't that true?"

Washburn knew that this was a compound question, and hence objec-
tionable, but saw nothing to gain by further interruption.

"Yes."

"So," Mills continued, "if you had a blackout for an extended period of
time, Doctor, say a couple of days, there is scientific evidence that it could
have been caused by alcohol, and no scientific support for the suggestion
that it was caused by PTSD alone, correct?"

"Yes."

"Thank you, Doctor. Now, you've said that Mr. Scholler told you that
he had abused both alcohol and Vicodin, isn't that so?"

Clearly frustrated now, Overton had come forward in the witness
chair, her hands on the balustrade of the box. "That's right."

"Did he also tell you, Doctor, that he had abused alcohol in Iraq before
one of these so-called traumatic experiences?"

"Your Honor!" Finally Washburn was moved to rise to his feet in out-
rage. "I object to Counsel's characterization. Most of us humans would
consider sustaining a severe head wound during a rifle and grenade attack
on foreign soil in defense of our country a traumatic event. There is nothing spurious or so-called about it."

This brought the gallery noise now to a full hum, and Tollson dropped
his gavel for the first time. Without a word, he glared around the room
until all the noise had ceased.

Mills broke the silence. "I'll withdraw the word *so-called,* Your Honor."
But she wasn't backing down. "Perhaps the court reporter can reread my
question without the offending word."

Tollson looked down over the bench at his reporter and nodded.

The woman pulled the tape up and read, "Did he also tell you, Doctor,
that he had abused alcohol in Iraq before one of these"—a pause—"traumatic experiences?"

Overton, her mouth set, shot a glance at Washburn, then came back to
her tormentor. "Yes, he did."

"In other words, Mr. Scholler's alcohol abuse preceded his PTSD, and by itself was capable of producing extended periods of memory blackout, isn't that so?"

"Apparently," Overton snipped out.

"That would be a 'yes,' then, is that correct?"

Through all but gritted teeth now. "Yes."

"And Mr. Scholler told you that the particular blackout after the death of the victim, Ron Nolan, lasted approximately four days, isn't that true?"

"Yes."

"Thank you, Doctor," Mills said. "No further questions."

LAWYER AND CLIENT sat knee to knee in a holding cell behind the courtroom during the lunch recess. Outside their two small wired windows, it was a bright and sunny day. Their view included a small city of media vans that had set up out in the parking lot. Washburn's mouth was full of liverwurst on rye, but it didn't shut him up. "It doesn't matter," he said. "What's important is she established the PTSD. Now we've just got to make sure we get Tollson to let it in. You gonna eat your pickle?"

"No. I'm not holding anything down. You go ahead."

Washburn stopped chewing. "You nervous?"

"Why would I be nervous? On trial for murder and all."

"You've got to keep your strength up." Washburn grabbed the pickle and took a bite of it. After he finally swallowed, he sipped from his bottled water and cleared his throat. "But we need to talk about what we do if he doesn't allow it."

"You mean Tollson?"

A nod. "And the PTSD. We get that, we're going to have the jury on our side. They're going to see what happened in Iraq, what you've been through . . . it's decent odds they don't convict. On the other hand, this morning I was hoping Ted would rule to let the PTSD in without a hearing, but he didn't do that. Which means he's thinking about it, maybe he thinks it's bogus."

"Why would he think that? He lost a foot himself."

"Yeah. But remember, whatever else happened to him, he didn't get any PTSD from it. Which means, maybe, that to him it's just a bunch of mumbo-jumbo from weak-ass lesser beings. Or shyster lawyers like me."

"Is this supposed to cheer me up?"

Washburn shrugged, took another monstrous bite of his sandwich. "Just running down the possibilities. Look," he went on, "don't get down about this. Half the world's on our side."

"Which means half isn't."

"But we don't need half. We just need one out of twelve. So get over it. The fact is you're a wounded veteran who's the victim of an extremely—now—unpopular war. The more we get the war in as a villain, the more we got Nolan as a victim of the war himself. Without the war, nobody would have been killed. Your guys in Iraq, Nolan, nobody. Plus we got our big surprise when you testify, which will sway some hearts and minds, since it brings it all around and gives them an alternative theory to think about. But all that's counting on the PTSD, without which it's a different ball game." Taking another drink of water, Washburn swished it around. "So the question is, Tollson doesn't let it in, we might want to talk about a plea."

Evan closed his eyes for a second, then shook his head. "No way."

"Wait. Before you—"

"Everett, listen. Mills's last offer was forty to life. I can't do forty."

Washburn looked at his client. He'd been here with other clients more times than he cared to remember, but it never got easy. Tollson's ruling to hold a hearing on the PTSD evidence was unexpected and perhaps ultimately disastrous. Washburn had truly believed that his argument in chambers, casually though he had phrased it, would carry the day and that Tollson would allow the PTSD evidence at the trial.

But now, possibly, that wasn't to be the case.

Washburn wasn't giving up. It wasn't in his nature to do that. But he had to get it through to Evan that they might, after all, lose. "I'm sure I could get Doug Falbrock to drop the gun," he said. Any use of a gun in the commission of a murder in California added an automatic twenty-five years to the sentence. "Plea to a second. Get them down to, say, twelve to life."

Evan was sitting back, arms crossed. "Wasn't it you who said the immortal words 'Anything to life equals life'?"

"I was being glib," he said. "You'd be a model prisoner, out in the minimum."

"Still," Evan said, "twelve years."

Washburn unfolded his hands, took his last bite of sandwich. "I'm just saying"—he chewed a couple of times—"I'm just saying you might want to think about it."

[21]

WASHBURN'S PLAN TO GET the war into the trial at every opportunity was behind his decision to call Anthony Onofrio as his next witness. Onofrio had come home six months ago and had immediately contacted Washburn's office asking if and how he could help with Evan's defense. As an older veteran, a father of three who'd left his Caltrans job and home in Half Moon Bay to do his duty, as well as the lone military survivor besides Evan in the Baghdad firefight, he was in a unique position to recount the traumatic event that was at the heart of this hearing.

But no sooner had the clerk sworn in the thick-necked, friendly looking workman than Mills stood to object. "Your Honor, the last witness has already testified and established to the People's satisfaction that Mr. Scholler suffers from post-traumatic stress disorder. We are willing to concede that point, though we still contend that it's irrelevant. The People fail to see what probative value, if any, this witness can bring to these proceedings. He wasn't even here in the United States during the time of the murder and his testimony can have no bearing on the defendant's guilt or innocence."

Judge Tollson leaned back in his chair on the bench, his eyes nearly closed. He inclined his head a quarter of an inch. "Mr. Washburn?"

"Your Honor, this witness is foundational. There can be no post-traumatic stress without an original trauma, and Mr. Onofrio was an eyewitness to the trauma that Mr. Scholler experienced and to the effects of which Dr. Overton just testified. We did not simply hire a rent-a-shrink to come in here and invent a condition following an event which never took place. Without the event, there can be no condition."

For a long moment, and against all reason, since he was basically correct, Washburn lived with the agonizing possibility that Tollson was going to dismiss his witness and call an end to his entire line of questioning.

He also had time to reflect that Mills's objection made little sense. In theory, by granting this hearing without the presence of a jury, Tollson had provided her with a bonus—she'd get to see all of his evidence before he could present it at trial. She should want to hear everybody he brought in so she'd, in effect, have two chances to take them apart—now and when the jury had been impaneled.

But then, he realized, she was probably running mostly on nerves and adrenaline herself. And the fact remained that if Tollson did side with her and preclude Onofrio from testifying, the same objection and rationale might get some traction regarding calling his following witnesses as well, and that would truly be problematic.

Tollson ended the suspense. "Ms. Whelan-Miille," he said, "this is a hearing. That means we get to hear what people have to say before we get to trial. Mr. Washburn is right. This witness's proposed testimony is foundational to the question of trauma. The objection is overruled. Mr. Washburn, you may proceed."

Trying to hide his sigh of relief from the Court, Washburn leaned his head forward, the merest hint of a bow. "Thank you, Your Honor." He turned to the witness. "Now, Mr. Onofrio, can you please tell the Court about your relation to Mr. Scholler?"

"Until he was wounded, he was my squadron leader in Iraq in the summer of two thousand three."

Over the next few minutes, Washburn walked Onofrio through the makeup of the squadron and its general duties as a military convoy unit, then came back to the main thrust. "Mr. Onofrio, you've said that Mr. Scholler was your squadron leader until he was wounded. Would you please tell us how that came about?"

"Sure. We were escorting Ron Nolan to a meeting with—"

"Excuse me," Washburn said. "You were escorting the same Ron Nolan who is the victim in this case?"

"Yes."

"He was with you in Iraq, was he?"

"He came and he went, but basically, yes. He was working for

Allstrong Security, which was handling the Baghdad Airport and doing other work over there. It was one of our regular jobs driving him where he needed to go."

"All right, so he was with your convoy on the day the Mr. Scholler was hit?"

"Yes, he was." Onofrio sat back in the witness chair and basically told it as he remembered it. The tension on the city's streets, Nolan firing on the purported suicide car, the discovery of what it had really been and who had been in it, the rock-throwing and then the sustained attack from the surrounding buildings and rooftops. "Just after it all started, though, the actual rifle firing and the first RPG, we had a chance where maybe we could have gotten out, but the lieutenant wouldn't give the order to pull out until we'd gotten the men who'd already been hit into one of our vehicles."

"He wasn't going to leave anyone behind?" This was important information, carefully rehearsed. Washburn wanted it to be clear in the jury's mind, when it came to it, that Evan was in grave danger, in the thick of it, and had acted nobly.

"No, sir. So he ran up to the lead car, which was still smoking, and tried to get out the guys who'd been hit."

"He did this while you were under heavy fire?"

"Yes, sir. But then the second car took a hit and a couple of the other guys went down, so it was obvious there wasn't going to be any chance for any of us to get out if we didn't move pretty quick. So Nolan kept firing through the roof and had me drive up to where Evan was pinned down. He still wanted to try to carry some of the guys out if he could get to them, but an RPG went off somewhere behind us and next time I looked over, he was down."

"What had happened?"

"He was hit by shrapnel, or something. In the head. There was blood everywhere. I thought he was dead. I thought we were all dead."

"All right, thank you, Mr. Onofrio. I'm glad you made it home alive." He half turned back to Mills. "Your witness."

* * *

MILLS SAW THIS as a no-win cross-examination and almost passed the witness, but decided she had nothing really to lose if she just took the judge's advice and heard what the man would say. No jury was listening now, and maybe she'd strike some promising vein that she could mine when she had him again during the trial. If Washburn was going to call up what she considered these largely irrelevant witnesses, she might as well take the opportunity to go fishing with them.

"Mr. Onofrio," she began. "First let me say that I, too, and all of us in the courtroom, are grateful that you made it home alive. Thank you for your service to our country."

Shrugging, embarrassed, Onofrio mumbled, "You're welcome."

"One of the things I was struck with in your testimony was the fact that you were not sent over to do convoy work. Did I get that right?"

Onofrio nodded. "That's right. We were supposed to be doing maintenance on heavy equipment transport vehicles, but when we got to Kuwait, they weren't there yet, so they farmed a bunch of us out as convoy units."

The questioning was getting far afield, but Washburn took his own advice and let it go. Better to hear the answer now than find out for the first time in front of a jury about some land mine in the witness's testimony.

"How did you feel about that?" Mills asked.

He smiled, either at her naïveté or at the question. "They didn't ask us. It wasn't like it was negotiable."

"No, I understand that. But the convoy work at the front, wasn't it more dangerous than the work you'd originally been scheduled to do?"

"Only by about a factor of ten. Maybe twenty."

"So? Much more dangerous, then?"

"Yes. Way more."

Mills paused, and kept casting. "Didn't you and the other men object to that?"

"Sure. But what were we going to do?"

"I don't know, Mr. Onofrio. What did you do?"

"Well, we complained about it to Lieutenant Scholler. We asked him to talk to the base commander and see if we could get transferred back to our regular unit."

"And did he do that?"

"He tried, but he couldn't get in to see him. Not in time, anyway." Then, trying to be helpful, Onofrio added, "He was going to see if Nolan could pull some strings with the brass, but again, that didn't happen in time."

"Mr. Scholler thought that Mr. Nolan might be able to pull some strings for him. Why was that? Were they friends?"

"I'd say so, yeah."

"Close friends?"

"Well, I don't know." He shrugged again, then unwittingly dropped his bomb. "Drinking buddies, anyway."

The words had barely registered as significant when Mills heard Washburn all but erupt behind her. "Objection! Irrelevant!"

But this was the purest bluff. No one in the courtroom thought the answer was even remotely irrelevant, and Tollson sealed that opinion in an instant. "Overruled."

Mills kept her mouth tight to avoid telegraphing her pleasure. "Thank you, Your Honor," she said. Then, back at the witness. "Mr. Onofrio, when you characterize the friendship between Mr. Nolan and Mr. Scholler as that of drinking buddies, do you mean that they literally drank together?"

Onofrio, picking up the panic in Washburn's tone, flashed a quick look over to the defense table. "Occasionally, I think, yes."

"Do you think they drank together, or did you see them drinking together?"

"Yes, they drank together."

"Mr. Onofrio, is there a rule in the military against drinking on duty, or in a war zone?"

"Yes."

"But Mr. Scholler broke this rule?

"I suppose so."

"You witnessed this yourself, personally?"

"Yes."

"How many times?"

"I don't know exactly. A few."

"More than five times?"

"Your Honor," Washburn said. "Badgering the witness."

"Overruled."

Mills nodded. "More than five times, Mr. Onofrio?"

"Maybe."

"More than ten?"

"I didn't count the times," Onofrio said. "I really couldn't say for sure."

"Once a day? Once a week? Once a month?"

"A few times a week."

"All right, then. Did Mr. Scholler drink to excess?"

"Objection," Washburn sang out. "Calls for a conclusion."

"Overruled," Tollson said. "A lay witness can give an opinion as to sobriety."

Mills slowed herself down. She was close to something very good here and didn't want to blow it. "Did Mr. Scholler ever appear drunk to you when he was on duty?"

"Objection. Conclusion."

"Sustained."

Mills tried again. "Did you, personally, ever see Mr. Scholler intoxicated after he'd been drinking with Mr. Nolan?"

Onofrio threw another worried glance over to Washburn and Evan. "Yes, ma'am."

"And by intoxicated, do you mean that you heard him speak with slurred speech or have trouble walking?"

"Yes, ma'am."

"Mr. Onofrio. When was the last time you remember noticing these things—defendant's slurred speech or the uncertain walk?"

Onofrio looked down at his lap. "His last night over there."

"The night before this incident at Masbah, is that what you're saying?"

He blew out and slowly nodded. "That's what I'm saying."

"Mr. Onofrio, on the day the shooting started, when Mr. Scholler was leading the convoy that got ambushed, did he appear to be intoxicated?"

"No, ma'am," Onofrio answered strongly.

Mills paused, then came out with it. "But he certainly was hung over, wasn't he?"

STEPHAN RAY, the language and recreational therapist from Walter Reed, nodded enthusiastically at Washburn from the witness stand. "He is definitely one of the success stories. He worked very hard and was also very lucky. But his success doesn't take away from the seriousness of his injuries. There was a real question for at least a couple of months as to whether he'd live, and then a further question about how completely, if at all, he'd recover."

"What were the areas most affected?"

"Well, most obviously affected were speech and memory, although there were also some coordination issues early on that cleared up more or less on their own."

"So how did these memory problems manifest themselves?"

"Well, at first, just after the surgery, of course, he remained pretty much continually unconscious for three weeks—in fact, I believe they kept him in an induced coma until they were confident that he'd gotten sufficiently well to handle consciousness, although I'm not a hundred percent sure of that. I wasn't on his medical team. I'm not a doctor. But when I first encountered Evan, he had what I'd call severe memory and cognition issues. He didn't know where he was, he thought I worked for the CIA, he didn't know what had happened to him exactly. But mostly, he didn't have a vocabulary."

"No vocabulary at all?"

"At first, very little. But then over time, as the healing progressed, he recovered the use of most common words."

"Was this a natural event?"

"To some degree, yes. But a lot of it was a matter of training the brain again, or relearning what he'd once known. We used flash cards, just the way you would if you were learning a new language, and Evan made really remarkable progress, especially compared to many others of our patients who never recover their ability to talk or to reason."

Washburn nodded. "Even with all this progress, how long did Evan remain in therapy with you at Walter Reed?"

"Nearly six months."

"Six months. And during those six months, while he was progressing so well, did he also suffer from blackouts?"

"I'm not sure exactly what you mean by blackouts."

"Periods when he could not recall what he'd done or where he was. As you described when he'd first come out of surgery."

"Ah. Well, yes. They were not infrequent."

"Not infrequent. So they were common?"

"Yes, but that's always to be expected in a case of traumatic brain injury."

"And how long could a blackout period last?"

"Again, it would vary. I remember a time with Evan, this was after three or four months of therapy, when he woke up one morning convinced that he was in Baghdad. He didn't understand why there was snow outside when it was summer in Baghdad. I thought it was a serious enough setback to bring it to the attention of the doctors, but he woke up on the third morning and was fine."

"He didn't think he was in Baghdad anymore?"

"No. He knew he was in Walter Reed. He picked up just where he'd left off in terms of his recovery."

"But for those three days, he was different?"

"As far as he was concerned, he was in Baghdad."

"I see. Now let me ask you this, Mr. Ray. After Evan woke up, realizing that he was in Walter Reed and not in Baghdad, did you ask him about his memory of the time he'd imagined he was in Baghdad? In other words, did you ask him about his memory of his past three days?"

"Yes, I did. He remembered none of it."

"None of it?"

"None. In fact, he thought I was playing a joke on him. Those days were just gone, as though he'd never lived them."

"Thank you, Mr. Ray. Ms. Whelan-Miille, your witness."

* * *

"Mr. Ray, did Ron Nolan visit Mr. Scholler at Walter Reed?"

"Yes, he did. I met him on that occasion."

"Did you play a part in their conversation?"

"Not really, no."

Mills went right on. "Would you describe Evan's demeanor after Mr. Nolan left?"

"He was very upset and angry to the point of tears. I remember distinctly that later he developed a migraine headache so severe that he had to be sedated for a time."

Mills stood still for a moment, wondering how far she could push this point. Surely, if she got Ray at trial, she could take Evan's anger and jealousy further, but today she didn't want to overplay her hand. She knew he'd be there for her if she needed him at the trial.

"Thank you, Mr. Ray," she said. "No further questions."

Because she was on the People's witness list, Tara wasn't allowed in the courtroom. Now, at five-fifteen, in the jail's visiting room, she bit her lip and tried to keep up a brave smile every time she met Evan's eyes.

And then they were at the window that would be theirs for today, one chair on either side of it, the hole in the Plexiglas through which they had to talk. It was by now all so familiar, and still so awful. But Tara wasn't going to concentrate on the bad. She could take her cues from Eileen, upbeat and positive. "I saw you on TV in a coat and tie."

"I thought I told you. I get to look like a regular person in court."

"You look like a regular person now."

"If you took a poll, I bet most people would say I look like a regular jailbird, what with the jumpsuit and all. What'd they say about things on TV?"

"They said it was a mixed day. What do you think?"

He shrugged. "There's no jury yet, so really none of this counts, but it didn't feel too mixed to me. This prosecutor woman is pretty tough. She's pounding on the drinking theme."

"Why does she want that so much?"

"Everett says it's all positioning for the jury. They're not going to be disposed to like or believe a drunk. Whereas if I'm suffering from PTSD and blacking out, then I'm a wounded war veteran with a mental illness who's caught in a terrible situation he didn't really create, and the sympathy flows like honey. I know, it's a little cynical. But the point is, if we get the PTSD, then to some extent it explains the drinking. Not that I'm using that as an excuse for myself. The drinking, I mean." He lowered his gaze for a moment. "I still don't know what got into me that night, why I didn't just go home with you."

"Did it ever occur to you that maybe what Mr. Washburn's arguing is actually true and not cynical after all? That your physical brain wasn't healed yet so you weren't completely rational—your cognitive powers just weren't all there. And you put PTSD on top of all that, I don't see how a jury could ever get to first-degree murder."

"Well, let's hope." He fell silent, seemed as if he were about to say something, but held it back.

"What?" she asked.

He drew a breath and let it out. "At lunch today, Everett said that I might want to start thinking about if I wanted to take a plea bargain after this hearing phase if the judge doesn't let in the PTSD."

"A plea bargain? Why? He's been saying all along we were going to win."

"Apparently it's not such a sure thing without the PTSD."

"Well, why wouldn't the judge let it in?"

"I don't know. Everett didn't even think it would be an issue until Tollson ordered the hearing this morning. But now it is, and if we lose it . . ." He lifted his shoulders.

"What would you plead to?"

"Second-degree murder. Everett thinks he could talk them into dropping the gun charge."

"So how long would that be?"

He hesitated for a beat. "Twelve to life."

Tara's head dropped as though she'd been struck. After a minute she looked up again, her eyes brimming with tears. "If you do plead, isn't that admitting you did it?"

"Yeah."

"You can't do that."

"No, I don't think I can."

"You don't remember anything about those four days?"

"Tara, we've been over that a thousand times."

"Well, maybe the thousand and first . . ."

He shook his head. "It's not going to happen. I remember going to Ron's after I left you. I remember hitting him and him hitting me back, both of us getting into it. Then nothing until I woke up in jail. I'm sorry. I'm just so sorry, but there's nothing there. It's like I disappeared into those damn bottles."

Tara bit down on her lip. "You can't plead that you did it, Evan. We can't let ourselves accept we're going to get beaten here."

"That's what I was thinking too. But if we do—get beaten, I mean—then I'm going to be in prison for a lot longer than twelve years."

"I'd wait, Evan. I really would."

"I could never ask you to."

She was rubbing her hand back and forth over her forehead. "God God God."

"I don't think He's listening," Evan said.

OVER THE NEXT TWO and a half very tedious days of technical testimony, Everett Washburn called two psychologists who had administered batteries of tests to Evan over the previous several months. Personality tests, neuropsych tests, intelligence tests, perception tests, concentration tests, memory tests. Both agreed with Dr. Overton that Evan clearly suffered from symptoms that were consistent with PTSD. Washburn called several members of the Redwood City Police Department who had worked with Evan and who had specific recollections of times when he'd exhibited PTSD symptoms in their presence—particularly inappropriate laughter and speech aphasia—an overlong pause in the stream of his conversation. Lieutenant Lochland described his irrational anger and some of the complaints he'd fielded about Evan related to the defendant's work in the DARE program.

Now it was Friday, the lunch recess was over, as was the PTSD hearing, and Judge Tollson had both attorneys back in his chambers. In contrast to his usual out-of-courtroom affability—perhaps worn down by the gravity of the issues, perhaps chastened by the enormity of the decision he had to make—today the judge sat all the way back in his chair, his arms crossed over the robe at his chest. Still and expressionless, he waited until both Washburn and Mills had taken their seats and the court reporter set up her machine.

Finally, he looked over, got a nod from her, and cleared his throat. "Mr. Washburn," he said, "for the record, have you called all your witnesses related to the PTSD evidence that you're seeking to place before the jury?"

"Yes, Your Honor."

"Ms. Miille, do the People have any evidence they wish to offer on this issue?"

"No, Your Honor."

"All right. And before I make my ruling on the People's four oh two motion, do you have any comments that you'd like to make?"

"Just what I said at the beginning, Your Honor. That my witnesses proved beyond a doubt that Mr. Scholler suffers from PTSD and this in turn supports his claim that he can't remember anything about this period."

Tollson turned to the prosecutor. "Ms. Whelan-Miille? Comment?"

"After hearing all the evidence, Your Honor, the People still believe the entire issue of PTSD is irrelevant and highly prejudicial to this case. The defendant's position here is that he didn't commit the murder. So he's not arguing a quarrel with the victim, or heat of passion, or even self-defense. The only possible result of allowing this PTSD evidence will be to create sympathy for the defendant with the jury."

Tollson sat still for another few seconds, then came forward and rested his arms on his desk, his hands clasped in front of him. "Mr. Washburn, I substantially agree with Ms. Whelan-Miille. I've given this matter long and hard thought in terms of weighing prejudice against probative value. And my ruling is that I'm not going to allow this PTSD evidence."

Washburn, staggered by the ruling, brought his hands up to both sides of his face, then rested them on the side of his chair while he got control of his emotion. "Your Honor," he said, "with all respect, this evidence needs to be admitted."

"For your purposes, perhaps, but not as a matter of law, Counselor. It's inadmissible because it has no relevance to the evidence related to Mr.

Nolan's murder. Beyond that, it has the strong possibility of wasting a lot of time and confusing the jury. If I let in your expert testimony on psychological issues, the jury is necessarily going to have to hear about a lot of hearsay which would not otherwise be admissible, would not be subject to cross-examination, and would be likely to prejudice the prosecution by exciting sympathy for the defense and a dislike of the victim. When you balance that against the entirely speculative argument that the defendant *might* have been undergoing an episode of PTSD when he killed the victim, which by the way he entirely denies doing, the whole thing is just designed to turn this trial into a circus. Until you tell me your client or somebody else is going to testify to a self-defense claim now at this eleventh hour, this evidence does not come in."

"Your Honor." Washburn uncrossed his legs and moved to the front of his chair. Normally unflappable, the old barrister had broken a sweat over a flush during the judge's monologue. He wiped at his neck with the handkerchief from his jacket pocket. Looking over at the court reporter, he sighed in pure frustration. "Of course, this guts the defense, Your Honor, and I hope the Court will keep an open mind toward reconsideration as the case comes in."

"Of course, Counsel." Tollson at his most brusque. "This Court's open-mindedness is legendary."

[22]

"LADIES AND GENTLEMEN of the jury." Today—a Wednesday, two weeks after the PTSD ruling—Mills wore a subdued blue suit over a white blouse, no jewelry, low black pumps. Jurors knew she had a government salary and she was expected to dress in a "lawyerlike, ladylike" fashion. Her presentation was supposed to be professional. Any sign of flamboyance might be taken for disrespect, or even arrogance. Representing the People of the State of California before this jury of seven men and five women, she wanted nothing to call any undue attention to herself. Neither aggressive nor hostile, she was to be the plainspoken voice of truth and reason, recounting the prosecution's case.

Starting in the middle of the courtroom, Mills walked a short course up to the foreman's position, along the front row of the jury panel, and then, after a quick stop at her desk to turn the page in her binder and check her notes, back to where she'd begun. She did this as a kind of timing device to slow herself down; she also believed in making eye contact with each and every member of the jury. The message was clear—she was leveling with them, person to person, looking them right in the eye and telling them the unblinking truth.

"Good morning. As you know from the questions you answered during your selection as members of this jury, we'll be here for the better part of a couple of weeks hearing the evidence that proves that this defendant"—here she turned and pointed to Evan—"murdered a man named Ron Nolan. The defendant hated Ron Nolan. There's no doubt about it. He thought Ron Nolan had stolen his girlfriend. He hated him for being a business success in Iraq, where Defendant had been injured while serving in the Army. He blamed Ron Nolan for the injuries he'd received, injuries that actually occurred because Defendant, after a long night of drinking, led his men into an ambush in Iraq. Evan Scholler hated Ron Nolan.

"He made no secret of it. He told his parents, he told his girlfriend. He hinted as much to some of the police officers with whom he worked. He stalked Ron Nolan by illegally using police information to keep track of his whereabouts. He broke into Ron Nolan's house and tried to frame him for the killing of two Iraqi citizens murdered in the United States.

"Finally, the evidence will show that Defendant carefully planned and premeditated this murder. Several days before his attack on Mr. Nolan, Defendant, *while on duty and in uniform as a policeman for the city of Redwood City,* contacted a locksmith and tricked him into letting him into Mr. Nolan's townhouse. The locksmith admitted Defendant into the home. In a subsequent search, the FBI found planted in that house evidence related to the murders of Ibrahim and Shatha Khalil. Unfortunately for Defendant, his plan failed when Ron Nolan found the evidence that was planted and called the FBI, who then discovered Defendant's fingerprints in Mr. Nolan's home.

"The defendant hated Ron Nolan, and when he couldn't frame him for murder, in a drunken rage he went to Ron Nolan's house and killed him. The actual cause of death was a single gunshot wound to the head. Not just to the head, mind you, but fired from a gun held just inches from the skull.

"But Defendant didn't just murder Ron Nolan. First, he administered a savage beating. He broke his jaw. He broke his wrist. He broke at least two of his ribs. He left bruises and cuts and injuries over a lot of Ron Nolan's body. The evidence will show that this defendant hated Ron Nolan, and he killed him.

"But if that is what happened, how do we know he did it? Well, for openers, he told his girlfriend he was going to. He left his fingerprint on the murder weapon found by the body. And within hours after Nolan's body was found, the police found Defendant cowering in his apartment, Ron Nolan's blood still on his hands and clothes, the injuries he'd received in the fight still unhealed, and the murdered man's blood still on the brass knuckles he used to inflict the beating I've described.

"This defendant hated Ron Nolan and he killed him. And he killed him in a way that the law defines as first-degree murder. At the close of the evidence in this case, I'll stand before you and that is the verdict for which I will ask."

Mills was doing it by the book, dispassionately laying out the elements of the People's case. Like all prosecutors, she would consistently refer to the deceased as "Mr. Nolan," and later, sometimes, even Ron, to humanize him to the jury—a living, breathing human being whose life had been prematurely taken from him. By the same token, Evan Scholler would forever after remain "the defendant," or even, less familiarly, simply "Defendant"—a clinical term denoting the place in society to which he'd fallen. A nameless, faceless perverter of the social order who deserved only the most cursory acknowledgment as a human being and no sympathy.

In the center of the courtroom one more time, she paused, noting that Washburn had let her go on this long without objection. It was a calculated technique, she knew, to signal to the jury that, in spite of this apparently damning litany condemning the defendant, the defense remained confident—nay, unconcerned by these allegations.

Letting out a theatrical sigh, Mills again allowed herself a glance over to the defendant's table, but this look communicated sadness and resignation. No one would have enjoyed putting on the kind of recitation she'd just completed. The human condition was sometimes a terrible burden. Mills had done her disagreeable though imperative job, hoping to bring justice to the evil defendant and closure to the victim and to those who had loved him.

WASHBURN HAD THE OPTION of coming out swinging now with his defense opening statement, or waiting until the People had presented their case and delivering it then. After Mills had sat down, Tollson asked him what he wanted to do, and he said he'd be going right ahead with his statement now. He didn't like to let the jury sit too long with one story without being made aware that there was another one, or another version of the same one. He found that if the prosecution got to make an unrebutted opening statement and then followed it with up to a week or more of its own witnesses, all he could do was play defense. And this passive style didn't win too many cases.

But, furthering his earlier strategy of avoiding interruptions and objections, he no sooner indicated to the judge his decision to give his opening statement—enthusiasm to defend his innocent client!—than he got the gallery chortling by commenting, in his folksiest manner, "But after Ms. Whelan-Miille's eloquent opening statement, Your Honor, the bladder of a poor old country lawyer could sure use a short recess." Which of course, reflected his opinion that the prosecution's opening had not in any way threatened his client, or even called into question Evan's innocence. Washburn would get to all that in just a minute in his own opening statement and clear up any nagging little inconsistencies that might point to Evan's guilt.

But first he had to pee.

Though, actually, he didn't.

The judge gave them fifteen minutes, and Washburn and Evan took the opportunity to walk out the courtroom's back door to the small holding cell, where they sat across from each other on the cold cement blocks that served as benches. Washburn had shaved carefully but had missed a fairly obvious spot along his jawline for three days running now. Beyond that, never sartorially close to splendid, in a too-large wheat-colored suit with a ludicrous orange tie, he looked particularly disheveled today, as he would every day of the trial. His ten-year-old brown wing-tips had frayed laces and holes in both soles, so he could cross either leg and get the regular-guy message out. Juries, he believed, didn't like fancy dressers as defense lawyers. They liked real people who talked straight and respected their intelligence. And it didn't hurt if you had a personality either.

But now his immediate concern was his client. Evan had cleaned up pretty good. In contrast to defense attorneys, juries tended to like handsome and decently dressed defendants. Not too handsome, especially in a jury with seven men, but respectable. Evan's body language already spoke with an accent of defeat and dejection—not unexpected, given Mills's effective castigation of him—but troublesome nonetheless.

They both sat with their elbows on their knees, heads nearly touching. "You don't look good," Washburn said. "That get to you?"

Evan raised his eyes. "I can't believe I did so many stupid things."

"You were injured," Washburn said with apparent sincerity. "You weren't back to yourself yet. You are now."

"You believe that?"

"I do."

A pause. "You believe *me*?"

"I wouldn't be here if I didn't."

"Is that true?"

Washburn took a long beat. "That is God's truth, my son. You may not know what you did, and you know what that's consistent with?"

"What's that?"

"Innocence. If you weren't there, you wouldn't know what happened, would you?"

Evan sighed. "Everett, I broke into his house."

"You did not break into his house. You let yourself into his house."

"Either way. That was just stupid."

"Granted. It's one of the things I find fascinating about this case, all the stupidity." He held up a hand. "No, I'm serious. You've admitted to a lot of stupid behavior, plus you were drinking way too much, which never helps, but you've never admitted planting that evidence at Nolan's, have you?"

"That's because I didn't."

"You know that. I know it. And that would have been another stupid move. So it's not the stupidity that's keeping you from copping to it. You see what I'm saying? Staying drunk for four days after your fight with Nolan was stupid. Not going to work all that time was stupid. But you didn't drive up to Nolan's in an alcoholic stupor, somehow get into his home without alerting him, get ahold of his gun, and kill him. You couldn't have done it. Your state of mind, pardon me, was too stupid. Whoever did this planned it, timed it, did it right. And call me a soft-hearted romantic, I don't see that being you."

Evan almost broke a smile. "You going to argue that?"

"If I can get the right spin on it, which might be a trick. But, listen, the main thing . . ."

"I'm listening."

"I need you to buck up in there. You don't have to be indignant, or angry, or anything negative. But you've got to sit up straight and don't let the weight of all the shit she's piling on you get you down. You'll look guilty and pathetic."

"You want me to look happy?"

"No! God, no. You're unjustly accused. Nobody's happy with that. But you're a soldier. You're fighting the good fight. You've been through battle, betrayal, brain injury, bottle-epsy, and now this bullshit. You beat every other one of 'em, and now you're standing up to this one. That's the message. Stick with it. Those jurors are going to try to be objective, okay, but they're twelve unpredictable human beings. Don't forget that. And if they're inclined to like you, that's not a bad thing. Every one of their votes is going to count equally. You get one of 'em on your side, it's over."

Evan sat up straight, his back against the wall. "You really think we can still win this thing?"

"We're not in it to lose, Evan. So when I go out and razzle-dazzle 'em in the next few minutes, it'd be good to have an enthusiastic fan in the peanut gallery. You think you can do that?"

"I'll give it a shot. If I knew what the peanut gallery was."

"You know. The peanut gallery. Howdy Doody, Buffalo Bob, Clarabelle the Clown. All those guys." But clearly, Evan was clueless about *The Howdy Doody Show*. Washburn hit him on the shoulder. "Anyway, so forget the peanut gallery. Just hang tough out there and remember that the jury's looking at you. We're doing good."

"If you say so, Everett. If you say so."

At that moment, the bailiff knocked and opened the courtroom door, telling them their time was up. Washburn let Evan precede him, then stopped short in the doorway. His heartbeat stuttered. And again. He'd had a heart attack about five years previously, and this did not feel like that. There was no pain. The arrhythmia caught his breath, that was all, and then the moment was over. But suddenly he found that the confidence he'd been exuding in his pep talk with Evan had vanished. The harsh reality, as his body took another opportunity to remind him, was that he was getting old. He persisted in living each day with the myth that he was still at the peak of his powers and would live forever. When in truth, he was even older than the Howdy Doody generation, maybe even older than Buffalo Bob himself, now long deceased. He'd lost the PTSD fight to a far younger opponent and now, no matter what he'd told Evan, he faced a far more difficult uphill battle against Mills. It struck him that he might not have the advantage this time, that age and treachery might not overcome youth and skill.

As he stepped into the courtroom behind his client, he realized that he'd allowed his shoulders to slump, that his right hand had lingered at his chest. He willed it down, squared himself away, caught the eye of the young and confident Mary Patricia Whelan-Miille at her table, and flashed her a mouthful of teeth that would have done a horse proud.

"MY FRIENDS, I'm going to speak to you for just a few minutes to tell you about the rest of the evidence in this case—things that the prosecution chose not to mention because they don't fit Ms. Miille's version of what happened, and things that at the close of this case will still be unexplained. This evidence will make you wonder whether Evan Scholler killed Ron Nolan, and will leave you with a reasonable doubt and will require you— require you if you fulfill your oaths as jurors—to find Evan Scholler not guilty."

Washburn stood with his hands in his pockets, relaxed and genial. He'd actually won a round or two with Tollson in chambers, though it really didn't feel like it. But the whole question of Iraq, he'd argued, had to be part of the trial. It was relevant on its face, and essential if the jurors were even going to begin to grasp any of the complexities surrounding both the defendant and the victim. And Tollson had agreed with him. To a point.

He intended to find out where that point exactly was.

"This case and the issues surrounding it began in Iraq," he intoned. "It's important to understand the significance that Iraq plays in the affair, because so much of the evidence presented by the People that appears to cast Mr. Scholler in a negative light in fact paints a very different picture when viewed in its true context, the context of what happened in Iraq.

"You will hear testimony that the deceased was a highly trained mercenary with a long history of both overt and covert operations in some of the most violent places in the world—Afghanistan, Kuwait, El Salvador, and Iraq. At the time of his death, he was working as a government contractor for Allstrong Security, which has offices both here in California and in Iraq. All of his adult life, the man was surrounded by death and violence. This was his livelihood and he was good at it.

"Evan Scholler, on the other hand, worked as a Redwood City police patrolman until he was called up for deployment to Iraq in the first months after the invasion. He served over there for about three months before he was involved in a firefight against Islamic insurgents in Baghdad in which he suffered a head wound and traumatic brain injury. In a coma that lasted eleven days, he was airlifted first to a field hospital in Iraq, then taken to Germany, and finally brought to Walter Reed Hospital. In March of two thousand four, he came back to work for the police department here in this city."

He paused to meet a few more eyes in the jury box. There it was, he thought with some satisfaction and relief. Short and sweet, and he'd gotten it in. He'd hoped that bringing in this information first thing and right up front might catch Mills in a first-inning lull, and sure enough he'd pulled it off.

Dang! He loved the drama of a trial.

Taking a breath, his heart palpitations forgotten, he moved on to the more pressing evidentiary issues. "Ms. Miille has described at some length the evidence that she says will compel you to convict Evan of first-degree murder. That evidence is neither as clear nor as uncontradicted as she might have led you to believe. She talked a lot about the day of the killing. Just for openers, we don't know the day of the killing. Mr. Nolan was last seen on Wednesday, June third. He was found dead on Saturday, June sixth.

"Now, the prosecutor says he was killed on Wednesday, the third. If so, that would be convenient for the prosecution because that is a date when my client spoke harsh words about Mr. Nolan. The evidence will show, and it is in fact undisputed, that Evan had too many drinks that night, at a bar a few blocks from here called the Old Town Traven. There he learned that the deceased had tried to implicate him in the murders of two Iraqi citizens. Tara Wheatley, Evan's girlfriend, will tell you that, drunk and in a rage, he told her that he was going to go to Mr. Nolan's house and kill him. And in fact, Evan has never denied that he went to Mr. Nolan's house that night, and that the two men fought.

"So the prosecution says, and wishes you to conclude, that that's the night the deceased was killed. But as the saying goes, wishing don't make it so. There is no evidence that Mr. Nolan was killed on Wednesday, as opposed to Thursday, as opposed to Friday.

"And let's take the two motives that, according to the prosecution, caused Evan Scholler to commit murder. First, jealousy. Ms. Wheatley will testify that on the evening of June third, she came to find Evan at the Old Town Traven. She invited him to come back to her apartment for the night. She told him that she had stopped seeing Mr. Nolan, and that she was in love with him."

As though taken by an apparition, Washburn stopped in his tracks, spread his palms to the jurors. "Now, it's been a few years since I've experienced some of the finer emotions such as young love, but if my memory serves, when a woman tells you she's dropped another boyfriend in your favor, that's when jealousy's much more likely to go away than to make you want to go and duke it out with your rival."

This last witticism produced a gratifying hum from the gallery. Several of the jurors broke smiles as well. Feeding off those vibes, Washburn went on. "Now, anger. The evidence will indeed show that Evan was angry— angry enough to drive to Mr. Nolan's house and engage him in a fistfight. He was angry, the evidence will show, because he believed he was being framed for a murder he didn't commit. That's a good reason to be angry," Washburn added. "It might make any of you angry."

"Your Honor! Objection."

Washburn turned and took the opportunity to glance out at the gallery, always a reasonable litmus for how he was doing. Nobody snoring yet, anyway. He produced his patented half-bow, acknowledging the objection, and turned back to the jury box, without even waiting for the judge to rule. "I'll withdraw that last comment, Your Honor," he said.

And continued. "Why, you may ask, did my client illegally let himself into his rival's house? He had come to believe that Mr. Nolan was in fact the killer of Ibrahim and Shatha Khalil. He will testify that he accompanied Mr. Nolan on a kill-and-destroy mission in Iraq that featured the same type of fragmentation grenades as were used in the Khalil murders. This might have been an error in judgment, but it was not a prelude to murder. Had he intended to kill Mr. Nolan, he could have simply waited in his home and done it instead of gathering evidence against him to send to the authorities.

"These are all points that the prosecution has presented to you as facts, and they simply are not.

"Did my client hate Ron Nolan? Yes, he did.

"Was Evan Scholler struggling to recover from the physical injury and mental anguish he sustained as a result of fighting for his country in Iraq? Yes, he was.

"As a result of the pain, both physical and mental, did he sometimes drink too much during the months of his recovery? Yes, he did.

"And as a result of the combination of these things, did he display bad judgment? Without a doubt.

"He did misuse his authority as a policeman to keep track of Ron Nolan's whereabouts. He did break into Ron Nolan's house in the belief that Ron Nolan had a hand in the deaths of the Khalils. He did give way to despair and alcohol and anger, and threaten Ron Nolan. He did go to Ron Nolan's house and fight with him on the night of June third. He did all of these things and has freely admitted doing all of these things.

"But these are not the things for which he is on trial.

"Ladies and gentlemen of the jury, at the close of all of the evidence, you will find that what Evan Scholler did not do was kill Ron Nolan. That is something the evidence does not show. And when, at the close of the evidence, you can see that this has not been proved against my client, you will be obliged by your conscience and by the laws of this state to find him not guilty."

[23]

AFTER THE OPENING STATEMENTS, they got right down to it as Mills called her first witness.

The medical examiner, Dr. Lloyd Barnsdale, had been in his position for fifteen years. Dry as dust, pale as the corpses in his lab, the bespeckled and weak-chinned coroner wore what was left of his graying, dirty blond hair in a combover. Today, though the warm Indian summer days of September continued outside, he wore a cardigan sweater over a plain white shirt and a snap-on bow-tie.

Mills waited impatiently for the ME to be sworn in. The confidence she'd felt in the morning when she'd finished with her opening statement had pretty much dissipated under the amiable onslaught of Washburn's monologue. The truth was that she had her work cut out for her. It would never do to become complacent. Washburn would eat her alive if she gave him any opportunity at all.

"Dr. Barnsdale, you did the autopsy on Ron Nolan, did you not?"

"I did."

"Would you please tell the Court your ruling as to the cause of death?"

"Certainly. Death was caused by a gunshot wound fired at close range into the head."

Barnsdale had, of course, been a witness a hundred times before. This did not necessarily make him a good witness. He spoke with a wispiness that was very much of a piece with his looks. Mills, from halfway across the room, found herself straining to hear him.

She saw that the jurors had, to a person, come forward in their chairs. It did not help that outside the building, road construction continued

unabated on Redwood City's never-ending downtown beautification project. The noise of the heavy equipment was nearly as loud as the building's
air-conditioning.

Mills backed up a couple of steps, to just beyond the last juror in the
box. If she could hear the witness, so could all the jurors. She raised her
own voice, hoping to lead by example. "Doctor," she asked, "were there
other marks or injuries to the body?"

"Yes. There were multiple signs of blunt-force and sharp-force trauma—
contusions, bruises, and lacerations on the torso, the groin, and the
face."

"Approximately how many separate injuries were inflicted on the victim?"

"I counted twenty-eight separate injuries."

"And did each of these appear to be a separate application of force?"

"There were a couple that might have been the result of a single blow.
For example, the same blow with an instrument could have hit the victim
on the forearm and the head. On the other hand, from the size and ir-
regular features of some of the injury sites, it appeared that some bruises
might have resulted from multiple blows landing in approximately the
same place on the body. I would have to say the man was hit at least two
dozen times."

Mills went back to her table and brought forward a large piece of card-
board on which she'd taped some 8½ × 11 color photographs from the
autopsy and had it entered into evidence as People's Two, since the autopsy report was People's One.

When they had gotten to it, Judge Tollson had hand-picked the six
autopsy photos that he was going to allow the jury to see. Mills considered
his choice a partial victory for herself—whoever had done this to another
human being barely deserved to be called one himself. Even without the
head wound, the damage to Nolan's body was severe.

"Doctor," Mills began, "using the photographs to illustrate your testimony, can you characterize these injuries more particularly?"

"Well, yes," Barnsdale whispered. "As we can see in Photograph A,
there were quite a few injuries that either raised bruises, or cut the skin, or
both. Although the gunshot wound, particularly the exit wound in the

back of the head, no doubt obliterated some of these, there still remained a profusion of them, particularly on the head."

Using the laser pointer, she walked him through the other five photographs.

"Do you know what caused these bruises and contusions?"

"Not specifically. It was my finding that there appeared to be more than one type of bruise, caused by different objects, some blunt and some less so."

"Doctor, were you given any implement or implements in an effort to determine whether they might have caused the injuries you observed?"

"Yes. I was given a fireplace poker and a pair of brass knuckles from the evidence locker of the Redwood City Police Department."

Two more exhibits marked and presented to the doctor.

"Yes," he said, "these are the items I compared."

"What was your conclusion, Doctor?"

"Several contusions, particularly on the jawline, appear to be the result of contact with the brass knuckles. These particular knuckles have a piece or fragment missing from one edge. You can clearly see the pattern injury in several locations that match this implement. Further, in a general sense, the damage inflicted at those injury sites is consistent with what one might expect from being struck with this sort of an object."

"And what damage is that?"

"They both cut and bruise. They leave a distinctive imprint."

"Were there a lot of these brass knuckle contusions?"

"Distinctly, there were three. Perhaps five. I could not rule them out as having been used to cause other injuries, but there was not enough detail to tell you definitively that this was the weapon used."

"What about the poker?"

"I could only find one injury across the forearm that definitively appeared consistent with the poker or something very like it. But all of the injuries to the top and side of the head were consistent with a blow from a hard, cylindrical object that could have been this poker. Further, I understand from the lab that the victim's blood and tissue was removed from the poker, which also supports the suggestion that this was the weapon used."

"As to the injuries you've discussed so far, were they consistent with having been inflicted with a man's fist?"

"No. I don't think so. The injuries I've attributed to the poker and brass knuckles were far too extensive typically to have resulted from a simple blow from the fist."

"But that leaves, Doctor, does it not, many other bruises on Mr. Nolan's body?"

"Yes, it does."

"Could they have been inflicted by a man's fists?"

"Well, yes they could, although they are very nonspecific and might have been inflicted by any blunt object, including a glancing blow by the poker or brass knuckles, or even by the impact of Mr. Nolan having hit the ground or a table or anything else as a result of one of the other blows."

"Doctor, could you describe the gunshot wound in any greater detail?"

"Yes, it was what is called a close contact wound, meaning the gun was fired right up against the skin of the forehead."

"Doctor, are you able to tell us the order in which the injuries were inflicted?"

"Not really. Logically, it would seem likely the gunshot wound would have to be last because it would have been immediately lethal. As to the blunt force trauma, it appeared that some had actually started to heal slightly, and therefore might have been inflicted before some of the others which showed less signs of healing. But the body heals more or less quickly at different times and at different places on the body. This isn't a very reliable way to sequence injuries. All I can say is that all of these injuries were *perimortem*, meaning that they were inflicted around the time of death."

"Thank you, Doctor. No further questions." Mills, apparently shaken by the photos and the testimony in spite of herself, had gone nearly as pale as the medical examiner. She turned back to the defense table. "Your witness."

WASHBURN HAD THE IMPRESSION that Mills had cut her questions short because she was getting sick. Beyond that, he'd barely heard the testimony of the witness from back where he sat, and he doubted that the jurors, intent on the photographs, had heard too much of it either. He normally didn't like to spend too much time with this more or less pro forma witness, the medical examiner, since typically all his testimony served to do was prove that a murder had been committed, and that wasn't at issue here. But this time, he thought he might pry a nugget loose from this normally unpromising vein.

And if he was going to go to that trouble, he wanted the jury to hear what the man had to say. So when he got to the middle of the room, he pitched his own volume down to the nearly inaudible. "Doctor," he said, "can you tell how old a bruise is?"

"I'm sorry," the witness replied, cupping his ear. "I didn't hear the question."

Washburn barely heard the response, but came back with his question just a few decibels louder than the first time.

Barnsdale leaned forward, his face scrunched in concentration. "Can I what?" he asked. "I'm sorry."

Behind Washburn, the gallery was getting restive. Tollson brought his gavel down one time firmly. "I want it quiet in this courtroom!" He brought his focus back inside the guardrail that separated the gallery from the bullpen of the court. "And I need you two gentlemen both to speak up, is that clear?"

"Yes, Your Honor," Washburn straightened up and nearly shouted.

Shaking his head—this was rank theatrics, circus behavior—Tollson looked down at the witness. "Doctor?"

Barnsdale looked around and up at him. "Sir?" A whisper.

"Louder, please. The jury needs to hear you."

Back to Washburn. "Go ahead, Counselor."

"Thank you, Your Honor. Doctor." A smile meant they were friends. "You've talked about these bruises on the body of the victim, that we've seen now in these photographs. My question is can you tell the age of a bruise?"

"As I just said, only within very broad limits."

"Please humor me, Doctor. Explain in some detail how you can tell that one bruise is older than another."

Clearing his throat, Barnsdale complied. "Yes, certainly. Bruises begin healing as soon as they are made, so the degree of healing, diminishing of swelling, thickness and solidity of scabbing, color, and so on, can tell you roughly how long it is since the bruise was sustained. We all know that some people bruise more easily than others. And it's also true that the same person might bruise more easily on a different part of his body, at a different time in his life, or depending on his general health. But all things being equal, we can get some idea from the bruises themselves."

Tollson, from the bench, intoned, "Louder, please."

Washburn went on. "And these bruises to the victim, were they all the same age, so to speak?"

"No."

"No? What was the greatest difference you observed between them?"

"Impossible to say."

"Impossible, Doctor. You can't give us any information? Are you telling me one of these bruises could have been inflicted on Mr. Nolan when he was five years old, and another a few minutes before his death, and there would be no difference."

A small round of laughter from the gallery.

"Well, no, of course not."

"Then could some of these injuries been inflicted a month before Mr. Nolan's death?"

"No."

"A week before?"

Some hesitation. "I doubt that seriously."

"But it could have been a week before."

"I doubt it."

"Well, certainly, Doctor, some of the injuries could have been inflicted three or four days before Mr. Nolan's death. That's true, isn't it?"

Washburn knew he had the doctor, and knew what the answer had to be.

"Well, I'd have to say yes."

"And, Doctor, did you make any effort at the time specifically to note in your autopsy the age of the various bruises?"

"I didn't record a specific analysis of that for each bruise."

"Why not?"

"It seemed irrelevant at the time. It certainly was irrelevant to the cause of death."

"Because none of these blows killed him, isn't that right, Doctor? Mr. Nolan died from the gunshot wound, whenever that was inflicted. True?"

"Yes."

"Thank you, Doctor. No further questions."

NEXT UP was Shondra Delahassau, a forensics sergeant with the police department. A dark ebony woman in her early thirties with her hair in cornrows, projecting competence and confidence, she couldn't have been more of a contrast to Dr. Barnsdale.

"We got the call on a Saturday afternoon after the groundskeeper, who was blowing leaves off the back patio, saw evidence of a fight and what looked to be splashes of blood in the living room."

"And what happened next?" Mills asked.

"Well, the first responders to arrive were a patrol team, who entered the townhouse to see if there were injured persons or suspects still on the premises. They found only a dead body and left without disturbing anything. Once the house was cleared, they waited out front for other officers. My unit, which is crime scene investigation, got there about the same time as Lieutenant Spinoza, who had obtained a search warrant, at around four-thirty."

"And what did you find inside?"

"First, of course, the blood, a lot of blood. In the rug and on the walls and so on."

"Did your unit take samples of this blood for analysis, Sergeant?"

"Yes. We took samples from every location for testing in the lab."

Mills spoke to the judge. "Your Honor, I believe the defense is prepared to stipulate that DNA testing matched blood samples from the premises to either the defendant or Ron Nolan."

This was bad news, and a buzz arose in the gallery, but Washburn had been only too happy to enter the stipulation after Mills had told him that the lab tech who had actually done the DNA testing was out on maternity leave. It wasn't to his advantage anyway to have a half day of scientific evidence putting Evan's blood and Nolan's blood all over Nolan's home.

"Thank you, Sergeant," Mills said. "Now, back to the townhouse itself, what else did you find?"

"Well, furniture had been knocked over in the living room and in the office. We found a fireplace poker that was stained with the victim's blood on the floor in the office. Then we discovered the victim's body on the floor in the bedroom. There was a nine-millimeter Beretta semiautomatic on the bed."

"What did you do next?"

"While Lieutenant Spinoza called the medical examiner's office, I supervised while members of my unit started taking photographs of the scene, collecting blood, hair, and fiber samples and fingerprints if any were available. My usual drill at a murder scene."

Mills duly marked and had her identify almost two dozen samples with the trace evidence from Nolan's place. When they'd finished, Mills pulled the gun out of a protective firearms box and gave it to the bailiff to clear, demonstrating on the record that it was unloaded and safe to handle. "Now, Sergeant, did you personally dust the gun for fingerprints?"

"I did."

"Did you find any usable latents?"

"Yes."

"And were you able to identify whose fingerprints were found on the gun?"

"We did. It held the fingerprints of Mr. Nolan, as well as those of the defendant, Mr. Scholler."

Again, a rush of comment swirled across the gallery. Mills let it go on for a satisfying moment before she turned to Washburn and gave him the witness.

WASHBURN HAD ALWAYS believed that there were basically only two ways to defend against a murder charge. The first was to present an affirmative defense case that, on its own merits, created either mitigation or reasonable doubt. This former approach had been Washburn's stock-in-trade over the years and he'd done exceedingly well with it. He would listen to all the prosecution's facts and theories, and then introduce his own defense case, which might include self-defense, diminished capacity, temporary insanity, or any other of the many psychiatric defenses (including PTSD). In San Francisco, over time, these became pretty much slam dunks. But even in San Mateo County, such a strong affirmative defense would often convince a jury to convict only of a lesser charge. Washburn believed this was because people basically wanted to believe in the goodness of their fellow man. Even if they had done something truly heinous, if there was a semiplausible reason that they'd been driven to it by events outside of their control, jurors tended to give them a break.

The second way to win was, in Washburn's experience, both far more difficult and far less effective; this was the reactive defense, which challenged every fact and assertion made by the prosecution. Naturally, good defense attorneys also did this automatically even when they had a strong affirmative case, but debunking a carefully built prosecution was never an easy task. In most cases, of course, this was because the defendant was guilty. But beyond that, it was a huge hurdle for most jurors to disbelieve government testimony and to doubt the sworn testimony of authority figures such as doctors, forensics experts, and the police.

When Tollson had taken PTSD away from him, Washburn knew he was stuck with a reactive defense, and this was what had filled him with such a sense of dread. Now here he was with his second witness on his first day—a woman whom he normally would have dismissed without a crossexamination because she had nothing of substance that would help his case—and he was rising to question her, grasping at straws just to keep up the charade that he was putting on an enthusiastic, even passionate, defense.

"Sergeant Delahassau," he began, "you've testified that you tested Mr. Nolan's townhome for fingerprints, blood, hairs, and fibers, isn't that so? Your usual drill, I believe you called it."

"Yes, that's right."

"And you discovered matches with Mr. Scholler's blood and fingerprints?"

"Yes."

"What about his hair?"

The gallery let out what seemed to Washburn to be a collective chuckle.

"Yes, we found samples of his hair too."

"Did you find any other hair, besides Mr. Nolan's and Mr. Scholler's?"

"Yes. We found traces of hair from at least three other individuals."

"Can you tell if that hair was from a male or female?"

"Under some circumstances, DNA can determine that. You need a follicle."

"And to your knowledge, did anyone run DNA tests on these hair samples?"

For the first time, Delahassau's face clouded. She threw a troubled look over to Mills, then came back to Washburn. "Uh, no, sir."

"Why not?"

Another hesitation. "Well. We had no other suspects with which to match samples."

"But these hair samples surely indicated that someone else had been in Mr. Nolan's townhouse, isn't that true?"

"Well, yes, but they could have been years old, or . . ."

"But, bottom line, Sergeant, you do not know if the three hair samples found in the victim's home came from men or from women, do you?"

"No."

Unsure of what, if anything, he'd just proven, Washburn decided he'd take his small victory now and move on to his other minuscule point. "Sergeant," he asked, "did you recover the bullet that had killed Mr. Nolan?"

Letting out a sigh of relief that the other line of questioning had ended, Delahassau reverted to her confident self. "Yes. It was embedded in the floor directly under the exit wound in his head."

"So he was shot while he was already on the ground?"

"That appeared to be the case, yes."

"And did you run a ballistics test on the Beretta?"

"No. The bullet was deformed too much for that."

Washburn brought his hand up to his mouth in an apparently genuine show of perplexity. "Sergeant," he asked with an exaggerated slowness, "are you telling me that you do not know for an absolute certainty that the bullet that killed Mr. Nolan came from the weapon that had my client's fingerprints on it?"

"No, sir, but . . ."

"Thank you, Sergeant. That's all."

He'd barely gotten the words out when Mills was on her feet. "Redirect, Your Honor?"

Tollson waved her forward. "Sergeant," she began before she'd even reached her place, "what was the caliber of the bullet that killed Mr. Nolan?"

"Nine millimeter."

"And what was the caliber of the recovered weapon?"

"Nine millimeter."

"And was the recovered weapon a revolver or a semiautomatic?"

"It was a semiautomatic."

"Now, sergeant, when a nine-millimeter weapon is fired, what happens to the casing—the brass jacket behind the actual bullet that holds the gunpowder that propels the blast?"

"It gets ejected."

"You mean it pops out of the gun?"

"Yes."

"And did you find a casing for a nine-millimeter round in Mr. Nolan's bedroom?"

"Yes. It was among the sheets on the bed."

"Were you able to match that casing to the recovered Beretta?"

"Yes."

"So there was one nine-millimeter bullet and no others recovered from the scene, one nine-millimeter casing and no others recovered from the scene, and although the bullet itself was not capable of comparison, the only casing at the scene that could have contained that bullet was fired by the nine-millimeter Beretta with the defendant's fingerprints on it."

"Yes."

"Thank you."

[24]

WHEN THEY ALL GOT BACK to their tables after a short afternoon recess, Washburn noticed that Mills seemed to be losing her sense of humor as the day wore on. But whether Mills was enjoying it or not, she was putting on the kind of straightforward, linear case that juries tended to like. Her next witness was Evan's direct superior in the police department, Lieutenant Lochland, who, alarmed at Scholler's absence from work, had found him in his apartment, drunk and covered in blood, and eventually placed him under arrest.

"Lieutenant," she began, "Defendant was under your direct supervision while he worked with the police department. Isn't that so?"

But Washburn and Evan had talked about this coming testimony on the break, and the old lawyer was on his feet before she'd finished her question. "Objection! Relevance. Three fifty-two, Your Honor."

Tollson turned a questioning look down to Mills. "Counselor?"

"Foundational, Your Honor," she said.

"That's fairly broad. Can you be more specific?"

"Goes to Defendant's state of mind leading up to the act. Also foundational to the break-in at Mr. Nolan's."

The judge, in what Washburn was beginning to recognize as something of a pattern, pulled his glasses off to ponder for a minute.

Before he could put them back on and render his decision, Washburn said, "Your Honor, if you will, I'd like to request a sidebar." If Mills was getting tired or losing her chops due to low blood sugar, if this was her afternoon tendency—and her body language made it appear to be—Washburn wouldn't hesitate to use that against her.

A shorter pause this time, until Tollson nodded. "Very well. Counsel may approach." When the two attorneys had gotten in front of the bench, Tollson peered over it. "What's the problem, Everett?" he said.

"Your Honor, there's no possible relevance to Lieutenant Lochland's relationship to my client. The only thing this will get the People is negative character stuff. That Evan was angry, that he lied to his superiors when he broke into Nolan's place, that he disobeyed orders, maybe got drunk on duty. There's nothing possibly relevant there and even if it is, it's far more prejudicial than probative and opens up a whole number of cans of worms."

"Ms. Whelan-Miille?"

Clearly, Washburn's attack on this point had blindsided her. But she wasn't about to give up any ground without some kind of a fight. "The lieutenant's a hostile witness, Your Honor. You think he wants to be up here testifying against another cop, and one that worked for him? He's not going to say anything bad about Evan's character. At worst, he'll say he was mixed up and still recovering from the wounds in Iraq. And that will, if anything, incite sympathy from the jury. This is all part of Mr. Washburn's case anyway. How can he want to put it in through his own witnesses and keep it out with mine?"

"If it was all that sympathetic," Tollson said, "I doubt if Mr. Washburn would object to the testimony. And in that case, why do you want it?" the judge asked. When Mills couldn't come up with an answer in the next ten seconds, Tollson stepped back in. "Let's move on, shall we? How's that sound?"

Washburn inclined his head. "Thank you, Your Honor."

Back at the defense table, he pulled his yellow legal pad over in front of him and drew a happy face that he showed to his client under his hand. At the same time, Mills tried to pick up with her witness. "Lieutenant, it was you who arrested Defendant, was it not?"

"Yeah. That was me."

"Can you tell the jury the specifics?"

"Sure." He turned to face the panel and began in a conversational tone. "Lieutenant Spinoza—he's the head of the homicide detail—called me at home as a courtesy on that Saturday to tell me he was worried about Patrolman Scholler. He'd been called on the Ron Nolan homicide and remembered that Patrolman Scholler had looked up that name on the police computer in the past few days. Spinoza wondered if I'd heard from him and I told him I hadn't. Patrolman Scholler hadn't been into work on Thursday or Friday, so when I got Spinoza's call, I was a little worried myself.

"I thought the best bet would be to go check out his apartment, so I drove up there—he lived in one of those units along Edgewood Road. All the blinds in the windows were pulled down, so there was no seeing in. I knocked and called out his name, and nobody answered, but I heard some movement inside, like something, some object, falling over.

"Now I'm starting to think something's wrong. I get out my cell phone and call his number and the phone inside starts ringing, and I started pounding on the door, calling for him."

Washburn could have objected to this narrative, but again knew it was coming in, and was just as happy to get through it as quickly as possible.

"And finally I hear, 'Yeah, one minute,' and a few seconds later Patrolman Scholler opens the door, just like that. Then I take a look at him and he's all beat up. So I ask him what happened? But he didn't seem to understand the question. So then I asked him if he knew about a guy named Ron Nolan, that he'd been killed." Lochland stopped, sat back, clasped his hands in his lap.

But Mills wouldn't have called him up if he didn't have something she needed. So she asked. "And did he have any reaction to that, Lieutenant?"

"Yes, ma'am. He swore."

"He swore. What exactly did he say, Lieutenant?"

Washburn knew the answer to this question, and came halfway out of his chair as he objected and, much to the displeasure of both Mills and Tollson, requested another sidebar.

When both attorneys were again in front of the judge, Mills started right in. "Your Honor, this is a frivolous objection if we've ever heard one. Mr. Washburn knows what Defendant's words were upon learning about Mr. Nolan's death, and the jury needs to hear them."

Washburn shot back at her. "There is no need to subject the jury to vulgarity, Your Honor. The defense will stipulate that Evan used language that some might find offensive, in spite of the fact that even that admission might taint him in the eyes of some of the jury members."

"Oh, please." Mills rolled her eyes. "The man's on trial for murder, Your Honor. He's broken into the victim's house. He's admitted to beating him with brass knuckles—"

"*Fighting* him with brass knuckles," Washburn replied calmly. "The evidence supports a fight between two professional warriors, not a beating."

"This is hair-splitting of the most obvious kind, Your Honor. And in fact, on reflection, I wonder if Mr. Washburn didn't help prepare Lieutenant Lochland in his testimony so that he would set up this objection, rather than simply repeat Defendant's words, which he'd always used with me in my preparation."

"Your Honor." Washburn's face reflected his sadness that his opponent had stooped so low as to accuse him of coaching her witness, although of course he had done just that. If he could somehow keep Evan's unfortunate choice of words, uttered in an alcoholic stupor, out of the record, it would be a significant victory. "I strenuously object to Counsel's intimation that I may have acted unethically."

"I'm not saying that, Your Honor. I'm saying that the jury knows that Defendant did all these other pretty questionable things, plus he lied to his boss and his locksmith friend. The fact that he used a mild swear word isn't likely to stain his reputation at this point."

Tollson put his glasses back on and scowled down through them. "I agree, Counselor. The witness can answer the question."

"Your Honor," Washburn said, "allowing a witness to use vulgarity on the stand is a slippery slope that . . ."

"Counselor, I don't believe . . . we're not talking about the f-word, the c-word, or the n-word, are we?"

"No, Your Honor," Mills said.

"We can't know that yet, Your Honor, the witness hasn't answered yet."

But this last comment, finally, got under Tollson's skin. "Don't toy with me, Counselor. I've made my ruling. Stop wasting the Court's time."

"Of course, Your Honor. Apologies."

Tollson ignored him. "Ms. Whelan-Miille," he said, "you may proceed."

So after all that, Mills was back at her place ten feet in front of the witness. "Lieutenant, would you please tell the jury Defendant's exact words when you asked if he knew a Ron Nolan, and that he had been killed?"

"Yes, ma'am." Frustrated that he wasn't going to be able to keep it out, Lochland put the best face he could on it. He turned toward the panel and spoke directly to them. "He said, 'I kicked his ass.' And I said, 'Jesus, Evan, he's dead.' And he said, 'Goddamned right.'"

Mills dared a glance over to Washburn, and certainly knew that she risked incurring the judge's wrath as she nodded, directing the words as much to her opponent as to the jury. "'Goddamned right,'" she said. "Thank you, Lieutenant. No further questions. Your witness, Mr. Washburn."

Fresh as a teenage boy, Washburn all but hopped up and over to his place to begin his cross-examination. "Lieutenant Lochland, after Patrolman Scholler reacted to the news, what did he do next?" The decision to refer to Evan by his police rank with this witness was, of course, intentional.

"He kind of folded himself down to a sitting position, then lay back all the way."

"On the floor?"

"Yes."

"Was he resisting arrest?"

"No, sir. His eyes were closed. I rolled him over and put handcuffs on him and he still didn't wake up."

"So he was asleep, then?"

"Asleep, maybe, but also drunk. We tested him at the station and his blood alcohol was point two four."

"And what, Lieutenant, is the blood alcohol level at which a person is considered legally drunk in California?"

"Point oh eight."

"So Patrolman Scholler was at something like three times the legal limit for driving?"

"I don't know the math, but he certainly was very drunk."

"Incoherently drunk?"

Mills jumped all over the question. "Objection! Conclusion."

"Sustained."

Washburn took a short beat, came at it another way. "Did Evan respond immediately to your question about what had happened to him?"

"No."

"At his apartment, did he ever call you by name?"

"No."

"Was his speech slurred?"

"Yes."

"And did you have to repeat your questions before he answered?"

"Yes."

"Now, Lieutenant Lochland, he never said he killed Ron Nolan, did he?"

"No, he did not."

"The only thing he said was that he kicked Nolan's ass, correct?"

"Right."

"And to repeat that colorful phrase, Evan Scholler looked like he'd gotten his ass kicked as well, didn't he?"

"Yes. He was seriously beat up."

"Now he said something else," Washburn continued, "after he said he'd kicked Mr. Nolan's ass, didn't he?"

"He said, 'Goddamned right.' "

"Before he said that, you said that Ron Nolan was dead, correct? But you have no way of knowing whether he understood you when you said that, do you?"

"Well, no, not for sure."

"He was drunk, beat up, and more than a little incoherent, correct?"

"Yes."

"So to repeat my question, do you have any way of knowing whether he heard or understood you when you told him that Ron Nolan was dead?"

"He was pretty out of it. I can't honestly tell you that he understood anything that was going on."

"Did Patrolman Scholler say anything else while you were transporting him to the police station?"

"Nothing coherent. Just gibberish."

"Your Honor!" Now Mills was on her feet, truly enraged. "Sidebar, please."

Clearly, tempers all around were fairly raw by this time. Tollson gave the request a full thirty seconds before, muttering, he nodded and waved the two attorneys forward for their third sidebar of the afternoon.

When they got to the front, Tollson was waiting, pointing a finger at them as though he were a schoolteacher. "I'm getting more than a little tired of this bickering, Counselors. This is not the way we do a trial."

But Mills, fire in her eyes, came right back at him. "I'd prefer we didn't have these issues, either, but Mr. Washburn's conduct here is unconscionable! You just sustained my objection about the word *incoherent* and now the witness gets it in, barely disguised."

"In such a way that his answer was not conclusory as to my client's mental state, Your Honor. That was, I believe, the objection. Lieutenant Lochland is certainly qualified to call gibberish incoherent."

But Mills wasn't giving up. In a restrained voice, she said, "Your Honor. Obviously, if Defendant was incoherent, then his earlier words don't have nearly the same power."

Washburn had a great deal of experience in situations like this one. The temptation was to begin responding directly to your opponent, and this invariably infuriated judges. So he kept his eyes on Tollson, his voice modulated and relaxed. "That is, of course, more or less my intention in pursuing this line of questioning, Your Honor. The distinction between an incoherent epithet and an incriminating answer to a question, though perhaps too subtle for my opponent to grasp, is hugely significant."

"All right. That's enough of that, both of you. I'm going to allow the question and the answer to stand. Ms. Whelan-Miille, you, of course, may redirect." He pointed down at them once again. "I will not be entertaining any more sidebar requests today. This witness has been up here for nearly an hour, and two-thirds of that time we've been up here arguing about four or five words. It's got to stop. If you have objections, raise them in the usual way and I'll rule as best I can. But that's the end of this quibbling nonsense. Understood? Both of you?"

Washburn nodded genially. "Yes, Your Honor."

Mills stood flatfooted, apparently still too angry to talk.

Tollson brought his hard gaze to rest on her. "Counselor? Clear?"

At last she got the words out. "Yes, Your Honor."

* * *

LOCHLAND WAS STILL on the stand, having established that on the Saturday of his arrest, Evan had been a fount of incoherent and meaningless babble. Washburn could be forgiven for feeling that things were going his way. After he passed around to the jury the booking photo, Defense Exhibit A, in which a completely disheveled Evan stared blankly at the camera, further establishing his incoherence, Washburn, in his courtliest manner, half turned to Mills. "Redirect."

Mills looked up at the clock, which read four forty-five. She could probably get in a question or two about whether or not Scholler's "Goddamned right" had sounded coherent or not to the lieutenant, but in the end she decided that this would only serve to underscore Washburn's thrust—that nothing Evan said that day meant much of anything. Even "Goddamned right," which she had worked so hard to get in. It was what he'd said, and she had no doubt what it had meant—it was tantamount to an admission that he'd killed Nolan and Washburn knew it. But whether or not the jurors would come to see it that way was anyone's guess. She was going to have to trust that they would use their common sense.

All she wanted at the moment was to put this day behind her. She'd get another hack at Washburn tomorrow, and she had the cards—Evan Scholler was guilty and the jury was going to see it and that was all there was to it. Raising her eyes to the judge, she felt the urge to smile begin at the corners of her mouth. She looked over to the jury, to Washburn, back up to the judge. "No questions," she said.

Tollson brought down his gavel. "Court's adjourned until nine-thirty tomorrow morning."

[25]

FRED SPINOZA WAS a far cry from being a hostile prosecution witness.

In fact, he felt seriously abused that someone who worked for his department, played on his bowling team, got his help finding the address of the house he was planning to break into, where he would then commit murder, and had even come to his own home and played the war hero with his children . . .

Every time Spinoza thought about it, it roiled his guts. He believed that there was a special section in hell reserved for someone who could have done that to his kids.

Never mind what Evan Scholler did to Ron Nolan.

Resplendent in his dark blue uniform, Spinoza settled himself into the chair hard by the judge's platform. He'd put in a lot of time on the witness stand in his career, and rarely had he looked forward to the experience more than today. Now here came Mary Patricia Whelan-Miille up from her table in the packed courtroom, to a space about midway between him and the jury.

Mills and he had shared drinks on several occasions, once they'd gotten to know each other over this case. There had been a short time in the first weeks when he thought she might be coming on to him, but though he found her quite attractive, he loved Leesa and had made that clear enough to Mills that, if she was in fact trolling, she chose to back off.

But some chemistry, he knew, still sparked between them.

He knew that this would play well for a jury—it was just another one of those intangibles that sometimes came into play during a trial. A major People's witness and an assistant DA working in ·understated sync could bring a sense of rightness, of unassailable conviction, to a prosecution case.

Mills seemed rested and confident as she nodded to the jurors, then smiled at her witness as though she meant it. "Lieutenant Spinoza, what is your position with the police department?"

"I'm the head of the homicide detail."

After she went over the details of his service, she got down to it. "Defendant was a patrolman, was he not, Lieutenant?"

"Yes. He'd been a patrolman working a regular beat before he went overseas, and when he came back, he went back to his former position."

"How was it, then, that you came to know him?"

Spinoza shot half a grin at the jury, then shrugged. What was he going to do? It was the truth. "He was on my bowling team."

"Can you tell the Court, please, Lieutenant, about the first time you ran across a connection between Defendant and the victim in this case, Ron Nolan?"

"Yes. I was in the office on a weekend. The Khalil murders had just taken place, so I was working overtime. I happened to run across the defendant at one of the computers, and I asked him what he was doing. He told me he was trying to locate the address of a drug dealer."

"Did you ask him the name of that drug dealer?"

"Yes. He told me it was Ron Nolan."

"Is that against department policy?"

"Well, it's a gray area. Of course, police are not allowed to use computers for personal reasons. He could use the computer to follow up on a narcotics tip, although, strictly speaking, he should have referred the whole thing to vice."

"How about using the computer to locate a romantic rival?"

"That would not only be against policy, but completely illegal. If he were caught doing that, he could expect to be fired and probably prosecuted."

"So Defendant's use of the computer in this case was illegal?"

"As it turns out, yes."

"And yet you helped him?"

In his prep work with Mills, they had both acknowledged that this would be an uncomfortable moment that they needed to address head-on.

"Of course, I didn't know the real reason he was using the computer at that time, but yes. He told me he was tracking a drug dealer and I believed him."

"So in what way did you assist him?"

Spinoza looked at the jury, spoke directly to them. "Well, I knew that he'd have to know how to work the system if he ever did need to find an address from a license plate. I suppose you could say I viewed it as more or less a casual thing, a training opportunity."

"Did Defendant tell you why he wanted to find Mr. Nolan's address?"

"Yes. But I thought his reason . . . I thought he was making a joke." This was an important clarification that Mills had wanted him to make sure he got in, since it served to underscore both Evan Scholler's arrogance and his premeditation.

"Nevertheless, what was the reason he gave you?"

"He said he wanted to hunt down Mr. Nolan and kill him."

A shimmer of reaction echoed through the courtroom, serious enough that Tollson dropped his gavel a couple of times.

Mills let the murmur die down and then resumed her questioning. "Did Defendant mention this killing of his rival any other times?"

"Yes."

"And where was that?"

Spinoza turned in the witness chair to face the jury again. "At my house. After work."

"Was this a usual occurrence, a patrolman coming to your home outside of work hours?"

"No. It was decidedly unusual."

"So what happened?"

"Well, we got ourselves some coffee and went outside and since it was something we'd joked about before, I asked him if he'd killed his dope dealer yet."

"And what was his answer to that?"

"He said he hadn't because Mr. Nolan was out of town."

"And yet you still considered this a joke?"

"Maybe not a funny joke, but it's the way we cops often talk to each other. It still never in a million years occurred to me that he was actually planning—"

Washburn was on his feet, not letting him finish. "Objection!"

Not missing a beat, Tollson nodded. "Sustained. Confine your answers to the questions, please, Lieutenant. Go ahead, Counsel."

Mills nodded, satisfied, and apparently ready to begin the next line of questioning they'd rehearsed, which was the aftermath of the murder itself, the FBI's involvement, and Scholler's arrest. But then, suddenly, she paused, threw a last glance at the jury, and must have seen something she liked, because her next words were, "Thank you, Lieutenant." And then to Washburn, "Your witness."

Spinoza knew Washburn well. As head of homicide in Redwood City, he'd sparred with the veteran attorney many times before, and he was particularly looking forward to it today. Confident that even a master like Washburn wouldn't be able to put a different spin on the events about which he'd just testified, Spinoza was settling himself in, getting psyched for a cross-examination he thought he'd actually enjoy, when Washburn lifted his head, shook it, and said to Tollson, "I have no questions for this witness."

"SPECIAL AGENT RIGGIO," Mills began with the next witness, "how did the FBI get involved in the Khalil case?"

Marcia Riggio had short, cropped dark hair. She wore a navy-blue suit that would not have looked out of place on a man. But the severe look was mitigated by a tan open-necked blouse of some soft and shimmery material, as well as by a plain gold chain necklace. She sat upright in the witness chair, her hands folded in her lap, and spoke with a formal and flat inflection. "Many witnesses at the scene reported hearing an explosion, which the arson inspectors concluded was consistent both with the damage to the bedroom and with the cause of the ensuing fire. Mr. Khalil and his wife were both naturalized citizens from Iraq, and so because of a possible terrorist angle, local officials deemed it prudent to contact Homeland Security, the Bureau of Alcohol, Tobaccco and Firearms, and the Federal Bureau of Investigation. Subsequently, analysis of the shrapnel from the explosion revealed that the blast was caused by a device called a fragmentation grenade, probably of domestic manufacture, the possession of which is against federal law. Effectively, the FBI took jurisdiction of this case, although we of course shared our findings with local police."

"And what were your findings?"

"Very little in the first few days. Besides the fragmentation grenade, we discovered that both victims had been shot before the explosion, with nine-millimeter caliber bullets which, when we found them, were too badly formed for comparison to a firearm. We interviewed several family members, of course, in the wake of the attack, and were beginning to process that information when my partner, Jacob Freed, and I received an envelope in the mail that contained a computer diskette with a photograph file that focused our attention in a different direction. Among the pictures in that file were photographs of the Khalils' home taken from several angles, with a handwritten note that the pictures had been downloaded from a computer belonging to a Mr. Ron Nolan. Subsequently, Mr. Freed obtained Mr. Nolan's telephone number and left him a message that we would like to have a discussion with him on a matter that might involve national security. There was no mention of the Khalils, or of the photograph."

"Did you in fact interview Mr. Nolan?"

"Yes."

"What did he tell you?"

Washburn was on his feet. "Objection. Hearsay."

Tollson looked at Mills. "Counsel?"

"You've already ruled on this, Your Honor," Mills said. "When Mr. Nolan's accusations to the FBI are repeated to Mr. Scholler, they give Mr. Scholler yet another motive to kill him."

Tollson looked over to Washburn. "She's right, Counsel. We did talk about this, and it's coming in. Objection overruled."

She went on in the same vein, meticulous as to every detail and nuance. Nolan's call to the FBI, his theory that his romantic rival, the defendant, might have broken into his house, his discovery of the frag grenades and 9mm Beretta weapon in his closet, the record of computer usage while he'd been away; then, following up on Nolan's theory, the FBI's discovery a day later of the defendant's fingerprints on the computer diskette. Finally, she came to an end.

"Trying to get the timeline correct, do you recall the day or date that you made the discovery about Defendant's fingerprints on the diskette?"

"Yes. Both. It was Thursday, June fourth."

Mills waited for more of a reply until she realized that Special Agent Riggio had answered her question and didn't need to deliver a speech about it. "And after you had that information, did you try to contact Defendant?"

"Yes, we did. We attempted to reach him through his job as a police officer in Redwood City, but he had not come into work that morning."

"Had he called in sick?"

"No."

"All right. Where did you try next?"

"We called him at his home, but there was no answer there. So we left a message on his answering machine."

"Did he ever answer that message?"

"No, he did not."

"Were you planning to place Defendant under arrest at that time?"

"No. At that time, we wanted to question him."

"Did you stake out his apartment?"

"No. We had no reason to suspect that he was avoiding us. We thought it likely that he would either call us or we would otherwise locate him in a day or so."

"Did you attempt to locate Mr. Nolan during this time?"

"No. He said he would call us if he got any more information. Beyond that, we had no reason to try and contact him during this period."

"So what did you do next?"

"We ran the fingerprints we'd picked up in Mr. Nolan's townhouse and determined that he had been correct. The Defendant had been in his house. Further, the defendant's prints were on the Beretta that was in Mr. Nolan's backpack."

"Did you find his prints on the fragmentation grenades?"

"No. They have a rough surface and did not contain usable fingerprints."

"But the Beretta with Defendant's prints was in the backpack with the fragmentation grenades, was it not?"

"Yes."

"And could you tell if that gun had been fired recently?"

"We could only say that it had not been fired after its last cleaning. But we have no way to tell when it had last been cleaned."

Mills, in a rhythm, kept it going. "Was the gun loaded?"

"Yes. There was a full magazine and a round in the chamber."

Mills knew she had covered a lot of ground with Riggio, who was in many ways the ideal witness, an uninflected, just-the-facts-ma'am kind of presence. But she still had a ways to go. "Special Agent Riggio, how did you discover that Mr. Nolan had been killed?"

SPINOZA AND RIGGIO ate up the whole morning, and court didn't resume until nearly two o'clock in the afternoon.

Washburn, who'd remained silent throughout the lengthy direct, showed little of the enthusiasm he'd displayed the day before as he slowly rose from his chair and advanced to make his cross. "Special Agent Riggio," he began sonorously, "you've testified that in the immediate aftermath of the Khalils' shootings, you interviewed several family members. What did you talk to them about?"

"We had the usual preliminary interviews following this kind of event."

"And what are these interviews comprised of?"

"Developing knowledge of the relationships between the family members and the deceased, as well as business, personal, political, or any other issues that might throw light on the investigation of the crime."

"How many of these interviews did you have?"

Mills spoke from behind him. "Objection. Relevance."

"Sustained."

Washburn couldn't entirely camouflage a disappointed grimace. "The Khalils have widespread business interests, do they not?"

Again: "Objection. Irrelevant."

This time Washburn replied. "Not at all, Your Honor. The People, while never charging Mr. Scholler with the murder of the Khalils, are attempting to insinuate without proof that he was somehow involved in their deaths. I'm wondering if Special Agent Riggio had interviewed anyone among Mr. Khalil's vast business interests who had any connection to Mr. Scholler."

"All right. Overruled. You may answer that question."

To Riggio, it was all the same. Unruffled, she nodded. "Yes, the Khalils had widespread business interests."

"Just here in this country?"

"No. Overseas as well."

"In Iraq?"

"According to the children, yes."

"But you didn't check that information yourself?"

"We were beginning to verify all the information we'd gathered when Mr. Nolan was murdered."

"So," Washburn said, "the answer is no, you didn't check the information about the Khalils' business interests in Iraq, isn't that so?"

"Your Honor!" Mills tried again. "Relevance?"

Washburn said, "It'll be clear in a second, Your Honor."

"All right, but it had better be. Overruled."

"Special Agent Riggio, Mr. Nolan worked for an American security contractor firm in Iraq, did he not? Allstrong Security."

Now Mills was on her feet. "Your Honor, please! We've discussed this before. This fishing expedition is going nowhere and the only purpose to eliciting this hearsay is to suggest a connection between Mr. Nolan and the Khalils, which is unsupported by any evidence."

Washburn knew he could probably get away with at least one outburst per trial. He figured this was as good a time as any, and whirled around on Mills. "There's a whole lot more evidence of Nolan's involvement with the Khalils' murders than of my client's. You just don't want the jury to hear anything that doesn't fit your theory."

Bam! Bam! Bam!

"Mr. Washburn!" Tollson exploded. "Both of you. Enough. Any more of this and somebody's going to get a contempt charge. You're to address your remarks to the bench and not to one another." Tollson stared them down, giving equal time to both. Then, glancing at the wall clock, he said, "I'm calling a ten-minute recess so everyone can cool off."

WHEN WASHBURN RESUMED, his was once again the voice of sweet reason. He produced a stack of documents received from the FBI and gave them to Riggio on the stand. "Special Agent Riggio. Using these business records, did you have an opportunity to investigate the fragmentation grenades that you discovered in Mr. Nolan's apartment?"

"Yes."

"And what did you discover?"

"These particular grenades were produced in late two thousand two—if you want the stocking and serial numbers, I've got them, but—"

"That won't be necessary. Go ahead."

"And they were shipped to Iraq in the early weeks after the invasion."

"Do you know if they were delivered to Mr. Scholler's patrol?"

"No."

"No, you don't know, or no, they weren't?"

"They were delivered as part of a consignment to Allstrong Security in Iraq."

"Is there any evidence that Mr. Scholler at any time had possession of these grenades, or shipped them back, by whatever means, to the United States?"

"No."

"Special Agent Riggio, have you any witnesses that reported seeing these grenades in Mr. Scholler's possession at any time?"

"No."

Even though he'd gotten the right answer on the last several questions, Washburn knew it wasn't much. But it was probably all he was going to get. He smiled at the witness. "Thank you," he said. "No further questions."

[26]

BY THE FOLLOWING TUESDAY AFTERNOON, the weather had turned. A violent early-season storm toppled trees and flooded many of the low-lying streets around the courthouse, playing enough havoc with the morning's traffic patterns that court couldn't be called into session until nearly eleven o'clock, and then only to adjourn almost immediately for an early lunch.

In the previous two trial days, Washburn hadn't had much to say to the witnesses Mills called. The other FBI agent, Jacob Freed, provided pretty much the same testimony as his partner, Marcia Riggio. Washburn hammered a bit at the provenance of the frag grenades again, at the lack of real investigation into the lives and motives of possible other suspects in both the Khalil and Nolan murders after they'd identified Evan as their main person of interest. But he knew that he'd inflicted little if any damage to the prosecution's case—the fact, and Washburn hated to admit it, was that the FBI and Spinoza had coordinated very well, and had fashioned an evidentiary chain that was pretty damn compelling. In the end, Washburn just wanted to get Freed off the stand as quickly as possible, although he still took the better part of half a day.

Likewise, David Saldar, the locksmith, came to the stand and, by far the most nervous and uncomfortable witness to date, gave his testimony without any surprises. He was talking about an unarguable point in any event—Evan Scholler had done exactly what Saldar was saying he'd done. He'd lied to a friend, he'd used the police uniform to buttress his credibility, he'd let himself into a home that was not his. It wasn't exactly a highwater mark for the defense, but Washburn couldn't do anything about that either.

Mills's final witness, who'd taken up most of yesterday's—Monday's—time, had been Tara. In spite of clearly conveying to the jury that she was involved with Evan, she not only reaffirmed the fact that Nolan had told her he was concerned and worried about Evan's break-in, but she also provided the crucial testimony of the overt threat to Nolan's life that Evan had made at the Old Town Traven.

Coming from a woman who so obviously did not want to hurt the defendant, Tara's testimony seemed to resonate with the jury in an especially powerful way. And Washburn, try as he might, couldn't get a handle on what he could cross-examine her about—that she hadn't believed Nolan's assertion about Evan planting the weapons in his house? That Evan hadn't really meant what he'd said about killing his rival? Neither of those opinions would be admissible, since that's all they would have been—the opinions of a woman, the jury would feel, who would certainly lie if lying would help her lover's defense.

Now the prosecution had rested and Washburn would get his chance to present an affirmative defense. But in the absence of a client who could even deny that he'd committed the crime, in the absence of an alternative suspect, and with the plethora of motive and opportunity weighing in against Evan, he knew that this might be the legal challenge of his entire career. He didn't have much, and what he did have was dubious at best.

The first order of business was to try to get the jury, to the extent it was going to be possible at all, into Evan's camp. Reminding himself that he only needed one juror, he settled on a woman in the back row named Maggie Ellersby, who was about the same age, and pretty much had the same suburban-housewife look, as Evan's mother, Eileen. More than that, during jury selection she'd revealed that she had two sons of her own; that she was opposed to the war in Iraq, although she supported the troops there. She might have a liberal streak, which in turn might extend to perceiving Evan as some kind of a victim of something, and hence not completely culpable. Beyond that, she had been married to the same man for thirty years, and so might in her heart be rooting for Tara and Evan to put this problem behind them and have a life together. All of this, of course, was extremely nebulous, but it gave Washburn hope to have a "litmus juror" to whom he could target his defense.

"Your Honor," Washburn said as a fresh squall of rain tattooed the courtroom's windows, "the defense calls Anthony Onofrio."

"MR. ONOFRIO, you knew the defendant, Evan Scholler, in Iraq, did you not?"

Washburn wanted Onofrio for a variety of reasons, not the least of which because he exuded such an appealing "regular guy" quality. This was an inherently friendly man who worked with his crew on California's roads. He had some, but not too much, education. Good-looking in a casual way, he might be able to bring Mrs. Ellersby, for example, along in his regard for Evan Scholler.

"Yes, I did. He was my squadron leader."

Over the next hour, Washburn led Onofrio over the same ground they'd covered during the PTSD hearing before jury selection. Mills objected to the same things she'd objected to at that time—that Onofrio wasn't even in the U.S. at the time of the murder and therefore his testimony couldn't possibly be relevant—but Washburn argued again that Onofrio's testimony was foundational to Evan's head injuries, which so far hadn't even made it into the record. Even without mention of PTSD, those head injuries were certainly relevant to his blackouts, and these, in turn, Washburn argued, and Tollson agreed, could be a core issue for the defense.

The gallery grew hushed as Onofrio began describing the firefight at Masbah, concluding with the observation, ". . . we could have gotten out, but two of our men had already been hit, and Evan wasn't going to leave without them."

"So what did he do?"

"He led a couple of the other guys up to the first Humvee and pulled out the driver of that vehicle, then carried him back to our car. Then they went back for the gunner."

"And was Lieutenant Scholler under fire at this time?"

"A lot of fire, sir. It was pretty hot, coming from all over."

"All right." Having established Evan's bravery as well as his concern for his men, Washburn let Onofrio get to the end of the Masbah story without further interruption. Washburn was happy to see that Mrs. Ellersby needed to dab at her eyes with a Kleenex several times during the recitation. When Onofrio finished, Evan bleeding profusely from the head and surrounded by his dead comrades, several other jurors were having similar reactions.

Washburn stood still for several seconds, moved as the jurors had been by the story. Then he turned the witness over to the prosecution.

THE LAST TIME Mills had cross-examined Onofrio, during the 402 hearing on PTSD, she'd hit pay dirt with questions regarding Evan's alcohol use in the war zone. Accordingly, she wasted no time broaching the topic again as soon as she was in front of the witness.

"Mr. Onofrio, did you personally witness Defendant drinking alcohol in Iraq?"

But this time, Washburn was ready for her. "Objection. Irrelevant."

"Sustained."

Mills was halfway back to repeating her question when she stopped herself in almost a double-take fashion. "Your Honor," she said, "with respect, Mr. Washburn made a similar objection during our four-oh-two hearing in this matter, and at that time you overruled him."

Tollson removed his glasses, leaned over the bench. "Yes, I did, Counselor. At that time, the question of Defendant's alcohol use, or not, was germane to the issues involved in that hearing. Here, unless you can show me that Defendant's alcohol use, or not, in Iraq in some way refutes Mr. Onofrio's testimony, or relates directly to the crime with which Defendant is charged, I'm not going to allow it. It's irrelevant, as Mr. Washburn has noted."

Mills stood flatfooted, then walked back to her table, checked her binder, turned a page or two of it, and looked back up. "All right, then." Determined not to let the jury see she'd been caught off balance, Mills smiled through clenched teeth. "Well, then, thank you, Your Honor," she said. "I'll tie this up and we'll come back to it later."

DENIED HIS USE of PTSD, Washburn's best hope was still some kind of a medical defense. If the jury didn't buy the fact that Evan had suffered a

severe and extended blackout, then he was left with no defense whatso-
ever, except that he was lying. So, to that end, over the past weekend
Washburn had spent several hours going over his next witness's testimony.
He could only hope that it was going to be enough.

"Dr. Bromley," he began. "What kind of doctor are you?"

"I'm a neurologist at Stanford Medical Center and at the Palo Alto
Veterans Center."

"A brain doctor, is that right?"

In his mid-fifties, though he looked ten years younger, Bromley dressed
impeccably. With a strong jaw, a prominent nose, fathomless eyes, and a
short, well-kept Afro, he exuded a steely confidence. Now he allowed a
breath of a smile to grace his features as he nodded. "That's the lay term,
yes."

"Doctor, did you know Mr. Scholler before his arrest?"

"Yes. He was a patient of mine at the Veterans Center after he was re-
leased from Walter Reed."

"According to your understanding, Doctor, what was his situation at
Walter Reed?"

"He was admitted there in September of the previous year. When he
arrived, he was still in an unconscious state from injuries sustained overseas. Doctors had already performed a craniectomy—removal of a section
of skull to allow the brain to swell—and his condition was poor. They
thought it highly likely he would die. Second prize was that he would
survive, but be a vegetable."

Washburn noticed several of the jurors flinch at this brutally matter-of-
fact account. He went on. "And when you first saw him here in California? When was that, by the way?"

"Mid-March, nine months after he was wounded. He had made,
frankly, a nearly miraculous recovery."

"In what sense?"

"In almost every sense imaginable. They'd replaced the disk of his
skull about three months before that, and already his speech patterns had
returned to almost normal. His memory still suffered small short-term
lapses, and specific words would evade him from time to time, but he
seemed to be improving in these areas with each test we administered. His
physical coordination was such that I had no problem recommending that

he go back to his work as a policeman, so long as his assignment was neither too strenuous nor stressful. In short, his was the most remarkable
recovery from traumatic brain injury that I've seen in my twenty years of
medical practice."

Washburn nodded, delighted that he had fastened upon Bromley. He'd
always been in the picture, of course, but the opportunities for Evan's
defense that involved PTSD had always seemed somehow sexier and more
compelling. Now, knowing what was going to come out, he started to
entertain a small ray of hope that a straightforward medical explanation
could produce approximately the same results as a PTSD defense. If he
could make his client any kind of a victim, he knew he still had a
chance.

"Doctor, did you have an opportunity to examine Mr. Scholler after he
was arrested?"

"Yes."

"How soon after?"

"A couple of days."

"And what was his condition at that time?"

"Well, mostly he was suffering from headaches. But he was also experiencing fairly severe disorientation as well as some speech aphasia. All of
this is, of course, consistent with trauma to the brain."

"But you have testified that the symptoms of his traumatic brain injury
had all but passed by a few months before that, isn't that so?"

"Yes."

"And yet these symptoms seem to have reappeared. Right?"

"Correct."

"And why is that?"

"Because of new trauma. At the time I saw him after his arrest, Mr.
Scholler had sustained several new head injuries."

"And how did he get those?"

"He told me he had been in a fight with Mr. Nolan."

"A fight with Mr. Nolan." Washburn half turned to bring the jury
along with him. He particularly noted Mrs. Ellersby, canted forward in
her chair, rapt. "Doctor, could a mere fight produce these kinds of debili-
tating injuries?"

"Of course. Any knock to the head can cause severe injuries, or even

death. And from examining Mr. Scholler's head, I found evidence—
bruises and broken skin—of several such blows. He also had a new concussion."

"Were these injuries enough to make a person pass out?"

"Certainly."

"At the time they were inflicted?"

"It could be then."

"Could it also be later?"

"Yes."

"Thank you." Washburn risked another quick look at the jurors. Everyone was still with him. "Now, Doctor," he continued, "in a case like
this one, where there had been previous traumatic brain injury within the
past year, might the ramifications of a beating such as the one endured by
Mr. Scholler be more serious than in someone without that history?"

"There's no might about it."

"So the symptoms of this kind of beating would be more serious than
they would be to someone who hadn't had the earlier trauma?"

"Well, not to say that a single beating couldn't be severe enough to
cause significant damage, and even death. But certainly the history of recent trauma would exacerbate any symptoms from the beating."

"And why is that?"

"Because the brain is an extremely complicated and slow-healing or-
gan." Bromley—bless him, Washburn thought—turned to address his
remarks directly to the jury. "It's common, in fact it's the norm, for a TBI
to cause neurological and physical problems forever. Other scenarios, particularly if they involve bleeding and clotting, can take two to four years
to clear up entirely. And even then, there may be scarring and other complications."

"What about blackouts?"

"Yes, of course, blackouts too. Although typically, medical profession-
als don't refer to them as blackouts. It's not a very specific term."

"Is there a specific medical term, Doctor?"

"Well, there is syncope"—he pronounced it sin-co-pee—"which is
more or less simple fainting. Then there are seizures, both epileptic and
psychogenic, that is, nonepileptic. And finally there are alcoholic blackouts, where you have anterograde amnesia during or following a drinking

binge. All of these would probably be called some sort of blackout by a lay person, and all of them might be affected by TBI."

"And what happens during any of these blackouts?"

"Either one or both of two things: temporary loss of either consciousness or memory."

"And how long can a blackout last?"

"Well, again, that depends. In some sense, lay people might call a coma a blackout, and they've been known to last a decade or more. Most, like fainting or epileptic seizures, last no more than ten minutes."

And suddenly, with this answer from Dr. Bromley, Washburn felt a sickening hollowness in his stomach so acute that he thought for a moment that he might have a period of syncope himself. He had known of the weakness of this blackout information, of course, for the better part of the year, and had gone over it again with Bromley over the past weekend, intent on getting this medical evidence into the record.

Struggling to get to his next point, all at once he saw this testimony now for what it was, and it was smoke. He could sense that it wasn't going to work. His idea had been to establish that Evan's loss of consciousness was a possible, and even common, result of his TBI, tying everything neatly back to Iraq, and the good soldier sympathy vote from Mrs. Ellersby. After the beating Evan had taken on that night, Washburn had assumed that he'd be able to supply at least a colorable argument that Evan's coming testimony held water.

And now, with a great and terrible clarity, he could see it just wasn't going to fly. The fact that Evan might have blacked out at some point was no proof that he actually had spent any or all of that time in an unconscious state. In fact, given his blood alcohol level at the time of his arrest, it was indisputable that he'd had at least flashes of consciousness during that time when he'd drunk himself into oblivion. Washburn's thought that he could slip this past the jury or that it would get lost in a wave of sympathy was just wishful thinking. He had believed it might work because he needed it to work to have any hope of winning this case.

Washburn still had Bromley's testimony about much of what Evan had been through because of his traumatic brain injury. He might go on to suffer effects from that for the remainder of his life. A few of the jurors initially might still give Evan the benefit of the doubt because they took pity on his situation. But Bromley's testimony offered nothing at all in the way of proof that Evan had been incompetent or unable to commit the murder of Ron Nolan. And eventually, this simple fact was very likely to convict his client. He'd been deluding himself to think otherwise.

He walked to his table and took a sip of water. Turning, he came back to his place in the center of the courtroom. Still, he hesitated.

"Mr. Washburn," Tollson asked with some concern, "is everything all right? Would you like to take a recess?"

"No, Your Honor. Thank you." Then he executed his trademark bow, thanked Bromley, and turned him over to Mills.

The prosecutor got up and advanced to her place with an enthusiasm that told Washburn that she hadn't missed the issue. And indeed, her first question honed in on it. "Doctor, with regard to these blackouts you were discussing. You said they usually lasted a few minutes, is that right?"

"Normally, yes, although it can vary."

"So you said. So your testimony is that a blackout can last for a few days, is that right?"

"Well, again, the terminology of blackout isn't precise. If we're talking about fainting or a seizure, I'd say no. They don't last more than ten minutes usually. True unconsciousness, however, can of course extend indefinitely, though I would hesitate to call that a blackout."

"So is there any way that you can assure the jury that Defendant in fact suffered any kind of blackout at all on the night of the beating?"

"No, I can't say that."

Mills threw a plainly gloating look over to the jury, then came back to Bromley. "Thank you, Doctor. That's all."

"WAS IT just me," Evan asked, "or did not that go very well?"

They were in the holding area behind the courtroom again, for the recess. In a gesture that Washburn took to be one of sympathy, the bailiff had delivered paper cups filled with fresh, hot coffee for both him and his client. Normally, this wasn't allowed since a suspect with a cup of hot coffee was a suspect who could attack people with it, but today for some reason—the change in the weather? the pathetic Bromley testimony?— the bailiff had offered and both men had jumped at the chance.

Washburn, of course, downplayed the problem. Shrugging, he said, "Between Onofrio and Bromley we got in a whole lot of what you've been through. Somebody on that jury is going to care, you watch." He sipped at the brew. The bravado he'd put in his answer wasn't just to buff up his own self-image. Evan was going on the stand next, and Washburn needed him to project both relaxation and confidence while he was up there. He was going to get to tell his story at last and, more importantly, sell it to the jury.

But it wasn't much of a story, and both men seemed to understand that.

"Don't take this badly." Unruffled, collected, Washburn leaned back against the wall and crossed one leg over the other. "I still think we've got a decent shot, but I also think the Court would look favorably on an offer to plead."

Evan turned his head and fixed Washburn with a glare. "We've been through that."

"Yes, we have. And now you're going to tell the jury that you didn't kill Nolan."

"That's right."

"Any idea who did? Because I don't have one."

"It wasn't me."

"Because you don't remember doing it?"

"Everett. Listen. I can't believe I beat him with a poker, then shot him in the head, and have no memory of it. I would remember that."

Washburn sighed. "Well, as you say, we've been all through it. But we could say you went back to talk to him after the fight and he attacked you. You were weak from the earlier beating and you had no choice but to grab the poker . . ."

Evan was holding up his hand. ". . . and execute him with a point-blank shot to the head. I didn't do that. That is not who I am."

"Yes, and that may not be the point." He tipped up his coffee and swallowed. "There's absolutely nothing about those days that you remember?"

"You don't think I've tried? You don't think I want to remember any little thing?"

"Maybe you were drunk the whole time?" Washburn rubbed his palms on his pants legs. "I want you to think about this carefully, Evan. If that's what happened, at least that gives the jurors something more to think about."

"If I change my story now, then I'm a liar before, though, right?"

"No. If you just remembered, it's come back to you in the stress of the trial."

"Damn conveniently. They'll see through that in a heartbeat."

"Okay. Suppose it happened that you were home the whole time, suffering from the beating, drinking to kill the pain. You never left the apartment."

"And how does that help me? They'd still have to believe me."

"No." Washburn shook his head. "*They* don't have to believe you. *One of them* has to believe you. It's a lot better to say 'I didn't do it' than 'I don't remember, but I probably didn't do it.' There's a real difference there."

Evan took a couple of breaths. "I thought it was about the evidence. Not what I say. What the evidence says."

"That's the problem," Washburn said. "The evidence, my friend, makes a very good case that you did it." Just at that moment, the bailiff appeared, and Washburn punched his client on the thigh. "Drink your coffee," he said. "We're up."

[27]

AFTER THE MONTHS OF BUILDUP, the endless coaching and strategy sessions, the arguments, disagreements, accords, and prognostications, Evan Scholler's time on the witness stand was really quite brief. Washburn saw no point in having his client go over again all of the reasons he might have had to loathe the victim. That had all been well-established by earlier witnesses. There were really only a couple of lines of inquiry that Washburn thought stood any chance of traction with the jury, if only because they provided an alternative theory to the case, and he got right to them.

"Evan," he said, "why did you break into Mr. Nolan's home?"

"First, let me say that that was wrong. There's no excuse, I shouldn't have done that. I should have advised the homicide detail of my suspicions about Mr. Nolan."

Mills got to her feet. "Your Honor, nonresponsive."

"Sustained." Tollson's glare went from Washburn over to Evan. He spoke to the defendant. "Mr. Scholler. Please only answer the questions that the attorneys put to you. You're not here to make speeches."

"Yes, Your Honor. Sorry."

"All right, Mr. Washburn, go ahead, and carefully, please."

Washburn posed the question again, and Evan responded. "Because I had found out about the Khalil murders from the paper, and then more about them from Lieutenant Spinoza. I had gone on a mission with Mr. Nolan when we were in Baghdad together, and he'd used frag grenades at that time. Then, knowing that Mr. Khalil was of Iraqi descent, and knowing what Mr. Nolan did for a living, it occurred to me that he might have had something to do with those murders."

"Why didn't you simply, as you say, go to homicide?"

"Because I might have been wrong, which would have made me look stupid both to the lieutenant and to Tara, and I couldn't have that."

"Why was that?"

"Well, one, I was a policeman myself. Two, I was hoping to reconnect with Tara."

"All right. So you broke into Mr. Nolan's home?"

"I did let myself in, yes."

"Trying to find evidence that Mr. Nolan had been involved in the Khalil murders?"

"That's right."

"Didn't you think that was a bit far-fetched?"

"Not at all. I'd seen Mr. Nolan kill other people."

Mills raised her voice. "Objection."

"Your Honor," Washburn responded. "Mr. Nolan was a security officer. Sometimes his job was to kill people. Mr. Scholler knew him in that setting in Iraq. There is nothing pejorative about it."

Tollson put his glasses back on. "Objection overruled."

"All right," Washburn continued. "Now, when you went into Mr. Nolan's home, Evan, did you find anything which in your opinion might have been connected to the Khalil murders?"

"Yes."

Evan ran through his actions and motivations in a straightforward manner—the frag grenades, touching the gun both in the backpack and in the bed's headboard, the computer files. As Washburn had coached him, he kept bringing his narrative back to the jury, and particularly—without being too obvious—to Mrs. Ellersby, three over from the left in the second row.

"So you copied the photographic computer file?"

"Yes."

"Presumably, now, you had your proof, or at least some possible proof, of a connection between Mr. Nolan and the Khalil murders. What did you do next?"

"Well, I didn't want to take away any of the proof, so that it would still be there when the FBI searched the house—"

Mills pushed her chair back with a resonant squeal and said under her breath, "Give me a break."

Tollson banged his gavel with some force. "If I thought you'd done that on purpose, Ms. Miille, I'd hold you in contempt right now. There will be no histrionics in this courtroom! You will live to regret the next outburst of any sort and I'm admonishing the jury to disregard your unprofessional comment." Then, to Evan, "Go ahead, Mr. Scholler."

Evan let out a long breath, for the moment apparently, and perhaps actually, unable to remember where he'd been in his testimony.

Washburn took advantage of the moment. "I'm sorry, Your Honor, my client seems to have blacked out for a second."

"Oh, Christ!" Mills whispered.

Bam! Bam!

"That's it, Ms. Miille, you're in contempt. We'll talk about what the sanction is going to be outside the presence of the jury." His mouth set in a hard line, Tollson pointed to both attorneys. "This ends here, I'm warning you. Mr. Washburn, does your client need a minute to compose himself?"

"Evan?" Washburn asked. "Are you all right?"

"Fine."

"All right," Tollson said, "let's have the reporter read back the last question, please."

The question got Evan back to where he was saying that he didn't want to take away any of the proof, so that the FBI would find it when they searched the house. "So I decided to make a copy of the photo file on the computer that held what I was sure was a picture of the Khalils' house. So I took one of the diskettes and made the copy and brought it home."

"Now, wait a minute. You were a policeman and you had what you considered strong evidence of a murder, and yet you didn't contact homicide?"

"Right, I didn't."

"And why was that?"

"Because I couldn't tell them what I'd found without admitting I got it in an illegal search. None of it would have been admissible in court."

"So what did you do?"

"I mailed the diskette to the FBI, who I heard were investigating the Khalil murders."

"And then what happened?"

"And then Mr. Nolan came home and must have realized that somebody had been in his house."

"In fact, he must have realized it was you, Evan. Isn't that so?"

"Well, the way it worked out. Yes, apparently. So he turned it all around to make it look like it was me who'd planted the evidence at his place and also, incidentally, killed the Khalils."

Washburn knew this was all inadmissible speculation but was betting that Mills, still reeling from the contempt citation and the reaming she had taken in front of the jury, would be keeping a low profile, at least for a while. He pressed on. "And did you, in fact, kill the Khalils?"

"No, I did not."

"Were you ever charged with killing the Khalils?"

"No."

"Did you at any time send fragmentation grenades or any other type of arms, ammunition, or ordnance from Iraq to the United States?"

"No, I did not."

"At any time, did anyone ever present you with any evidence that you had tried to send these items from Iraq to the United States?"

"No."

"Now, when you heard that Mr. Nolan had turned the tables on you and reported to the FBI, what was your reaction?"

"I was furious. I wanted to confront him and fight him."

"You did not want to kill him?"

"That never entered my mind. I was mad. I wanted to hit him."

"With brass knuckles?"

"I just happened to have them with me that night, and when I got there, I thought I might need them. Mr. Nolan had a great deal of training in hand-to-hand combat, more than me, and I wanted to level the playing field."

"So, by fighting him, did you want to stop him from telling his story to the FBI?"

"No. It was too late for that. He'd already done it." This was another critical point related to Evan's alleged motive. There would be no point in killing Nolan to stop him from turning over evidence to the authorities if that had already happened, which it had.

"So let me get this straight, Evan. On the evening of June third, two thousand four, Tara Wheatley told you that she had ended her relationship with Mr. Nolan and wanted to pursue one with you, is that correct?"

"Yes."

"And on that same night, you learned that Mr. Nolan had already supplied the FBI with evidence that supposedly connected you to the Khalil murders, right?"

"Right."

Washburn threw an open glance at the jury. Could his point be more plain? But it was, of course, necessary to nail it down in all its particulars so there could be no misunderstanding at all. "In other words, Evan," he said, "did you have any motive to kill Ron Nolan on account of your relationship with Ms. Wheatley?"

"No, I did not."

"And did you have any motive to kill Mr. Nolan to prevent him from talking to the FBI?"

"No. He'd already done that."

"So you had no motive to kill Mr. Nolan, is that right?"

"I had no reason to kill him."

Washburn cast one last sidelong glance at the jury box, fixed on Mrs. Ellersby for a second, and was pleased to note that she was nodding soberly, as if newly convinced of something. Evan's testimony had, he was sure, made a strong impression on her. And if on her, then maybe on one or more of the others.

MILLS ROSE SLOWLY from her table, her brow creased, her face set in an expression of deep concern. She came and stood in her spot and brought her right hand to the side of her face, then let it down. "Mr. Scholler, as you've testified, on June third, two thousand four, you went up to Mr. Nolan's townhome with the intention of fighting him, and then you did in fact engage in a fight with him, am I right so far?"

"Yes."

"What did you do after that fight ended?"

"I don't remember."

"You don't remember? Did you black out?"

"I don't remember."

"So it is not your testimony that you suffered a blackout, after all. Is it?"

"No. Whether I did or not, I don't remember."

"You suffered quite a beating yourself in this altercation, did you not?"

"Yes."

"And yet, with all the problems you've had, particularly with traumatic brain injury, you did not seek medical help?"

"Apparently not, but I don't remember."

Washburn raised a hand at his desk. "Your Honor, objection. Badgering. If he doesn't remember anything, it follows that he doesn't remember particulars."

This satisfied Tollson, and he nodded. "Sustained."

Mills pursed her lips and paused to phrase her question so it came at things from a slightly different angle. "Mr. Scholler," she said finally, "what is your first memory after you sustained your injuries on Wednesday night at the hands of Mr. Nolan?"

"I remember waking up in a hospital bed, I think it was the Saturday night."

"So Wednesday night through Saturday night is a complete blank, is that right?"

"That's right."

"All right." Mills paused for another second or two, and then—just like that!—her posture changed. Her back straightened perceptibly, a wisp of a grim smile tugged at the corners of her mouth. Obviously, she had reached some decision, as though she'd done everything in her power to get to this point, and now the time had come to commit irrevocably to her strategy. "So now, Mr. Scholler, as you are sitting here in front of me and the members of this jury, maybe you killed Mr. Nolan and maybe you didn't. You just don't remember. Is that right?"

Evan sat with the question for a long moment.

"Mr. Scholler," she prompted him. "It's a yes or no question. Can you tell me that you did not kill Mr. Nolan?"

Evan's eyes went to Washburn, who returned his gaze impassively. Coming back to face his prosecutor, Evan leveled his gaze at Mills. "I don't remember," he said at last.

[28]

AT EIGHT-THIRTY THE NEXT MORNING, Mary Patricia Whelan-Miille sat on the corner of her desk in her small office. Behind her, outside the window, the freak storm was into its second day and showing no signs of clearing. In the parking lot just outside, the cold and heavy rain slanted nearly horizontal in gusting sheets. In front of Mills, her secretary, Felice Brinkley, sat with a notepad on a folding chair that she'd set up by the door.

Felice was a no-nonsense woman who wore minimal makeup and had let her hair go almost completely gray. Mills thought she'd done this as a defense against being hit on by guys—with her finely pored skin, sculpted cheeks, and a hooded, sensuous cast to her eyes, and even with the gray hair and lack of fuss, she was a strikingly attractive woman. The curvaceous figure didn't hurt either.

Thirty-six years old, she was the mother of two boys and a girl, all under twelve. Mills also believed that Felice was among the smartest people she'd ever met and constantly tried to persuade her to take the LSATs and become a lawyer herself, but Felice would have none of it—perhaps in itself, Mills had to admit, a testament to her intelligence. The way it was now, Felice was explaining for the fiftieth time, she could come in early, work her regular hours, skip lunch, and be home just about in time to be there for the kids when they got home from school. Her husband, John, worked a swing shift in maintenance for the city for the pay differential, so one of them was always there for the kids. "That's just our priority."

"But with the extra money, and there'd be a lot more of it, John wouldn't have to work at all if you got in with a high-ticket firm, which you would," Mills replied.

"Sure. But I'd have to work twenty-hour days. And how would that make him feel, not working? He wants to work. Or if I made more money than him? I don't necessarily think that's a recipe for a happy marriage."

"But it's okay for him to make more money than you?"

"He doesn't."

"But if he did, that would be okay?"

"Sure. But it would also be okay if I made more than him, if that's just the way our lives work out. But why should I go for a new job that I wouldn't like as much and would keep me away from my kids just for the money?"

"Because money is what makes you safe, Felice." She held up an admonitory finger. "Okay, and I know you don't want to think about this, but what if he leaves you?"

"Who, John?" She laughed. "John is never going to leave me."

"How can you be sure of that? He's a man, isn't he?"

Felice had heard all of this before, and found it mildly amusing. Her poor, sad, driven boss who worked impossible hours and was never in a stable relationship trying to tell Felice how to have a more secure and happy life—there was something inherently funny, if also somewhat pathetic, about the situation. "All men don't leave," Felice said. "Both the kids' grandfathers are still around, for example, and married to the grandmothers. It happens. In fact, in both of our families, John's and mine, it's kind of a tradition." She brushed her hair back from her forehead, opened the notepad on her lap, snapped her ballpoint a couple of times, checked her watch. "Now, how about you show me this closing argument?"

Suddenly wide-eyed, bushwhacked by the time, Mills boosted herself off her desk. "Oh, God, is it really eight-thirty already? We've got to . . ."

Felice raised her hand. "You've got to just calm down, MP, and tell the story. That's all you've got to do. Slow and easy."

"You're right." Mills blew a strand of her hair away from her mouth. "You're right."

"Yes, I am." Felice clicked her pen again. "Okay, hit it."

"LADIES AND GENTLEMEN of the jury." Mills held her legal pad with her notes as a prop, although she knew pretty much exactly what she was going to say. "At the beginning of this trial, I told you that the evidence would prove to you beyond a reasonable doubt that Defendant killed Ron Nolan with premeditation and malice aforethought. I'd like to take a last few minutes of your time now to talk about the law and explain how the evidence has done exactly that."

For the next forty-five minutes, she focused on the elements of murder to help the jury wade through the verbose and sometimes arcane instructions that the judge would give them at the end of the case. Then she got to the core of the argument.

"So now I've explained what murder is. We've talked a little about what the legal definition of premeditation is, and I hope my comments have helped you understand what precisely the law requires be proved before the defendant may be found guilty. Now I'd like to talk to you about the evidence, the specifics of the testimony in this case, the exhibits, the reasonable inferences to be drawn from that testimony and from those exhibits that show the defendant's conduct meets the definition of first-degree murder.

"And what is that evidence? First, Mr. Nolan and Defendant were rivals for the attention of the same woman, Tara Wheatley. The defense would have you believe that on the night of Defendant's attack on Mr. Nolan—one that he freely admits, by the way—Ms. Wheatley, after a six-month relationship with Mr. Nolan, decided to suddenly change her allegiance and affections in favor of Defendant, and that because of this shift, Defendant no longer had a motive to want to kill Mr. Nolan. I submit to you that this is simply untrue."

"Wait a minute," Felice said. "Not 'untrue.' Be more earthy. Why not, 'Does this make any sense to you?' "

Mills nodded. "Better." She made a note, then resumed her pacing and her argument. "The defense is telling you that a man who lost his girlfriend to another man, who believes that that man lied and cheated and betrayed him, who knows that the man has enjoyed an intimate relationship with the defendant's girlfriend while he was laid up in the hospital, is suddenly told by the girlfriend that she intends to come back to him, and now everything is okay. No bitterness. No animosity. No hate. That's what the defense is selling. I hope you're not buying.

"First of all, because your common sense tells you that's nonsense.

Blood feuds don't end in a minute. Long-held hates don't vanish over-night, and the defendant must have known that Ms. Wheatley, who had already changed her mind once, could just as easily change it again tomor-row and prefer Nolan to him. But more to the point, all the evidence shows that as a simple fact, the defendant still did hate Ron Nolan.

"After he talked to Tara, he armed himself with a deadly weapon—and as you've heard from the evidence, those brass knuckles are a deadly weapon—and he went to Ron Nolan's place for the express purpose of beating him. Does that sound to you like someone who had given up hard feelings, someone who had forgiven his enemy, someone who did not still want revenge and to inflict pain? Of course not. That's just nonsense." She stopped by the window. "Is that enough on that?"

Felice nodded. "I think so. You don't want to beat it to death. Just move along."

Pacing again, Mills continued. "While I'm discussing motive, let me just say that motive alone is not . . ."

"No," Felice said. "The weight of motive evidence will be in the jury instructions. You don't have to go there."

With a nod, Mills started in again. "The defense would also have you believe that the second equally compelling motive—that Defendant wanted to stop Mr. Nolan from producing more evidence to connect him to the Khalil slayings—was moot because Mr. Nolan had already pro-duced such evidence. This is a spurious argument." She stopped. "Is *spuri-ous* okay?"

Felice considered for a second. "Maybe a little fancy."

"How about *specious*?"

"Maybe a lot fancy." The paralegal rolled her eyes. "How about going for the blue-collar vote and using *phony*."

"*Fake.*"

"*False.*"

Mills snapped her fingers. "That's it. *False.*" She went back to her for-mal voice. "This is a false argument because first, Defendant may well have believed that Mr. Nolan had more evidence. But more to the point, none of what Mr. Nolan had told the FBI about the Khalil evidence could be used against Mr. Scholler if Mr. Nolan was dead. If there's one thing you've learned in this trial, it's that we need to produce live witnesses to give testimony. I suggest to you that the defendant had an even greater motive to kill Mr. Nolan once it was clear that Nolan had turned him in and was prepared to cooperate as a witness against him.

"If the defendant did kill the Khalils, adding one more murder to the list to protect him from being caught wouldn't have been a big deal."

"Whoa up," Felice said. "You better be ready. Washburn's gonna light up on that one."

"I know. But I'm allowed to argue, and I want the jury to hear it."

"The judge won't let it in."

"No, probably not. But I'll talk fast and get as much of it in as I can before they shut me down."

"So long as you know."

"I know. Okay, moving on." Mills consulted her notes briefly. "So let's get down to what actually happened, what the undisputed evidence proves happened. Arming himself with brass knuckles, and admitting to Tara Wheatley that he was going to quote put an end to this unquote, Defendant drove to Mr. Nolan's house and attacked him. A fight ensued, and both men were injured. Three days later, a gun bearing Defendant's fingerprints was found on the bed in Mr. Nolan's bedroom, near to where Mr. Nolan lay on the floor with a fatal gunshot wound to the head from the same caliber weapon.

"Exactly what happened on the night of that fight? The only person in this courtroom who could tell us that claims that he has no memory of that time. No memory at all. And this in spite of his own doctor's testimony that blackouts last no more than ten minutes. That leaves a lot of conscious time for which Defendant has no explanation, and no memory. The evidence you've heard, and from his own witness, does not support his testimony.

"So with a lack of absolute certainty, we are left with the task of asking ourselves what is the most reasonable explanation for the facts in evidence. Is it more reasonable to assume that Defendant finished his fight with Mr. Nolan and then, inebriated and with a concussion, drove himself to his apartment, where he continued to drink for the next two days, while some unidentified third party, for some inexplicable reason—"

"Maybe *unexplained*."

"—for some unexplained reason, entered Mr. Nolan's home, beat him with a fireplace poker, and then shot him?

"Or is it more reasonable to assume that, armed with his set of brass knuckles, Defendant got the better of Mr. Nolan in their fight and, when he had finished that exercise, simply shot him in the head with a handgun he found at the scene? Then, ladies and gentlemen, and only then, after he had murdered Mr. Nolan in cold blood, did he drive himself home and proceed to drink himself into an alcoholic stupor." Mills stopped, locked eyes with Felice, and shook her head. "I hate this guy," she said.

"It's not coming across," her paralegal answered. "It's very clean and objective. I buy it completely."

"Not too short?"

"Not for me."

Mills glanced up at the wall clock. "Almost showtime. Imagine if I actually pull off beating Washburn."

"Don't get ahead of yourself. Just take it a sentence at a time." Felice stood up and gave her boss a quick hug. "You feel ready?"

"As I'll ever be."

"Okay," Felice said. "Go get 'em."

[29]

By late Friday afternoon, the tension was thick in the jury room. Ryan Cannoe, the foreman, had just counted the fifteenth ballot and the vote—from an original of eight to four to convict—now stood at eleven to one.

"Maggie," he said to Mrs. Ellersby, "we've got another forty-five minutes and then we're going to have to come back after a very long weekend. Now, I'm not trying to coerce any kind of a different vote from you, but if you're sure you won't budge, and you're never going to budge, maybe we should just send out the word that we're hung and leave it at that."

This brought a burst of invective from several of the other jurors. "After all the time we've put in on this!" "No way!" "That's bullshit!" "The guy's guilty as sin and we all know it."

"Maybe we don't all know it," Ellersby replied. The day—in fact, the whole jury experience—had been its own trial for her, especially since this morning when the last two defections from her camp had crossed over, leaving her as the lone vote to acquit.

"So that's your final decision, Maggie?" Cannoe asked again. "You really don't think he did it?"

"Not exactly that," she said. "I think he might have done it, as I've said all along. I just can't be sure in my heart that it's first-degree murder. If he went there to beat Nolan up and he died by mistake, that's second-degree."

Cannoe kept his patience. "Except he didn't die from the beating."

"No. I know that. Things got out of hand."

Juror #2, Sue Whitson, a woman of Ellersby's age who'd been an early voter for acquittal, now joined the argument. "Maggie, I'd be with you except that in the end, he put the gun up to the man's head and shot him. How do you explain that except to say that at some time, Mr. Scholler decided to kill him? And that's murder one."

"The point," Cannoe added, "is that you believe Scholler did it, don't you? Never mind all the legal distinctions. He pulled the trigger, right?"

Ellersby sighed and whispered, "I don't see how he didn't, but I don't know if they proved he did."

"It's not absolute proof, Maggie," Sue said. "It's proof beyond a reasonable doubt. And they've done that."

"You admit it yourself," Cannoe said. "You just said you don't see how he didn't do it."

"I know."

"Well, then . . ."

"Well, then, I just keep coming back to what Mr. Washburn said in his closing statement. That they could have come up with any number of other defenses that seemed to make more sense. Self-defense, for example, or heat of passion, or simply saying no, he didn't do it. But instead they went with the truth, which he admitted was maybe harder to believe . . ."

Sue reached out and put a hand on Maggie's arm. She spoke with a surprising gentleness. "Maybe because it wasn't, in fact, true, Maggie. Maybe Washburn's just playing on our gullibility, figuring we'll want to believe that this young man, Evan, who'd had such a terrible time in Iraq, that somehow his injuries there are to blame for the fact that he can't say he didn't kill Nolan. If it wasn't for all the Iraq stuff, would you have any doubt about what really happened? Would his story have made any sense at all? That's what I finally came to see. It just doesn't. I wish it did, but it doesn't."

"He came to beat him up," Cannoe said, "and wound up staying to kill him. If that's not what you see, Maggie, and you don't think you can ever say otherwise, I'll call for the bailiff and tell him we're hung. You want me to do that?"

Ellersby looked around the table at all of her intelligent, well-meaning fellow citizens. None of them cold-blooded, none out for vengeance. All of them had given nearly a month out of their lives to see that justice was done, that the system worked. And for her part, she knew that she had been irrationally swayed by the power of Washburn's simple argument in closing that he was too smart and too experienced to ever allow a ridiculous defense like Evan's "I don't remember" to be the centerpiece of his case, except that it was the truth.

That's why they had gone with that defense, because it was the truth.

And Maggie Ellersby's mind's eye could picture Evan passed out in his apartment, not from alcohol, but from his brain injury—not in a blackout but in a true state of unconsciousness, knocked out from the beating he'd taken.

But there was no evidence that that was what had happened. None at all. And what if Washburn, as another one of her colleagues on the jury had pointed out early on, was nothing more than a man who was paid to tell lies on behalf of his clients? That's what all lawyers were, right? She flashed on the O. J. Simpson case, the Dan White "Twinkie Defense" case in San Francisco. If she was the lone holdout, and her vote to acquit wasn't based on any evidence she could name, how would she be able to explain herself to her husband and her friends?

How could she live with herself?

"Maggie?" Sue softly queezed her arm again.

"Do you want me to call the bailiff?" Cannoe asked.

Ellersby looked up to the ceiling, said a quick prayer for Evan Scholler's soul, and brought her eyes back down to the table. "No," she said. "I think we need to do one more ballot."

PART FOUR
[2007]

[30]

DISMAS HARDY'S WINDSHIELD WIPERS couldn't keep up with the downpour. They thwacked as fast as they could go, but this latest in a series of March squalls reduced his visibility to near zero. He could barely make out the first gate until he was at it. He loved his little two-seater Honda convertible with the top down in the summer and fall, but it wasn't made for this kind of weather. The plastic back window had long since gone opaque and even with the defrost fan blasting, the inside surfaces of the door windows were fogged over too. He pushed the button to lower his driver's window so he could present his identification to the guard and the rain misted in over his face.

Behind him, someone honked, then honked again. His rearview mirror was useless; he couldn't see his side mirrors, either, through the condensation on the windows. The rain pounded down on the cloth roof. He was inside a drum. Blinded, cocooned, he had to lower his window another few inches so he and the guard could see each other. Opening the window allowed more water in, enough to soak through the fabric of his suit in seconds.

Another blast from the impatient prick behind him. Hell, Hardy was already wet; he had half a mind to jump out and confront the guy, pull him out of his ride, deck him, dump him into the churning brown stream that ran over the road's gutters.

Instead, he squinted out to see the guard, flashed his driver's license, and spoke so he could be heard over the rain. "Dismas Hardy, to visit one of your inmates, Evan Scholler."

The guard, all but invisible through the downpour, spoke loudly, too, from his semienclosed space, "I'll have to see your ID better than that, please, sir. Sorry."

Seething, Hardy handed it out. Waited. He had time to decide that if the car behind him honked once more, he would go take the driver out, but then his wallet was back at the window and he heard a crisp "Thank you, sir. Ahead to your right after the next gate."

And he rolled up his window and let the clutch out simultaneously.

When he'd left the city a couple of hours ago, the sky had been light gray, but it hadn't even been drizzling. So he didn't have an umbrella or a raincoat with him.

After he found his spot in the parking lot, he turned off the motor and parked to wait out the worst of the squall. Regain some of his composure. Whoever had been behind him—some delivery guy maybe—didn't follow him to this lot. He thought it was probably just as well.

Composure was an issue. Even before the rain, Hardy's physical reaction to the scheduled visit to the prison had caught him off-guard. It had been a while since he'd had a client in prison, and he was out of practice. He kept having to reach for a breath, his palms were sweaty, an unaccustomed emptiness had hollowed out his lower rib cage. Closing his eyes, he leaned his head back and drew in a long breath through his mouth, which he then exhaled with a certain deliberation. He did it again. And again.

When at last the drumming of the rain stopped, he opened his eyes. Now, suddenly, it was just a light drizzle. Seizing the moment, he opened the car door and stepped out onto the asphalt.

HARDY HAD SEEN pictures of Evan Scholler in the newspapers, caught some glimpses of him on the TV news as the trial had gone on, so he thought he'd recognize him on sight. But when the guard first opened the door to the very small room to bring the inmate in, Hardy took a quick glance and decided that this couldn't be his man; the guard must have gotten it wrong and this shackled guy must be going to see another attorney in a different room.

For one thing, Evan was younger, just thirty-one now; this inmate looked at least forty. Further, in photos and on television, Evan was far better-looking, with a stronger chin, lighter hair, a better complexion, smaller in the gut and bigger across the shoulders. This guy here was big, casually buffed, physically intimidating, especially wearing a flat-affect expression that made his thin mouth look mean, even cruel. At first glance, this guy looked like a stone killer.

But the guard, checking the slip of paper in his hand, said, "Dismas Hardy?" A nod. "Here's your mope."

Evan took the slur without reaction. He stood at attention, but relaxed in the pose, seemingly uninterested in what, if anything, happened next. He looked Hardy up and down as he might a side of beef hanging in a cooler.

"You can take the shackles off," Hardy said.

For the obvious reason, guards in prison did not carry guns on their persons, so in any one-on-one encounter such as this delivery, shackles on prisoners tended to be the norm. Hardy knew several attorneys who visited their clients here and most of them were happy to let the shackles stay put. A shackled convict was a controllable convict, and with many of these inmates, you couldn't be too careful.

The guard hestitated for an instant, then shrugged. "Your call." With practiced precision, he unlocked the handcuffs from the chain that was threaded through the Levi's belt loops encircling Evan's waist. The cuffs still dangled from the waist chain at his sides.

Now, though, his hands free, Evan rubbed at his wrists.

The room was four feet wide by about seven feet long. A heavy, solid, industrial gray metal desk squatted against Hardy's right wall and stuck out two-thirds of the way across the space; in a pinch it could serve as a first-line barrier in the event of a surprise attack. Folding chairs sat on either side of it. Hardy had a door with a wire-glass window in it behind him and another door just like that facing him. The guard who'd let him in had cautioned him to stay on his side of the desk, "just to be safe." He'd also pointed out the small button low in the wall in Hardy's side that could be pressed in the event of any trouble.

Evan's guard said, "I'm right outside the whole time," and then that's where he was, closing the door behind him.

Hardy said, "You want to sit down?"

Evan thanked him and sat. He put his free hands on the table, still looking through Hardy, until suddenly he focused. "You got a cigarette?"

"Sorry, I don't smoke."

"I didn't either," Evan said. "What a joke."

"What is?"

"Not smoking. Watching what you eat. Staying in shape. All that stuff outside. Then you wind up in here." Maybe he felt as though he'd given too much of himself away. As a cop or a soldier or at the prison or somewhere else, Evan had gotten good at the thousand-yard stare, and he reverted into it. After a minute inside himself, he came back to Hardy. "So who are you?" he asked.

"Dismas Hardy, your new attorney."

"Don't take this wrong," Evan said, "but it took you long enough."

"Yeah, well, it was a little complicated."

A beat. "What's that first name again?"

"Dismas. The good thief. On Calvary? Next to Jesus?"

Evan shook his head. "Don't know him. Dismas, I mean. I've heard of Jesus."

Hardy looked him in the face. If this was humor, it was damn subtle and wouldn't be a bad thing. But he couldn't tell. He could see, however, that his initial impression of the man's age was off—close up he came as advertised, thirty-one. Hard years.

"What happened to Charlie Bowen?" Evan asked.

"He went missing last summer. He's the equivalent of dead as far as the Court's concerned. My firm inherited his files, including yours. I got them about four months ago."

"You a slow reader?"

Hardy's glance came up at his new client again. The guy wielded words efficiently, short punches inside. First a wave at humor, then a cutting jab. A lot going on behind unyielding eyes. Hardy figured he deserved the rebuke—four months while he decided whether or not to take on the appeal himself must have felt a lot different to him than those same four months inside the prison had to Evan.

But Hardy was here now, and that's what mattered. Evan's trial had ended nearly two years before. Charlie Bowen obviously hadn't gotten too far with the appeal in the fourteen or so months that he'd worked on it. Nobody else had done anything on it for six months after Bowen disappeared. The four more months that Hardy had taken while he made up his mind after he got the files were the least of Evan's real problems.

So Hardy ignored the question. It was irrelevant now. He pushed his chair back from the desk, crossed his legs, started in a conversational tone. "I used to be a cop," he said. "Before that I was a Marine and did a tour in Vietnam. Sound familiar?"

"You enlist?"

"Marines," Hardy repeated. "They don't draft Marines."

"How old were you?"

"Twenty."

"Yeah, I was twenty when I joined the Guard, still in college."

"That was pre-nine-eleven?"

"Pre-everything," Evan said. "Different world. The Guard looked like easy money at the time. A good way to keep in shape. Who knew?"

"Did you go right into the Police Academy after school?"

"Pretty much. Couple of months off, maybe. You can only drink so much beer and do nothing else before it gets old."

"I don't know. I spent ten years doing that. I had a kid who died."

Hardy wasn't fishing for sympathy. He wanted Evan to know a little bit about who he was, why he might be taking on this case personally. The young man's history struck a chord in him. With his life apparently over, Evan was still seven years younger than Hardy had been when he'd awakened from his own long alcohol-powered slumber after the death of his first son, Michael. Starting over from scratch at thirty-eight, Hardy had resurrected himself and his life in a way he would have been unable to predict—success, wife, kids, even happiness. So he knew it could be done. You didn't want to bet on it, but the slim possibility was there. Maybe this kid—like Hardy an ex-cop, ex-soldier—could get another chance. "So how long," he asked, "did you walk a beat before they recalled you?"

"Three years, give or take. This isn't in my file?"

"How's it relate to your case?"

Perhaps unconsciously, Evan scratched with his right index finger at the surface of the desk. "I don't see how it would."

"That's why it's not in your file," Hardy said. "Not in Bowen's, anyway."

"What about Everett Washburn's?"

"It might be there, I don't know. I haven't talked to him yet. I wanted to meet you first. See what you had to say."

"Like what?"

"Like your own testimony at your trial. Was that Washburn's decision, or yours?"

"I don't remember, exactly. I think we agreed on it together."

"I don't understand why, when you were on the stand, you didn't take the chance to tell the jury yourself that you didn't kill Nolan. If you didn't."

The scratching stopped. Evan stared across at Hardy. "Maybe I did do it."

"Okay. That'd be a good reason. Did you?"

"You really want to know?"

"It's why I'm here."

"Washburn never cared one way or the other. If I actually did it, I mean. Said it didn't matter."

"That's what makes the world go 'round. I do care if you killed him. Did you?"

"I don't know," he said.

THE SECOND OFFICE out of which Everett Washburn practiced law was the lower flat of a Victorian building on Union Street in San Francisco. It was really more of a personal refuge than a business office. Everybody in Redwood City knew Washburn; aside from his managing-partner role in his own firm, he was a fixture at the Broadway Tobacconists down there, and sometimes the constant familiarity, having to be "on" all the time, got to be a little much for the old man. In San Francisco, he kept a secretary who came in for about ten hours every week. Her main job was to keep the plants watered. There were a lot of plants.

The place he favored most in the flat was all the way in the back. Twelve feet in diameter, octagonal in shape, with windows on four of the walls and bookcases stuffed with leisure reading—no law books—on the other four, the room was intimate and comfortable. It held his rolltop desk and slat-back chair, two small upholstered couches, a love seat, a large, square coffee table of distressed wood, and a couple of wing chairs. All of the furniture sat on a cream-colored Persian rug that had set him back twelve grand five years before.

"This is a great room," Dismas Hardy told him as he followed him in and stopped to admire it. "I could live in this room." ·

"It has a certain feng shui, I must admit. I do love the place. Have a seat, anywhere you'd like." Washburn plumped himself down in the middle of one of the couches, fixing Hardy with an appraising stare. "I've heard your name come up several times over the past few years, Mr. Hardy, but seeing you, I think we've met before, haven't we?"

Hardy took one of the wing chairs. "Yes, sir. And it's Diz, please. About five years ago in Redwood City. You put me in touch with an ex-client of yours and she wound up saving one of my associates' lives."

"Literally?"

"Well, the information she gave me. It solved a murder case about ten minutes before the guy could do it again."

Washburn pulled a look of pleased surprise. "I must say I don't hear that kind of story too often. An actual solved murder? My side of things, that never happens."

"Well, it did once. I probably should have gotten back to you, told you about it."

"You're telling me now. It's good to hear when a case turns out well. Did I charge you for the referral to my ex-client?"

"No."

Washburn clapped his hands together. "So much the better. Although as we all know, no good deed goes unpunished."

"I know," Hardy said. "I avoid them at every opportunity."

"And yet you've done me the courtesy to come down here to see me."

"That's not a good deed. I needed to talk to you and it was either my office or here. It gave me the chance to get out into the air in the middle of the day."

"Well, regardless, I appreciate your flexibility." And then, suddenly, as though he'd flicked a switch, Washburn shifted into business mode. He came forward to the very edge of the couch with his elbows on his knees, his hands clasped loosely. "You said it was about Evan Scholler."

"It is. I'm doing the appeal."

"Ahh. So you're the guy who comes in after the battle to shoot the wounded."

"I hope not. I've reviewed the transcripts. So far, from what I see, I'm not inclined to go with incompetence of counsel."

"That's magnanimous of you. Though in all honesty that trial wasn't one of my finer moments, I'm afraid. But what are you going to do when your client won't plead? I know I could have gotten him a manslaughter, and he could be out by the time he's forty. Now . . ." He shook his head. "Anyway, when I heard it was about Scholler, I thought you were coming here as a courtesy to tell me in person that I'd fucked it up and that was the basis of your appeal."

"Nope."

"So what are you thinking? The PTSD?"

Hardy nodded. "The judge shouldn't have kept it out. My call is that Ninth Circuit judges are going to fall all over themselves spinning this thing when it gets in front of them. Scholler had a legitimate disability of some kind that the jury couldn't hear about? And he did, right?"

"Oh, yeah. We had the experts. The diagnosis was cold."

"Are you kidding me? And the judge didn't let it in? How could it not be relevant and admissible?"

"How indeed?"

They both, of course, were familiar with the notorious liberal slant of the Ninth Circuit Court of Appeals, which had made countless rulings on the admissibility of extenuating circumstances in murder cases, such as childhood abuse, dysfunctional parenting, or exposure to violence on television. If PTSD being ruled inadmissible didn't get their attention, Hardy would eat his bar card.

"Well." Hardy held out his hands, palms up. "Need I go on?"

"Not to me," Washburn said. "I do think that PTSD's the best play, though that just might be my own self-interest talking. I've kicked myself a hundred times over some decisions I made in that case. If I were doing the appeal, I might go for incompetent counsel."

"What would you have done differently?"

"Well, fought harder with Evan to take a plea, is the main thing." Washburn focused on an empty space in the air between them. "Done more with the Khalil murders, maybe, although God knows what that would have been—I spent fifty grand on my private eye and he got nothing remotely usable. Then—this was my favorite—I got halfway through my own chief medical witness when I realized that his testimony, if anything, helped the prosecution. But the main thing, as I say, would have been a plea."

"But he wouldn't take one."

"Adamant. He didn't remember doing it and wasn't going to say he did. Period."

Hardy shook his head. "Dumb."

Washburn shrugged. "I don't know. Maybe he thinks he probably didn't do it."

"What do you think?"

The old man waved that off. "I never go there."

Going for levity, Hardy put on half a grin. "Even for fun?"

"Never, nohow, no way, ever."

"I can't stand a man who won't express his opinions."

"No. Me neither." Washburn sat all the way back on the couch. "But the poor fucking guy. You met him yet?"

Hardy nodded. "I went down there last week." A beat. "I bet he'd take that plea now."

"Yeah, I bet he would." Washburn had already given Hardy about twenty minutes of his time, call it two hundred dollars' worth, although he wasn't charging him for this visit. Still, time was money and if there was no business to be done between these two men, Washburn would not make any until Hardy left. "So. How else can I help you?"

"I was hoping to pick your brain a little."

"How little?"

"Six to eight hours over the next month or so."

Washburn came forward again. "My professional courtesy rate is two hundred."

"Sounds reasonable," Hardy said. "I don't know how much time you have right now, and I don't want to impose . . ."

Washburn held up a hand and looked over at the grandfather clock that stood sentinel where the windows met the bookshelves. It was quarter to four. "I'm comfortable going till five," he said. "Feel free. Pick away."

* * *

A MONTH into his new old job, his second hitch as head of San Francisco's homicide detail, Lieutenant Abe Glitsky walked alone down the fifth-floor hallway and turned into the small room—itself bisected by a counter—that served as the unit's reception area. It was five-twenty, and both of the clerks stationed here had left, probably gone home for the day. Glitsky, after his initial disapproval, was getting used to the idea of hourly employees putting in their time and going home. While he'd been deputy chief of inspectors over these past few years, he'd always felt it odd that even the clerical jobs were so personal—you got in early and you stayed until your boss went home because if you didn't, someone else might get close to him and then you might not rise in the bureaucracy when he did. Or she, of course.

In another few steps, he was in his office—a small room stuffed with file cabinets, crammed with a large flat working desk, windows high enough in the wall along the right to allow in a bit of natural light but that afforded no view of Bryant Street down below. Coming around the desk, Glitsky glanced up at his bulletin board of active homicides—nine of them today, about average, crimes committed in the past month or so on which his inspectors were still working. Settling into his chair, he sat back and wondered anew if his request for what amounted to a voluntary demotion had been a mistake.

He'd been on the job for more than a month now, and besides some of the personnel issues that had been and continued to be a bit troubling, he found that, much to his surprise, he somewhat missed his large official office with its bookshelves and plaques and wall decorations, its brace of leather chairs for important visitors, its reception area that discouraged passersby from stopping in to say hello. The deputy chief's office was that of an Important Man, and while he had occupied it, Glitsky often had not felt, at base, like he belonged there. Now, as head of homicide, he still had what he believed to be an important job, but it was mostly an invisible one. Could it be, he'd been wondering, that he'd grown accustomed to being in the public eye, to having his opinion matter to others, to being consulted by the chief and even the mayor about important civic issues?

He kept telling himself that he was in a period of adjustment to the new surroundings, that was all. Change itself was never easy. But two or three times already, he'd entertained the thought that maybe he'd made yet another mistake in a recent history of poor career choices.

And there was no getting around it. These new digs were different and they made the whole job, once so familiar, feel different. First, this office was physically separated from the inspectors' room. When the detail had been on the fourth floor, the internal windows in the lieutenant's office looked out over the crowded room that held the desks of the troops. Here, even if his new office had internal windows, which it didn't, he wouldn't have been able to see the inspectors, since the computer room was in the way. Inspectors could and did come and go, they never had to pass his door, and Glitsky might never know they'd been around.

The good news was that, barring emergencies, Glitsky's own hours had stabilized. As deputy chief, he'd considered it his duty to set an example of rigor, discipline, and enthusiasm, and he'd made it a point to be at work at seven-thirty. At the other end of the day, department meetings, press conferences, and public appearances often kept him out until nine, sometimes later. His weekends rarely were his own either. Deputy chief wasn't a job; it was a life.

And Glitsky was at a juncture—the crux of it, really—his desire in life was to be with his wife, Treya, and their two young children, Rachel and Zachary. The last couple of years, since Zack had been born, had been something of a strain. Treya worked as the secretary for San Francisco's district attorney, Clarence Jackman. She was at her desk at nine and left at five. There had been weeks while Glitsky had been deputy chief that they'd basically only gotten to speak to each other in this building, the Hall of Justice.

Now, having made sure that his desk was cleared, Glitsky was getting ready to check out for the day. He went out his door, closing it behind him. Passing through the empty computer room, he entered the inspectors' area and saw that fully eight of the fourteen homicide inspectors were in the room. This was unusual, since most of the time, these people were out interviewing witnesses, assessing crime scenes, building cases, and working out rebooking details and/or charges with assistant DAs.

Darrel Bracco looked over and raised a hand in greeting—at least one person in the unit apparently okay with the new status quo. As the vibe of Glitsky's presence passed through the room, other inspectors looked up. Glitsky caught a few nods from veterans who went back to their conversations and coffee, was ignored by a couple of others.

This was the way it had been since he'd come down here, his people misunderstanding his reappointment to homicide, wondering if in reality he was some kind of spy sent down by the brass to shake up the detail, screw up their jobs.

Glitsky hoped that this was simply the effect of change on his people, and that it, too, would shortly pass. But until it did, he wasn't having a good time. Getting up to Bracco's desk, he summoned a neutral tone. "I'm out the door, Darrel. Anything happening I might want to know about before I go?"

Bracco thought a minute, then shook his head. "Nothing new, Lieutenant," he said. "Slow day on the prairie, I guess."

"I guess so." Glitsky did a quick scan of the room. He didn't want to seem to be checking on anyone. In fact, he wasn't, but that didn't mean people might not think he was. "See you tomorrow, Darrel."

"Yes, sir," Bracco said. "Have a good one." Glitsky had turned and gone two steps when Bracco spoke again. "Wait a sec, Abe. I just remembered. There was something you might want to put back on your board." This was the active homicide board in Glitsky's office. Usually, once a name left that board, it stayed off forever, either because a suspect in the case had gotten arrested, or because the trail had gone too cold to waste the inspectors' time anymore, or if the only eyewitness fell terminally ill with lead poisoning, or if, for any of a zillion reasons, the case wasn't being actively worked anymore.

"Back on the board?"

"Yeah. One of my old ones. Bowen. But it's been closed since before your time. We can get to it in the morning. Here, I'm writing myself a note so I won't forget."

"How 'bout if I just walk back in there and write it back up?"

Sheepish, Bracco nodded, getting to his feet. "That would probably work too. I didn't want to keep you if you were leaving."

"How long can it take?" Glitsky asked. "B-O-W-E-N, is that right?

Five letters. Shouldn't take me more than a few minutes." He was already back at his door, turning the key in it. "So what's the case?"

"Hanna Bowen. Finally ruled a suicide by hanging."

Glitsky turned and faced his inspector. "What? She unhang herself?"

"It's more like I promised the daughter that I'd take another look at it. She can't seem to get her arms around it. That her mom killed herself, I mean."

"Okay. But the coroner ruled suicide? And you're going to help this daughter how?"

"I know it's a long shot, Abe, but the girl's still torn up. You know all the classes we take that tell us to be sensitive to the victim's pain, and all that. I figure what can it hurt, and it might help her."

"What, though, exactly?"

"Well, evidently the mother kept a diary. Or the daughter—her name is Jenna—Jenna thinks her mom might have kept a diary and she asked me if I could try to find it."

"And do what with it?"

"See if it gave us any reason to think her mom's death might have been a homicide."

Glitsky boosted himself back onto his desk. "This was your case originally?"

"Yeah."

"Anything point to homicide back then? When was this?"

"Maybe early February, and not really, no. Except that Jenna had such a hard time with accepting that her mother would do that."

"Well, God knows we've seen that before, Darrel. Not that I blame her. Your mother goes that way, you don't want to believe it. Maybe you honestly can't believe it, but that doesn't mean it didn't happen."

"I know. I told her I'd look, that's all. No promises."

"For this diary?"

"I don't know, Abe. That might not be all. I worked the case pretty hard when it was live. There were other elements at the time. Well, to be honest, mostly one other element, but it seemed worth checking out, although at the time I couldn't get anything on it."

"What was that?"

"The dad, Charlie. He disappeared last summer. That's supposedly why the wife killed herself."

"What do you mean, disappeared?"

"I mean poof, gone, vanished. No trace. Jenna thinks he wouldn't have just disappeared either. She thought he might have been killed."

"By who? Why?"

"No idea."

"Very strong, Darrel. So she thinks her father was killed, too, and that it's somehow connected to her mother's suicide?"

"Not suicide. She doesn't buy suicide. She thinks her mother was another homicide."

"Two homicides." Glitsky sat with it for another few seconds.

Bracco made a face. "The daughter lost both parents in the same year. If the diary turns up . . ." He shrugged. "Who knows. We might get something."

"So where are you gonna start?"

"I suppose I'll meet her and go through all the evidence again. Then maybe get to the father's files, which I never really looked into last time."

"What files?"

"His work files. He was a lawyer. Maybe it was something he was working on."

"What was?"

"The reason he was killed."

Glitsky scratched for a second at the corner of his mouth. Bracco had always been an enthusiastic cop, but he'd gotten promoted up to homicide originally because his father had been a driver to a former mayor, and sometimes his lack of experience showed. "You realize, I know, Darrel," Glitsky said, "that most middle-aged guys who disappear . . . I'm assuming this Charlie Bowen was middle-aged?"

"Fifty."

"There you go. Sometimes guys like him just walk away from it all on their own. They're not murdered."

"Right. I know that, Abe. Of course."

"And the wives of those men, who have been deserted by their husbands of, say, thirty years, might they find themselves depressed in the months following the desertion, even to the point of wanting to kill themselves?"

"Sure."

"Did we investigate Bowen as a homicide when he went missing?"

"No."

"And that was because . . . ?"

"He was considered a missing person."

"Not a homicide?"

"Not a homicide. No, sir."

"Okay, then. Just to make the point."

"I hear you." Bracco shrugged away his misgivings. "Anyway, I'll be logging some time to the case and I thought you'd want to know."

"Okay." Glitsky pushed himself off his desk and wrote the word BOWEN onto the board, with the name BRACCO in the investigating inspector's column. "But, Darrel?"

"Yes, sir."

"Maybe not too much time, huh?"

OVER THE PAST SEVERAL YEARS, Glitsky's grown boys—Isaac, Jacob, and Orel—and Treya's grown girl, Raney, had created a diaspora of their own to places as far-flung as Seattle, Milan, Washington, D.C., and—not so far-flung—Orel was living in San Jose. Now the new family unit with two toddlers ranged in the same old upper duplex on a cul-de-sac above Lake Street.

When Glitsky got home from work—driving his own car instead of being chauffeured by his driver in his city-issued vehicle—he and Treya and five-year-old Rachel had pushed Zack's baby carriage for a mile or so on the foot-and-bike path that ran behind their home at the edge of the Presidio's forest. In their backyard, in the still-warm evening, both kids swung on the new swingset Glitsky and Dismas Hardy and Hardy's son Vincent had built about three years before. Dinner was a store-bought roast chicken, the skin peeled off, with fresh steamed spinach and a side dish of noodles for the kids—since Glitsky's heart attack six years ago, Treya wouldn't let him eat anything with cholesterol in it.

By eight o'clock, both kids were asleep in their separate rooms down the hallway off the kitchen. Abe and Treya sipped tea sitting together in dim light on the leather love seat in the small living room. They had redecorated the room for the birth of Rachel, and now what had been a worn and dark interior sported blond hardwood floors accented with colorful throw rugs, yellow Tuscan walls, Mission-style furniture, plantation shutters.

Taciturn nearly to the point of muteness, Glitsky was happy to let Treya carry the conversational ball as she told him about her day, the machinations of the DA's office, Clarence Jackman's dealings with the board of supervisors, the mayor, the chief of police. It was endlessly entertaining because they both knew all the players and because the city was in many ways such a truly loony and fascinating place to live.

Today's drama featured Treya's boss on a tightrope walk between Mayor Kathy West's edict that declared San Francisco a sanctuary city for illegal immigrants, and the U.S. attorney's response that he was going to cut off every federal law enforcement grant to the city if she did anything to hamper the Justice Department's crackdown on arresting and deporting these people.

"That I'd like to see," Glitsky said. "What's he going to do, arrest Kathy?"

"If she actually does anything other than talk the talk."

"You think she will?"

"I don't know. She's talking about it." Treya's laugh was a low contralto. "Talking about not just talking about it."

"Very bold."

"*Très*. But you never know. She might really do something."

"So what's Clarence going to do?"

Treya laughed again. Sometimes Glitsky thought that her talent for laughter was what had attracted him the most about her. After his first wife, Flo, had died, he had thought for a long while that he would never laugh again. "Clarence," Treya said, "has got eight lawyer positions funded by federal money, but the rest of his budget comes from the city. He is going to wait."

"He's a good waiter," Glitsky said.

"One of the best." She put a hand on his leg. "But here I've been, me, me, me. You seem—I don't mean to spook you—but slightly more upbeat than you've been."

Glitsky shrugged. "Just getting used to the new world order. I actually had a possibly productive talk with Darrel Bracco today."

"I like Darrel. And possibly productive? Wow. The man gushes."

Sipping his tea, Glitsky gave her a sideways look. "Maybe saved him some hours of slog, that's all."

"Okay, retract the gush." She squeezed his leg. "And next you were probably going to tell me what Darrel talked to you about. If you were going to keep on talking, I mean. Not that you have to. No pressure."

This time his smile broke clear. "He was going to be spending half of forever looking into the case files of this lawyer who disappeared last summer because some poor heartbroken girl thinks maybe he didn't run away and desert her and her mother after all. Maybe he was killed instead."

"Is there any reason she thinks that?"

"Not that Darrel knows. But the thing that makes it so sad is that her mother killed herself over it a couple of months ago, and the girl just can't accept it."

Treya took a beat and sipped her tea. "And people say you're not really all that fun. How can that be?" She turned to him. "That heartening, upbeat story was what's made you feel better about the job?"

"Talking to Darrel," Glitsky said.

"Ah. The silver lining."

"I mean, first, you've got to believe Charlie Bowen was a homicide, which there's no sign of, so why are you even looking?"

"Charlie Bowen," Treya said. "Where do I know that name?"

"He's the father. The missing person."

"The lawyer? I knew him, Abe. He's the guy, Diz got all his files."

"Our own Diz?"

"Our own Diz." Treya gave his leg another squeeze. "Maybe Darrel ought to talk to him."

[31]

THE NEXT MORNING, Friday, May 4, Glitsky and Treya drove in to work together. Through the largesse of Clarence Jackman, Treya had a dedicated parking spot behind the jail that she considered perhaps the job's single greatest perk.

Yesterday's high pressure front had scoured the sky clean and banished the marine layer halfway out to the Farallones, so the sun packed an unseasonable warmth. Though there was no breeze at all, some fluke of nature had delivered a fragrant and powerful olfactory blast from the city's main flower market around the corner. Treya, getting out on the passenger side, looked over the car's hood at her husband and said, "This day is too beautiful. Do you smell that? If we were truly evolved spirits, no way would we go in to work today."

"No? What would we do instead?"

"Whatever we wanted. Dance, sing, take the ferry to Sausalito."

Glitsky met her in front of the car and took her hand as they started toward the Hall of Justice. "If we were truly evolved," he said, "we'd probably get fired. So, luckily, we're not."

"Well, maybe you're not." She ceased walking, effectively stopping them both, and sniffed the air aggressively. "But I'm at least taking one extra minute here to enjoy this."

"Smelling the roses, as it were."

"You should try it. Close your eyes a second, breathe it in."

Glitsky did as instructed, then opened his eyes. "Yep, roses," he said, "and then all that other stuff."

* * *

WHEN GLITSKY opened the door to homicide's reception area, he was looking at Dismas Hardy, who was dressed for work in his suit and tie and looking at his watch. "Two minutes late," Hardy said. "What kind of example is that to set for your team?"

"Treya held me up," he said. "We stopped in the parking lot to smell the flowers."

"How were they?"

"Really great. Flowerlike." Glitsky greeted the two clerks that sat at their desks and then swung open the door to the counter that divided the room, indicating that Hardy follow him in. Opening the door to his office, Glitsky asked, "Did we have an appointment?"

"No."

"I didn't think so."

"But you called me last night, if you remember, which I bet you do. I didn't get in till too late to call you back. Something about Charlie Bowen?" Hardy took one of the chairs from against the back wall and pulled it up to sit on it.

Glitsky got himself seated behind his desk. "His name got you down here first thing in the morning?"

"Not really. I've got a hearing downstairs at ten anyway." Hardy crossed a leg. "So you're going to tell me they found his body?"

"Why do you say that?"

"Let's see. You're homicide. You call me about a guy who went missing ten months ago. Call me crazy, but I figure maybe he's suddenly become a homicide."

"Nope. That's not it. Good guess, though."

"Thank you. You want me to make another one?"

"You could, or I could just tell you."

"Okay. Let's go with that."

Glitsky gave it to him in about ten sentences, at the end of which Hardy was frowning. "So your guy Bracco," he said, "wants to do what exactly?"

"Find this diary."

"Which may or may not exist?"

"Right."

"And then which may or may not have anything to do with Charlie's wife's death?"

Glitsky shrugged his shoulders. "This isn't my idea, Diz. Treya just thought you might save Bracco some running around."

"If I could, I'd be happy to. But we're talking like sixty large boxes of files, about a third of which we've already farmed out or returned to clients."

"Right. I know."

"Besides which," Hardy said, "the timing's wrong. If the wife died in February, I had the files in my office by mid-December. She couldn't have dropped the diary into any of them even if she wanted to. You want, though, I'll get one of my people to go through the boxes on everything we've got left, but I wouldn't get my hopes up."

"That's what I told Darrel."

"There you go," Hardy said, standing up. "Great minds. Oh, no, wait, that couldn't be it."

Glitsky was picking up his telephone. "Get the door on your way out, would you?"

HARDY HAD TAKEN up the habit of his now-deceased mentor David Freeman and, whenever the opportunity presented itself, walked the fourteen blocks between his office on Sutter Street and the Hall of Justice. Today, his morning hearing having ended sooner than expected, he was making pretty good time—not that it was a race or an opportunity for exercise or anything like that—when he got to Mission Street. There, a well-dressed, elderly woman caught his eye and moved just a bit over to get in his path. She looked into his face, beamed at him, and said, "Pardon me."

"Yes?"

"Are you all right?"

"I think so." She didn't look like it, but Hardy suddenly had no doubt that she was yet another in a city full of crazies.

"Then you ought to smile."

"Excuse me?"

"A day like this, a handsome man like you ought to be smiling."

"I wasn't?"

"Not really, no. More like frowning. More like the whole world's on your shoulders."

"Sorry," he stammered, trying to rearrange his expression. "Better?"

"Much," the woman said. "You watch. It'll help. Have a nice day."

After she disappeared into the crowd, Hardy stood for a long moment, unable to move. Catching his reflection in the store window next to him, he saw that the smile he'd dredged up had already faded completely away. Stepping all the way out of the foot traffic into the archway entrance to an ancient storefront, on an impulse he pulled his cell phone off his belt and punched in a number. "Hey," he said.

"Hey yourself. This is a surprise. Is everything all right?"

"Fine. Everything's fine. I just wondered what you were doing?"

"When?"

"Like, now."

His wife's laugh tinkled through the phone. "Like now I'm about to get in my car and go eat a salad someplace. Why?"

"Because I thought for a change of pace maybe you'd like to have some lunch with your husband."

Hardy waited out the short pause.

Then, "I would love to have some lunch with my husband. I think that's a great idea."

"You're not too busy?"

"I've got two hours and change. Where were you thinking?"

THEY DECIDED on Tommy's Joynt, Hardy by cab and Frannie by car, since it was about midway between Frannie's office on Arguello and Hardy's downtown. Fifteen minutes after the phone call, they sat down in one of the booths, Hardy with a bowl of buffalo stew and a beer and Frannie with a French dip and Diet Coke.

"You don't come to Tommy's Joynt and eat a salad," she said, biting into one of the place's homemade pickles. "I mean, it's legal and all, but it would be wrong."

"It's not that I don't agree with you," Hardy said. "But if you really wanted a salad, we could have—"

"Hey!" She put a hand over his. "We're here," she said. "This is the perfect spot right now. There couldn't be a better one."

Hardy looked around and nodded. "No." He sighed. "You said it. It's perfect."

Frannie cocked her head. "Dismas, are you all right?"

"You're the second person who's asked me that in the last half hour, so apparently not."

"The second one. Who else?"

He told her about the lady at the corner of Mission.

"You mean out of everybody walking down the street, she just stopped you and told you to smile?"

"Right. But first she asked me if I was okay. That I looked like I was carrying the weight of the world on my shoulders. Then after she left, I realized that that was pretty much the way I felt. I don't know why. I wasn't consciously down or anything. It's an absolutely glorious day . . ." He put down his fork, looked across at her. "Anyway, it hit me pretty good upside the head, almost like a message from on high."

"Saying what?"

"One thing, saying I ought to call you."

"I'm glad you did."

"Me too." He picked up his fork again, put it in the stew, stirred a minute. "I never thought I'd say this, but I think I'm having some trouble with this empty nest thing."

She put her sandwich down and again covered his hand with hers. "Yeah."

"And then I've been pretty pissed off at you for not being home when I get there, so I arrange not to be home when you are. Maybe I don't even consciously know I'm doing that, but I think that's what's been going on. It's wearing me down."

"I know. It's wearing me down too." She brought a napkin up to her eye and dabbed at it. "I don't really miss them so much, you know. I mean, I don't want them living with us anymore, God knows. We did enough of that. I just don't seem to know what to do with myself, so I fill up all my time with work, and then when I come home and you're not there either . . ."

Hardy finally got some of the great stew into his mouth, followed it with some Anchor Steam. "I'm thinking maybe we ought to reinstigate Date Night. Make it sacred again."

"I think that's a great idea. Maybe even go wild and have two a week."

"I would if you would."

"Deal."

She put her hand out over the table and Hardy shook it.

AN HOUR LATER, Hardy ascended the steps into the wide, marbled, circular foyer that marked the reception area of the law firm of Freeman, Farrell, Hardy & Roake, of which he was the managing partner. He marched up to the waist-high mahogany bullpen that demarked the territory of Phyllis, the firm's receptionist, and, obeying the finger she held up, waited while she placed a call to one of the other offices.

When she finished her business, she turned to him with her usual expectant petulance. "I told an Inspector Bracco that you would be here at one o'clock," she said. "Which is when you told me that you would be here."

"I know, Phyllis. I'm sorry. Something came up."

"And your cell phone broke?"

"You know, now that you mention it"—Hardy held his jacket down over the holster for his phone—"I've been looking all over for the damn thing. Have you seen it? Maybe I left it in my office somewhere. Or the car. I bet I left it charging in the car."

She shook her head with an icy disdain. "He waited forty minutes."

"I'm sure he did. Did he leave a number? We can get back to him."

"Of course, but I wanted to be sure you were here."

"As well you should, Phyllis. As well you should."

"Would you like me to call him now? He may not be far away. It's only been twenty minutes, after all, since he left."

Hardy considered that for a second. He had thought about driving down the Peninsula and getting some unscheduled time to ambush Mary Patricia Whelan-Miille on his Scholler appeal, but if Bracco was still close to the office, he was all but certain that it would be a short meeting. "Sure," he said, "call him back if he can make it."

Phyllis started punching buttons. Hardy made it to the door of his office when his cell phone rang on his belt, stopping him in his tracks as he lifted the phone and looked at the display screen. The call was from his office's main number. His shoulders fell and he turned around to face her.

Phyllis, her mouth set in disapproval, shook her head at him. "Maybe you left it charging in your car. Or maybe not."

Busted.

"I'll try to reach Inspector Bracco now," she said.

BRACCO COULD HAVE been the poster child for the good homicide cop. He went about five foot ten, a hundred and seventy pounds of muscle. He wore a tailored camel-hair sport coat over a pair of brown slacks, a light tan dress shirt with a plain brown tie. Under a close-cropped head of straw-colored hair, gray eyes animated his square, ruddy, clean-shaven face.

Now Bracco sipped a cup of freshly brewed coffee and sat comfortably in a leather chair by one of the windows that looked down on Sutter Street. This was in the more casual of the two seating areas that distinguished Hardy's office—the other, formal, more intimidating space with the Persian carpet, the Queen Anne chairs and lion's claw coffee table, complete with doily, claimed the area more or less in front of his large cherry desk.

Hardy went to the twin of Bracco's chair and sat down. He began on a conciliatory note. "I'm sorry you had to wait last time you were here. There was some confusion about my schedule."

Bracco turned up a palm, dismissing the apology. "You're doing me the favor, seeing me at all. I appreciate it."

"Sure. But I told Abe it'd probably be pretty slim pickins."

"That's what he said. He also said you offered to have one of your people go through Bowen's files, but that you didn't expect to find Mrs. Bowen's diary in them."

"Only because she would have still been writing in it, I presume, when the files had already been removed here to our storage. Glitsky said you weren't even sure there actually was a diary."

"No. Well, Jenna—Bowen's daughter—she's pretty sure there was a diary. Although I went through the house again this morning with a comb and nothing turned up."

"Well." Hardy wasn't sure where he fit in this picture, but he didn't want to give Bracco the bum's rush after his wait earlier. Let the man at least finish his coffee. "I can't speak for the files we've already finished with, but if you want me to light a fire under this, we can probably get through the rest of them in a couple of days. I've just gotten back to the office, otherwise I would have had somebody on it already. Is there some kind of hurry I don't know about?"

Bracco shook his head. "Just Jenna, to be honest with you. For the first few weeks after her mom's death, she was pretty much out of commission with grief. Now she's trying to process it, close the book one way or the other. If there's a diary and some clue . . ." He shrugged. "Anyway, so no, there's no real hurry, but I feel like a owe her another look if it's that important to her. And it is."

Hardy sat back and crossed his legs. "So I take it you had the mom's case?"

"Right."

"And you were okay with the coroner's call?"

"Pretty much."

"Did you see anything or talk to anybody that made you think it wasn't a suicide?"

"Generally, no. I mean, her husband had vanished a few months before. She'd made plans to go to Italy this summer, but the general feeling was that that was to try to put the desertion behind her, not to party. Most of her friends, and I talked to a lot of them, described her as devastated and depressed."

"So what's her daughter's take?"

"I think pretty much the usual. Her mother just wouldn't have done that. That's not who she was. Then she points to the Europe trip. Hanna— the mom—was evidently pretty frugal. Tight as a drum, Jenna says. She would never have bought tickets to Italy and not used them. She would have killed herself afterward."

Hardy allowed a small grin. "I know some people like that. Although putting off your own suicide until after you get your money's worth might be stretching it. And that's it? That's the daughter's reason she thinks it wasn't suicide?"

"Originally, basically, yes." Bracco drank some coffee, stared out the window for a moment.

Hardy had the impression he was trying to decide if he should say any more and thought he could help him along. "That's a lot of disclaimer you're throwing around. Originally. Basically. Do you have some doubts yourself? Is that why you're digging here?"

Bracco's mouth pursed as he continued to wrestle with whatever it was. "It was their rope, she slung it over a beam in the garage, got up on a little step-up ladder, and dropped off."

"But . . . ?"

Noticing that his coffee was finished, Bracco came forward in his chair and put the cup and saucer on the low table in front of him. Now he looked straight across at Hardy. "None of this worried me too much at the time, you understand. I had three other actives. This one went to the coroner and went away in a couple of days. It wasn't until Jenna called me back a few days ago that I looked at it again."

"And?"

"And her neck was broken." He paused, then made his point more clearly. "Regular slipknot, no hangman's noose, fifteen-inch fall."

"You're thinking she should have strangled."

"Most people, those same conditions, that's what happens."

"But not always? Did you ask Strout?" This was the city's medical examiner, who'd ruled the death a suicide.

"He says he's seen a few where the fall and the weight breaks the neck."

"Well, there you go."

"Nobody who weighed as little as she did, though. A hundred and five pounds." Hardy made no response; by itself this was interesting, certainly, but not conclusive. "And then," Bracco went on, "there was the other thing Jenna didn't think about originally, but remembers now."

"What was that?"

"That her mother had decided that Charlie didn't just disappear. That he'd been killed."

"Someone in her position," Hardy said, "that could easily be wishful thinking. That he didn't leave her, he was taken from her instead. Big psychological difference."

"Yeah," Bracco said, "but the main thing is that Jenna says her mom was on a mission to find out who killed her dad and wouldn't have killed herself in the middle of it."

"Maybe she got to the end and found he'd really run out on her."

"I said the same thing to Jenna. She totally disagreed. If her mom would have found that out, even then if she decided to kill herself, she would have left a note for Jenna so at least her daughter would know the truth."

A short silence settled between the two men. "You're saying you think it's not impossible somebody killed Mrs. Bowen."

"It's not the kind of thing I'd try to sell to Glitsky. Not on what I've got now."

"You got a motive?"

"You probably won't love it."

"Try me."

"Somebody—the same person—killed the husband, too, and Hanna got too close to finding out."

Hardy shook his head, suppressed the start of a smile. "A bona fide conspiracy theory. You're right, that would be a tough sell to Glitsky."

"That's why I'd like to find that diary. It would be something real."

Hardy thought that even if it existed, it still would be considerably less than a smoking gun. Stealing a quick glance at his watch, he decided he'd given Bracco enough time and a good listen. Bracco didn't wear a wedding ring, and Hardy wouldn't be at all surprised to find out that the daughter, Jenna Bowen, was a pretty young thing. As for him, it was time to get back to work. He started to get up.

But Bracco suddenly came forward. "Anyway, the reason I wanted to see you in person. I'm just saying there might be something else in those files."

"Some reason Bowen might have been killed, you mean?"

"Right."

This time, Hardy let his grin blossom. "You know how many big moving boxes we're talking about here, Inspector? Something like forty-five or fifty to go. Last time I checked, when he disappeared Charlie Bowen was covering two hundred and thirty-two active files, of which we've offloaded about eighty so far." He softened his tone. "Which is not to say we won't come upon something that looks fishy somewhere down the line, and if we do, I promise you'll hear from us. From me. But I think you're talking the original needle in a haystack."

Chagrined, Bracco sat back and nodded. "Yeah, I can see that. Well . . ." He pushed himself up to his feet.

Hardy, rising himself, said, "If you get anything specific attached to some probable cause, you could always subpoena the files and have a special master go through them."

"I could do that, but I don't have any idea what I'm looking for."

"Well, there's that." Hardy brightened. "Except the diary."

"Right. Except the diary."

"I'll get somebody working on that before you hit the street."

"I appreciate that," Bracco said, extending his hand. "Thanks again for your time."

Hardy nodded. "And we find anything on the other matter, you'll be the first to know. But as I told Glitsky, I wouldn't hold my breath on any of this."

Bracco broke a small smile. "I never do."

[32]

HARDY HAD A SPY in Redwood City.

His old law school buddy Sean Kelleher worked as an assistant district attorney in the same building as Mary Patricia Whelan-Miille and told Hardy that she wasn't calendared for any trials and should be in or about her office for the whole day. As soon as Bracco had walked out of his office, Hardy had made the day of Michael Cho, one of his paralegals, by assigning him to start looking through the boxes of Charlie Bowen's files for a woman's diary. Then he'd picked up the phone and called to make double sure about Mary Patricia, told Kelleher he owed him one, and hightailed it down to his garage.

Ten minutes later, top down on his S2000, Hootie blaring from his car's speakers, Hardy cleared Candlestick Point and twenty minutes after that was parking in the courthouse lot twenty-five miles south. If San Francisco had been warm and pleasant all day, Redwood City, in the mid-eighties, was positively balmy. As he brought the roof back up over the convertible, he found himself humming out loud. He felt like a different person from the stoop-shouldered slug who'd attracted the attention of the possibly-not-crazy elderly woman at the corner of Seventh and Mission that morning. The lunch with Frannie, her receptiveness, maybe the start of the next phase of their lives together after the unexpected hollow emptiness of the recent one.

The little dance he was doing around Mary Patricia Whelan-Miille was not frivolous. He thought it so likely as to be certain that she would not consent to a regular scheduled appointment with him. After all, he was the man who was trying to undo all of the hard work she'd put in on what was to date still one of the most successful moments of her career. In fact, he considered it not impossible that even his planned ambush of her would be rebuffed. Certainly, there was no reason, other than professional courtesy, that she need feel compelled to see him. He wasn't kidding himself. He knew who he was. He was the enemy.

When he arrived in Redwood City, he called Kelleher, who came out and walked him past the receptionist into the offices in the back. He had a cup of coffee and shot the breeze a little and then asked Kelleher to point him toward the lair of Mary Patricia Whelan-Miille.

Her door was open and Hardy stood for a second in the hallway, trying to take her measure. Younger-looking than he'd expected, with a very appealing profile, she was sitting forward in her chair, her elbows on her desk, one hand playing with a loose tendril of blondish hair, apparently reading. Her feet, shoeless, were tucked back under her chair. It was a Friday-afternoon scene similar to one he'd seen a thousand times in the legal world—the alone, as opposed to lonely, time every good lawyer needed to keep up on facts, to study cases, to stay current on changes in the law, to recharge.

Part of him hated to bother her.

The rest of him stepped forward and knocked softly on her door. "Excuse me."

She turned to face him, her expression just short of querulous. Yes, it said, he was interrupting her. But she could be serene about it. The petulance gave way to a mild curiosity. "Can I help you?"

"I think so." He pointed to the name on her door. "If you're Mary Patricia Whelan-Miille."

"That's me."

"That's some name."

"Tell me about it. Sometimes I wonder what my parents were thinking. Mississippi and all of New York."

"Pardon?"

She straightened up in her chair, put her hands behind her lower back, and arched herself briefly. Getting out the kinks or showing off the merchandise. "Nine syllables," she said. "Mary Patricia Whelan-Miille. Mississippi and all of New York. Imagine having to ask people to say 'Mississippi and all of New York' every time they wanted to address you by name. You'd never talk to anybody." She broke a nice smile. "People call me Mills. Who are you?"

Hardy came forward and introduced himself.

"Dismas?" she asked.

"Dismas."

"I don't think I've ever met a Dismas."

"You're not alone. He was the good thief on Calvary, next to Jesus. Also, he's the patron saint of thieves and murderers."

"Good for him. I'm proud of him. I've always wanted to be patron saint of something, except I understand first you've got to be dead, and that's got limited appeal." Mills swung in around to face him. "So, Dismas, how can I help you?"

"Well, speaking of appeal, I wanted to ask you for a few minutes of your time to talk about the Scholler case. I'm doing the appeal."

The mildly flirtatious personality dropped off her like the calving of a glacier, leaving only the cold, flat ice behind. "I have nothing to say about that. I won the case. I don't think there are any legitimate appealable issues."

"You don't think PTSD should have been let in?"

"If you've read the transcripts, you know I argued against just that and prevailed. That was the right call. And now, I'm sorry, but I'm in the middle of—"

"You spoke to Charlie Bowen. I'm only asking for the same courtesy."

"Charlie Bowen made an appointment with me and we set ground rules."

"I'll go with ground rules," Hardy said. "Same as Charlie's."

"Do you even know what they were?"

"It doesn't matter. I'll agree unseen."

"There's a desperate offer." She folded her arms over her chest. "Look, Mr. Hardy . . ."

"Dismas."

"Mr. Hardy, please. I don't want to be a hardass, but I'm not going to talk to you about Evan Scholler. He was guilty and I got him convicted and I hope he rots away in prison. That's all I've got to say, all right? Please."

Hardy counted five of his heartbeats. Of course, there always had been the make-an-appointment-and-set-ground-rules option, but he'd never before had a conference like that produce anything of real substance. If you wanted your soda to fizz and bubble, you had to shake it up.

But now he was looking at turning around and driving back home, facing a weekend with absolutely nothing to chew on and work with. The words and the idea came out of his mouth before he was aware that he'd thought of them. Anything to keep her talking with him. "How about if I don't talk about that case at all?"

She cocked her head, still wary. "Then what exactly would we be talking about?"

"Charlie Bowen."

"What about him?"

"Anything he might have said to you before he disappeared."

That stopped her. She combed her hand through her hair, made a face at him that could have meant anything, looked down at her desk, back at Hardy. "Why do you want to do that?"

"He disappeared while he was working on this appeal. Before I get too far with it, I don't want to have the same thing happen to me."

She shook her head, chortling. "Don't be ridiculous. He'd barely started even the preliminary work. I don't think he'd even finished the transcripts when I talked to him."

"So what did you talk about?"

"He wanted to review the evidence that hadn't been used at the trial. To see if I had any working papers not included in the defense discovery. Stuff like that. Just to make sure the record was complete while he was going ahead. Housecleaning."

"He didn't mention any personal conflicts?"

"No. If I recall, the meeting lasted under the hour. We didn't get too close."

"But he was going ahead with the appeal?"

"Of course. That's why we were talking at all."

"He didn't seem nervous or overly concerned with his safety?"

"Why would he be? The bad guy was already in jail." Shaking her head as if to clear away that thought, she went on. "I hate the appeals process, you know that. They ought to give our side an appeals process if we lose a case—try the scumbags again until we get 'em and put 'em away."

"YEAH, THAT'S MILLS," Washburn said. "She's a bit of a zealot, but she's also only the second person in thirty years to whip me in court, so she's got my respect." Hardy had thought it was late enough in the day that there would be a good chance he'd find Washburn at the Broadway Tobacconists, and he was right.

Now they sat in a cloud of cigar smoke in the back of the unpretentious little store. Except for Greta, the female proprietor, they had the place to themselves, a situation—Washburn assured him—that would change in the next hour, when his acolytes and his girlfriend would appear from their various offices to drink "from the vast fount of my knowledge."

Not entirely sure Washburn was poking fun at himself, Hardy said, "Well, whatever time you and I get together here, it's on the clock."

"Goes without saying." Washburn savored his smoke, drawing on it, exhaling another plume. He twirled the cigar around between his lips, then dipped the unlit end into a small glass of amber liquid which, from the bottle next to it, was Armagnac. "Sure you won't join me?"

"Thanks, but then I'd just want a little nip of your nectar, and I'm going to be driving."

"Probably wise. So how can I help you today?"

"Well, this is odd, but it came to me when I was trying to get to Mills. I didn't even see a draft of Charlie Bowen's appeal brief in the file, so I'm assuming he hadn't gotten to it. I'd also been assuming that he was going to go with the PTSD. But now I'm wondering if he'd mentioned anything about that to you."

"What?"

"What he was basing his appeal on. Especially if it wasn't PTSD."

Washburn sat back, drew on his cigar, held the smoke. "Actually," he said, "you raise a good point." Another pause while he dipped the cigar again in the Armagnac. "You know, he seemed to think that it might be more fruitful to attack the competency of the local constabulary as well as the FBI."

"How's that?"

"Well, the Khalil murders." Turning the cigar between his lips, Washburn sat back, pensive. "I mean, here you had two murders intimately connected with the Scholler case—there was no question of that—and a blatant assumption that Evan had committed them with the frag grenades and so on. But the DA never charged him with those murders. You see the issue?"

Hardy saw it plainly, and it struck him as unusually powerful. "So the police and the FBI never questioned anyone else?"

"And, on one hand," Washburn added, "why would they? They had a suspect they could convict, and may as well send him down for one murder as for three, without the risk of losing on the other two."

"You mean they never questioned anyone else about the Khalil murders?"

"I assume they must have, a few people anyway. But certainly not everyone they could have." He took in a huge lungful of the pungent air. "You're forgetting, though, and I wonder if Mr. Bowen did as well, that you can't base your appeal on evidence that isn't discussed in the record. The Court doesn't know anything that the court reporter hasn't taken down."

"I'm not forgetting that," Hardy said, "but then who killed the Khalils?"

"Well, if you believe Evan, Ron Nolan did."

"Did you believe Evan?"

Washburn seemed to be considering it for the first time in a long while. "You know, now that you mention it, yes, I think I do. Evan just didn't smuggle small arms and grenades out of Iraq as souvenirs. He was only over there a matter of weeks. In the brief time he had there, he couldn't have both found a source for these things and arranged to find a way to send them home. Especially when you consider he was airlifted out of there unconscious and with no warning. I'd be surprised if he got out with his own socks, much less all this hardware." He studied his cigar's lengthy ash. "No," he repeated, "it beggars belief. That just didn't happen."

"So where did that stuff in Nolan's closet come from?"

"It must have been from Nolan himself, wouldn't you think? He could move about a lot more freely, and he had both more time and a lot more contacts than Evan ever did."

Hardy sat back in his chair, his elbow on the armrest, his hand resting over his mouth, in deep thought. "Okay," he said in a faraway voice, "let's go with Nolan killing the Khalils for a minute. I don't want to jump too far ahead of ourselves here. Can we take that as fact?"

After a small hesitation, Washburn nodded. "I do."

"All right, then, here's the million-dollar question. Why did he do it?"

"I don't know."

"Was there any speculation you heard?"

Washburn shook his head, now troubled by this as well. "Somehow that just never became part of the discussion, did it?" Asking himself. He turned to face Hardy. "Even when everyone was taking it for granted that Evan had killed them, I don't remember anyone stopping to examine the why of it too closely." He drew on his smoke. "I think there was more or less an assumption that it was something that had happened in Iraq that we would never find out about. Maybe it was something personal or maybe he just hated Iraqis in general for what they had done to him. And at the same time he could frame Nolan for the murders and eliminate his rival for Tara. It was a great opportunity to kill two birds with one stone if you happened to be a psychopath, which some people thought Evan was."

"But nobody asked the hard questions?"

"Apparently not."

"Even though the FBI was all over this thing?" It wasn't really a question. "Does that strike you as the FBI we all know and love?"

Clearly, Washburn, too, had caught the bug. His eyes were alight with possibility. "If Nolan did in fact kill the Khalils," he said contemplatively, "then certainly anyone in the Khalil family—Iraq being the tribal culture that it is—would have had not just a motive but an obligation to kill him."

Hardy, low-watt electricity running through him, leaned forward, elbows on his knees. "What do you think are the odds that the FBI never talked to any of the Khalils?"

"Zero. And yet now that you mention it, all the interviews we got were from the Redwood City police. And it was a pretty perfunctory job."

"So you're telling me the FBI would have relied on the locals to talk to witnesses in a potential terrorism case? I don't think so."

Washburn nodded and nodded. "Son of a bitch," he said, unmistakable glee in his voice. "You're talking *Brady.*"

Hardy, his mouth set, tried to keep his elation low-key. "You're damn right I am."

The reference was to what was commonly called a *Brady* violation. In *Brady v. Maryland*, the Supreme Court held that a defendant had a right to any evidence that was in the possession of the prosecution that might cast doubt on his guilt, whether or not it was eventually to be used at trial. The prosecution was absolutely required to turn over any background, testimony, evidence, interviews—anything—that could exculpate a defendant. If the prosecution withheld any of this discovery, *and the withheld material was reasonably likely to undermine confidence in a guilty verdict,* then these were grounds to reverse a conviction. Of course, evidence of such a violation was never found in the court's records. The whole point was that the prosecution had withheld the evidence and the defense didn't find out about it until sometime after the trial.

This opened up an entirely new strategic element.

Hardy and Washburn both keenly understood the situation. If in fact the FBI had interviewed witnesses in the Khalil killings and did not supply either the witnesses or the testimony, or both, to the prosecution, which the prosecution was then mandated to turn over to Evan's defense, it was highly possible that they were looking at a *Brady* violation. The added beauty of the situation was that Mills didn't even have to know about the withheld evidence. The FBI was legally construed to be part of the prosecutor's team and Mills was responsible for turning over that evidence whether or not the FBI told her about it.

Of course, proving not only that the FBI had held back evidence but also that the withheld evidence was likely to undermine confidence in the guilty verdict against Evan Scholler was another problem.

But Hardy would face that when he came to it.

For the moment, the *Brady* possibility, if he could get it off the ground by finding an FBI witness or two that hadn't made it into the Scholler record, meant that he could file a writ of habeas corpus with declarations and get it in front of the court of appeals in relatively short order. The court of appeals could then remand it back down to Redwood City, probably back to Tollson's courtroom, where—if they were hearing new evidence—anything might happen.

Washburn tapped Hardy's knee, snapping him from his reverie. "It's still going to be a long shot proving the evidence is exculpatory," he said. "Essentially you'll have to prove somebody else other than Evan might well have killed Nolan. Which, I must tell you from bitter experience, is a tough nut." He lowered his voice. "It might even be contrary to fact."

"Maybe not," Hardy said. "It might be enough for the court if I prove that somebody else had a reason to."

The old lawyer shook his head. "That, I'm afraid, is wishful thinking."

"Not at all. If there was another plausible suspect the jury didn't get to hear about . . ."

Washburn frowned. "And the FBI, which withheld it last time, and which is immune to state process, is going to hand it over now? How are you going to make them do that?"

"I don't know," Hardy said. "It's a work in progress."

[33]

HARDY DROVE BACK up to the city on the 280 Freeway, got off on the ocean side of town at Nineteenth Avenue, and, at a couple of minutes after the official beginning of the cocktail hour, walked into the front door of the bar he partly owned, the Little Shamrock. Moses McGuire, his brother-in-law, out of rehab now this past year or more, was behind the bar at the far end by the beer taps. To Hardy, he looked impossibly fit, although maybe it was simply the fact that he'd lost thirty pounds and cleaned up his appearance along with his bloodstream.

Perennially shaggy and long-haired, often bearded, McGuire had cultivated more or less the look of a biker or a mountain man since his twenties—which is to say for nearly forty years. Faded, often tattered blue jeans and some crummy T-shirt seemed as much a part of his personality as his justly fabled temper, his casual disdain for convention, his fondness for altered states of consciousness.

Down at the end of the bar today, passing the time with a pretty young woman, he might have been a mid-forties banker on his day off. The still-full head of salt-and-pepper hair was short and neatly parted, the mustache trimmed in an otherwise closely shaved face. He'd tucked the tails of his blue dress shirt into a pair of khakis. He'd had his nose broken often enough in bar fights that Hardy thought he'd always look a bit battered, but today his eyes were clear, his skin nearly devoid of the capillary etching that had been a regular feature of his face in the heavy drinking days that had comprised the majority of his adult life.

As a sometime bartender and part-owner, Hardy could have gone around the bar and helped himself to whatever he wanted, but occasionally you got back there and found you couldn't easily get yourself out, and tonight was supposed to be the first of his new Date Nights with Frannie, and he didn't want to start it off on the wrong foot. So he pulled up a stool and gave McGuire a casual nod, which brought him right on down.

"What's the word, Counselor?"

"Hendrick's, over. One onion."

"That's four words, and I've got cucumber."

Hardy nodded. "Even better. And while you're pouring, I've got a question for you."

"Hazel." McGuire didn't miss a beat. "Although some people think they're more green. But I'd call them hazel. Kind of a bedroom hazel." McGuire grabbed a glass, threw in some ice, reached up behind him to the premium gin row, and brought down the round dark bottle of Hendrick's gin. After a quick free pour to an eighth of an inch below the rim, he cut a fresh slice of cucumber and dropped it on top. *"Santé,"* he said, placing it on the cocktail napkin he'd laid down on the bar. "Okay, what's your real question?"

"It's a long one."

McGuire scanned the length of the bar and around the corners of the room, none of which were very far away. The Shamrock was a small, neighborhood place that had been in its same location at Lincoln and Ninth Avenue since 1893. The grandfather clock against the wall behind Hardy had stopped during the Great Earthquake of 1906 and nobody'd set it running again since. The pretty girl had gone back to her friends by the dartboards, and all of the other twenty patrons seemed comfortably settled at the bar or on the couches in back. "That's all right," McGuire said. "The crowd's pretty much under control."

On the drive up from Redwood City, after he'd wrestled with some of the problems raised by the *Brady* violation issues, Hardy had returned to the question that he still hadn't answered, and that, in his and Washburn's enthusiasm for *Brady,* they'd inadvertently let drop. So, after filling in his brother-in-law on some of the background—with a doctorate in philosophy from UC Berkeley, McGuire's ability to grasp facts and concepts had always been impressive even when he was in the bag; now that he was sober, it was formidable—Hardy came out with it again. "So, the question is, why did Nolan kill the Khalils?"

"Piece of cake," McGuire said. "It was his job."

Hardy drank off some of the rose-scented gin—he'd come to love this stuff. "Just like that, his job?"

"Sure. He's a SEAL, right? He's a trained assassin. You remember the SEALs in 'Nam. Shit. Killers. And now he's working for this security company in Iraq?"

"Allstrong."

"Right, Allstrong."

"But he was a recruiter over here, Mose, hiring people. No way was he doing wet work."

"Right. I'm sure. With his background? No way he wasn't, if it was needed."

"And why would it have been needed with the Khalils?"

"I don't know. Not enough information. But they were Iraqi, *n'est-ce pas?*"

"Yep."

"Well, then, you check it out, I bet you find they have family or something over there and they were somehow getting in the way of Allstrong's business."

"So they kill the father over here?"

McGuire nodded. "Sending a message."

"Pretty long distance, wouldn't you say?"

"The father was probably running the business from over here. Cut off the head, the body dies. This isn't brain surgery, Diz. All this didn't come out at the trial?"

"None of it did."

"Why not?"

"Well, the easy answer is that everybody on the prosecution team thought my guy had been the killer, and the motive was mostly personal, about him and Nolan."

"But you think it was Nolan?"

"I'm beginning to."

"And you're thinking, then, that this stuff about him ought to have been in the trial?"

"Precisely."

"Hmm. Let me think about it." He walked down the bar and saw to a couple of drink orders. Shooting himself a club soda from the gun, he came back down to Hardy. "Okay," he said, "I've got it all figured out."

"Hit me."

"Nolan killed these Khalil people, and then their family killed him in retaliation."

"How'd they know he did it?"

"They put it together that it was Allstrong because of what was going on in Iraq, whatever that was. Once they knew that, they found out Nolan was Allstrong's man over here. Even if he wasn't the actual killer, they were striking back and getting revenge."

"How'd they know where he lived?"

"Diz, please. It's cake to find people nowadays. You got a computer? They probably knew where he'd be living before he moved in. Come on, this doesn't sing for you?"

"No, it does, that's the problem."

"Why's it a problem?"

"Because if it happened the way you say, my client's innocent."

"And this is bad news because . . ."

"Because he's about three years into life in prison right now."

Moses tipped up his club soda. "Could be worse."

"True," Hardy said, "but it also could damn sure be better."

"BUT WHY didn't the prosecution look into that?" Frannie asked between bites of her calamari. "I mean, I can see them finally deciding it was probably your guy Evan, but you'd think they'd at least question some of the victims' family, too, wouldn't they? If only to find out some background on them."

"More than background, Frannie. These were two murders. Just thinking it was Evan shouldn't have been nearly enough. They would have wanted to prove it and maybe send him to death row."

They were at Pane E Vino, back on Union Street not far from Washburn's office, and here it had finally chilled down enough to make them decide to eat inside. They were up right in the window. Dusk hadn't yet progressed into dark. Frannie's shoulder-length red hair brought out the contrasting green in her eyes, which were the same color as the silken blouse she wore—a visual that, even after all of their time together, still captivated Hardy.

Dipping some of the fresh warm bread into the restaurant's little dish of olive oil, Hardy pinched some salt from the open bowl and sprinkled it over his upcoming bite. "But just because we have no record that anybody from the FBI talked to them doesn't mean that it didn't happen. Washburn and I have developed a theory about that."

"Which is?"

"That the FBI interviewed these people and didn't pass their information on to the police or the DA."

"Why wouldn't they do that?"

"Well, the simple answer is because they didn't have to. But another answer is maybe they just didn't want to. And finally, Washburn's personal favorite and maybe my own, is perhaps they were ordered not to."

"Why would that be?"

"Evidently, that is not a question for us mere mortals."

Frannie chewed thoughtfully, sipped at her Chardonnay. "So what are you going to do?"

"Well, first thing, I've already done it. Driving up, I called Wyatt"—this was Wyatt Hunt, Hardy's private investigator—"and asked him to try to find anybody in the extended Khalil family that the FBI actually talked to. And the beauty of it is that it doesn't even really matter too much what they said. If the FBI talked to them at all about the Khalil murders and didn't see fit to tell the DA, then we've got a real discovery issue." Hardy put his wine down. "Moses, you know, thinks Evan might even be innocent."

"And why does my brilliant brother think that?"

"Well, the great thing about Mose, as you know, is that he can build these complex theories without any reference to the facts. Or maybe with just one teensy little fact."

"And which one was that?"

"In this case, that Nolan killed the Khalils."

"You think that's a fact?"

Hardy considered, nodded. "Close enough. I don't think Evan did, that's for sure. So based on that, according to Mose, Evan didn't kill No-lan. The Khalils did."

Frannie's face grew dark. She placed her hands carefully apart on either side of her plate. "And these are the people you're hoping to go talk to? These same people who killed Nolan?"

"We don't know they killed Nolan. That's just Mose's theory." But even as he said it, Hardy knew where his wife was coming from, and why she suddenly was so concerned. He couldn't deny the sharp tickle of apprehension that washed over him as well.

And, he realized, it was not altogether ungrounded.

Frannie was already concerned, and she wasn't even aware yet that there was any question about what had happened to Charlie Bowen, whether he'd in fact actually disappeared or whether he'd been the victim of foul play.

Perhaps following the same path upon which Hardy was thinking to embark.

He sucked in a quick breath—he didn't want Frannie to worry about that—then picked up his wineglass and took a sip. "I know what you're saying," he told her, "but if these guys were a real problem on that level, I've got to believe the FBI, with all of its resources, would have gotten some inkling of it. Wouldn't you think?"

"I would think that, yes. But then what?"

"Then I'd think they would have arrested somebody. That's what they do, Frannie. They find bad guys and put them away."

"Except if this one time they, in fact, didn't."

"Why wouldn't they?"

"For the same reasons you just gave me why they didn't tell the DA about these interviews you're pretty sure they had." She ticked them off on her fingers. "They didn't have to, they didn't want to, or they were ordered not to."

Hardy acknowledged the point with a small nod. "Well," he said, "I've got to believe there's a quantum difference between not turning over interview notes and not arresting someone they knew was a killer."

"Dismas." She put her fork down and met his eyes. "I never actually thought I'd say this, but you don't watch enough television. On *The*

Sopranos, the FBI turn mobsters all the time and leave them in place for years, hoping to scoop up the big fish. Meanwhile, all these other people are getting beat up and killed. This happens in real life too. Everybody knows this."

He nodded again. "True. It just seems a ways off on this case. At least at this point when everything's speculation."

"Do me a favor, would you?"

"Anything, my love."

"If it moves beyond speculation, take a little extra care. If these people killed Nolan, they could kill you."

Hardy knew that she might be right, but so was he—this was a long way from being established. "I'm not a threat to the Khalils," he said. "I don't want to prove anything about what they did or didn't do. I just want to know if the FBI talked to them and didn't tell the Redwood City cops about it. So I don't think we have to worry too much about anything happening to me."

"Oh, okay," she said with an edge, "then I'll be sure not to."

ANOTHER OF THE CHANGES in Frannie's life after her own children had moved out was that she had turned into a baby junkie, so after dinner, since they would be driving right by the Glitskys' flat on their way home anyway, she suggested that they should call their friends and see if they wanted company. Back a few years ago when Date Night had been truly sacred, especially during Rachel's first year, this postprandial visit had become a weekly ritual.

Now, while Frannie and Treya and even Rachel passed the infant Zachary back and forth with suitable enthusiasm in the living room, the two men sat on the steps overlooking their swingset project in Glitsky's small backyard and talked quietly, very quietly, about Charlie Bowen.

"You really think he's a homicide?" Glitsky was nowhere near as defensive as he might have been if either Bowen or his wife had disappeared on his watch, rather than on Marcel Lanier's. So Hardy's theories were interesting and maybe even fun to talk about, but they weren't—yet—Glitsky's problems.

"Not exactly," Hardy said. "It's just suddenly I'm finding myself a little more curious about what happened to the guy."

"You're building the whole thing on a bunch of ifs. You see that, don't you?"

"Well, not all of them are ifs. Scholler didn't kill the Khalils, for example. That just didn't happen."

"That doesn't mean Nolan did."

"No. That's true." Hardy rubbed his palms together. "But let's say that a homicide professional such as yourself had a hunch somebody had been killed, even if there was no body and no evidence. How would you go about finding out if you were right?"

Glitsky didn't hesitate. "I'd trace his last days, his last hours if I could."

"So do you know anything about Bowen's? Last days? Last hours?"

In the light from the bulb over the back door, Glitsky turned to his friend. His face, partly in shadow, with its hatchet nose and the whitish scar coursing through both of his lips, might have been some kind of terrible tribal mask, fearsome and powerful. "I don't know anything about Bowen, period, Diz. As far as I'm concerned, he's a missing person."

Hardy sat, musing. He wasn't here to argue.

An animal scurried through the brush on the Presidio's grounds.

"Your man Bracco came by my office today too," Hardy said. "On this Bowen thing."

"Charlie?"

"No, the wife."

"Right," Glitsky said. "He wanted this alleged diary."

"He did. But he also had a few other concerns that had just come up." Hardy went into it in some detail, Bracco's discoveries that the very light Hanna Bowen had broken her neck in a relatively short fall without a hangman's noose, that she'd come to believe her husband had been murdered. Bracco also apparently did not think it inconceivable that Charlie Bowen had been murdered, and that it might have had something to do with one of the cases he'd been working on.

"I told him," Hardy concluded, "that Charlie had a couple of hundred cases and identifying any one of them as connected with murder was going to take a bit of doing."

"But now," Glitsky said, "you're starting to think it might be Scholler."

"I don't know if I'd go that far yet. I wouldn't try to take it to the bank, but there's starting to be a hell of a lot of questions, don't you think?"

After a minute, Glitsky nodded. "It's interesting," he said. "I'll go that far." Then, "You want me to do anything?"

Hardy shook his head. "I don't know what it would be, Abe. Bracco's already on it, even without the diary. Since you trained him, he's probably doing that last-hours-and-last-days thing with Mrs. Bowen. Maybe he'll come up with something."

"If Darrel finds something that leads back to Charlie, Diz, and he starts to look like a homicide, I'll jump all over it."

"That'd be good. I'd appreciate it." Hardy fell into a silence again.

"What are you thinking?" Glitsky asked after a minute.

"Nothing."

"Yeah, but it's a loud nothing."

Hardy took a breath. "I was just wondering if it was possible that the FBI knew who killed the Khalils and didn't say anything about it because it was part of a bigger case."

Glitsky looked over at him. "I missed a segue here. I thought we were talking about the Bowens."

"Now we're talking about the FBI. But it's still Scholler."

"Guy gets around."

Hardy shrugged. "It's a complicated case. But part of it is how much the FBI didn't tell the DA. Or even if they had another suspect they forgot to mention."

"Whatever it is," Glitsky said, "you'll never know."

"But you think it's possible they'd deliberately withhold that kind of evidence?"

"As my father would say, 'Anything's possible.' If it's the FBI, I'd go a little further. Nothing is impossible."

"They'd screw up a murder case on purpose?"

"Not every day, certainly. Not usually. But for the right reason . . ."

"Like what?"

"I don't know. Say maybe the guy's a valuable snitch. Or he's a mole in a terrorist group." Glitsky snapped his fingers. "There you go. He's giving the Feebs good information on a terrorist cell, I bet they wouldn't blink if he killed his girlfriend on the side. Say 'national security' to these guys and anything goes."

"You think?"

Glitsky chewed his cheek. "Would I bet on it in this case? Maybe not. Do I think it's ever happened? Definitely, and more than once."

And if it happened here with the Khalils, Hardy thought, perhaps Charlie Bowen hadn't figured it out in time as he was preparing his appeal. Maybe the Khalils had seen him—justifiably—as a threat, a loose cannon who wouldn't hesitate to accuse them of murder if it would help get his client off. And if they had, or if one of them had, in fact, murdered Ron Nolan . . .

"Okay, then here's another angle you might want to put in your pipe and smoke," Hardy said. "Moses is of the opinion—again, based on nothing, but still, he's not dumb—he thinks that Nolan killed the Khalils because it was his job. They were Iraqi, and he worked for this company that does a lot of business in Iraq. Allstrong Security, which is evidently—"

But Glitsky put a hand on his arm, stopping him. "Allstrong Security?"

"Yeah, headquartered here and in—"

"I know where they are, Diz. I know who they are." Unconsciously, he tightened his grip on Hardy's arm. "Nolan worked for Allstrong? How could I not have heard about that?"

"Maybe because it's a small detail about a trial in another county three years ago. Could that be it? And why would it have mattered, anyway?"

But Glitsky, a muscle working in his jaw, was inside himself, putting something together. He let go of Hardy's arm, staring ahead of himself into the darkness.

"Abe? Talk to me."

Slowly, he began to spin it out, as though to himself. "I'd bet my life it's close to the same time frame, something like three years ago, right? But I'll check that."

"What?"

Still, Glitsky hesitated. "We had a homicide here in the city of a guy who'd been over in Iraq working for Allstrong. His name, if memory serves, was Arnold Zwick. Somebody snapped his neck in an alley down in the Mish. Left his wallet on him."

"All right. And this means . . ."

"No, wait. The same weekend, a day or two later I think, three more guys, all together, all muggers with sheets, turn up dead on the street in the Tenderloin. Two of 'em with their necks broken."

"Three broken necks?"

"That's what we said. Batiste thought it might be a serial killer starting out, but nothing else happened. No clues, no suspects. Eventually it all just went away."

"So what was the deal with Allstrong?"

"Nothing, really." Glitsky still trying to process his memory. "We never found anything, anyway. The investigation never went anywhere."

"But?"

"But witnesses told us Zwick seemed to be rolling in cash before he got killed. But we never found any of it, except a couple of hundred in his wallet. Debra Schiff thought he'd embezzled it from Allstrong in Iraq, then split. They were getting paid mostly in cash back then. Her theory was that Allstrong sent somebody back over here to find Zwick, make an example of him, get the money back. But as I say, we never got a lick of proof."

"And now you're thinking . . ."

"I'm not thinking anything yet. Except maybe Moses might not be all wrong about Nolan."

Hardy sat, elbows on his knees, mulling over this new information. "Let me ask you this, Abe. You've got friends in the FBI, right?"

Glitsky hit a one-note chuckle. "Local cops like myself don't have what you call bosom buddies in the FBI, Diz. But I know a few guys, yeah."

"Maybe you could ask them a couple of discreet questions?"

"About this Khalil case?"

Hardy shrugged.

"And what," Glitsky asked, "makes you think they'd tell me anything at all about that? Especially if they've kept something about it hidden all this time?"

"Well," Hardy said, "I know the two agents who were involved in my case. Maybe you could just put in a good word and see if they'd talk to me."

"I could do that, sure. Which doesn't guarantee they will."

"No, I know that. But it might help."

Glitsky shrugged. "Couldn't hurt, unless it does. And we'll never know either way, anyway. But I'll put in the word."

At that moment, the back door opened behind them. Frannie was standing there holding Zachary, with Treya in the hallway behind her.

"What are you guys plotting out here?" Frannie asked.

"Violent overthrow of the government," Hardy replied. "It's time we took control and fixed everything."

"Good idea," Treya said. "Maybe Abe could start the revolution with that squeak in our refrigerator door. It's been driving me crazy for weeks."

WHEN THEY GOT HOME, while Frannie was in the bathroom getting ready for bed, Hardy moseyed on downstairs and picked up the telephone in the kitchen. After three rings, he got the answering machine for the Hunt Club, Wyatt's private investigation agency.

"Wyatt." His voice a whisper. "I just wanted to give you a heads-up about the Khalils. You might want to keep a low profile. And if you find out if and when somebody talked to the FBI, go easy from there. Get as much detail as you can, but if you meet any resistance at all, don't make anybody mad at you. Just report back to me. We don't want to raise any flags with them. If you're getting the impression that the risk factor's gone up around this thing, that would be accurate. So be careful. Just treat that as the word of the day—careful."

When he got back upstairs to the bedroom, Frannie was in her pajamas in the bed. She put her book down. "Where'd you go off to?"

"Just downstairs, locking up, that's all."

She gave him a quizzical look. "Is everything okay?"

"Fine," Hardy said. "Everything's fine."

[34]

THE QUESTIONS ATE AWAY at Hardy for the rest of the weekend, and at seven-thirty Monday morning he called Darrel Bracco on his cell phone from home. The inspector seemed glad to hear from him at such an early hour, and told Hardy that they still hadn't located Hanna Bowen's diary but that yesterday he'd talked to one of Hanna's best friends, a woman named Nora Bonner, and gotten what he called pretty strong corroboration for Jenna's opinion that her mother had not been suicidal. Bonner and Hanna had gone out to dinner two days before she died, and all she'd been able to talk about was what she kept calling her husband's murder.

"Hanna didn't by any chance mention who she thought had killed him?"

"She thought it was something he was working on, but didn't know what. Evidently, he didn't talk about his cases at home."

"So why did she think it was that?"

"The last couple of days, he told her he thought he was onto something big, that he might actually be doing some real good."

"But he didn't say what it was?"

"He didn't want to jinx it before he had some answers."

"So why didn't she, Hanna, tell that to the police earlier? If Charlie was looking into something big—"

"Because nobody was looking at Charlie's case, that's why. It wasn't a homicide, remember?"

"All right," Hardy said, "let me ask you this. If Hanna was trying to find what Charlie was doing, how was she investigating it?"

"That's what I'm trying to find out. If it were me, I'd probably have gone to Bowen's secretary. Or maybe he was using a private eye. But the problem is this is all ancient history now. Bowen's gone most of a year. Who's gonna know, or remember?"

"The secretary might."

"Right. And she was?"

"It'll be in his admin records. While we're looking in the files anyway. Then you just track her, or him, down. Hopefully still in town, probably with another firm. Or—here's a possible shortcut—maybe the daughter knew."

"That's worth checking. I'll ask her." Bracco paused. "Can I ask you one?"

"Sure."

"Last time we talked at your office, you didn't seem too enthusiastic about the odds of getting anything out of all this. Now you're calling me before I'm in at work. Did something happen I might want to know about?"

Hardy took a beat. "That's a fair question. The answer is yeah, although it's all still pretty nebulous. I'm working on the appeal for one of Bowen's cases that was hanging fire when he disappeared. Evan Scholler. Some of the witnesses I'm hoping to talk to might have developed a motive to kill Bowen."

"You're shitting me."

"It's a long way from established, but it's something I'm looking at. I talked to Glitsky about it over the weekend."

"What does he say?"

"What does Abe usually say?"

"Not much."

"That's what he said this time too. But I'm thinking if you can find some independent confirmation looking into Hanna's last days, maybe that she had tried to contact these same people—"

"What are their names?"

"It's a family. The Khalils." Hardy spelled it for him. "The father and mother were killed about four years ago in Redwood City, and everybody thought my guy Scholler had done it. Now, maybe not."

"So these Khalils killed their own parents?"

"No, but they might have killed the guy Scholler got sent up for. If you're keeping score, his name was Ron Nolan. Anyway, I've got my investigator looking into this too. So, yeah, I'd say it's heating up, but it might all fizzle and go away."

"I should talk to these people too. The Khalils."

"Well." Hardy temporized. "First we've got to find out exactly who we're talking about, and at this point, we don't have any idea. It's a big family. And you're already well along on Hanna's last hours. If you get something solid there, you're ahead of me and then you've really got something to talk to these people about. Meanwhile, I keep scratching. And call you if I get anything real."

"With respect, sir. If Charlie Bowen's a murder, it's police work."

"I couldn't agree more, Inspector. I'm just trying to find grounds that'll fly for my appeal. But Hanna Bowen's murder, if it was that, is police work too. And it's way fresher."

Bracco paused a little longer this time. "We ought to stay in touch."

"That's my plan. If you notice, I made this phone call, for example. I've got no desire to work your case, Inspector. Really. I just want to get my client out of jail."

Bracco let out a little laugh. "God, that just sounds so wrong. My clients, all I want to do is put 'em *in* jail."

AT LUNCHTIME, Hardy was down the Peninsula again. Though he might have been able to get the information from his client, Everett Washburn also knew Tara Wheatley's address and phone number and even where she worked. He'd left a message, identifying himself as Evan's attorney, and she'd called right back on her break and agreed to meet him in front of her school at a quarter to noon.

As soon as he saw her, as she walked out of the building and got close to where he'd parked, Hardy understood a lot better what all the fuss had been about. He'd just read a book called *Silent Joe* by one of his favorite authors, T. Jefferson Parker, where one of the underlying concepts was the idea of the woman who possessed what one of the characters called "the Unknown Thing"—an attractive force so powerful that it altered the orbit of every man it encountered. It wasn't mere physical beauty or sexuality, though they both were part of it. It was something bigger, more inclusive, subtler, and far more dangerous.

Whatever the Unknown Thing was, Tara Wheatley had it in spades.

When she got to the passenger door, she stopped and beamed a smile down at Hardy that, at another time in his life, would have melted him. She wore sunglasses against the bright day. Her hair was down. The plain pale-orange cotton dress she wore revealed nothing—it came to below her knees—and yet stirred something that, to his old bones, felt primal.

"What is it about guys and convertibles?" she asked. "I'm assuming you're Mr. Hardy."

"That's me."

Hardy started to reach over the seat, but she opened the door on her own—bare tanned legs and sandals—and plopped herself in. Hardy had the rogue thought that it was lucky she was teaching fifth-graders—any further into adolescence and her boy students would probably riot.

"Where to?" Hardy put the car in gear, got moving. "Can I buy you lunch someplace?"

She shook her head. "I've only got one period off for lunch—forty-five minutes. Just away from here, anywhere. Wherever you find shade."

Out of the parking lot, he turned right and crested a hill, following the main road until it dipped into an area where the homes were surrounded with old oaks.

"You can turn anywhere in here," she said.

Hardy did as he was told, and parked at the curb on a shady street in an established neighborhood of large attractive homes set on small lots. As soon as he'd set the brake and turned the motor off, she turned toward him in her seat, her near leg tucked up under her. "Sorry to hustle you out of the lot back there," she said, "but people don't need to see me talking to another man outside the school. I'm already pretty much the fallen woman. I almost lost the job over it back during the trial."

"Over what? Having a boyfriend?"

"Having *two* boyfriends, Mr. Hardy. Not exactly at the same time, but close enough for some people."

"Who?"

"Suburban moms, Mr. Hardy. Never underestimate the power. Some

of them really never liked me. I think I must have threatened them somehow, though I don't know how or why that would be." Hardy had a pretty
good idea, but he said nothing. "Anyway, thank God the nuns supported
me. I love the work. I love my kids. But you didn't drive down here to talk
about me. What can I do for you? Is everything all right with Evan?"

This had been her first question to him on the phone this morning,
too, as soon as she'd heard who he was. But this time the question
prompted an unexpected one from him. "Have you not seen him recently?"

Clearly, the answer made her uncomfortable. "Two weeks."

"That's not so bad."

She shrugged. "It's not good. Not if he's the man you love, and he is.
But he's already been in prison for two years, and in jail another year before the trial." She lowered her head, shook it slowly back and forth, let out
a deep sigh. "It's a hard one, the whole thing."

"I can imagine."

"I mean," she went on, "if he stays in prison. I don't know what we're
supposed to do. He won't marry me. I've offered that a hundred times. I
think he's starting to lose hope. I don't know what he wants out of me
anymore. Sometimes I'm not even sure what I want. I know I wanted
him—I *do* want him—but I wanted a life with him. You know? Not this."
Suddenly her eyes flashed. "But I'm not giving up on us. I'm not. Don't
think that. It's just . . . it's so hard. It's so endless."

"I believe you," Hardy said.

She raised her eyes and looked over at Hardy. "Do you think you're
going to have any luck? Do you think he's ever going to get out?"

"To be completely honest with you, I don't know. I don't want to give
you any false hopes, but I'm starting to think we might have a prayer."

"Is that what was so urgent?"

Hardy nodded. Maybe he'd exaggerated about needing to see her right
away, but here they were now, and he couldn't feel bad about it. He felt
that things had begun to move quickly, and he didn't want to lose his
momentum. "There's a good chance that the FBI talked to the Khalils
and didn't let the prosecution know. If that's true, we've got an appealable
issue."

"Well, I'm glad. But I don't know anything about that."

"No. I didn't think you did." Hardy hesitated for a moment. "I wanted to ask you a few questions about Ron Nolan."

She rubbed her hand across her forehead, brushed a hair away. "I knew it was going to have to come to that again someday."

"Why did you know that?"

"I don't know. He was such a mistake. I still don't know why . . ." Letting the thought hang until there was no other way to complete it. "I feel like the whole thing is my fault."

"How is that?"

"If I hadn't gone and told Evan about Ron tipping off the FBI. Ron knew I'd do that once he told me. He just played me. And then Evan went up to his place . . ."

"So you think Evan did kill him?"

"Well, I mean . . . I don't think he was himself at the time. But I guess . . ."

"You guess so?"

She shrugged again, then nodded. "I don't know what else could have happened."

"A lot else could have happened, Tara. Nobody seems to know what happened. So unless Evan told you something that didn't make the trial—"

"No! He didn't do that. He didn't remember."

"I believe him. You might be happier if you believed that too. But what I'm wondering is if Ron ever talked to you about his work with Allstrong? You went together for how long?"

"September to May. How long is that? Eight months? What do you want to know about his work?"

"Whatever you can tell me."

"Well, he liked it, it paid very well, he was gone a lot."

"Back and forth to Iraq?"

"Sometimes."

"Even though he was under suspicion for causing the blow-up at Masbah?"

"I never knew about that until Evan told me just before Ron and I broke up. But that really didn't worry Ron. Nothing worried Ron. I'm pretty sure he went over to Iraq at least three, maybe four times. To get paid in cash if nothing else."

"In cash?"

"Yes." She adjusted herself in the seat. "He showed me a wrapped-up brick of something like fifty thousand dollars in cash after one of his trips."

"What did he get that for?"

"I think it was just how he got his regular pay sometimes. That's what he told me."

"How did he get that back into the country?"

"What do you mean?"

"I mean, you can't enter the country with that kind of money in cash. You've got to claim it at customs."

She shook her head. "No. Ron didn't have any problem with that. He always flew by military transport out of Travis. He knew all the pilots and the commanders and everything. It was just part of how Allstrong did business."

"Tara," Hardy asked, "didn't it ever occur to you that Ron brought those frag grenades over from Iraq the same way, and that he'd killed the Khalils with them?"

"Of course. I knew Evan hadn't done that anyway. But there wasn't really any proof that Ron had either. But then, he was such a liar. He lied about everything to me. And to Evan."

"Did you ever hear him mention anything about the Khalils?"

"No. Not really. Not until they were dead, anyway." She looked at Hardy in a pout of frustration. "I wish I knew what you were trying to get me to say. If it would help Evan, I'd say it. But I didn't know much about Ron's work at all."

"I'm not trying to get you to say anything, Tara. I'm trying to get a handle on Ron Nolan, on what was going on around him. See if that leads me anywhere on this appeal."

"Well, for a handle, I can help you there. He said he was a warrior."

"A warrior. What did he mean by that?"

"Oh, we talked about that a lot. I really didn't like it, or agree with him, but when he talked he could make it sound like it made perfect sense."

"What did, exactly?"

"That the world needed warriors, and the job of the warrior was to kill. And that's who he was, how he defined himself."

"As a killer?"

"A killer." She nodded. "And I'm sure he was. One time . . . well, no, never mind."

"What?"

She paused, then shrugged. "Well, it was one of our first dates . . ."

[35]

GLITSKY WAS ON THE PHONE at his desk, talking to his closest connection in the FBI, Bureau Chief Bill Schuyler, with whom he'd had many previous, nearly amicable dealings. Now the tone didn't ring with cooperation and friendship.

"Bill," Glitsky said, "you're telling me both agents quit?"

"Yes, sir."

"At the same time?"

"I'm not at liberty to disclose that, Abe. They're no longer with the Bureau. That's all I know."

"Could I talk to their superior?"

"I am their superior, Abe. What else do you want to know?"

"I want to know where they are."

"I just told you. They quit."

"You just also told me that you were their superior. And two hours ago when we last talked, you didn't know they'd left the Bureau."

"I hadn't worked with them personally in a while, Abe. I guess they got away from me."

After a small pause, Glitsky tried again. "This is a murder case, Bill. Freed and Riggio testified a couple of years ago down in Redwood City and it would be helpful to know who they talked to."

"Wouldn't that all be in the record?"

"We were wondering if any of their reports dealing with that case happened not to get turned over to the DA."

"I'm sure they turned over everything they were supposed to. And you're investigating a homicide in Redwood City? Isn't that outside of your jurisdiction? And who is we?"

"The Redwood City case might be connected to a couple of San Francisco homicides, Bill. And we is me and the lawyer I've been working with on this stuff."

"Well, whoever it is, Freed and Riggio aren't going to be available."

"Because they've left the Bureau?"

"That's correct, Abe. Anything else?"

"When you say they left the Bureau, Bill, do you mean they joined another federal agency? Or are you telling me a couple of thirty-something FBI agents opened a Dairy Queen in Texas and didn't tell you where?"

"Always a pleasure to talk to you, Abe. Have a nice day."

IN SPITE OF Schuyler's best wishes, Glitsky wasn't, in fact, having a nice day. He sat at his desk in the early afternoon. He had gotten up five minutes earlier and turned off his overhead lights, closing and locking the door behind him. Both of his hands were cupped on the blotter in front of him and from time to time, irregularly, he would drum the fingers of those hands. His mouth was tight and a muscle in his jaw worked at the side of his cheek.

He hadn't been kidding when he'd told Hardy that one didn't really have bosom buddies among the agents of the Federal Bureau of Investigation. But Hardy's request, to put the word out to Agents Jacob Freed and Marcia Riggio to talk to him if he called, had been so benign that Glitsky never expected any sort of bureaucratic runaround. He and Schuyler had worked portions of several cases together and, jurisdictional squabbles apart, had always before gotten along reasonably well as human beings.

When Hardy had told him on Friday night that the number of questions surrounding the Bowens, which might or might not be connected with the Scholler case, was sufficient to get his attention, Glitsky still had had no problem reserving his judgment. Questions came with the territory. They were what investigations were all about. Few people had the good taste to disappear or die in such a way as to leave all questionable issues in their lives resolved.

But now this unexplained and almost certainly spurious disappearance of the two FBI agents who'd been instrumental in the Scholler case forced Glitsky up against one of the other cardinal rules of investigation: There is no such thing as a coincidence.

It wasn't a coincidence that Ron Nolan worked for Allstrong, and so had Arnold Zwick.

Three broken necks in one weekend wasn't a coincidence.

Beyond those new and disturbing items, it was one thing to have Charlie Bowen, who was working on the appeal in the Scholler case, vanish without a trace. There was a reasonable and plausible explanation for the suicide of his wife six months later.

And certainly FBI agents had been known to leave their jobs.

But for all of these things to come together in an apparently random set of coincidences stretched Glitsky's credulity far beyond its normal capacity for elasticity.

A relationship existed here among these parts. He just didn't know what it was. But he was starting to get a good idea that it probably involved at least one homicide in his jurisdiction, possibly two. And maybe more. This made it his business.

But more than that, the FBI and Allstrong connections significantly enlarged the playing field. Whatever had originally happened in the Scholler case, and Glitsky was woefully ignorant of all but the most general of those details, it had appeared more or less parochial—essentially two guys duking it out over a woman. Now, suddenly, Hardy's theories involving the Khalils, and whatever business they were doing in Iraq, and perhaps even some kind of U.S. government involvement, did not seem so incredibly far-fetched. And though Abe's opinion of the FBI's methods included his belief that it would ignore the taking of a life by a snitch or a prospective witness if it suited its agenda, it it did not extend to the possibility that its agents would actually sanction or commit murder.

So—the only conclusion he could draw—the FBI knew more about this case than they were willing to divulge. They possibly knew who had killed the Khalils. And who had killed Ron Nolan. And if it wasn't Evan Scholler, this meant that the FBI had let the wrong man be sent to prison for life.

If one of the Khalils instead had killed Nolan in retaliation, and then either or both of the Bowens because they'd picked up that trail, and the FBI knew about it . . .

He pulled over the phone on this desk, lifted the receiver, and punched in a number he knew by heart. "Hello, Phyllis," he said, "it's Abe Glitsky. I need to talk to Diz, please."

HARDY'S PRIVATE INVESTIGATOR, Wyatt Hunt, did his research primarily on his computer in the large converted warehouse by the Hall of Justice that he called home. He had no trouble finding the details of the Khalil murders on the net. Over the weekend, he also spoke to Hardy to clarify exactly what his assignment was. It had evolved somewhat from Friday's first phone call, when Hardy merely wanted to know who, if anyone, among the Khalil family had had an interview with FBI special agents in regard to the Scholler case. Now, Hunt's personal priority had shifted to finding out, without putting himself in danger, what those interviews had been about.

By now, on Monday afternoon, he knew that the extended Khalil clan consisted of twenty-three separate families strung out between South San Francisco and San Jose, and then across the Bay over to Hayward and Fremont. The typical arrangement was that each family owned its own franchise of the 7-Eleven chain, although four of them owned more than one store. The family had been in the country since Ibrahim and Shatha had emigrated with their four children in 1989, before the first Gulf War.

The eldest surviving brother, Abdel Khalil, had been the spokesman for the family in the aftermath of the murders of his parents and seemed the likeliest source of information. Abdel owned three stores along the El Camino Real between the two northern Peninsula towns of Millbrae and San Bruno, but conducted his corporate business out of a low-slung stucco-and-glass building set down in a former landfill by San Francisco Airport.

Hunt got out of his Mini Cooper and walked in the flat glaring sunshine across a treeless parking lot and into the nondescript reception area of AMK, Inc. A swarthy, somewhat disheveled young man in shirtsleeves sat at the only substantial piece of furniture, a cluttered desk in the middle of the room. He was sorting some kind of paperwork. A cup of tea steamed at the side of his desk. The screen saver on his computer showed an artist's rendering of a 7-Eleven store in a typical urban strip mall. A radio, turned low, played what Hunt would have called Middle Eastern, perhaps Iraqi, music.

Hunt had made the appointment this morning, probably with this same young man, under slightly bogus conditions, saying that he was a writer who was doing an article on successful immigration stories. Now, after he introduced himself, the boy gave him a nervous smile and disappeared through a door behind him, leaving Hunt standing alone in front of the desk.

A minute later, Hunt was shaking hands with a good-looking man in his mid-thirties. With his mustache he bore a slight resemblance to Saddam Hussein, although he was dressed in American clothes—black slacks that looked to be the bottom portion of a man's suit and a light blue dress shirt with an open neck. "Mr. Hunt, I'm Abdel Khalil. Would you like something to drink? A cup of tea, perhaps, coffee, Coke."

"Coffee would be nice. Black, please."

"Fine. We can take it in my office." Khalil snapped his fingers twice quickly and the boy jumped, bowed, and disappeared.

Hunt followed Khalil to a more spacious room in the back corner of the building. From the chair he was directed to in front of the standard wooden desk, he had an unimpeded view of the Bay and of planes landing at the airport.

The room itself, like its counterpart outside, was functional in the extreme. An oversized map of the Bay Area was pinned to one of the walls above a low credenza. A computer had its own small table at a right angle to the desk, which Khalil went around and sat behind. He'd barely gotten settled when the receptionist knocked and entered with a cup of coffee and handed it to Hunt, then closed the door behind him on the way out.

"Now." Khalil clasped his hands on the desk. He spoke educated and uninflected English. "Mr. Hunt. How's the coffee? Good. Now, how can I help you? I understand you're writing an article of some kind?"

This was always the tough part. Hunt placed his saucer on the tiny table next to him. "Actually, sir, that's not the case, and I apologize. I'm a private investigator working with a lawyer who's doing the appeal on the Evan Scholler case and if you'd like to kick me out of here, I'd understand."

Surprised, but not completely unamused, Khalil waved that off. "You've barely gotten settled. Why would you think I wouldn't talk to you about Evan Scholler?"

"It could be a touchy subject."

"And why would that be?"

"I think the assumption was that he killed your parents."

"Yes." Khalil's face darkened. "That was a difficult time. But I hope we've put that behind us. Did you say Scholler was appealing his conviction?"

Hunt nodded.

"Well, I wish him luck."

"You do? That's a bit of a surprise."

"Why is that?"

"If he killed your parents."

"But he was never charged with killing my parents. And frankly, it didn't seem to make much sense at the time, unless you bought the idea that after what happened to him over there, he hated all Iraqis and just picked them as a random couple to sacrifice." Khalil shook his head. "I never really saw that."

"So who do you think killed them?"

"I think it must have been Ron Nolan."

"Why do you say that?"

"Well, the fragmentation grenades, for example. His work, I understand, brought him to and from Iraq frequently, where he would have access to that stuff and would have been able to bring it back here by military transport without having to bother with customs."

"But why?"

"Why what?"

"Why your parents? What was Nolan's motive?"

Khalil grimaced, the memory of it all beginning to play back. "I believe he picked up a contract to assassinate them in Iraq. Our family has business interests over there and I think—well, I had heard this, and when I told the FBI—"

"Wait a minute, please! Excuse me. You're saying you talked to the FBI, then?"

"Of course."

"And you told them that you believed Ron Nolan had killed your parents because of information that you got from Iraq?"

"Well, yes."

"And what did the FBI say?"

"They seemed to already know, and didn't disagree that that was probably what happened. They assured us they would look into it. But then, of course, after what happened to Mr. Nolan . . ."

"So they talked to you about the Scholler trial?"

This seemed to stump him for a minute. He half turned and looked out his window, his brow furrowed, then came back to Hunt. "I don't really recall that."

"So what did they talk to you about?" Hunt sat back, lost for a beat in his own perplexity. "But I'm sorry, I interrupted you. So you're saying the FBI didn't think Scholler killed your parents?"

"Right. That's probably a large part of the reason he never got charged with that. Everyone I've talked to in the FBI agreed that it was Nolan."

"But Nolan was never—"

"Nolan was dead, Mr. Hunt. What was anybody going to do about that? It was over, a done deal. Even if some of my brothers and cousins wanted to kill him, he was already dead."

"So you're saying Scholler did kill Nolan?"

Now Khalil showed genuine surprise. "Well, yes, of course. I don't believe anyone has any doubts about that. Do they?"

Well, as a matter of fact, yes, Hunt was going to say, *my boss does.* Which would have led to Khalil's next question, *Then who did kill Nolan?* And Hunt's answer—Hardy's answer—would have been: *Uh, you guys. The Khalils.* But suddenly, that was not how this was going.

Instead, Hunt scrambled. "Okay. Nobody doubts Scholler killed Nolan. And the FBI told you that Nolan probably killed your parents. Did they know why? Or who put this contract out?"

"The short answer is not at first, they couldn't find anything, although I heard from relatives that they interrogated a lot of people over there."

It was all Hunt could do to keep his mouth from dropping open in amazement. "In Iraq? The FBI interrogated people about your parents' death all the way over in Iraq?"

"Of course. That's where the trail led."

"But they didn't find out who did it?"

"Eventually, they believed they did, yes." Now Khalil allowed a small smile. "And we—my family—verified that they were right. Your FBI, they know what they are doing, you know. They're extremely competent and efficient."

Hunt sat back. "What did they find out?"

"Well, as I say, eventually it became more or less obvious. But first you have to know that my father, Ibrahim, was a brilliant businessman. He directed his youngest brother, Mahmoud, in some of his widespread business dealings in Iraq. Mahmoud was trying to supply contract workers on a reconstruction job over there, a very lucrative one, but the main supplier—Mahmoud's chief competitor, in fact—was a Kurd named Kuvan Krekar. The FBI became satisfied that Mr. Krekar took out the contract on my mother and father to disrupt our business over there, and to a large extent he was successful. In the short term." When Khalil's small smile returned, it had a chilling aspect. "I received word about two years ago that Mr. Krekar had died from an improvised explosive device. My country, as you know, is going through some very violent times. But the good news is that Mahmoud and his business have been thriving lately, and we believe we have turned the corner over there."

[36]

AT FIVE-THIRTY, Hardy and Hunt were sharing one of the window booths at Lou the Greek's, a bar and, in some people's opinion, restaurant located just across the street from the Hall of Justice. The squabble over whether it was in fact a true restaurant worthy of the name derived from the uneven quality of the food they served at the place. Many of the regular patrons came in only to drink at the tiny bar in the front, and didn't ever try to eat the constantly changing Special that Lou's wife, Chui, created every single day.

The Special was the only food item on the menu, and in deference to Chui's Chinese and Lou's Greek ethnicities, she most frequently tried to make different combinations of ingredients that included both of these two cultures' rather violently disparate culinary traditions. Thus, on any given day, the Lou's Special might be taramasalata (fish roe) wontons in an avgolemono broth, moussaka potstickers, or the oft-requested Yeanling Clay Bowl, the ingredients of which had once stumped a panel of six of the city's all-star chefs after DA Clarence Jackman had publicly referred to it as his "favorite lunch in the city."

Because Lou's was semi-subterranean—the entrance off Bryant descended eight steps from the street level—the booth where Hardy and Hunt sat had windows high in the wall above them, which at the same time were at the ground level of the alley that ran alongside the building on the outside. The view out the windows, which few took advantage of, was of passing feet, garbage cans, the occasional horizontal homeless person.

Today, neither Hardy nor Hunt was paying attention to the ambience. Hardy, who had spent most of the afternoon working on the first draft of his argument on the PTSD issue for Evan's appeal, sat with his shoulders hunched over slightly as though he were brooding, his hands cupped around a mug of coffee. Hunt sat sideways in the booth, slowly revolving a pint glass of beer on the table. Hunt had already made his report to Hardy at his office, and this had prompted Hardy's call back to Glitsky, and ultimately the decision that they should all meet down here and see what they had.

"You don't think the fact that the Khalils talked to the FBI is going to be enough for you?" Hunt asked. "Friday that was all you wanted."

"I remember it well," Hardy said, "those halcyon bygone days. And absolutely I'm going to make the argument. The Khalils had a strong motive to kill Nolan. The jury should have known about that and decided for themselves whether that caused them to have a reasonable doubt about Evan's guilt. It's up to the jury, not the FBI, to decide what's important and what's not. But for *Brady* to work, the withheld discovery has to be reasonably likely to cast doubt on the verdict. And the idea that some unknown third parties had a motive to kill Nolan probably isn't going to convince the court to give Evan a new trial. We're just going to need something stronger if we want to argue that the Khalils killed Nolan—"

"Which I just don't see, Diz. Really. Still possible, I know, but you had to have heard this guy. If he didn't absolutely believe Scholler killed Nolan, he's gotta get himself an agent."

"Well, if the alternative option was either himself or one of his relatives, it might sharpen his thespian skills a little bit, don't you think?"

Hunt shrugged. "Possibly. But still, it's against my gut."

"All right, then, let's go with that for a minute. Say whoever killed Nolan, it wasn't the Khalils and it wasn't Scholler. Who does that leave?"

"How 'bout the FBI? Maybe there was way more money involved and these two agents who have disappeared found it and left the country."

"Maybe," Hardy said without enthusiasm. "And a good story. But I kind of doubt it."

"Me too," Hunt said, pointing at the entrance. "And I hate that. But here comes Glitsky. Maybe he'll know something."

IT WASN'T ONLY GLITSKY. Bracco came in with him. Hardy introduced Hunt around—he hadn't met either of the cops before. Lou came from behind the bar and took their orders, Glitsky's green tea and Bracco's Diet Coke. In the next few minutes of show and tell, everybody got reasonably caught up. The story Hardy had heard from Tara about the mugging incident in San Francisco's Tenderloin, implicating Nolan in those three deaths, significantly upped the buzz quotient around the table.

Bracco went last, revealing to the civilians what he'd already told Glitsky—that he'd located Bowen's secretary, Deni Pichaud, and talked to her for an hour or more about what her boss had been working on during the last few days before he disappeared. Ms. Pichaud didn't have much to offer. Bowen, as everyone already knew, had a varied and substantial practice, and according to Pichaud he tended to flit from one case to another as clients called and demanded his attention. She had no special memory of anything about Evan Scholler or his appeal.

When Bracco finished, the four men sat looking at one another for a long moment. Hardy finally broke into the silence. "So where does that leave us?"

"Is shit creek already taken?" Hunt asked.

Glitsky, who eschewed profanity, gave the detective a quick bad eye but then blew on his tea, sipped, and said, "It's the FBI and Iraq. That's all that's left."

Hardy shook his head. "The FBI didn't kill Nolan, Abe."

"Maybe Scholler did." Bracco held up a hand. "I know he's your client and all, but—"

"Yeah, but that almost doesn't matter at this point," Glitsky said.

"I'm afraid it still does to me, guys," Hardy put in. "That's why me and Wyatt are here. So if everybody's good with it, maybe we can just leave the whole question of who killed Nolan open and see where that leads us."

"Good by me," Glitsky said. "I want who did the Bowens, and we know that wasn't Scholler."

"So you're going with the Bowens being murders?" Hunt asked.

Glitsky nodded. "Until I get proven otherwise." He pointed a finger across the table at his inspector. "Which means, while I'm thinking of it, Darrel, feel free to put in more time on both these investigations. Treat 'em both like they're righteous one eighty-sevens. Witnesses if you can find 'em, evidence ditto, phone and financial records, the whole ball of wax."

Bracco, determination all over his face, nodded. "Got it."

"Meanwhile," Glitsky continued, "how are the FBI and Iraq connected to the Bowens?" In a rare display of humor, he channeled the line from *Ferris Bueller.* "Anyone? Anyone?"

"I've got a thought," Hardy said. "Let's go back to Nolan. The FBI talked to him in person and his employer works in Iraq, which puts FBI and Iraq in the same sentence anyway."

Hunt picked it up. "All right. And Abdel Khalil says Nolan picked up the contract on his parents in Iraq from a guy named Kumar or something."

Hardy, who rarely forgot anything, chimed in. "Kuvan."

"Okay, Kuvan. Kuvan paid Nolan forty or fifty grand to take out the Khalils. Then the Khalil family over in Iraq took out Kuvan."

The four men sat with their thoughts and drinks. Finally, Hardy cleared his throat. "My, what a tidy little package," he said.

Glitsky turned to him. "What are you saying?"

"I'm saying that this is all a nice cleanly closed circle, except for two little things—Charlie and Hanna Bowen. And I think we're all in agreement that, no matter what, the FBI didn't kill them. Right?"

Nods all around.

"Well, check me if I'm wrong on anything here, but how about if the trail leads to Iraq, all right, but instead of Kuvan paying for the hit, the order came from Allstrong?"

"The way it did with Zwick," Glitsky added.

"Do we know that for sure?" Bracco asked. "And even if we do, what does it get us?"

"Nothing with Zwick, as you say. The FBI never got involved in that investigation," Hardy answered. "But with the Khalils, it gets us the FBI covering for an American company with contracts over there, deflecting the blame—and the retaliation—on this Kuvan guy. Just another Iraqi businessman who got squeezed in the war. This totally satisfies the Khalils—they get their tribal revenge and they're happy. And over here, now nobody's looking at Nolan anymore, or at Allstrong. The story's completely over."

"And the FBI did this, again, why?" Glitsky asked.

"Because Allstrong is connected high up in the government, both over there and back here. High enough that they could call off the FBI."

"Uh-oh." Glitsky was shaking his head.

"I know, I know," Hardy said. "You hate this conspiracy stuff. Which doesn't mean, Abe, that it doesn't happen."

"I don't hate it," Bracco said.

Hunt chimed in. "Me neither. In fact, I kind of like it."

"Maybe I'm missing something," Glitsky said, coming back at Hardy. "So, Diz, you're saying that the FBI went over to investigate what? Nolan's murder?"

"No. The Khalil murders."

"I thought they'd concluded that was your client?"

"No," Hunt corrected Glitsky. "Redwood City, not the feds, concluded that that was Evan. According to Abdel, the FBI thought it was Nolan pretty early on."

"So they went over to Iraq? Why?"

"To find the source of the frag grenades," Hardy said, "if nothing else. Interview Nolan's associates, maybe his boss, who has, it turns out, in fact actually ordered the hit."

"But again, Diz, why?"

"Well, and here I'm extrapolating a little bit, but see if it doesn't sing for you, because Allstrong had a profitable relationship with this guy Kuvan. And the Khalils were getting in Kuvan's way. This is all stuff, by the way, that Wyatt more or less verified this afternoon with Abdel. So Allstrong orders its guy, Nolan, to do the hit. Which is, P.S., what he basically did for a living anyway."

"So." Glitsky, trying to make the tumblers fall into place, slowly swirled his teacup in front of him. "How does this get us to Bowen?"

"Bowen gets Evan's appeal," Hardy said, "just like I did. He starts asking the same types of questions I've been asking, except instead of sending Wyatt here down to talk to Abdel Khalil, he starts with the assumption we're working with right now—that Nolan and not Evan killed the Khalils. So that changes his equation about who would need to cover that up if it comes out, and what's the answer?"

"Allstrong," Hunt said.

Hardy nodded. "Ten points."

"Who needs to cover what up?" Glitsky asked.

"Allstrong. They can play fast and loose all they want in Iraq and nobody asks too many questions as long as they're fulfilling their contracts. But if it comes out—and it would be a huge story over here—that they're killing naturalized American citizens on American soil to promote their business interests in Iraq, I've got to believe that screwed up as things are over there, Allstrong would at least stop getting new contracts. They might even lose the ones they've already got, and that's if they don't get charged for murder first."

Bracco slurped at the end of his Diet Coke. "How much money are we talking about? For Allstrong, I mean, their contracts over there."

Hunt spoke up. "I got curious checking out some stuff on Nolan and Googled them over the weekend. Their first year in Iraq, when Nolan was on the payroll, they got about three hundred and fifty million dollars in government contracts."

"You've got to be kidding me," Bracco said. "Allstrong Security? I mean, who are they? Nobody's ever heard of them. They're not exactly Halliburton."

"No, but they're trying harder," said Hunt, "that's for sure."

"Maybe they'd actually kill to get work," Hardy deadpanned.

Glitsky sat back, his body language saying that he was still reserving judgment. "Okay, okay. So you're saying Bowen went to Allstrong first, not the Khalils, with these questions?"

"That's my guess," Hardy said.

"And Allstrong killed him?"

A nod. "Or had him killed, yes."

"That's pretty drastic, don't you think?"

"Maybe from our perspective, granted. But these guys are a bunch of mercenaries. They're hired guns. That's how they solve problems." Hardy came forward in his enthusiasm. "Look, Abe, Allstrong had already dealt with the whole Nolan thing and put it behind them. The world believed it was Evan Scholler who'd killed the Khalils for his own twisted reasons. Someone with the government who had major juice—a general, a congressman, I don't know, somebody who was in Allstrong's pocket and helping it get its contracts—had either ordered or convinced the FBI to offer up Kuvan privately to the remaining Khalils."

Glitsky was still shaking his head. "I know we're not all big FBI fans here, but I've got to say that I don't see them doing this. Ever. Sometimes they might get a little overzealous, but they're not going to frame an innocent Iraqi and stand back while someone else kills him."

Hardy nodded, conceding the point. "How about if they didn't know, Abe? How about if someone way up, like the general or senator or whoever I was talking about earlier, got to the director of the Bureau, say, and vouched for Allstrong, meanwhile selling him a bill of goods about Kuvan? So your agents solve the case and then they're ordered off it."

"And when somebody else wants to talk about it," Bracco said, "like you, this morning, sir, the agents don't work there anymore."

"And Allstrong stays off the hook," Hardy said.

"Until Bowen showed up," Hunt added.

"That's it," Hardy said. "And then here it was again, the threat to Allstrong, to its very existence, and a lot closer this time. So they had to make Bowen disappear before he could make any kind of public stink. Or even ask any more questions. He just had to go away." Hardy looked around the table. "Anybody see an egregious flaw here?"

Glitsky looked across at Bracco. "Don't worry about it, Darrel, he always uses words like that." Then, back to Hardy. "Do you know that Bowen ever actually got in touch with Allstrong? I mean, any actual proof?"

"No, but we can find that out. Those phone records you were talking about." Hardy turned to Bracco. "And you might want to check Hanna's too."

Glitsky snapped out a curt defense of his inspector. "I'm sure Darrel's got some sense of the drill, Diz."

"Sorry," Hardy said to Bracco. "I tend to get excited. This may really be something."

"Let's get some evidence first," Glitsky said. He sipped at the last of his tea, put his cup down gently. When he spoke, his voice was heavy with discontent. "I really don't want to believe there's a conspiracy here. And a cover-up. From somebody high enough up to have influence with the FBI. I keep believing our guys don't do that kind of stuff."

"With all respect, are you kidding, sir?" Hunt said. "These are the same swell folks who brought us Abu Ghraib and all the other disasters over there. Giving up Kuvan for the greater good, and that means pumping more money into a hardworking, God-fearing company like Allstrong—

that's a no-brainer. We're the good guys, remember, so whatever we do is right."

"Yeah," Glitsky said, "so let's hope we're wrong on this one."

Hardy, thinking about Evan Scholler doing life without parole in prison, didn't hope they were wrong. He didn't see another plausible alternative, and he'd long since lost faith in the essential goodness of man. Some were good, true, maybe most. But others, particularly those drawn to war zones and to chaos, would sometimes do anything—lie, cheat, and kill—for more money and more power, either or both. The basic rules of civilization did not apply.

That, Hardy was now all but convinced, was what had happened here. The moral rot that festered in Iraq and in the halls of power both here and abroad had poisoned the communal well over there. What distinguished Allstrong was that it had had the arrogance and irresponsibility to bring the rot and the chaos home.

And that, Hardy felt, could not be allowed to stand.

[37]

HARDY SAT IN HIS READING CHAIR, his feet up on the ottoman, in the dark living room in the front of his house. He wore the same black gym shorts that he'd put on before he'd gotten into bed six hours before. When he had started awake about an hour ago—he'd dreamt that he'd been pushed from an airplane out over the Pacific Ocean—tossing off the covers, he had lain still in the night until his heart slowed down, listening to his wife's breathing beside him, taking what comfort he could from the peaceful regularity of it.

Finally giving up on the idea of sleeping, he eased himself out of bed. Downstairs, he looked into the refrigerator out of habit, then closed it and went into the adjoining family room and watched his tropical fish swimming in their dim, gurgling home.

He'd spent most of the evening after dinner back next to his fish at his computer, finding out everything he could about Allstrong Security. Hunt's analysis of their financial success early in the war was accurate as far as it went, but he'd failed to mention that to date, the company's government contracts in Iraq totaled eight hundred and forty million dollars.

Allstrong was in charge of security at sixteen of the country's airports, as well as guarding electrical grids in twenty-two administrative areas. They had been in charge of the currency changeover for the entire country as well as the rebuilding of the power lines in the extremely violent Anbar Province. The company's Web site boasted of 8,800 employees in Iraq, 465 of whom were former American military men, most of them officers.

The company had also become active in several other countries, with more than 500 ex-commando operatives in Indonesia, Afghanistan,

Kuwait, Nigeria, and El Salvador, where it specialized in corporate as well as government logistics and security. Over 200 more employees worked at a sprawling new headquarters complex near Candlestick Point in San Francisco, where the concentration was mostly on programs to guarantee the integrity of municipal water supplies and, incongruously, on raising catfish as a sustainable and inexpensive food source for developing countries.

Jack Allstrong, the founder, president, and CEO, had evidently relocated back to the home office in March of 2005. He lived alone in a mansion in Hillsborough and presided over the business out of San Francisco, although the home page stressed that Allstrong was ready and able to embark to trouble spots anywhere in the world at a moment's notice in one of the corporation's fleet of private aircraft, which included two Gulfstream V jets.

When he went to bed, Hardy's brain had been spinning with the possibilities that Allstrong presented for his Scholler appeal. As soon as Bracco could forge the link tying Allstrong to Nolan's involvement in the assassination of the Khalils and to the deaths of the Bowens, Hardy would have an unassailable argument that the jury in the original trial never saw crucial evidence that reasonably could have affected the verdict. He'd get his appeal granted on the *Brady* violation, and then probably a new trial. And further, he doubted that a new jury, given the reversals in the case, would convict Evan again.

Now Hardy's subconscious had rejected all of these optimistic conclusions. As he sat slumped down in his living room chair he found himself scavenging for any kind of salvageable something that could tie Allstrong—either the person or the company—to any crime at all.

If Jack Allstrong had personally ordered Nolan to eliminate the Khalils, and paid him in cash, which is exactly what Hardy conjectured had happened, he could count on there being no record of it whatsoever. Especially after all these years.

Or—Hardy corrected himself—Charlie Bowen had come up with the only evidence there might have been, and perhaps had inadvertently passed it on to his wife. But by now, whatever that had been must be gone. And similarly, the murders of Charlie and Hanna had been carried out with professional efficiency.

Even if Bracco discovered that Charlie and/or Hanna Bowen had called or gone down to visit Allstrong on the last day of their lives, what would that prove? Would it lead to a discovery of Charlie's body, which had probably long since become fish food? Or would it place an Allstrong mercenary in Hanna's garage pulling her body down to make sure to break her neck as she dropped from her stepladder?

Hardy knew it wouldn't.

And so long as Allstrong didn't confess to anything—and if there was no proof he'd ever done anything wrong, why would he?—then in the face of all the accusations in the world, he'd remain untouchable. In fact, Hardy realized, with the size of the operation Allstrong was running, by now he'd undoubtedly have surrounded himself with protection—administrative assistants, senior staff, his own lawyers—to keep him insulated from riffraff such as Hardy himself or even Sergeant Bracco who might come calling on him with impertinent questions. Hardy might never even get to talk to him.

At the sound of the newspaper hitting the porch, he opened his eyes again. The darkness outside had lessened by a degree.

It was going to be a long day.

THREE AND A HALF HOURS into the work portion of that day, Hardy glared malevolently at the phone as it buzzed at his elbow. He was eight pages into his brief about the *Brady* violation. He made a good case that the FBI's information should have been disclosed to Washburn. This would have allowed him to cross-examine the now-disappeared, allegedly ex–FBI agents on the entire question of Nolan's involvement with the frag grenades. He'd turned off his cell phone and left strict instructions with Phyllis to hold all of his calls. He needed to concentrate.

But here was the phone, buzzing at him. Hence the glare.

He put his pen down and reached for the receiver. "This must be an emergency," he said in a mild tone. "Is the building on fire?"

"No, sir. But Lieutenant Glitsky said I should disturb you. Apparently somebody tried to kill Evan Scholler at the prison this morning. Lieutenant Glitsky is holding now. Shall I put him through?"

"That would be a good thing, Phyllis. Please." He heard the click of connection. "Is Evan all right?"

"He's alive, though he's cut pretty bad. He was lucky. The shiv hit a rib or he'd be room temperature by now."

"So he's going to live?"

"No promises, but good chance, evidently."

"So what happened, Abe? He get in a fight?"

"Well, finding out what really happened is always a little iffy there, but by first reports, it's starting to look like he was a target of some kind. The guy who went for him was a Salvadoran gangbanger out of L.A. named Rafael Calderon. Nobody had ever seen these two guys together before this morning."

"So you're saying somebody ordered this?"

"I'm not saying anything. I'm telling you what I've heard so far. And I've heard that your man Evan had been an ideal inmate. No word about any enemies, or what he might have done to make them."

"So the order came from outside?"

"Don't know. It could have been something personal we don't know about. I'd hesitate to conjecture. But maybe you've got something you want to tell me?"

Hardy, recalling his research the previous night, couldn't keep the thought from jumping to the front of his mind—Allstrong Security was developing a presence in El Salvador. Beyond his net surfing last night, he'd read several lengthy magazine articles and even pieces of a couple of books delineating the relationships between U.S. mercenaries and the Salvadoran gang networks in that country, and took it as gospel that the connections between them ran deep. He took a minute to get Glitsky up to speed, then asked, "Did they question Calderon?"

"Calderon wasn't as lucky as Scholler."

"Are you telling me he's dead?"

"That's right."

"Did Scholler kill him?"

"No. Scholler was on the ground, bleeding. When the guards heard the screaming and yelling from the assault and got there, they got Calderon surrounded and he went more or less insane. He still had his shiv on him and he charged them. They reacted with what, after the hearing, I'm sure will be called appropriate force in self-defense."

Hardy realized that he was gripping the phone so tightly that his knuckles were white. He knew that if Calderon had taken the job of assassinating Scholler in prison and either botched it or got caught afterward, both of which had happened in this case, he could expect to be killed by his handler or by another gang-connected inmate before he could be questioned and give anything away. And he knew that whoever had put out the contract would just as easily put out another one.

AFTER THE PHONE CALL, Hardy couldn't get his mind back on the draft of his brief. He decided to walk down to the Hall of Justice to clear his mind. The fine weather continued, and if Glitsky had already gone to lunch, Hardy could walk down a couple of blocks and catch a meal at any one of a number of the good new joints in SoMa, South of Market. But Abe was in, at his desk drinking a bottled water and eating a rice cake. Glitsky opened his desk drawer, pulled out a handful of peanuts in the shell, and slid them across his desk.

Hardy cracked a shell. "This is Allstrong again, Abe."

"Calderon? It might be at that."

"It is, absolutely."

Glitsky shook his head. "Don't get me wrong. I want it to be with all my heart, but I don't have enough, Diz. If makes you feel any better, I think it's possible, and I didn't think that a few days ago. I'm waiting for Darrel before I jump to any conclusions."

"I made that jump when I heard about the stabbing. There is no other conclusion."

"Not to be disagreeable, but don't kid yourself. You were all over this at least yesterday, maybe before."

Hardy chewed reflectively. "You want to hear how it works? Why it's Allstrong?"

"Sure, but the short version, please."

"Okay, six weeks ago Hanna gets killed. Allstrong's now had to kill two people involved in the Scholler appeal. He thinks it's probably all done as far as getting rid of evidence is concerned, but he knows that as long as Evan Scholler's in prison, there's going to be this appeal coming up again and its attendant risks, meaning people like Bowen or me coming around asking him provocative questions. Maybe there's even more evidence someplace that he was actively involved in a domestic homicide."

"Let's hope," Glitsky said.

Hardy nodded. "So Allstrong gets another idea."

"Kill Scholler."

"You're reading my mind." Another peanut. "Scholler dies, the appeal is over. Cuts it off at the source. But of course, the problem is that Scholler's in prison. Not untouchable, but more complicated, through El Salvador and backup through one of the L.A. gangs." Hardy held up his hands in a *voilà* gesture. "There's your six weeks between Hanna and now."

"Brilliant." Glitsky ate another peanut. "You've got it all figured out."

"I've got Bowen figured out too. They dumped him out in the ocean."

This brought Glitsky forward in his chair. "How do you know that?"

"I dreamed it," Hardy said, grinning. "But it's what happened, Abe. You're going to find his DNA in one of their airplanes, I promise."

"Just as soon as I get to look in one of them." Sitting back, Glitsky folded his hands on his lap. "I want to believe you, Diz, I really do. I'll jump on all of this with both feet as soon as I can go to a judge to give me a warrant. Or I get any other reason to send Bracco to talk to the guy. But until I do . . ." He shrugged. "I'm waiting on Bracco. He finds something or he doesn't. Usually, if something's there, he does."

"Yeah, but meanwhile, my client's still a target."

Glitsky glanced at the wall clock. "Diz. I think that's a reach. I really do. Or, at worst, by your own math, the next attack is six weeks away."

GLITSKY WAS HALF JOKING, but the next attack felt far closer than six weeks away to Hardy.

Back in his office, galvanized, he told Phyllis to hold his calls again and spent the next two hours working on his brief. One thing he could do, as a lawyer, was actually file his appeal and get things shaking. He, too, had been waiting for Bracco to come up with actual evidence that either of the Bowens had called Allstrong, but there was another, and much more direct, way to go about getting this information. He could pick up the phone and ask.

It wasn't Glitsky's way, and Hardy, in his enthusiasm to simply figure out what had happened, had gotten hung up with that process. But Glitsky was trying to solve two homicides in his jurisdiction and bring a killer to justice. Hardy, on the other hand, had only one job. He was working to free his client.

It was a crucial difference, and it now had gained added urgency with the prison assault on Evan this morning. Hardy had been hoping that once the police could somehow prove an Allstrong/Bowen connection, it would strengthen the argument in his appeal. But he really didn't need that to file—the FBI and the Khalils might eventually lead to Allstrong and Nolan, but the issue was whether or not those initial interrogations should have been part of the prosecution's discovery, and on this point there was little doubt.

Easy though it might be to make an actual phone call to Allstrong, there was another component to the equation that Hardy could ignore only at his peril. These guys had proven themselves seriously proactive about people who threatened their business interests. If Hardy's theories were correct, and he was by now all but certain that they were, they had killed both the Bowens and made an attempt on the life of Evan. And all of this without leaving behind a shred of evidence that would tie them to these crimes.

Hardy realized that as soon as he made that one simple phone call, the threat level in his own life was going to go up in a hurry. He would be putting himself exactly where Charlie Bowen had gone before he disappeared forever.

But he needed the information. He had to know for sure; he couldn't file his appeal until he knew.

Reward; risk.

Hardy had written the Allstrong office number down in his notes as a matter of course while he was doing his research last night. Returning from word processing where he'd dropped his draft marked URGENT, he closed his office door, went behind his desk, sat down, took out his notes, and pulled the phone over in front of him, punching the numbers with a steeled deliberation.

[38]

"JACK ALLSTRONG, please."

"I'll see if he's in. Can I tell him who's calling?"

"I don't know. How can you tell him who's calling if he's not in?"

"I beg your pardon?"

"You said you'd see if Mr. Allstrong was in. But if you were going to tell him who was calling, then you must know he is in. Isn't that right?"

Hardy hated to launch this logic assault on the poor receptionist, but with the attack on Evan, he believed he was running out of time. "Please tell Mr. Allstrong that my name is Dismas Hardy and that it's extremely important that I speak with him as soon as possible." He spelled his name out for her. "I'm an attorney working on the appeal in the Evan Scholler matter, with which I'm sure he's familiar. Please also tell him that I'm continuing the work begun last summer by a lawyer named Charlie Bowen. If he's busy, tell him I'll be happy to wait here on the line for as long as it takes."

As it turned out, it took less than a minute. A voice with an undefinably Southern accent and devoid of nervousness, anger, or fear came through the wire. "This is Jack Allstrong."

"Mr. Allstrong, my name is Dismas Hardy and—"

A big, booming laugh. "Yeah, I already know that. You made quite a first impression on our Marilou, I must say. And normally she is some kind of a tough nut to crack. She says you're working with Lieutenant Scholler?"

"Evan. Yes, sir."

"Evan, right. I always think of him as Lieutenant. That's what he was when he worked with us." He paused. "God, that whole quagmire with him and Ron Nolan just turned into a hell of a thing, didn't it? The messes people get themselves into. And two better young men you couldn't have imagined. But I don't suppose you ever had a chance to meet Ron?"

"No, I didn't."

"That's a shame. He was a fine man, a fine soldier, a loyal employee. What happened to him was just nothin' less than a goddamned tragedy, Mr. Hardy, I'll be honest with you. And I know it was because of the lieutenant's head wound to some extent, so I don't blame him the way I might otherwise. War, and this one's no exception, it can do horrible things to people. Anybody's been in one knows that for a fact. You a veteran, Mr. Hardy?"

"Yes, sir. Vietnam."

"Well, then, you know what I'm talking about. But at least this war, the soldiers themselves, the men on the ground, they're getting some respect. And about goddamn time, wouldn't you say?"

"Yes, I would," Hardy said. "But I'm calling because I'm about to file an appeal to see if I can get Mr. Scholler out of prison and—"

"Wait!" Allstrong's voice hardened up. "Now, wait just a second here. You say you're trying to get the lieutenant out of prison? I thought nobody doubted that he had killed Ron."

"Well, the jury thought it was beyond reasonable doubt, which is not—"

"Now, hold on. We don't need to be splitting hairs here, Mr. Hardy. I think I've made it clear that until he was injured and even after that, Lieutenant Scholler had my complete respect. He was a good soldier, a natural leader, good to his men. But I don't think I'm comfortable with the idea that the man who killed one of my first employees, and a damn good friend, is going to be out walking the streets again, a free man. And I certainly don't think I'm inclined to help with this appeal of yours."

"Sir, I don't believe Evan Scholler did kill Ron Nolan."

"Well, that's a good one. You might be in the minority with that opinion. I haven't talked to anybody else who thinks that."

"Not even Charlie Bowen?"

Allstrong didn't hesitate for an instant. "Not him either."

"So you talked to him?"

"Couple of times, at least. Last summer sometime, was it? I don't know.

Whatever happened to him anyway? One day he's here asking me all kinds of questions, I'm thinking he's moving forward on this appeal like you are, and next thing you know he's gone."

"That's what happened," Hardy said. "He disappeared."

"Just like that?"

"Apparently." Hardy found his temper starting to flare, and decided it was time to push on Allstrong, see if he could get a bit of a rise. "Did you know Charlie Bowen's wife?"

"I don't believe so."

"She never called you there?"

"She might have called here, although I don't know why she would have. But if she did, she never talked to me. Why do you think I would know anything about her?"

Hardy laid out his conjecture as factual truth. "She was working on some of the files Charlie was working on when he disappeared. Then, I don't know if you've heard, but six weeks ago, she committed suicide."

For the first time, Allstrong hesitated, then made a little kissing noise. "Well, I'm sorry to hear that, of course. Over Charlie walking out on her?"

"That's the general assumption, I presume. Although there are other theories."

"About why she killed herself?"

"Not just why, but whether. There's some evidence that she might have been killed by someone who wanted to make it look like a suicide."

"Why would anyone do that? Want to kill her, I mean?"

"Maybe because she'd found out something to do with her husband's death. And in that case, maybe Charlie Bowen wasn't a simple disappearance either. Maybe he was murdered too."

"That's a lot of maybes."

"Yes, it is. And here's another one. Maybe Charlie's work on this appeal is what convinced somebody they needed to kill him."

"Who would that be?"

"Whoever actually did kill Ron Nolan."

"Ahh." Allstrong mustered up a kind of chortle. "And this is what brings us around to where you don't think it was Scholler who killed him."

"That's right. These are my theories about the Bowens, both of them. I think they were both murdered, and I think the person behind those murders also tried to have Evan Scholler killed this morning at Corcoran Prison. But that one didn't work." Hardy didn't know if Allstrong had already received this news from his sources within the prison, and he thought it wouldn't hurt to hear it now from him.

And while there was no sign that this information registered as anything but another unimportant detail about Hardy's case, by degrees the superficial warmth was leeching out of both men's tones. When Allstrong spoke next, his easy Southern geniality was entirely missing. "Well, all of this is interesting, I'm sure, but it really doesn't have shit-all to do with me. And I'm afraid, as I told you, I'm not going to be too disposed to help you get Ron Nolan's killer out of prison. So if there's anything else specific I can help you with, let's hear it. Otherwise, I got a business I'm trying to run here."

"I appreciate that," Hardy said. "I thought you'd be interested in finding Ron Nolan's killer in any event, though. Whether or not it was Evan Scholler, you'd want to know who really did it, I presume. And whatever you can tell me now might help me get to the truth. I'm basing my appeal on stuff I think the FBI discovered that they didn't reveal to Evan's prosecutors at the time of the trial. I assume you're familiar with fragmentation grenades?"

"Sure."

"Well, then you may know that Nolan, who was in your employ at the time, had several of these in his home."

"I understood that Scholler put them there to frame Ron."

"No, sir." Hardy easily came out with the next untruth. "Since the trial, that's been pretty much discredited. The FBI concluded there was no way Evan could have gotten these things back home, whereas Nolan could have just packed them in his duffel."

"And why would he do that?"

"Because he liked them to cover his tracks after he assassinated people."

Allstrong laughed out loud, although through the phone Hardy picked up as much nerves as humor in it this time. When he got his breath, he said, "That accusation is really beneath contempt, Mr. Hardy. Ron was my recruiter out here. He didn't assassinate people."

"Yes, he did. The FBI has made that clear enough to the Khalil family, who were among his victims. That's the evidence I'm trying to get in front of the court this time around. If Nolan was killing people on contract, then revenge becomes a motive for his own death, and that might give Evan an out."

Allstrong came out with the question Hardy had been leading him toward. "You say Nolan was killing people on contract? That's absurd."

"The FBI doesn't think so."

"So who was paying him?"

"Well, the FBI makes the case to the Khalils that it was one of your former clients in Iraq, a man named Kuvan Krekar."

"Kuvan is dead. He's been dead now a couple of years."

"I know that. He was killed by the Khalils over in Iraq, but I don't think Kuvan was paying Nolan anyway. For what it's worth, a couple of inspectors with San Francisco's homicide department think the same thing I do, and they won't be giving up on their investigation anytime soon. They think that whoever paid Nolan to kill the Khalils also had a hand in the deaths of Charlie and Hanna Bowen. You got any idea who that might be?"

"None at all."

"That's funny, because all of us have the idea that it's someone in your company, Jack. Allstrong Security."

After a long pause, Allstrong said, "If that ridiculous accusation ever sees the light of day, Mr. Hardy, I hope you're prepared to spend the rest of your life defending the lawsuit I'll bring against you."

"I'M GLAD I did it," Hardy said. "I had to shake something up. It was kind of fun."

Frannie sat next to him at the bar of the Little Shamrock. Her brother, Moses McGuire, was standing across from them both behind the bar. "It was kind of fun," Frannie said to Moses, mimicking Hardy's voice with heavy irony. "*I think it's kind of fun* to threaten a man who's already killed at least two people and tried for three trying to keep this information from getting out. *I think it's kind of fun* that he can put me on his kill list next so me and my family can live in fear of being murdered every day from now on. I really think that's kind of fun." Frannie's color was high, her eyes shining with anger.

Hardy put a hand over his wife's. "That's not going to happen, Frannie. And you know why? Moses knows why, don't you, Mose?"

McGuire sipped his soda and lime. "Because you told Allstrong the cops were on it too. Killing you the way he'd done the Bowens wouldn't get him anything. But"—he held up a finger—"here's the tiny flaw my smart little sister has picked up on in your strategy, Diz. If this guy is juiced enough that he can pull strings inside the FBI, and apparently he is, what on God's good earth makes you think that he can't get around Abe Glitsky and Darrel Bracco?" He turned to Frannie. "Did I express that succinctly enough, you think?"

She bobbed her head once, still furious. "Perfectly," she said.

"Guys, come on," Hardy said. "He's not going to kill two cops, for Christ's sake. And who knows who else is in on the investigation. That's just not going to happen."

"He doesn't have to kill them," Frannie replied. "But what about if he has them ordered off from on high? Where does that leave you then?"

"Me, me, Monty, call on me." Moses wasn't smiling, either, though. He leaned over into his brother-in-law's face. "That leaves you hanging out there alone in the breeze, Diz."

"Okay, but if that unlikely event happens, which I doubt—"

"Then you'll have an accident, like Charlie Bowen did," Frannie said.

"No, Abe would never rest if—"

Frannie slammed her palm down on the bar. *"You'd already be dead, you idiot!"*

In the silence that descended, Hardy put his hand gently over Frannie's again. "Well," he said, "then I'd better get this whole thing done fast, shouldn't I?"

HARDY COULD BE GLIB all he wanted, but in fact Frannie and Moses weren't all wrong, or even mostly wrong. He knew that he'd possibly put himself in an elevated state of jeopardy and could live with that—he also thought he'd mitigated the problem dramatically by telling Allstrong that the police were already involved in this same investigation.

But the more he lived with it, the more he found himself worrying. He hadn't adequately considered that his phone call to Allstrong might also have put Frannie in danger. That had not been his intention, though it might very well be the result.

So Date Night, even at their old favorite restaurant Yet Wah, ended early. Frannie, still very upset over Hardy's call to Allstrong, went straight up to bed. Hardy went to his chair in the living room and punched up Darrel Bracco's number on his cell phone. The inspector picked up and Hardy told him his story—putting a press on Jack Allstrong in person—to a considerably more enthusiastic response than Frannie had given him. When he finished, Bracco said, "So we know both the Bowens were talking to Allstrong. I got that from the phone records too. But so what?"

"So what is what else this tells us."

"What's that?"

"This is close to him, personally. It's not just some corporate thing."

"How do you know that?"

"Mostly," Hardy said, "because he came to the phone to talk to me when there was no reason he needed to. He's got two hundred people under him down there. I guarantee he's got several levels of bureaucracy between him and the front desk. But I call him up out of thin air and mention Evan Scholler and the Bowens and he came right away. He wanted to know what I knew, to see how exposed he was. And I'm confident that I made it pretty clear."

"Why did you want to do that?" Bracco asked. "Warn him we're coming."

"My wife had the same question," Hardy said. "But maybe rattling his cage gets him to do something stupid."

"Something stupid to do with you, maybe."

"Maybe, but unlikely. I made it clear to Allstrong that now it's not just one lone attorney, and then several months later, his wife, also acting alone. The police are part of it now. If any of us disappears or has an accident, the heat only goes up on him. So he's got to figure another way out, make this investigation go away, and I'm trying to make it easy for him."

"He's not going to confess to ordering a domestic murder. Or anything to do with the Bowens."

"True. But I don't need that. I just need to get my client off. As far as he's concerned, that's going to be all I want."

"I want these murders," Bracco said.

"Of course you do," Hardy replied. "And you should. But you'll admit that building any kind of winnable case on the evidence we see so far after all this time is pretty long odds. Meanwhile, Allstrong knows this whole thing is driven by Evan Scholler. That's what was behind the attack this morning in prison. He already believes that if Scholler goes away, all his problems go away."

"I'm not going to go away," Bracco said.

"You won't have any choice if he's left you no evidence to work with. I got the feeling this guy's built his business by getting around local authorities everywhere he sets up shop. Now he's got political clout and the veneer of respectability. We're not going to take him head-on."

"So you've got a better idea?" Bracco asked.

"As a matter of fact," Hardy said, "I think I do."

AS HE TIPTOED into his bedroom at a little after eleven o'clock, Frannie switched on the light next to the bed.

"Hey," Hardy said.

"Hey." She patted the bed next to her. "I'm sorry," she said. "I was worried. I'm still worried, but I don't want to fight about it."

He crossed over to her and sat down, put a hand on her shoulder. "I don't either."

After a minute, she let out a long breath. "So how'd it go?"

"I think I've got Darrel talked into it. He really wants this guy. As do I."

"What about Abe?"

"I didn't get around to talking to Abe. He might have reservations I'd rather not entertain at this point in time."

Frannie closed her eyes and sighed again. "It's really that important?"

"Charlie Bowen told his wife it was the most important thing he'd ever worked on. It was his biggest chance to do some real good in the world."

"In the world, huh?"

"The big old world, yeah." He kept rubbing her back. "I didn't pick this fight, Frannie. It just came and fell in my lap. And now it turns out that this guy's just the smiling face of evil in this world, and what makes it worse is he cloaks it all in patriotism and loyalty while he deals away lives so he can make another buck. It makes me puke."

"And it's all up to you? It's got to be you, Dismas Hardy?"

"I think I've got the cards," Hardy said. "I can beat him and take him down."

"And what about the people protecting him politically?"

"Well, with any luck, them too. But Allstrong's enough for my purposes. I'm just trying to do the right thing here, Frannie, mostly for my client."

"I'm not sure I believe you, babe. I think you want to save the world."

"But if I did that," Hardy said, "I'd need personal theme music."

[39]

HARDY DIDN'T SLEEP as well as he would have liked. He woke up for the first time at two-sixteen to the sound of squealing tires out on the street below his bedroom. Wide awake, he went downstairs to check that the house was locked up front and back, which it was.

Behind the kitchen, he turned on the light and went to his safe under his workbench, opened it, and brought out his own weapon, a Smith & Wesson M&P .40. He hesitated for a moment, then picked it up and slammed a full magazine into the grip, racked a round into the chamber, and took off the safety. Then, quietly and methodically, he went through the downstairs, checking the kids' rooms, the family room, back up through the dining and living rooms. Nobody there.

Back upstairs in his bedroom, the gun's safety on, he put it in the drawer next to his bed and lay down again.

The sound of a Dumpster slamming shut, or a garbage can being dropped—something loud and clanging—woke him up at four thirty-eight. He grabbed the gun again and made another tour of the house, with the same result.

Up for the day, he realized, he put on a pot of coffee and went out to get the newspaper, but stopped at the front door first and looked down the street in both directions. Only after satisfying himself that it was clear did he go outside and grab the paper.

This was not turning out to be the way he had planned it.

ABOUT FIVE MINUTES before Frannie's alarm was going to go off, he went upstairs again and laid a hand on her shoulder, gently waking her up.

"Is everything all right?" she asked him.

"So far everything's fine. But sometime in the middle of last night, my subconscious must have decided that you were right. I've been awake half the night worrying. I shouldn't have put us in this situation. I'm sorry."

She reached out and took his hand. "Apology accepted. So what do you want to do?"

"I don't think it would be the worst idea in the world to check into a hotel for a couple of days. Treat it like a vacation."

She sat up, letting go of his hand. "Did something else happen last night that I didn't hear about?"

"No. I've just had time to think about these guys some more. Until it's clear to Allstrong that Glitsky and Bracco are really in on this investigation with me, which I hope ought to be by today or tomorrow, it's like Moses said—we're hanging out there all alone in the breeze."

Frannie shuddered. "I think I liked it better when you were pretending there was nothing to worry about."

"Me too. But I don't think that's the smart move right now. I think we'd be wise to lie a little low."

Sitting with the idea for another moment, Frannie finally sighed. "A couple of days?"

"Probably no more than that."

"Probably." She shook her head. "Do you have any idea how much I wish you hadn't called him?"

"Pretty much, yeah. If it's any consolation, I didn't feel like I had much of a choice."

"Right," she said. "That makes me feel much better."

ALLSTRONG WOULD ALSO know that Hardy went into his office every day, but Hardy had convinced himself that he could minimize his risk on that score by pulling directly into his parking place in the gated and locked parking garage underneath the building and taking the inside elevator up to his office. Once he was inside, he had a reasonable faith in his firm's security system.

As he pulled in about to park, though, he noticed a brown paper lunch bag lying against the wall just in front of his space. For a minute, the sight of the thing froze him. It was just the kind of harmless-looking item, he imagined, that might in actuality be an improvised explosive device. Turning on his lights, he illuminated the bag, which looked to be nothing more than what it was.

Setting the brake, Hardy opened his door and walked over to the bag, touching it gingerly with his foot, then leaning over to pick it up. It weighed almost nothing, and contained only a few napkins, an apple core, and a couple of Baggies.

Forcing a small nonlaugh at his paranoia, Hardy got back in to his car and parked, then crossed to the elevator and pushed the button to call it down.

IN HIS OFFICE, Hardy went over the final draft of his appeal, which explicitly laid out his argument on the *Brady* violation in such a way as to maximize Allstrong's connection to Nolan and to the Khalils. He attached a declaration from Wyatt Hunt detailing the conversation Hunt had had with Abdel Khalil. Included in the narrative was Tara Wheatley's information about the cash Nolan had brought back from Iraq, buttressing the idea that perhaps he'd been paid to carry out a contract on the Khalils. Of course, the FBI's interrogation of Abdel Khalil, which the agency had not seen fit to share with the prosecution team, was at the crux of his discussion.

In toto, Hardy believed that the appeal raised enough questions about important evidence that had not been admitted in the trial that he thought he'd at least get a hearing out of it. And possibly, if things worked out with Allstrong between now and then, a new trial for Evan.

Satisfied with his work, he sent one of his paralegals down to the court of appeals to file the brief, and then sent registered copies of it, as required, to Mary Patricia Whelan-Miille down in Redwood City, and also— although there was no mandate he do so—overnight to Allstrong Security marked "personal and confidential" for Jack Allstrong. He wanted Allstrong to know what he was doing, when he was doing it, and how it was likely to affect him if he didn't step in and do something to stop it.

Next, calling the prison, Hardy learned that Evan was still in the infirmary and that his condition had stabilized. There was some chance that he would be able to have visitors, perhaps as soon as the next day.

Hardy's cell phone went off—Bracco calling him. "It worked," he said. "I used the old 'Surely you'd want to cooperate in a murder investigation' and he opened up some time for me and I'm on the way down there right now."

"Have fun," Hardy said, "but be careful."

"Right." Bracco barked out a short, nervous laugh. "I'm all over it."

ALLSTRONG AND HIS ATTORNEY, who introduced himself as Ryan Loy, led Bracco back through a maze of hallways into a beautifully designed medium-sized oval conference room containing an apparently custom-made table with twelve matching chairs around it. An enormous spray of fresh flowers claimed the center of the table; at the counter under the tinted windows, someone had set up a full coffee service with pastries and fruit. When Bracco sat down at last with his coffee and Danish, he had a view of the entire South Bay as it shimmered in the sunshine.

Jack Allstrong had played the gracious host in his garrulous style as they moved back through the building, pointing with pride to the headquarters of the other divisions that now made up much of the company's work—computer security, water safety, privatization, logistics consulting, aquaculture. Loy, bookish and reserved in his suit and bow tie, nevertheless came across as another truly nice guy. Everyone they passed in the hallways was well-scrubbed, nicely dressed, young.

Loy closed the door to the conference room behind them and went around the table to Bracco's left while Allstrong sat two chairs over from him on the right. Bracco took out his pocket tape recorder and without comment placed it prominently on the table out in front of everyone.

"Excuse me, Inspector"—Loy had stopped in the middle of raising his cup—"but I understood this was to be an informal discussion and not a formal interrogation."

"Either way," Bracco said with a matter-of-fact tone, "I'm going to need a record of it. I understood that you wanted to cooperate. Mr. Allstrong doesn't have to answer any question he doesn't want to. You both understand that, right?"

Loy looked at Allstrong, who nodded.

Bracco picked up the tape recorder and spoke into it. "This is homicide

Inspector Sergeant Darrel Bracco, Badge Number 3117, conjoined case numbers 06-335411 and 07-121598, talking with Jack Allstrong, forty-one, and his attorney, Ryan Loy, thirty-six. It's eleven forty-five on Wednesday morning, May ninth, and we are at the offices of Allstrong Security in San Francisco. Mr. Allstrong, did you know an attorney named Charles Bowen?"

"Yes."

"How well did you know him?"

"Not well at all. I met him two or three times here in these offices to talk about an appeal he was working on."

"Evan Scholler."

"Yes."

"How did you figure in that case, that Mr. Bowen wanted to talk to you?"

"One of my past employees, Ron Nolan, was the victim. Scholler was eventually convicted of killing him."

"Do you know the grounds that Mr. Bowen planned to base his appeal on?"

"No idea."

"But he talked to you two or three times?"

"Yes. Is that a problem?"

Bracco shrugged. "Was he talking to you about the same things each time you talked to him?"

"Yes."

"And what specifically was the subject of those conversations?"

"I think he may have been trying to connect Nolan in some way to another couple who had been murdered a few days before Nolan himself was killed. I have the memory that he was trying to implicate Nolan in those murders somehow, which was ridiculous, and I told him so."

"Do you remember specifically any questions that he asked?"

"No. I couldn't really give him answers to the questions. This was a long time ago, and it didn't seem very important."

"When was the last time you saw him?"

"I don't know. Sometime last summer."

"And when was the last time you spoke to him on the phone?"

"I don't remember."

"Do you know that Mr. Bowen disappeared last summer?"

"Yes, I believe I did hear something about that just recently. Certainly I stopped hearing from him."

"Were you aware that his records indicate that he called you on the morning that he disappeared?"

Loy decided he had heard enough. Holding up a palm, he said, "Just a minute, Jack. What's your point here, Inspector?"

"Mr. Allstrong was apparently contacted by Mr. Bowen on the day he disappeared. I was wondering if he remembers any of the substance of that last phone call."

Allstrong reached out his own hand. "That's all right, Ryan." Then, to Bracco, "I don't remember any last phone call at all. I didn't know until just now that this last phone call was on the day he was supposed to have disappeared. As far as I know, Mr. Bowen might have just called the office on a routine housekeeping matter. I wouldn't know that. In any event, I don't remember talking to him. And while we're on this, Inspector, why didn't anybody ask these questions last summer when they might have been a little fresher in my mind?"

"The Bowen case has been reopened as a possible homicide, and we're going into more detail than when it was a missing person."

Loy sat up straighter, as if prodded. "If Mr. Allstrong is a suspect in a homicide, Inspector, I'm going to advise him to stop talking to you right now."

"Mr. Allstrong can stop speaking to me anytime he wants. And I never said he was a suspect. But he does appear to be someone who might have had contact with Mr. Bowen on the day he disappeared." Bracco talked straight at Allstrong. "But this leads to my next question, about Mr. Bowen's wife. Did you ever meet her or speak to her on the phone?"

"No."

"Are you quite certain?"

"Yes."

"Well, it appears she made a number of phone calls to your number. Do you have any explanation for that?"

"Again," Loy said, "he already told you he doesn't remember speaking to her. Mr. Allstrong gets a hundred calls a day, Inspector. He doesn't have time to speak to most of those people."

"Mr. Loy. Your client indicated he wanted to cooperate in this investigation. I have a number of questions I want to ask him." Bracco nodded. "He doesn't have to answer any questions, but what I need are his answers and not your suggestions as to what might or might not have happened. So again, Mr. Allstrong, do you have any explanation for phone calls that Mrs. Bowen made to your phone?"

"Well, of course, Mr. Loy is right. I get lots of phone calls."

"I can appreciate that. But the last call Hanna Bowen made in her life was to here. And it was the day before her death. I think you can understand why we are curious about two people who call Allstrong Security, one of whom disappears and the other dies immediately after the contact. It does appear an unlikely coincidence." It also wasn't true, but Loy and Allstrong didn't have to know that. Hardy's plan was simply to have Bracco show up and make it clear that the cops, too, were now part of the picture.

"Well, okay," Loy said. "You've asked your questions. Mr. Allstrong has told you what he knows. If you don't have anything further, I think it's time to end the interview."

But Bracco ignored Loy again. "Mr. Allstrong," he said, "if you didn't receive these calls, to whom in your company might Mrs. Bowen have spoken?"

Allstrong shrugged. "I could ask Marilou, our receptionist. She's the first line of defense. If Mrs. Bowen was hysterical or nonspecific about what she wanted or who she wanted to talk to, her calls would have stopped at the front desk. But as Ryan here says, we can always ask and make sure."

Bracco finally reached for his coffee and took a sip. It had gone tepid and he made a face.

"Is something wrong, Inspector?" Allstrong asked.

Bracco reached over and turned off his tape recorder. He decided he'd give the shit one last stir. "This doesn't seem to be going anywhere, gentlemen. I came here under the impression that you'd like to cooperate in these homicide investigations, but I'm not picking up much of a spirit of cooperation. In fact, frankly, you both seem pretty darn defensive for people who've got nothing to hide."

"That's ridiculous," Loy said. "We've answered every question you've asked. The plain fact is that Mr. Allstrong doesn't know anything about the Bowens other than what he's told you. He runs a huge corporation with branches all over the world. He doesn't have time to get involved in these small parochial matters. Look, Inspector, we're sorry Mr. Bowen disappeared, and about whatever happened to his wife. But to imply that there's any real connection between Allstrong Security and these events is just an absurd flight of fancy."

"Amen to that," Allstrong intoned.

"Well, then"—Bracco pushed his chair back—"thank you for your time."

At THREE-FIFTEEN, Glitsky was standing in front of a video monitor in the tiny electronics room between the two similarly minuscule interrogation rooms that fed off a narrow hallway that, in turn, was separated from the homicide detail by a glass wall. "I give up," he said to Debra Schiff, "what is it?"

"That, sir, is the top of your head."

Glitsky looked again. He wore his graying hair short and close to his skull. Leaning over, he squinted into the seven-inch monitor. "Could be," he said. "I couldn't prove it isn't."

"You see any identifiable part of your face?"

"No." He turned to her. "This is all the camera got in there?"

"Yes, sir."

"Lord." Glitsky walked out of the electronics room, took one step to his left, and reentered the interrogation room he'd left a minute before.

The room was four feet by five feet, so it was really more like a closet. It had no windows. Suspects in homicide investigations were often brought in for questioning and placed in these rooms, where they could be left alone and theoretically observed as they fidgeted or talked to themselves or otherwise did things that might be both incriminating and admissible in court. The problem was that the camera that was supposed to record all of this activity was cleverly hidden within the ceiling and the room was so small that the only image captured on tape, ever, was the top of the head of the suspect. As Schiff had just demonstrated to Glitsky.

"It's hopeless," Schiff told him. "We can't do business like this. We need a new room."

"I thought this *was* the new room." Glitsky was right. The entire homicide department had transferred to the fifth floor from the fourth only a little over a year before. Newly designed and supposedly state of the art. "But you're right, it's a little small too. Who approved the plans for this thing?"

"Well, nobody, which is kind of the problem. There's a couple of guys in robbery who moonlight doing construction here in the building."

"We didn't bid this out?"

Schiff laughed. "Are you kidding me? We have employees that do the maintenance in the building. We try to bid this out, the union's going to have a fit. We'd be taking their jobs."

"Well, then, why didn't we have the people in maintenance do it?"

"Because they said there's a three-year backlog on maintenance, and they'd need to charge us seventy-five thousand dollars from our budget. So we got the two guys from robbery to do it."

"Perfect," Glitsky said. "So where do you propose we put it, this new room?"

"I don't know, Abe. Anyplace else. Maybe out where the lockers are. Or take part of the computer room, which is way too big anyway. But this thing is just crazy."

"I agree with you." He tried a small joke. "I'll try to bring it up to somebody in facilities."

Schiff didn't laugh. "Sooner would be better, Abe."

"I hear you, Debra, I'll see what I can do. Really." But even as he was finishing up with this unwelcome bit of housekeeping, Glitsky saw that one of the clerks from reception was hustling his way. "Yo, Jerry," he said. "What up?"

"I've got Bureau Chief Bill Schuyler with the FBI holding for you, sir. He says it's important."

THE DOORBELL RANG in Hardy's hotel room. They'd gotten a small suite at the Rex, not far from Hardy's office, and Hardy had checked in at a little before five o'clock.

He crossed to the door and, taking no chances, looked through the peephole. Glitsky frowned at nothing in the dusky light. When Hardy opened the door, the lieutenant focused the dark look on him. "When Phyllis told me you were here, I thought maybe she was kidding me."

"Yeah, she's a great kidder, that Phyllis."

Glitsky threw a quick look around. "Obviously, you think this is necessary."

"Precautionary, that's all."

Glitsky nodded, his expression set and hard. "In any event, we've got to talk."

"And, lo, as if by magic, here we are talking right now."

Abe tightened his lips enough that his scar stood out in relief. "Would you like to know the result of your ill-advised encouragement to Darrel Bracco that he go down and have a chat with the Allstrong people?"

Hardy's face grew sober. "Is he all right?"

"Physically, he's fine." Glitsky pushed on the door and Hardy stepped back to let him in, then followed him into the sitting room. Grabbing the chair behind the desk, Glitsky spun it around and straddled it. "But he's slightly ticked off at you. As am I, I might add."

"And why is that?" Hardy sat down on the love seat.

"Because he was starting to get a feeling about this Bowen case, or cases. That he could crack them if he just had some time. And now that's not going to happen, ever."

"Why not?"

"Because I got a call this afternoon from Bill Schuyler. You remember Bill Schuyler? He's the FBI bureau chief who couldn't find the agents who'd testified in the Scholler trial."

Hardy's eyes lit up, although he tried to keep any sign of enthusiasm out of his face. "Tell me the FBI's taken over the cases."

"Lock, stock, and barrel."

"Citing national security issues?"

"Citing they're gonna do it and we can't stop them. I think the actual line was 'I don't got to show you no stinkin' badges.' But even Schuyler went so far as to say that he didn't really like it, but the order came from high up and there was nothing he could do about it. You know what a huge concession that was from him?"

"I can imagine."

"I bet you can. So you know how me and Darrel have spent the last three hours? Packing up all our files on either of the Bowens and delivering them over to the Federal Building. These are two now very probable homicides in my jurisdiction, Diz, and now I'm off them for no reason that I can understand."

"Which accounts for your less-than-stellar mood, not that you normally need anything specific. But that was faster than I would have thought." He held out a hand. "I'm not talking about the three hours. I'm talking about Allstrong getting someone to pull the FBI's strings. He's got to be seriously highly connected, which is what we figured, anyway."

"So you knew this was coming?"

Hardy nodded. "I hoped something like this would happen. This soon is a surprise, but that's not a bad thing either."

Glitsky's face remained hard. "Well, I'm glad you're so happy about it. Darrel and I are feeling just a little bit used and abused."

But Hardy shook his head. "I told Bracco last night, and I'll tell you now, you weren't going to get Allstrong on either of the Bowens. Never. Those cases are old, Abe, what evidence there might have once been is gone. And since these guys are stone pros, I'm guessing there wasn't much in the line of evidence anyway to begin with. So this FBI takeover, it's actually very good news."

"Yeah, I'm trying to keep my celebration pretty low-key. But just for the record, what's good about it?"

Hardy sat up straight. "All of a sudden the whole situation, which from Allstrong's perspective was under control and stagnant, is fluid again. It's a live issue. He's going to have to react and keep reacting if he wants to keep it where he can control it, which means he's going to have to deal with me."

"Like he dealt with Bowen?"

Hardy shook his head. "Not if I can help it, Abe, not this time. He's tried that approach and now it's come back to bite him. He's going to see that."

"I hope you're right, but even so, if the FBI is protecting him from prosecution, what difference can anything you do matter to him? Best case, you're a nuisance. He's never going down for murder if the Feebs won't let anybody build a case."

"Ah, but that's just it, you see? I don't want him for murder. I want his help to try to get my client out of prison. Then I'll just go away."

Glitsky's brow came down and hooded his eyes. "I hope I'm not hearing that all this has been about all this time is getting your *damn* client off."

Hardy's head snapped at Glitsky's rare use of a swear word. If he'd come to that, he was far angrier than Hardy had perceived. "Abe," he said quietly, "listen to me. Like it or not, my client's the only leverage we've all got. The Bowen murders pose no threat, they're ancient history. The attempt on Evan at San Quentin, same thing. That assailant's dead and it's never going to be anything more than a prison beef anyway. So what's the only other crime we know about that he's done here on U.S. soil? Putting out the hit on the Khalils, right? Which means Ron Nolan. And who's the only guy interested in connecting him to Nolan? Me. He's going to have to come to me."

"And then what?"

Hardy leaned forward in his chair. "Then I play him."

[40]

EVAN CAME TO THE VISITING ROOM in a wheelchair. He was going to recover completely, he told Hardy, although he joked that he never wanted to hear those particular words again. Still, it was a good sign that he could make a joke about anything. The attack, he told Hardy, had been completely unexpected and, except for his rib, professionally executed as he walked into what he thought was the empty bathroom. As far as he remembered, there were no witnesses.

Hardy brought him a copy of the brief to look over, and they discussed some of the finer legal points that he didn't understand at first, but in the end he seemed satisfied that this was an approach that possibly had legs. Hardy also brought him up to date on the developments in the Bowen cases, the FBI takeover, and they talked about who the mysterious higher-up might be.

"We may never know," Hardy said. "Somebody who believes that it's more important for guys like Allstrong to build companies that grow and prosper than worry about if they exactly adhere to the letter of the law. So they need to kill a few people? Look at all the jobs they're providing, the infrastructure. Totally worth the price, right? Damn straight."

"I love the national security angle. Like if Allstrong goes under, what happens exactly?"

"At the very least, it hurts the war effort, all the good work Allstrong's doing over there. That's always a good one they pull out." Hardy had his grin on. "But I'm also guessing that the big guy, whoever he is, loses a decent portion of his discretionary cash income."

Evan drew a pained breath. "I don't like to think that's really happening." He looked around at the prison walls. "But then again, I don't like to think that any of this is really happening either."

THE CALL CAME in at a little after one o'clock, just after Hardy arrived back at his office.

"Mr. Hardy. Jack Allstrong." He had his hearty good-guy voice back on. "This morning I received a copy of the appeal that you're filing in this Evan Scholler case. Mr. Loy says we can probably expect an application for a writ of habeas corpus to follow. He admires your work, Mr. Hardy, and advises me that there is a fair chance the court will at least order a hearing into your issue. I think we might have gotten off on the wrong foot in our last conversation, and I wondered if you might be free to come down to my headquarters office this afternoon."

Hardy didn't think it would hurt to play a little hard to get. "If you don't know anything about Mr. Nolan's connection to the Khalils, and last time you made it pretty clear that you didn't, I'm not sure we have much to talk about."

"Well, you seem fairly certain that Scholler didn't kill Ron Nolan, and if that's the case, there might be something we can do to help. I think it might be worthwhile to discuss it."

Hardy let him hang for a few more seconds. "I could give you a couple of hours this afternoon, but I really think this meeting should take place in my office."

HARDY SAT at his desk with his legal pad in front him. He'd already written a few notes to remind him of things he needed to cover in his upcoming conversation. Feeling mostly embarrassed at himself for believing that he might actually have the need for it, he'd placed his gun in the top desk drawer on his left, in easy reach if in fact it came to that.

As Phyllis let Allstrong into the room, he pretended to be writing. Looking up—"Excuse me, a few more seconds"—he motioned to the straight-backed Queen Anne chair that he'd placed in front of his desk, indicating that Allstrong take it. While he did, placing his briefcase down next to the chair, Phyllis closed the door on her way out. Scrawling some more lines, Hardy finally put down his pen and pushed the pad to one side.

"It appears," Hardy said, "you've got a guardian angel someplace in Washington who's taken care of making the police investigation into the Bowens go away. But as long as Evan Scholler is alive and in prison, either me or someone like me is going to be digging into the connection between Allstrong, Ron Nolan, and the Khalils. Whoever tried to have Evan killed has missed his chance and, with him held in protective custody from now on, isn't likely to get another one. And as you've recently found out, appellate lawyers are interchangeable. And, trust me, Mr. Allstrong, anyone who reads my file and my notes, of which there are several copies, will start this inquiry right where I left off. Does that about sum up the situation?"

Allstrong, wearing alligator cowboy boots with his light green gabardine suit, sat back and crossed a leg, his facial features relaxed, nearly friendly. "It adequately elucidates your understanding, certainly," he said. "Although, as I said in our conversation the other day, any assumption you're making that I've committed any kind of crime at all is false. I'm sure that federal investigators will find no evidence implicating me or Allstrong Security in what's happened to either of the Bowens."

"I'm sure they won't," Hardy said.

"And likewise they'll find no evidence that I ordered Ron Nolan to kill anybody. That's not the way I do business." His pro forma pitch completed, he flashed a quick salesman's smile.

"Since you've arranged to have Stevie Wonder and Ray Charles assigned to the investigation," Hardy said, "I'd be surprised if they could find Allstrong in the phone book. But that's not the point. What I'm going to uncover is the evidence the FBI already gathered that connects Nolan and your company to whatever it was that happened in Iraq that got the Khalils murdered. And if, in getting to Nolan, your company gets mixed up in a very public scandal, that's just an added bonus."

Allstrong sat impassively. "What makes you think the FBI has evidence tying Allstrong to these killings?"

"The agents told the Khalil family. What the agents found, I can find."

"I understood that the agents further told them that the contract had come from Kuvan Krekar. Isn't that so?" Allstrong asked.

Hardy nodded. "That's my understanding too."

"Well, then?"

"Well then what?"

"Well, then, it's obvious where the contract originated, isn't it? With Kuvan, not with me, and not with Allstrong."

"That would be obvious except for one thing. Or rather, except for two people. The Bowens. The whole thing with Nolan and Kuvan and the Khalils was a closed circle until Charlie Bowen pried it open again. If the Bowens were still alive, I might have believed that killing the Khalils was Kuvan's idea and Kuvan's contract. But Kuvan was already dead when Charlie Bowen started sniffing around, and that kind of neatly eliminated the possibility that Kuvan was Bowen's killer. But somebody still needed Charlie dead because he was going to find out and expose who'd really put out the contract on the Khalils. And you know who that was, Jack. You know because that was you."

Allstrong let his shoulders sag for a moment. "Back to that," he said.

"I'm afraid so." Hardy met his adversary's eyes, unyielding.

Allstrong shrugged, nodded, leaned down, picked up his briefcase, brought it up to his lap, and snapped it open. "Regrettably," he said, "this has become a very inconvenient situation."

And for an irrational moment, Hardy thought he'd miscalculated and in another half second he would be dead. Before he could even react to reach for his own gun, which he'd so stupidly, stupidly placed in the closed top drawer, Allstrong's silenced bullet would explode with no warning at all through the expensive briefcase and blow Hardy into oblivion. That would put an end to Hardy's threat right here, right now.

Hardy's left hand went to his drawer, started to pull it out.

He wasn't going to have enough time.

It was over. His life was over.

But in the moment Allstrong would have taken his shot if he could, instead of firing a weapon he'd perhaps concealed in his briefcase, he simply continued talking. "I have to admire your tenacity and industry. In fact, I'd like to offer you a retainer to take on some of my legal work. Mr. Loy is a fine corporate attorney but lacks the killer instinct sometimes required in my business. Like all our senior employees, you will be paid in cash."

Allstrong turned the briefcase around, showing Hardy the neatly stacked packages of one-hundred-dollar bills. And no sign of a gun.

Hardy quietly exhaled and brought his shaking hands together, clasped now white-knuckled on his desktop.

And Allstrong continued. "This is two hundred thousand dollars, Mr. Hardy. I'd like to offer it to you against billings for the first year. If you prefer, I could arrange to have this deposited in an offshore account, a Swiss bank account, or any other place that you choose. You would in fact be retained by one of our Iraqi subsidiaries, who do not file tax returns in the United States. So whether you choose to report this to the IRS as income is completely up to you."

"I wonder how many of those are my tax dollars," Hardy said.

"Don't be naïve," Allstrong countered. "And don't trifle with me." The bribe offer having already, albeit tacitly, admitted his complicity in everything that Hardy had accused him of, he went on. "I'd strongly advise you to consider what I'm offering. As you yourself have noticed, other alternatives, though perhaps risky and more costly, are still available to me."

Hardy clucked and cracked a grin. "I really thought we'd moved beyond that, Jack."

Allstrong slowly and carefully closed up the briefcase, setting it down again beside him. Sitting back, he eyed Hardy for a long moment. "So, Mr. Hardy, do we have an understanding?"

"Oh, we understand each other, Jack. But, no, we don't have a deal. I thought I'd made it clear. I want Evan Scholler out of prison. I don't care how it happens, but that's my price."

"What if the FBI suddenly found evidence that did implicate Nolan in the Khalils' deaths? What if there were surveillance reports linking some members of the Khalil family to terrorist organizations? And wiretaps where they discussed killing Ron Nolan? Do you think that would do the job, Mr. Hardy?"

"I think it might. So what you have to do, Jack, is get me that evidence."

"And then what?"

"And then I lose interest in you."

But Allstrong still wasn't quite ready to give it up. "And what if the evidence just doesn't exist?"

Hardy inclined his head. "Ah, but we know it does. Remember? The FBI found it before they talked to the Khalil children. You saw it when you decided to sell out Kuvan."

A lengthy silence settled.

At last, Allstrong nodded once. "He should have never used the grenades," he said quietly, as though explaining a complicated process to a child. "That was his own decision and just tactically stupid. But he didn't care. He'd become a liability. He loved to blow things up. He thought it was fun. The fool thought he was invincible."

"YOU WANT my opinion," Hardy said, popping a peanut into his mouth in Glitsky's office, "he did Nolan too. Not personally. Allstrong himself was still over in Iraq back then. But one of his guys took out Nolan. Just another job."

"Why?" Glitsky asked.

"Allstrong said it himself. Nolan had become a liability. He used the frag grenades that could be traced back to Allstrong."

Bracco, sulking, stood against the wall, arms crossed over his chest. "You're not telling me he's giving you something that can be traced back to him? I'm talking about the frags."

"No. He won't do that. They might get back to the company, but old Jack will be able to say that Nolan stole them or something, that he was acting on his own when he killed the Khalils. It was a freelance gig."

"It doesn't matter anyway." Glitsky sat all the way back, exuding frustration. "He's got protection, remember? He might as well have immunity. I'm still having a hard time getting my arms around the fact that the Feebs are part of this. Schuyler wouldn't go along with any of this on his own."

"I wouldn't take it personally, Abe," Hardy said. "And it's not on his own. He's being told it's national security, too, and he believes his bosses. There's a greater good involved. So everybody winds up being good guys."

"Peachy," Glitsky replied.

"So what about the Bowens?" Bracco asked. "What about those murders? Collateral damage and we leave it at that? Does that seem right to either of you guys?"

Hardy turned to him. "You were never going to make the case anyway, Darrel. Never, ever, in a million years. Ask Abe if he agrees."

For an answer, Glitsky shrugged.

Hardy held up a hand. "I'm not saying I'm happy with that, but it's reality."

"It sucks," Bracco said. "What am I supposed to tell Jenna the next time she calls? That fat cats like Allstrong walk? Sorry, but that's reality. Your parents don't count." He slammed his hand hard against a metal locker. "This just pisses me off." And he walked out the door.

"It's not over yet," Hardy called after him.

In the ensuing silence, Glitsky growled. "It's not over. What's that supposed to mean?"

"I mean I'm going to be getting this evidence in the next few weeks. And the great thing about evidence is that it speaks for itself."

Glitsky glared at him. "Oh, yeah, your *client*. Good for him. Good for you too."

"Not just us," Hardy said.

"No?" Glitsky asked again. "Then who else?" Sitting up, he shook his head in disgust. "Get the door on your way out, would you? I've got real work I got to do."

[41]

HARDY WAS IN HIS OFFICE opening his mail, having just finished reviewing the documents that he had received over the past three weeks via registered mail from the local FBI office in San Francisco. The FBI had done its usual efficient and thorough job and, from fragments found at the Khalil home, had matched the grenades used in that attack to a cache of them at the Allstrong warehouse at BIAP. Beyond that, they had recovered a bullet from the Khalil scene and matched it to the gun that had been in Nolan's duffel bag with the grenades. Downloads from Nolan's hard drive revealed not just the photos of the Khalil house from various angles, but also photos of the eventual victims that looked as though they'd been scanned in. Nolan's bank records memorialized regular biweekly automatic deposits of ten thousand dollars and another deposit, four days before the Khalils were killed, of twenty-five thousand. There was a handwritten quarter page in Nolan's handwriting, noting the victims' names and address, some indecipherable scribbling and doodling, and the notation "$50,000" circled several times.

The evidence tying the Khalils to a plot to kill Nolan was equally impressive. The wiretaps arrived, accompanied by neat binders of translations from the Arabic. There were informant reports, with names blacked out due to national security, but which clearly identified some of the Khalils as involved in a plot to murder Nolan in retaliation for the Menlo Park killings.

Hardy had to admire Jack Allstrong's own thoroughness, as well as his caution. All of this evidence would be valuable to Hardy when the hearing came up for Scholler's appeal. And none of it directly implicated either Allstrong himself or his company.

Of course, during the same time period, Hardy had been reading in the local press about the agents involved in the FBI's handling of the

Scholler case. The debate raged in the media about whether the agents had been merely grotesquely incompetent or criminally derelict in suppressing such critical evidence in the trial of a bona fide war hero. Agents were being transferred, suspended, and demoted.

Glitsky, following it daily with Hardy, could barely suppress his own glee. Hardy had tried to point out that it was unlikely that anyone truly culpable in the affair was ever really going to be punished, but Glitsky exulted in the random carnage the agency was inflicting on itself.

Now Hardy reached for an 8½ × 11 envelope. It had arrived addressed to him, personal and confidential, by regular mail with no return address, but postmarked in San Francisco. Reaching in, he pulled out two sheets of faxed copies of e-mail correspondence between *Rnolan@ sbcglobal.net* and *JAA@Allstrong.com*. Dated the day after the Khalil murders, it acknowledged that Nolan had accomplished his most recent assignment and requested payment of the remainder of his fee into a certain bank account. Allstrong should advise Mr. Krekar that "the situation has been resolved, as promised; Krekar should expect to move on the Anbar contracts without competition."

Although there was nothing remotely humorous about any of this, a ghost of a smile tickled the side of Hardy's mouth. Maybe he ought to tell Glitsky that Bill Schuyler wasn't the gullible, gutless G-man he needed to pretend to be if he wanted to keep his job. On the other hand, Hardy had no proof that Schuyler had had anything to do with this latest evidence. Any mention of his name would probably just get the man in more trouble. And in fact, the evidence could have come from any other FBI agent between San Francisco and Baghdad who had a sense of what was happening and a disgust at the role that the Bureau had been forced to play in it.

Hardy realized that without a witness or some other way to authenticate the documents, what he had in his hand were just two pieces of paper, worthless in a court of law. He sat at his desk pulling the tight skin at his jawline as for the hundredth, the thousandth, time he considered the ramifications of his intentions.

He had made no promises to Allstrong. To the contrary, he'd made it abundantly clear that whatever information he received would be his to do with as he pleased. Additionally, this wasn't information he'd gotten from Allstrong anyway. He owed Allstrong nothing. As Allstrong himself had said, it was an inconvenient situation.

He got up and, without a word to anyone, walked across his office and out to the copy room, where he copied the two pages. Coming back to his desk, he put the copy in his file and began searching through his notes for the address of Abdel Khalil.

HARDY AND FRANNIE were trimming the roses that bounded the fence in their backyard on a cool Sunday afternoon in the second week of June, talking about the arrival of their children, who'd both be returning home from their respective schools in the next couple of days. "I think they should both work," Hardy said. "I worked every summer of my life."

"Of course you did," Frannie said. "I can see you now, four-year-old Dismas out plowing the fields. To say nothing of walking ten miles to school every day, in deep snow."

"Leave out the snow part," he said. "This was San Francisco, remember."

"Yeah, but back when you were a baby, wasn't the climate different here?" Frannie enjoying the little joke at the expense of the eleven-year difference in their ages.

"You're a very funny person." He reached over and clipped a newly budded rose just at its base.

"Hey!" She turned on him.

"It's my old eyes," he said, backing away. "I was aiming for lower down on the stem."

"Yeah, well, keep it up and I'll aim for lower down too." She took a quick and playful swipe at him with her cutting tool.

Hardy backed up another step, then cocked his head, looking over her shoulder. "Well, look what the cat dragged in."

Glitsky was just emerging into the yard from the narrow walkway between their house and the neighbor's. He was in civilian clothes, hands in the pockets of his battered leather jacket. Getting up to them, he gave Frannie half a hug and accepted her kiss on the cheek, then turned to her husband. "You should leave your phone on."

"I know. It's bad of me," Hardy said. "But it's Sunday, I figured whatever it is can wait. But maybe not."

"Maybe not, after all. You know anything about this?"

"About what?"

"Jack Allstrong."

Hardy felt his stomach go hollow. He caught his breath, cleared his throat, tried to swallow. "No. What about him?"

"He got in his car this morning down in Hillsborough and turned it on and it blew up him and half his house. It's all over the news."

"I don't watch TV on Sunday either."

Glitsky just stood there.

Frannie touched Glitsky's arm. "Abe? What's wrong?"

"I don't know, Fran. I don't know if anything's wrong. I was thinking Diz might be able to tell me." He kept his eyes on Hardy.

Who drew another breath, then another, then blew out heavily and went down to one knee.

EPILOGUE
[2008]

ON A WARM LATE-SUMMER DAY about fifteen months after Jack Allstrong's death, an excellent jazz quartet was doing arrangements of big band material in her backyard as Eileen Scholler came out of her house. She wended her way under the balloons and through the large crowd of well-wishers, touching an arm here, a back there, smiling and exchanging pleasantries and congratulations with her guests. At last she came to the table under one of the laden lemon trees where Dismas and Frannie Hardy sat drinking white wine with Everett Washburn.

"Ah, here you are, way in the back. Do you mind if an old lady pulls up a chair?"

"I don't see any old ladies," Washburn said, "but glowing mothers of war heroes are always welcome."

Hardy pulled out the chair and as she sat, her eyes started to tear up at Washburn's words. She smiled around the table. "War hero. I never thought I'd hear anybody say that about Evan again. And now . . ." She indicated the overflow crowd and turned to Hardy. "How am I ever going to repay you?" she asked.

"Believe me, Eileen," he said, "the result was plenty payment enough." After the court of appeals had ordered a new trial for Evan, the San Mateo County district attorney declined to prosecute further. The FBI, it seems, was reluctant to cooperate, citing national security and the need to keep its own internal investigation confidential. Over the impassioned objection of Mary Patricia Whelan-Miille, the DA had been only too happy to use that as a reason to dismiss the charges. "Seeing Evan walking around a free man. Look at him over there, laughin' and scratchin'."

They all looked to where Evan stood with his arm around Tara in a knot of people comprised of his father, several other guys and women about his own age, Tony Onofrio, and even Stan Paganini.

"I still feel like it's a dream," Eileen said. "Like I'm going to wake up and he's going to be in prison again."

Frannie reached over and put a hand over hers. "That's not going to happen. What's going to happen is he and Tara are going to get married next month and I wouldn't be at all surprised if you become a grand-mother in pretty short order after that."

Eileen squeezed Frannie's hand, looked briefly skyward, then came back to her. "Your mouth to God's ear," she said, "but I almost can't bring myself to hope after all this time."

"You'll get used to it," Hardy said.

"No." Eileen smiled across at him. "You don't understand. I never want to get used to it. I want to just be glad he's back in our lives every day and never forget how today feels and how lucky we are. We really never believed we'd see this, and now that it's here, it's just . . . well, it's just a miracle. We're living in a miracle and we can't forget that and I'm just so grateful."

Suddenly she stood up, walked around behind Washburn, leaned over and hugged Hardy for a long moment, then gave him a kiss on the cheek and straightened up. "Thank you," she said. "Now I think I'm going to go hug my son again."

"That's a great idea," Hardy said. "Hug him for me too."

When she'd gone off, Washburn sipped his wine. "I must confess to both of you that I feel a little awkward being here. She should have been able to have this party four years ago."

Hardy shook his head. "The government cheated, Everett. They cheated him out of a fair trial. I wouldn't beat myself up over it."

Frannie leaned over. "Yes, he would," she said. "But that doesn't change the fact that you shouldn't."

"Well, in any event," Washburn said, "justice delayed is justice denied and all of that, but today I've got to go with it's better late than never." He glanced back over in Evan's direction. "The boy's paid some pretty mean dues, I'll give him that. Whatever's up next, I've got to believe he's going to be able to handle it."

"Odds are good," Hardy said. "The odds are pretty damn good."

* * *

EVAN KNEW that he was dealing with an expert in hand-to-hand combat and couldn't afford to hesitate. As soon as Nolan started to open the door, he lowered his shoulder and rammed as hard as he could. The impact knocked Nolan backward, the back of his leg caught the edge of the coffee table, and he went over and down backward. Evan was on him, a knee into his chest, almost before he hit the floor, and he followed with two or three near-instantaneous metal-knuckled fists to the jaw.

But all the alcohol he had on board wasn't to his advantage. Nolan came up with a vicious karate chop to Evan's neck that pitched him off to the side and onto his back, by the fireplace, while at the same time it cut off his ability to breathe.

Nolan twisted and leapt across the distance separating them, maybe five feet. Evan swung wildly in a huge roundhouse that Nolan blocked with his arm, but scored with a knee to the groin that allowed him to go inside, then jab twice at Nolan's head with the knuckles, glancing blows that nevertheless moved Nolan back. But not for long. Nolan got to his knees and actually produced a vacant smile of determination. "You are so fucking dead," he said.

Scrambling to his own feet, still gasping for breath, Evan grabbed the poker by the fireplace and held it to the side for an instant and then stepped forward and slashed with it. Nolan jumped back out of the way and, as the poker got past him, twisted half around and delivered a kick to Evan's stomach that knocked more air out of him, though it left Nolan exposed to the backhand slash of the poker.

But between the loss of breath and his drunken state, Evan's reflexes weren't responding as they usually did. Nolan got his hands on the poker as it came at him and brought it over his own shoulder and he turned and leveraged himself into Evan's torso, pulling him over his back, slamming him down, judo-style, half against the coffee table and half onto the floor. Evan felt as though he'd broken his back, but if he simply lay there and let Nolan come at him, he knew that he would have no chance and that his enemy would kill him here and now. So in desperation he kicked out again, this time hitting Nolan hard in the knee, spinning him half around and down against the brick of the fireplace, clattering in the tools still left against the hearth.

When Evan tried to move to get up again, though, his body wouldn't obey the frantic commands of his brain. Pushing against his own inertia, he rolled himself over and over again, hoping to use the coffee table as a shield as Nolan picked himself up, slowly now, as though sensing his advantage.

Still struggling for breath, the images of Nolan straightening up doubling and blurring before his eyes, Evan forced himself to a knee, hoping to get his hands on something he could use for a weapon. The only chance was the poker, on the floor midway between them. With an animal growl, lunging, he got his hands on it just as Nolan's one foot came down, pinning his hands to the floor, while the other foot cocked and exploded at Evan's left ear, knocking him headfirst against the wall, from where, now unconscious, he crumpled to the ground.

THERE WAS NO TIME. He woke up again and, with his swollen tongue, tasted blood in his mouth, felt its crusted residue on his dry and cracked lips. Through the room's door, although the room itself was dark, he could see Nolan fumbling in the closet, where Evan knew he kept the gun.

The pain in his head had now spread to his back, his neck, his legs. He could not move a muscle. The slightest effort—opening his eyes the smallest crack, a quarter-inch twist of his head, a twitch in his knee—and the world, for his sanity and protection, went black.

THE FOOTSTEPS came closer, almost shuffling with a slow deliberation.

Even in the darkness, Evan felt a shadow fall over him. Nolan had the gun in his hand.

Then the whispered words. "You stupid son of a bitch."

Evan did not move or respond in any way. Did not feel that he could.

Nolan stood over him. Whatever damage Nolan had done to him, and Evan realized that possibly it was severe enough to be life-threatening, the fight had not been without its own consequences for the commando. From the way Nolan was moving, he was clearly hurt, physically compromised. With one arm so badly injured, it took him a couple of tries to rack a round into the chamber.

Evan had no option but to attack again, and he twisted and kicked, hit-

ting Nolan below his knees, knocking him down. Evan scrambled, grabbing for Nolan's gun hand with both of his. Getting ahold of it. With his one free hand, Nolan swung in tight again and again, hard jabs to the side of Evan's head.

But even to protect his head, Evan didn't dare release his grip on Nolan's gun hand. To let go of the gun was to die.

Grabbing the barrel with all of his strength, grunting with the exertion, he finally lifted enough to get the gun and the hand that held it off the ground. And then he twisted it, and twisted again.

And at last the gun was free and in his hand, the barrel now tight against Nolan's forehead.

It was over.

Nolan went limp, the fight suddenly all out of him. He held his arms out against the floor in an I-give-up gesture. For a full second that felt like a minute, neither man moved.

And then in a lightning strike, Nolan screamed and threw a last jab in the direction of Evan's head.

And the gun went off.

ACKNOWLEDGMENTS

In preparation for this book, I spoke to many veterans of the fighting in Iraq and read a lot of books about that country and the war that, as this book goes to press, is still claiming American and Iraqi lives every day. I'd particularly like to acknowledge and thank Mike Dufresne for his early insights into the role of the National Guard in Iraq; Don Currier for his general overview of the war and his terrific photographs; T. Christian Miller, author of *Blood Money: Wasted Billions, Lost Lives, and Corporate Greed in Iraq;* Aaron Moore, First Sergeant, U.S. Marine Corps; Craig Denton, and Rick Tippens.

Other books that contributed in one way or another to *Betrayal* include *Blood Stripes: The Grunt's View of the War in Iraq,* by David J. Danelo; *Ambush Alley: The Most Extraordinary Battle of the Iraq War,* by Tim Pritchard; and *Licensed to Kill: Hired Guns in the War on Terror,* by Robert Young Pelton. In spite of all of this research, it is of course possible that there may be inaccuracies and/or errors of one kind or another in this book, and any of these are the fault of the author.

As with all of my other Dismas Hardy books, I owe a huge debt of gratitude to my great pal Al Giannini, an assistant district attorney in San Mateo County. Al is brilliant, tireless, and endlessly enthusiastic, and he contributed mightily to every part of this book from its inception to its final draft. His knowledge both of the law and of human nature is second to no one's, and whatever verisimilitude this work contains, particularly in the legal realm, is because of Al's keen eye and sagacious judgment.

At Dutton, I am blessed with a wonderful sales, marketing, publicity, and editorial staff. My deepest thanks for their commitment, enthusiasm, taste, and intelligence goes out to my publisher, Brian Tart; my new and excellent editor, Ben Sevier; Lisa Johnson, Trena Keating, Beth Parker, Erika Imranyi, Kara Welsh, Claire Zion, Rick Pascocello, Susan Schwartz, and Rich Hasselberger for another superb book jacket design. Though he has moved on to another publishing house, I would also like to tip my hat one last time to Mitch Hoffman, who was my editor at Dutton for many years, and who was instrumental in getting this book off the ground.

My assistant, Anita Boone, continues to perform her yeoman's work on a daily basis, creating a sense of calm and efficiency in my writing environment that makes it all possible. She is a great person, and I'm blessed to have her with me. Peter S. Dietrich, M.D., M.P.H., contributes not only his medical expertise, but his knowledge of clear libations. Karen Hlavacek and Peggy Nauts are both world-class proofreaders. I'm also lucky to have several other friends to keep books and other things in perspective in my day-to-day life. These include the very talented writer Max Byrd, my perennial best man Don Matheson, Frank Seidl, and Bob Zaro. Also, I must acknowledge my two great children, Justine and Jack, both of whom continue to inspire and inform these novels in many ways.

Several characters in this book owe their names (although no physical or personality traits, which are all fictional) to individuals whose contributions to various charities have been especially generous. These people, and their charities, include Ryan Loy, the Borders Group Foundation; Marcia Riggio, the Santa Clara Valley Chapter of Brandeis University National Women's Committee (Science for Life Campaign); Felice Brinkley, the First Amendment Project; Mary Patricia Whelan-Miille, Yolo County Court Appointed Special Advocates (CASA); and Arlene and David Ray (for the respective character Stephan Ray), Stop Cancer.

My agent, Barney Karpfinger, embraced the idea for this book at the very earliest stage and guided me through many moments of its inception and structure. I consider him a great friend and true collaborator in my work and my career, which would be significantly diminished without him.

I very much love hearing from my readers, and invite all of you please to visit me with any comments, questions, or interests on my Web site, *www.johnlescroart.com.*

ABOUT THE AUTHOR

JOHN LESCROART is the author of eighteen previous novels, including *The Suspect, The Hunt Club, The Motive, The Second Chair, The First Law, The Oath, The Hearing,* and *Nothing But the Truth.* He lives with his wife and two children in northern California.